EXILE

Denise Mina

An Orion paperback

First published in Great Britain in 2000
by Bantam Press,
a division of Transworld Publishers
This paperback edition published in 2011
by Orion Books Ltd,
Orion House, 5 Upper St Martin's Lane,
London WC2H 9EA

An Hachette UK company

1 3 5 7 9 10 8 6 4 2

A CIP catalogue record for this book
is available from the British Library.

ISBN 978-1-4091-3531-9

Typeset by Input Data Services Ltd, Bridgwater, Somerset

Printed and bound in Great Britain by CPI Mackays, Chatham ME5 8TD

The Orion Publishing Group's policy is to use papers
that are natural, renewable and recyclable products and
made from wood grown in sustainable forests. The logging
and manufacturing processes are expected to conform to
the environmental regulations of the country of origin.

www.orionbooks.co.uk

Acknowledgements

This is my opportunity to express my gratitude to everyone at the Strathclyde Police Media and Information Service Department, and to Superintendent Iain Gordon especially, for their help in researching this book; to Philip Considine for technical advice and support; and to Gerry Considine who'll push us both over if he doesn't get a mention. Also, many fervent thanks to Rachel Calder, Katrina Whone, and, of course, to my mum for holding my coat while I did all this. Ursula, so long, baby. Finally, special thanks are due to Stephen Evans for matters which are no concern of yours.

The End

'Kick it and see,' he said.

She felt the foot going into her side, a dull thud ripple through the crippling pain.

'She's dead,' said the woman.

But she wasn't, she was still alive and she heard them. The ground was warm and wet beneath her. Her dry eyes were stuck open and she could see across the floor to a dirty glass by the skirting board. The woman crouched down by her. She was pulling at her wrist, tugging at the bracelet.

'Leave it,' he said, but she ignored him, tugging again. '*I said leave it.*'

The woman dropped her arm and backed off. The man shuffled into her line of vision, worn trainers, grey trousers. They were talking about her, about how to get rid of her, about getting Andy's van. The pain surged and she spasmed at the shrieking trill on her spine, the scalding whiteness behind her eyes. The searing light grew brighter and brighter until there was nothing.

I

Postie

It was minus five outside the bedroom window and Maureen's face prickled against the cold. She wanted to get out of bed, wanted a cigarette and a coffee and to be alone, but his leg was pressed tightly against hers and his hand was under her thigh. The cumulative heat was itchy and damp. She peeled their skins apart, trying hard not to wake him, but he felt her stir. He peered around at her through sleep-puffed eyes.

"Kay?' he murmured.

'Yeah,' breathed Maureen.

She waited, watching her milky breath hover above her, listening to the wind hissing outside. Vik's breathing deepened to a soft, nasal whistle and Maureen slid into the bitter morning.

She flicked on the kettle, lit a cigarette and looked out of the kitchen window. January is the despairing heart of the Scottish winter and black clouds brooded low over the city, pregnant with spiteful rain. It came to her every morning now; it was the first thought in her head when she opened her eyes. After a wordless fourteen-year absence, Michael, her father, was back in Glasgow.

They only found out afterwards that their elder sister Marie hadn't bumped into Michael in London. She'd gone looking for him, contacting the National Union of Journalists and putting adverts in the *Evening Standard*. She found him living in the Surrey Docks in a high-rise council flat carpeted with empty lager cans. He was troubled with his health and hadn't worked for a long time so Una paid his fare home. Maureen told them she wouldn't see him but her insistence was needless. Liam said Michael never mentioned her, had never once spoken her name and ignored it when anyone else did. Even their mother, Winnie, was starting to wonder about that. Maureen couldn't get over the injustice of it. Michael was back in the bosom of the family and she was outcast.

The moment she heard he was home everything changed for her. It wasn't like the breakdown: she wasn't flashing back all the time and she knew it wasn't depression. It was a limitless, aching sadness that marred everything she cast her eye over. She couldn't contain it: her eyes had become incontinent, dripping stupid tears into washing-up, down her coat, into shopping trolleys. She even cried while she slept. When she stood at the window in Garnethill and looked down over Glasgow she felt her face might open and flood the city with tears. Grief distracted her entirely; it was as if her life continued in an adjacent room – she could hear the noises and see the people but she couldn't participate or care about any of it.

Vik snored loudly once and stopped. He was the only thing in her life that wasn't about the past but it was the wrong time for a fresh chapter and coy new discoveries. Maureen was seeing her father everywhere, grieving for Douglas and missing Leslie desperately. Vik knew almost nothing about her, nothing about Douglas being murdered in her living room six months ago, or Michael's late-night visits to her bedroom when she was a child, nothing about the schism in her family. Telling about Michael was the worst moment with new boyfriends: she saw them change towards her, saw them feel confused and implicated.

Douglas had been different because he was a therapist. She'd never had to explain away the nightmares or the irrational phobias. Douglas was as soiled and melancholy as herself and Vik was a big, jolly boy.

She looked out of the window, took a deep draw on her fag and heard the swish of paper scraping through metal, followed by a light thud on the hall carpet. She recognized the blue hospital envelope at once – Angus was keeping busy. She picked it up and went back into the kitchen, sat down and lit a fresh cigarette from the dying tip of the old one. The envelope was made of cheap porous paper, her name and address written in a careful hand. She leaned across to the bills drawer and pulled out the pile of blue envelopes, laying all fifteen in chronological rows on the table. The writing was changing, becoming more controlled. He was getting better. Some of his letters were threatening, mostly they were gibberish, but the threats and the gibberish were evenly interspersed, regular and anticipatable. She knew the voice of random insanity from her own time in mental hospital and this wasn't it. He was a rapist and a murderer, but she wasn't afraid of him and she didn't give a shit. He was locked away in the state mental hospital. It was like being challenged to a dancing competition by a brick. Wearily, she gathered the unopened letter together with the old ones and shoved them into a drawer. She could read it later.

'Maureen?' Vik called sleepily from the bedroom. 'Maureen?'

She stubbed out her fag and tried to find her voice. 'Yeah?' She sounded tense.

'Maureen, come here.'

She stood up. 'What for?' she called.

'I've got something for you.' Vik was grinning.

She brushed the hair off her face. 'What sort of thing?' she said, forcing the playfulness. If she could act normal she might feel normal.

2

Daniel

London is a savage city and she didn't belong there. She might never have been found but for Daniel. She would have disappeared completely, a missing splinter from a shattered family, a half-remembered feature in a pub landscape.

Daniel was having a good morning. It was a sunny January day and he was on his way to his first shift as barman in a private Chelsea club favoured by footballers and professional celebrities. The traffic was sparse, the lights were going his way and he couldn't wait to get to work. He slowed at the junction, signalling right to the broad road bordering the river. He took the corner comfortably, using his weight to sway the bike, sliding across the path of traffic held static at the lights. He was about to straighten up when he saw the silver Mini careering towards him on his side of the road, the wheel-trim spitting red sparks as it scraped along the high lip of the pavement. He held his breath, yanked the handle-bars left and shot straight across the road, up over the kerb, slamming his front wheel into the low river wall at thirty miles an hour. The back wheel flew off the ground, catapulting Daniel into the air just as the Mini passed behind him. He back-flipped the long twenty-foot drop to the river, landing on a small muddy island of riverbank. The tide was out, and of all the urban rubble in the Thames he might have landed on, Daniel found himself on a sludge-soaked mattress.

He did a quick stock-take of his limbs and faculties and

found everything in order. He thanked God, remembered that he didn't believe in God and took the credit back for himself. Staggered at his skill and reflexive dexterity, he pushed himself upright on the mattress, his left hand sliding a viscous layer off the filthy surface. Gathering the mulch into his cupped hand, he squeezed hard with adrenal vigour. A crowd of concerned passers-by were leaning over the sheer wall, shouting frantically down to him. Daniel waved. 'Okay,' he shouted. 'Don't worry. Other bloke all right?'

The pedestrians looked to their left and shouted in the affirmative. Daniel grinned and looked down at his feet. He was sitting on a corpse, the heel of his foot sinking into her thigh.

He scrambled to his feet, shaking the mattress, making her arm fall out on to the muddy bank. She was wearing a chunky gold identity bracelet with 'Ann' inscribed on it. He staggered backwards towards the river, keeping his eyes on her, trying to make sense of the image.

He could see her now, a bloated pink and blue belly and a void of a face framed by stringy grey hair, drained of colour by the rapacious water. A ragged handful of custard skin was missing from her belly. Daniel called out, a strangled animal cry, and flailed his left hand in the air, scattering her disintegrating flesh. He crouched and splashed his hand in the brown water, trying to wash away the sensation. Panting, he turned back and pointed at the rotting thing hanging out of the mattress.

A man shouted to him from the high river wall. 'Are you injured?'

Daniel looked up. His eyes were brimming over. The man's head was an indeterminate blob floating above the river wall. Daniel's eyes flicked back to the corpse, startled afresh by its presence.

The well-meaning man was shouting slowly, enunciating

carefully. 'Can you hear me?' he yelled. 'I am a first-aider.'

Daniel tried to look up but each time his eyes flicked back to her. He imagined she had moved and fear took the breath from him. He started to cry and looked up. 'Are you the police?' he shouted, in a voice he barely recognized.

'No,' shouted the man. 'I am a first-aider. Do you require medical attention?'

'Get the fucking police!' screamed Daniel, his eyes streaming now, his nose running into his mouth. He shook his hand in the air, his skin burning with disgust. *'Get the fucking police.'*

3
Winnie

A stark wind streamed into Glasgow tugging black rain-clouds behind it. Litter fluttered frantically outside the strip of glass and the close door breathed gently in and out. The students kept their heads down as they worked they way up to the art school. Maureen cupped her scarf over her ears and turned up her stiff collar before opening the door and venturing out. The bullying wind buffeted her, making her totter slightly as she turned to shut the door. She kept her fists tight inside her silken pockets and made her way down the hill to the town, cosy in her rich-girl overcoat.

She had bought the coat in a pre-Christmas sale. It was pure black wool with a grey silk lining, long and flared at the bottom with a collar so stiff that it stood straight up and kept the wind off her neck. It was the most luxurious thing she had ever owned. Even at half-price it had cost more than three months' mortgage. She swithered in the shop but persuaded herself that it would last three winters, maybe even four, and anyway, she enjoyed losing the money. On the day Angus murdered him, Douglas had deposited fifteen thousand pounds in her bank account. It was a clumsy act of atonement for their affair and the money compromised her. She knew that the honourable thing to do was give it away but she was dazzled by the string of numbers on her cashpoint receipts and kept it, justifying her avarice by doing voluntary work for the Place of Safety Shelters. She was haemorrhaging money, leaving the heating on all night, smoking fancy fags, buying endless new cosmetic products, fifty-quid face creams and new-you shampoos, trying to lose it without having the courage to give it away.

The biting wind made her eyes burn and run as she crossed the hilt of the hill. Leslie would be coming into the office today and Maureen was dreading meeting her.

'Maureen?'

Someone was shouting after her, their voice diluted by the wind. She turned back. A woman in a red headscarf walked quickly over to her, keeping her head down, stepping carefully over the icy ground. She stopped two feet away from Maureen and looked up. 'Maureen, I love you.'

'Please,' said Maureen, fazed and wary, 'leave me alone.'

'I need to see you,' said Winnie.

'Mum, I asked ye to stay away,' insisted Maureen. 'I just want ye to leave me alone.'

Winnie grabbed her, squeezing her fingertips tight into the flesh on Maureen's forearm. She was drunk and had been crying for hours, possibly days. Her eyes were pink, the lids heavy and squared where the tear-ducts had swollen beneath them. A gaggle of pedestrians hurried past, coming up the steep hill from the underground, walking uncertainly on the slippery ground.

'I love you. And look,' Winnie held a silver foil parcel towards her and clenched her teeth to avert a sob, 'I've brought you some roast beef.' Winnie poked the package towards her but Maureen's hands stayed in her pockets.

'I don't want beef, Mum.'

'Take it,' said Winnie desperately. 'Please. I brought it over for you. The juice has run in my handbag. I made too much—'

A passing woman skidded slightly on the frosty ground, let out a startled exclamation and grabbed Winnie's arm to steady herself. She dragged Winnie over to one side, jerking her hand and knocking the lump of silver on to the pavement. The cheap foil burst, scattering the slices of brown meat, splattering watery blood over the white ice.

'Oh, my.' The woman giggled, nervous with fright, patting her chest as she stood up. 'Sorry about that. It's so icy this morning.'

Winnie yanked her arm away. 'You made me drop that,' she said, and the woman smelt her breath, greasy with drink at nine in the morning.

She glanced over Winnie's shoulder to Mr Padda's licensed grocer's, shot Winnie a disgusted look and stood up tall and straight. 'Didn't mean to touch you,' she said perfunctorily.

'Go away,' said Winnie indignantly.

'I'm sorry,' the woman addressed Maureen, 'I slipped—'

'We didn't ask for your life story,' snapped a suddenly nasty Winnie.

Maureen couldn't help herself. It was a big mistake but she smiled at Winnie's appalling behaviour and gave her quarter. The disapproving woman took to her heels and scuttled away, watching her feet on the icy ground. Maureen took Winnie's arm and guided her out of the busy thoroughfare and into the side of the pavement.

'Thank you, honey,' said Winnie, covering Maureen's hand with her own.

Maureen wanted to turn and walk away. Every time she had seen Winnie before the schism Winnie hurt her or freaked her out or had done her head in one way or another. She dearly wanted to walk away, but looking at her mum's badly applied makeup, at her shiny nose and big mittens, Maureen realized that she'd missed her terribly, missed all the fights and the high drama and the mingled smells of vodka and face powder. 'Mum,' she said, 'I'm not staying away from you because you don't love me.'

Tears were running down Winnie's face and her chin began to tremble. 'Why, then?' she demanded, catching the eye of a workman on his way into the newsagent's.

'You know why,' said Maureen.

Winnie wiped her face with her mittens, scarring the beige suede with her tears. 'You know about Una?' she asked.

'I know she's pregnant. Liam told me.'

Winnie sniffed, wringing her hands. 'And what did you do on Christmas Day?' she asked.

Maureen shrugged. 'Had dinner with friends,' she said.

She had spent the day alone with a packet of Marks & Spencer's sausage rolls, which she had eaten and hadn't liked at all. An hour later she had read the back of the packet and realized she was supposed to have cooked them. Liam had come over in the evening and they had watched the tail end of the good television together and had a smoke. He had refused to eat with the family because Michael would be there. Liam said George, their stepdad, had almost come out with him. George didn't like Michael either and he liked everyone. George would have liked Old Nick if he could hold a tune and got his round in.

'It's because of your father, isn't it? We hardly see him now,' said Winnie. 'He isn't very nice.'

But Maureen didn't want to know. She didn't want one more scrap of information for her subconscious to build nightmares around. 'Mum,' she said, trying to stick to the point, 'it pains me to see you, do you understand?'

Winnie pressed her hankie to her mouth. 'How do I pain you?' she said, as her face crumpled. 'What have I ever done?'

'You know fine well.'

'No,' wept Winnie, 'I don't know fine well.'

'How could you have him back in your house after what

he did to me? I'll never understand that. I know you don't believe me but if you even wondered about it—'

Winnie took a deep wavering breath, snapped her wrist out and slapped Maureen's arm. 'At least phone—'

'Don't fucking slap me, Mum!' shouted Maureen. 'I'm an adult. It's not appropriate.'

Winnie began to sob, making Maureen into the sort of person who would shout unkind things at her crying mother. She had promised herself peace from this but here she was, falling into the old traps, playing the bad guy again, coming to hate herself on a whole new level.

'We don't see him any more,' Winnie struggled to speak through convulsive sobs, 'and Una's angry and George won't speak to me ... I miss you, Maureen. I don't want you to not see me.'

Maureen wondered at Winnie's resilience. If Winnie had set her mind to world domination she could have done it. Unhampered by the twin evils of manners or empathy, Winnie could railroad an acre of salesmen into charity work if she set her mind to it.

'Mum,' she said softly, 'I don't want to see you for a while and that continues to be true, whether or not you're all having a nice time together.'

Winnie clocked the condition. She looked up when Maureen said it would only be for a while and looked away again. She blew her nose and narrowed her eyes at Maureen. 'Don't you tell me what to do,' she said, hope twitching at the corners of her mouth. 'You're still a cheeky wee besom. And I'll slap ye if I want to. I could take you in a fight any day.' She looked at the spilled meat, scattered and trampled by passing feet. 'Are ye sure ye won't have a slice?'

Maureen started to smile but her eyes began to water and she had to breathe in deeply and blink hard to stop herself crying. It was good news: they weren't getting on, he had nothing to keep him here, no reason to stay. Winnie took off one of her mittens and played with her hankie, pulling at the corners, looking for a dry patch. The wedding band George had given her was loose on her finger Winnie was losing weight; her skin looked thin and a watery grey liver spot was developing on a knuckle. Maureen reached out suddenly and held her mum's hand, cupping it in her own, trying to hold the warm in. The wind blew freezing tears across her face like racing insects. 'Mum,' she breathed. 'My mum.'

They stood close, looking at Winnie's hand, chins trembling for love of each other, crying for the pointless sadness of it all.

'I can't stand this,' whispered Maureen.

'Me neither,' said Winnie

But she meant the moment and Maureen meant her life. Winnie reached up to Maureen's face, dabbing at her wet ear like a drunken St Veronica, letting her fingers linger on her cheek.

Maureen sniffed hard, dragging the cold air up to her eyes, waking herself up. 'Is he going back to London, then?'

'Don't think so,' said Winnie.

'Who's keeping him here?'

Winnie tutted at her. 'No-one's keeping him here,' she said. 'He's got a flat, a council flat, in Ruchill.' She pointed over Maureen's shoulder to the horizon, to the jagged red-brick tower of the old Ruchill hospital.

Maureen could see it from her bedroom window. She dropped Winnie's hand. 'What the fuck did you tell me that for?'

Winnie shrugged carelessly. 'It's where he is.'

'I don't want to know anything about him and you come here and tell me he lives near me?'

Winnie knew she was in the wrong. She tugged her

mitten back on and pressed her face up to Maureen's. Did it ever occur to you,' she said, 'that the rest of us know him as well?'

'What?'

'It's not all about you,' shouted Winnie. 'He's their father too. Don't you think they wonder about him? Don't you think I wonder?'

'Wonder?' shouted Maureen. 'You stupid cow! D'ye think I was committed to a psychiatric hospital suffering from pathological wonder?'

'Don't you cast that up to me.' Winnie held up her hand. 'Your breakdown wasn't just about him. You were always a strange wee girl. You were always unhappy.'

They hadn't seen each other for five months and although Maureen vividly remembered how angry her mother made her, she had forgotten the sanctimonious bulldozing, the utter disregard for her feelings, the vicious kindness and blind denial of what Michael had done.

'Think about it, Winnie,' she said, talking through her teeth, the fury reducing her voice to a whisper, 'think about what he did to me. If it wasn't for him I'd never have been so unhappy. If it wasn't for him I'd never have been in hospital. I'd have gone on to a real job after my fucking degree. I might be happy, I might be married. I might even have the nerve to hope for children of my own. I might be able to sleep. I might be able to look at myself in the fucking mirror without wanting to scratch my fucking face off.' She was out of control, shouting loud and crying in the street. Art students stole glances at her as they came out of Mr Padda's with their newspapers and lunchtime rolls. 'And what did he sacrifice all of that for? For a fucking tug.'

Winnie had never believed in the abuse and had never flinched from saying so before. But this time she pursed her lips and clasped her hands prissily in front of her. 'Is that all you want to say?' she said, grinding her teeth and looking off into the middle distance.

Winnie was trying to listen. She was actually trying, and Maureen had never known her do that. Not when they were children, not when they were adults, not even when Maureen was in hospital. 'Mum, that man and the memories and stuff. I know what he did. He knows he did it too.'

Winnie looked nervously around her. 'Do we have to discuss this here?'

'Does he ever ask for me?'

Winnie swallowed hard and looked away. She muttered something into the wind.

'What?' said Maureen.

'No,' said Winnie quietly. 'He never asks for you. Ever. It's as if you were never born.'

'How likely is that, Winnie? Doesn't it make ye wonder?'

Winnie couldn't think of an answer. It must have bothered her terribly. She looked angrily over Maureen's shoulder. 'I'm sick of this,' she said.

'Why did you tell me he lives there? God, am I not troubled enough already?'

'You can't blame me for that—'

But Maureen was backing off into the street. She leaned forward in case Winnie missed anything. 'Stay away from me,' she said slowly, pointing at her mum's soft chest. 'And stop phone-pesting me when you're steaming.'

'If I was that bad of a mother,' Winnie shouted after her, 'how come none of the rest of them had breakdowns?'

The vicious morning frost had numbed Maureen's ears before she was two hundred yards down the hill. She turned a corner and the wind ambushed her, parting her eyelashes. She stopped and waited at the lights, staring at the patchwork tar on the road. The nervous cars and buses jostled each other for road space, speeding across the twenty-foot yellow box, afraid of being left back at the lights. If she threw herself into the road she'd be killed instantly, a five-foot jump to an eternity of peace and no more brave ploughing on, no more shouting over the storm, no more nightmares, no more Michael. She thought of Pauline Doyle and envied her.

Pauline was a June suicide. She had been in psychiatric hospital with Maureen. Two weeks after she was released, a walker had found her dead under a tree. Maureen couldn't stop thinking about her. Her thoughts kept short-circuiting straight from worry to the happy image of Pauline at peace on the grass in springtime, oblivious to the insects crawling over her legs.

She glanced up, conscious that something around her had changed. The green man was flashing on and off and the other pedestrians had almost crossed the road. She jogged after them, clutching the fag packet in her pocket, bribing herself on with the promise of a cigarette when she got to work.

4
Work

The morning dragged by like a stranger's funeral. Maureen found herself picking over everything Winnie had said, looking for clues about the family, guessing what she really meant. Liam had told her that Una was pregnant, but Maureen wasn't concerned: she knew the baby would be safe from Michael because Alistair, Una's husband, was so even-tempered and he had always believed Maureen about the abuse. What jarred more intensely was Winnie trying to listen to her. Douglas used to say that Maureen was hypervigilant with her family, always looking for signals and signs, clues about what was going to happen next, because nothing was predictable. He said it was a common behavioural trait in children from disturbed backgrounds.

She couldn't remember Douglas's face properly any more. All she could picture were his eyes as he smiled at her and blinked, a strip of memory floating in a void, like an animated photofit strip. Maureen looked across the desk at Jan.

Jan was tall and blonde and plump around the middle. She had an inexplicable penchant for wearing green and purple together and giggled about it, as if she was a great character. She stayed with her parents on the south side but resented living in their warm home and eating their groceries. Her parents had retired recently and seemed to spend their days kicking about the house, bickering with each other about minutiae. Jan kept trying to engage

Maureen in the dull stories by asking about her own parents: did they fight, were they happy, who took out the rubbish? Maureen made up a story about a close family of two with an adoring mother who was very religious. Their father had left them when they were very young. She didn't remember him but he was a sailor with a gambling habit and a beard. When Maureen saw her fictional father in her head she always imagined him steering a fishing-boat and wearing a yellow sou'wester and joke glasses with pop-out eyeballs on springs.

'Smoke?' said Jan.

'Two minutes,' said Maureen, and went back to staring at a chapter in the housing-law textbook. It didn't make any sense. A regulation had imported a double negative into the legislation. She was crap at this. When they had given her the job it was because of Leslie and the posters, not because she had shown any capacity to map housing legislation or write summaries. The few reports she had submitted were politely bounced back for revision by the committee and she knew their buoyant faith in her was flagging.

In anticipation of the funding cut, the Place of Safety Shelters had moved to the cheapest city-centre office in Glasgow. It was an ugly, grey, windowless room. The funding cut had been deferred because of the poster campaign but the PSS stayed there, saving their money as best they could, getting ready for the hard times ahead.

The poster campaign was one of the few selfless things Maureen had done with Douglas's money. Leslie didn't tell the committee they were doing it. They plastered the city with the posters in one long night, working from west to east and finishing at dawn. Not many people phoned the funding committee number at the bottom of the poster to protest. The picture was quite obscure and most people didn't know what it was about but, still, the funding cut had been deferred for six months. Everyone in the office had been speculating about the posters after the decision was announced; Leslie called a meeting and admitted responsibility. She told them that her pal had masterminded the scheme, paid for it all herself, and now she'd like to work for them on a voluntary basis if they could find a place for her. They saw that Maureen had a degree and gave her the housing job. She'd been a hero two months ago – everyone in the office wanted to talk to her. The desk she shared with Jan was right by the door and she could hardly get a full hour's work done on any given day because women kept stopping by for a chat. She had a lot more time now.

Work was a reluctant ten-minute stroll from Maureen's house. She hated the ugly office, the endless river of broken women they had to turn away, and her occasional strained run-ins with Leslie. Once or twice in every working day Maureen wanted to get up and walk out but she stopped herself. She'd be letting Leslie down if she chucked it and she was doing something that mattered. She could stay for a short while, until the money ran out. So she was spending her days trying not to cry in front of Jan, avoiding Leslie and writing reports on housing-law regulations with exceptional incompetence.

Jan stood up from her chair and pulled on her coat.

'Benny Hedgehog?' she said, picking up her fag packet.

'Naw,' said Maureen, taking one from her own. 'I'll just have a Silkie.'

They made sure they had a light and headed downstairs to the street.

Staff weren't allowed to smoke in the grey open-plan office. The air-conditioning didn't work well so the committee had decided that only the waiting women could smoke. Jan and Maureen spent large portions of their days downstairs trying to think of something to say to each other. Cliques of exiled smokers are usually intimate and pleasurable, coming together as they do in ten-minute bursts of addicts' camaraderie. At the PSS Maureen found herself spending a lot of time with Jan and other women in whom she had no interest, trying to participate in conversations without crying, grasping for the appropriate response when Jan upped the friendship gears with whispered confidences.

'You all right?' asked Jan, as they took the first flight of stairs. 'You look a bit pale today.'

'I need a fag.'

'I think you're getting flu.' Jan lowered her voice. 'Did ye hear about Ann?'

'Ann?' said Maureen.

'Ann Harris, remember? She came to us, she was all cuts and bruises and didn't want to go to Casualty. She moved into Leslie's shelter.'

Maureen did remember Ann because of her peculiar colouring. Ann's pink skin clashed with her yellow hair, making her look angry or ashamed or on the verge of throwing up. She wore a big yellow gold identity bracelet that accentuated the discord, as if she was decorating the mistake. Maureen had noticed that wearing big jewellery was a feature of the very rich and the very poor for essentially the same reasons. But she remembered Ann most vividly because so few women came in after a bad beating. For most the decision to leave was a long, slow dawning.

Ann had come in wild-eyed and badly beaten, smelling like a long binge on cheap drink, asking for the pictures to be taken before she was even assured of a place. The Criminal Compensation Board photographs were always offered to the women. They provided evidence for interdicts and criminal prosecutions. Usually the women didn't want proof, they just wanted to get away and feel safe, but Ann wanted them. She didn't want to prosecute, she said, just wanted a record, just in case. She sat next to Maureen on one of the plastic chairs, waiting to be interviewed, and then waiting again for Katia to set up the camera. She sat staring at the floor, taking the fags Maureen offered her, smoking around the split on her bottom lip. The swelling was as thick as a thumb, like a localized collagen implant.

'Well,' continued Jan, 'she's disappeared.' She looked shocked, as if the end of the story had come as a complete surprise to her.

'She's probably lying drunk somewhere,' said Maureen.

'No,' said Jan, 'because she emptied her locker and she's gone.'

'Well, she's left, then,' said Maureen. 'What's surprising about that? Lots of women leave without saying anything.'

Jan had heard the story from someone else and they had been very surprised. She didn't remember why but she knew that they were. She opened the glass door and slipped out into the street, feeling sure she had forgotten part of the story.

Katia's pillar-box-red hair bobbed out of the doorway and Maureen was tempted to turn round and go back upstairs.

'Oh, hi,' said Katia, leaning out. 'How's it going?'

Katia was very pretty with a perfect figure and Krazy-Kolor red hair, which she wore in bunches.

'Not bad,' said Jan, huddling in next to her.

The deep doorway was the best spot for winter smoking. A vent at the back exhaled warm air from a bakery, carrying the sweet smell of hot bread. It was only big enough for two people, and Maureen had to stand in the cold, wet street, huddling her face in beside them so that she could catch a light in the windless vacuum.

'Hi, Maureen,' said Katia. 'Are you not talking to me?'

Maureen bared her teeth.

'I think she's coming down with a flu,' said Jan kindly. 'My dad's got it.'

'Yes.' Katia let off an asinine smile and touched Maureen's cheek. 'You look very pale.'

Maureen lit her cigarette very suddenly, half hoping she might burn Katia's hand, and sucked all the badness down, away from her mouth.

'Bloody freezing,' said Jan, nodding and stamping her feet.

'Yeah,' said Katia, pulling up the furry hood of her parka, watching Maureen all the time, 'freezing.'

A lorry backed up in front of them, deafening them with a loud reversing beep, and Maureen took a deep draw.

'And how's the lovely Vikram?' asked Katia, when the lorry had come to a standstill.

'Fine,' said Maureen.

'Good,' said Katia tartly. She saw that the conversation wasn't going anywhere and sucked the last life out of her cigarette, flicking the butt out into the road. 'See ye later, then.'

Neither Jan nor Maureen answered her. Katia went back inside.

'I don't know why,' said Jan, looking guilty, 'but I don't like her very much.'

Maureen huddled next to her in the coddling calm of the doorway. 'Me neither.' She had been nursing a caustic resentment of Katia since Vik's band played Nice and Sleazy's. Katia and Maureen had passed each other in the office; they didn't know each other at all. Vik sat Maureen at the girlfriends' table and Katia spotted her from the bar. She slipped lithely between the tables, sat next to Maureen and shouted over the music that she didn't expect to see her here, did she like the band? Yeah, Maureen did like the band. Katia had been following them for ages, she'd heard their session on the radio, and she'd taken their first band pictures for them. Through innuendo and references to other brilliant nights Katia made it clear that she had gone out with Vik very recently and was surprised that Maureen had managed to nip him. When Vik came over at the end Katia made a big play of kissing him and hanging on his neck. Maureen sat at the table, pulling her coat tight around herself, affronted at being roped into a demeaning competition over a boyfriend she'd only known for a minute and a half.

'You do look pale, though, Maureen,' said Jan.

'I'm fine, really.'

'You might get the flu.'

'Honest, Jan, I'm fine.'

'Dad's half dead with it,' said Jan. 'It's a bad bug.'

'Yeah, I need another fag. Have ye got your packet with ye?'

Jan dished them out and saw the tremble in Maureen's hand as she lit it.

'I think you're right,' said Maureen, 'I think I am getting flu.'

'Maybe you should take a few days off.'

Pedestrians scuttled past them, carrying shopping, hurrying to work, and Maureen looked out of the doorway. Every face was potentially Michael's. She didn't know what he looked like now; all she remembered about him was that he was twice as tall as the rest of them. He knew what she looked like. He would have seen her graduation photo hanging on Winnie's wall. She thought her way around the streets of Ruchill, trying to imagine where the council would have put him. The hospital was an STD clinic with a needle- exchange in the gatehouse. Maureen had been to the hospital once for an HIV test, one of the worried well, and the nurse had told her that it had been built on the isolated hill overlooking the city because it was a fever hospital. During the height of one epidemic the wards held a hundred at a time, she said, they were top to tail in the beds, dead for hours before they could clear them out. Ruchill was a burnt- out, boarded-up area with no shops and a notorious pub built from concrete slabs, painted black with high, mean windows. It looked like a machine-gun nest and she thought Michael might drink there.

Maureen and Jan had finished smoking but stood about in the freezing cold, warming the backs of their heads on the baker's vent, watching the traffic pass.

'I can't be annoyed with this today,' muttered Maureen.

'I know what ye mean,' said Jan.

They left the warm doorway, climbing the stairs slowly and shedding their coats.

It was late afternoon, minutes before the house managers' meeting was due to start, and Leslie swaggered in through the double doors wearing her leathers and carrying her crash helmet. Leslie's hair was short and dirty and stuck up like a windswept hamster's. Her skin was sallow, her big round eyes were black, and she was always mistaken for taller than she was. She walked into every room as if she was there to get her money.

'All right, Mauri?' she said, and nodded, surprised and apparently pleased to see her.

'All right yourself?' said Maureen.

Leslie glanced at Jan. She leaned over Maureen's desk and muttered, 'What ye doing later?'

'Nothing.'

'Come for something to eat?'

'Aye,' said Maureen, blushing with pleasure.

'Let's go to Finneston,' said Leslie, and stood up. 'I'll get ye when I've finished. Did ye hear about Ann Harris?'

'I did, aye.'

Leslie was about to say something but she noticed Jan watching her and stopped herself. 'I'll get ye on the way out, then,' she said and strode off to her meeting.

Jan smiled uncomfortably at her desk, irritated that Leslie had excluded her. Maureen could have explained that Leslie didn't mean to be rude, she just was rude, but Jan might come around the desk for a chat so she left it. Jan tried a pleasant smile. 'Leslie's always taken a personal interest in Ann, hasn't she?'

'Oh, yeah,' said Maureen, shuffling her papers.

'I heard she asked the committee for Ann to be placed in her shelter, is that true?'

Place of Safety Shelters was broke and the house managers were all working to aspirational budgets. No-one asked for new residents: they tried to palm them off on each other.

'Dunno,' said Maureen, puzzled. 'Dunno about that.'

She went downstairs to the toilet for a private smoke and a think.

5
Ann

Ann hadn't been seen for a month. She had left the shelter
five days after Christmas and never come back. The other
women in the shelter weren't worried. They thought she'd
gone back to her man. The kids were still with him and it
must have been hard for her to stay away, especially over
Christmas. The police weren't worried either. They took
her man's word for it that he hadn't seen or heard from her.
But Leslie was worried. Ann had left behind a bundle of
photographs. They were childhood pictures, birthday and
anniversary snaps. Young Ann with workmates in a factory.
Ann sitting up in a hospital bed smiling softly down at
the newborn in her arms as if the whole world lay there.
Among them was a Polaroid of a big man standing in
a school playground. He wore a camel-hair coat and
brown Reactalite glasses. He was grinning and holding
the hand of a sullen six-year-old boy. Maureen came to a
series of badly focused pictures that were all the same size
and shape: Ann with a sore lip and some other women in
front of a Christmas tree with Leslie behind them, her arm
raised in mid-gesture, the flash turning her pupils a demon
red.

'These are in the shelter at Christmas, aren't they?' asked
Maureen.

'Yeah,' said Leslie.

'How did ye get the women to stand for a picture?'

'I just asked them if they wanted to be in it.' Leslie

shrugged. 'It's Christmas Day. We try and keep it as normal as possible.'

It was late. The meeting had run over and the other house managers had hurried home quickly to warm houses and hungry children, leaving Maureen and Leslie alone in the office. They were sitting on the edge of Maureen's desk, listening as the wind whistled up the stairwell, tapping illegal fags on the floor and stepping their ash into the carpet. Leslie was in a different mood now, efficient and formal after her meeting, and she wouldn't look at Maureen.

'She wouldn't leave these,' said Leslie, taking the photographs back from Maureen. 'I know she wouldn't.'

'Were you quite close?' asked Maureen, trying to catch her eye.

Leslie blew a brisk cloud of smoke at her. 'No,' she said, rubbing her eye with the ball of her hand. 'Not really.'

'Well, how do you know she wouldn't leave the photos?'

Leslie dropped her fag end into a dry Radio Clyde mug. 'I just know she wouldn't. She'd only leave them if she thought she was coming back.'

The mug oozed smoke like a beaker in a crazy professor's lab. 'Maybe she just forgot them,' said Maureen, reaching in and stubbing out the butt, getting the sticky smell on her fingers.

'She wouldn't forget pictures of her kids – she talked about them all the time.'

'Maybe she wanted to start a new life,' said Maureen, 'and she just got pissed, snapped and fucked off. Loads of people do that. It was Christmas, that's bound to be an emotional time.'

Leslie shook her head. 'I think it was something to do with the card she got. It was delivered on the thirtieth of December and it freaked her out. She left an hour later.'

'Do women get mail delivered to the shelter?'

'Some women get application forms for jobs and things but hers didn't look formal.'

'Did you see it?'

'I saw the envelope. Most of the mail we get is bills and stuff so it comes to me and I dish it out. She didn't tell anyone what it was.'

'How do you know it was a card, then?'

Leslie thought about it. 'The envelope was square and stiff and Christmassy. It was red.'

'And she disappeared just afterwards?'

Leslie nodded. 'Hours afterwards,' she said, formal. 'I'm worried about her. I'm worried something's happened to her.'

Maureen looked at Leslie. She had the distinct impression of being lied to, of Leslie giving her limited information and herding her into a corner. 'Well, other women have left the shelter without saying anything and ye didn't worry about them this much.'

'But it's not usually this sudden. There are usually signs that someone's going to leave, like they drop hints or withdraw emotionally.' Leslie sounded as if she was giving a presentation. 'Usually they leave the shelter for longer and longer periods, stay out an odd night, take some of their belongings, and then they just don't come back. Ann didn't do that. She was just there and then, suddenly, she wasn't there.' She glanced sidelong at Maureen, gauging the impact of her speech, and went back to pretending to pore over the photographs.

'But Ann was a steamer,' said Maureen, 'and steamers do crazy things.'

'How do you know she was a steamer?' said Leslie quickly

'Because,' Maureen pointed at the row of plastic chairs next to her desk, 'she sat next to me. She was there for an hour on and off while they filled out her forms and set up the camera. I smelt her.'

Leslie shrugged resentfully. 'So, what does that mean?' she said. 'We're both steamers too.'

'We're not quite in Ann's league, though, are we?' said Maureen, thinking that Leslie might have been. Maureen didn't know how much she drank any more. 'Did Ann drink when she was staying with you?'

'Sometimes.'

'That's against the house rules, isn't it?'

Leslie glanced at her. 'She never drank in the house.' She sounded defensive. 'She'd say she was going to the shops and come back drunk.'

Maureen stubbed out her fag in the mug, compounding the smell on her fingers. She shouldn't have to do this, waiting behind in the horrible office, trying to guess what Leslie really meant. If Leslie didn't trust her any more she should fucking find someone she did and bore them with it.

'I heard you asked for her as a resident,' said Maureen.

'No, I didn't.'

'I heard ye did. I thought you were strapped for cash.'

'That's utter shite,' said Leslie, belligerent and annoyed, 'I didn't ask for her, I just happened to have a space.'

Maureen looked at her and sucked a hiss through her teeth. 'Leslie,' she said, 'do you know Ann?'

'No.'

'Why are you so interested in her, then?'

Leslie paused and pulled another cigarette out of her packet, but Maureen knew she wasn't a consecutive smoker. She was lighting up so that she'd have something to fiddle with, so she wouldn't have to look at Maureen.

'I don't know Ann,' said Leslie slowly, measuring her speech, 'but I'm worried about her.' She pursed her lips tight around her cigarette, lifting the lighter to the tip. The orange flame cast her face in stark relief and Maureen saw a miserable tremor on Leslie's chin. Whatever she was holding back wasn't keeping her warm at night.

Leslie was looking at the Polaroid of the big man and the small boy. The boy had Ann's fluffy yellow hair and pink skin. He didn't look happy and Maureen could tell from the strain in his forearm that he was trying to pull his hand away. His free hand clutched a handmade Christmas card decorated with glitter and gluey cotton wool. 'Is that Ann's kid?' she asked softly.

'Yeah,' said Leslie, her voice a little higher, a little uncontrolled. 'She's got another three, all boys.'

'He's like her, isn't he?'

Leslie nodded, clearing her throat, regaining her composure. Maureen sat next to her on the desk again, pretending to look at the picture but letting their hips touch, staying by her. 'I didn't see her again after she left the office,' said Maureen gently. 'Did her lip heal okay?'

Leslie nodded again. 'Yeah. She got a scar on it but the swelling went down pretty quick.' The colour rose in her face. 'Mauri, I'm frightened she's dead,' she blurted.

Maureen looked at her and snorted with surprise. 'Where did ye get that from?'

'From these.' Leslie slapped the photograph in her hand emphatically. 'They're pictures of everything big that ever happened to her. She wouldn't leave them. I think someone was after her.'

'Come on, Leslie, it's a shelter for battered women, there's someone's after all of them.'

'This is different.'

'Why is it different?'

But that was exactly the question Leslie didn't want to

answer. 'I think we should look for her,' she said, 'see what we can dig up.'

'We wouldn't know where to start.'

'We did it last time.'

'Yeah,' said Maureen, 'but you weren't lying out of your arse the last time.'

They sat side by side, looking around the office, as if the answer had been misplaced on someone's desk. Maureen rubbed her eye. 'Winnie came to see me this morning,' she said, falling into the old way of telling Leslie everything at the forefront of her mind. 'Michael's got a flat in Glasgow.' She wished she hadn't said it. She was opening up to Leslie through force of habit, telling her most intimate worries when Leslie wasn't there and Leslie didn't care.

Leslie looked at her aggressively. 'If he bothers you at all,' she said, 'I'll kick his teeth in.'

'Aye,' said Maureen sceptically. 'Right.'

Leslie had crapped it when they were chasing Angus. It was the one and only time Maureen had asked her to lift her hands but Leslie still talked like the world's hardest gangster. Maureen had begun to suspect that she needed to feel hard in response to a deep, souring fear. Leslie had been working at the shelter for a long time and she needed to differentiate herself from the women. If Leslie couldn't handle herself she would be a candidate for everything she saw there, a victim in waiting, as vulnerable as the rest of them, waiting to be raped and ripped, waiting for fate to ambush her.

'Are you hungry?' said Leslie, pulling on her leather jacket.

Maureen shrugged. She didn't want this, spending an evening with new, distant Leslie, being lied to and feeling like a mug and pretending that it didn't matter. She wanted to be alone, at home with a bottle of whisky and the

33

unquestioning companionship of the television.

'Well, are you coming, or what?'

Wearily, Maureen picked up her coat and her bag and followed Leslie down the stairs.

It was seven o'clock but as dark as midnight. A thin drizzle was falling, wafted up and down and sideways by the high wind, clinging to every surface. Leslie's bike was parked across the street. She gave Maureen the spare helmet from the luggage box and kick-started the engine on the fifth go. Maureen held on to her waist, resting her head on her shoulder.

A slick of rain covered the road and Leslie was driving too fast. She ducked between vans and cars, revving the engine angrily before changing gear. At the foot of a high hill she skidded on a sharp turn, bristled with fright and corrected herself, steadying the bike at the last minute. Maureen thought they were going to crash, that they might die, and the possibility left her feeling strangely elated. She let go of Leslie as the road slid away beneath her, holding on to nothing, feeling the wind push and pull her off balance. She swayed like a reed on the pillion as they drove through the dark, sodden city to the west.

6

Forever Friends

Maureen had always known that Leslie could be a cheeky bitch but she'd never turned on her before. She would never have believed that a boyfriend could come between them because they weren't those sort of women. They were bigger than that, they had a heroic history, and they were too close. She wrongly assumed that Cammy would be just another blow-through. She went out with them a couple of times but afterwards she was always left with the uncomfortable impression of having been talked about, kindly perhaps, but still talked about.

They had only been together a couple of months but Leslie had changed. She didn't want to spend time with anyone but Cammy any more and was always leaving early to hurry home to him. She started talking about having children and had changed the way she dressed. She bought a new pair of leather trousers for casual wear, offence enough in itself, but she coupled them with low-cut sexy tops with a deep cleavage that made her look cheap and vulnerable.

The last time they had arranged to go out together Leslie stood her up. Maureen waited at the bar, drinking slowly at first, checking her watch every five minutes, every three minutes, every indignant fucking minute as she realized that Leslie wasn't coming. She phoned the house. Leslie said she'd forgotten. Sorry. But Maureen said how could she forget? They'd only made the fucking arrangement the day before. Leslie giggled and whispered to Cammy to stop it and Maureen blushed as she listened to them, intimate and exclusive, sniggering at her. She slammed down the receiver and tramped up the road to her house feeling like a tit.

Maureen and Leslie had met through a mutual fear of the Slosh. It was a horrible wedding. Lisa and Kenny were barely twenty and had only been together for seven months of drunken fights and public sex acts. The food was bland, the bride was drunk and the groom spent the reception making faces into the video camera. The communal knowledge that the marriage was ill-advised added a hysterical edge to the reception. Everyone laughed too loud, acted drunk before they really were, danced confidently. Maureen and Leslie were sulking alone at adjacent tables while everyone else congoed in an ungainly stagger around the room, whooping and yanking at each other's clothes. Leslie scowled over at Maureen, tapped a fag from her and warned her that the band were threatening to do the Slosh. The Slosh is a graceless women-only line dance and non-participation is illegal at Scottish weddings, punishable by ritual dragging on to the dance floor.

'Let's get the fuck out of here,' said Maureen, and they retired to the bar for the rest of the evening.

They drank whisky and smoked cheap, dry cigars they bought from behind the bar. Maureen thought they were just big fags and inhaled vigorously. She could hardly speak the next day but that was down to the shouting as well; it was the most stimulating pub argument she had ever had. Leslie thought that women and men were born different but Maureen believed that gendered behaviour was learned. Leslie made sweeping statements about the nature of men and women on the flimsiest of evidence: all men were bad drivers; all men were arrogant and bullish; all women were kind and helpful. It was like listening to a bigoted misogynist in reverse. Maureen said that if women did have an essential nature it wouldn't only encompass good things, some characteristics would have to be bad, like being crap at sums or too simple-minded to vote. Leslie didn't have an answer but got round it by shouting the same points over and over. They swapped numbers and stayed in touch. They went to Lisa's divorce dinner together. By the time Maureen had finished her degree they had become so close that Leslie and Liam were her guests at the graduation dinner.

The art-history class was not a representative cross-section of society. It was an intellectual finishing school for posh lassies, a grounding for careers in auction houses and other jobs so badly paid and highly prized that only the very rich could consider them. Maureen wasn't moulding a career, she just loved the subject, and didn't think she'd live to see twenty-one. The girls were mostly from London and Manchester, they all had long flickable hair, timeless clothes, family jewellery. The milk-fed girls were slightly afraid of Maureen and she enjoyed it. It was probably the only social group in Glasgow where she would be thought of as a rough local. Leslie, who actually was a rough local, took umbrage at the graduation dinner and tried to insult all of her classmates, picking on Sarah Simmons particularly because she had misjudged the evening and worn her dead mother's filigree tiara. The girls conceded most of Leslie's points, taking it all in good part, and suggested moving the evening on to a cheesy disco, looking for a gang of horny medics who were known to hang out there. Maureen, Liam and Leslie deferred the invite. Trying to spoil it for them, Leslie told the girls that the disco was known locally as 'a-pint-and-a-fuck'. The girls got even more excited and left before the coffee arrived.

Maureen didn't work hard for her finals. She knew that something was happening to her. The flashbacks, the disorientation and the night terrors were building to a pitch. All her time in the university library was spent on the sixth floor reading books and articles about mental illness. She thought she was becoming schizophrenic but she didn't tell anyone what was happening. She was afraid that they would put her away, afraid that Leslie would disappear and take all the cosy, normal nights with her. It was almost a year later, when Maureen had her breakdown, that Leslie's true nature became clear.

After Liam found her in the hall cupboard in Garnethill and carried her into hospital wrapped in a blanket, whispering comfort and baptizing her with his tears, Leslie was the first person to visit and she kept on coming. She worked her shifts at the shelter around visit times, bringing magazines and nice food and spending time with her. But even Leslie couldn't stop the dreams or the fear or the panicked terror or the screaming at night. Winnie came to visit, sobbing loudly, drunk and drunker, attracting pitying glances from the patients. Una came to visit and brought Alistair. They smiled nervously and left quickly. Marie, their oldest sister, couldn't make it up from London. Busy time at the bank.

Maureen had been in hospital for weeks when Alistair came to visit alone. He betrayed his promise to Una and told the doctors that this had happened before. Maureen was ten when the family found her locked in the cupboard under the stairs. Winnie jimmied it open and pulled her out by her leg as Marie and Una stood by. Maureen had a long bruise on the side of her face and when they gave her a bath they had found dried blood between her legs. No-one knew what had happened but Michael left Glasgow for good, taking the cheque book, and never contacted them again. Winnie didn't have to tell them it was a secret: the children knew instinctively. No-one had mentioned it again until Una took Alistair into her confidence and he took it upon himself to tell Maureen's doctors.

It made sense of everything – Maureen's horror of people stealing into her room when she was sleeping, of the smell of drink in a certain light, of the dreams of prying fingers and hush and fumble in the dark. He had panicked when he saw the blood. She remembered the fist on the side of her head, the blankets of white behind her eyes, being lifted and locked in and left alone with the smell of blood, hoping she would die before he got back. When the fresh horror of the hospital and the breakdown subsided, what hurt her most was that in her memory Michael hadn't been responding to an uncontrollable urge. The abuse was half-hearted, as if he was just having a go, just road-testing a fresh form of dissipation.

Since the day Alistair came to see the doctors in hospital Maureen had always believed that Michael had made her bleed by ripping her inside with a ragged fingernail. It wasn't until later, much later, when she attacked Angus and he had shouted it at her, that she considered the other possibility. Angus said that Michael had raped her. The dreams and the signs all pointed to it, and in her heart she knew it might be true. It shouldn't matter, she told herself, it hurt and she bled and that was all. She was a child, and children don't perceive sex as centring on penetration. Priests and lawyers and gynaecologists do, but children don't. The possibility that he raped her shouldn't make any difference but it did, it mattered terribly. The possibility violated her in ways she couldn't name.

Winnie had made it clear at the hospital that she didn't believe Michael had abused Maureen, and Maureen dearly wanted her to be right. It was easier to believe that she herself was wrong and leave the world intact. She slid back into darkness like sand into the second chamber. And all this time Leslie came, as inexorable as a lava-flow. She got Maureen to write a list of the reasons why she wasn't making it all up. She brought books about surviving and articles about families' reactions to disclosure. She told Maureen that she wasn't the only one who didn't want to believe it: no-one wanted to; no-one wanted to know about abuse.

Maureen was at a disadvantage because Leslie had seen her at her lowest point. She saw Leslie pity other patients, avoiding them, grimacing openly as Pauline walked towards them in the grounds wearing shorts. She had never once looked at Maureen like that but, then, Pauline was hard not to pity. Admitted to the hospital weighing five stone and aiming for three, Pauline could never bring herself to tell the police what her father and brother had been doing. If her mother found out it would kill her. She had been discharged for all of two weeks when she was found in the scraggy woods near her house. She was under a tree, curled up into a ball, her face covered by her skirt. She had dried spunk on her back and the police thought she had been murdered until they found the letter in the house, a vague, heartbroken ramble about bad feelings and difficulty coping.

Leslie hadn't come to the funeral, she had said she wouldn't be able to keep her mouth shut, and they had all decided not to tell her mother. It had been Pauline's only ambition. Her mother cried so hard she burst the blood vessels in her eye. The father stood next to her on the bench, squeezing her shoulder when her sobs became too loud. The brothers wore cheap suits and hurried to get outside and have a fag, missing the line-up by the door. No-one at the funeral knew which of the brothers had been raping her. Pauline never told. The family huddled in the pub after the service, silently sipping whisky and smoking hard. Liam insisted on buying the father a pint and slipped two tabs of acid into it. Months later, they heard through the grapevine that the father had gone mad with grief and had been hospitalized himself.

Leslie relished that small, vicious gesture. In all the time Maureen had known her, Leslie had always talked lovingly about direct action and how she'd like to blow this up and stab that one and lead the revolution. The only time either of them had attempted anything was when they came up against Angus Farrell. Angus had killed Douglas and a dear man called Martin but they couldn't turn him in. He had done it to cover up his systematic rape of the women on the ward at the Northern psychiatric hospital, knowing that none of the deeply damaged women could give credible evidence against him. Maureen and Leslie went after him themselves, luring him to the tiny seaside town of Millport on the Isle of Cumbrae, but Leslie lost her bottle at the last minute, saying she knew she'd freeze if she had to do anything but sit with Siobhain. Maureen had attacked Angus alone.

They had all that history between them, knew so much about each other and Maureen felt sure they would get over Leslie's bad-choice boyfriend. It was Hogmanay before she finally realized that Cammy wasn't a blip, that their friendship was really dying.

Millennium Hogmanay was not Liam's most auspicious social outing. There was a bad dry on, and demand for party drugs was exceptionally high. It seemed that everyone in Glasgow wanted to celebrate two thousand years of the Christian message by getting completely out of it. Liam had retired from dealing several months before; he still had a lot of contacts but even he couldn't get a deal. Unused to drinking without chemical enhancement, he got completely off his face by half ten.

Liam had never hosted a party before; he'd only recently

admitted to having access to the rest of the house. During his dark, dealing days, he had left the ground floor of the three-storey town-house as worn and dirty as it was when he bought it. He kept the partition at the foot of the stairs to give his many dodgy visitors the impression that upstairs was a separate flat. He had been raided during the investigation into Douglas's murder and the police had scared the living shit out of him. They brought dogs and ripped up the floorboards. They strip-searched him and his girlfriend. They talked to all his neighbours and told them why they were there. They emptied every cupboard in the house, tipped over every box and container. It was a long time afterwards before he told Maureen that they'd found his scuddy mags under his towels in the bathroom. They weren't anything special but they showed them to Maggie and made her look at them. He didn't need to explain to Maureen why it hurt him so much. They'd searched her house too, found her vibrators and gone to the trouble of leaving them in a neat pile. She hadn't had a carefree wank since.

Liam retired almost immediately afterwards. He managed to get back into university to study film, despite having accepted several grant cheques before dropping out of law school years before. He spent his free time between lectures renovating the house. It was beautiful. He unnailed the wooden window shutters so that they worked again, stripped the flock wallpaper and painted the bare plaster vellum yellow. The carpets, sticky from thirty years of shuffling feet and a thousand small spills, were lifted, the floorboards sanded and varnished. He bought a job lot of Victorian armchairs in an auction and the millennium party was his chance to christen the house. Leslie arrived at ten past eleven with Cammy.

Cammy had all the equipment: he was tall and slim and blond but nature had played a cruel joke and made him an idiot. He smeared his fringe into a spiky comb on his forehead, wore a football top over straight-leg denims and had a recurring spot on the back of his neck that required urgent medical attention. Intimidated by the grand surroundings, he decided that Maureen and Liam were massively over-privileged parasites. He asked Liam whether his daddy had left him the house and Liam, pissed and unaware of the accusatory tone, laughed like a drain and said, yeah, that was right, his da gave it to him. Then Leslie took off her biker's jacket Liam took in her change of style and asked why she was dressed like a whores' shop steward. Leslie's offence was lost in the memory of the night because Liam went on to greater glories. He chucked Maggie twenty minutes before the bells, saying she was too good for him, too good, and anyway, he was still in love with Lynn. Lynn heard him and was furious, said he'd made her look like a scheming cow, and she told Maggie that she'd never go out with him again. Unconsoled, Maggie locked herself in the only functioning toilet, causing a fifteen-minute queue and an inch of urine in the back garden. Half the party saw in the new century waiting in a queue with their legs crossed.

Leslie and Cammy left Liam's Hogmanay party at one o'clock, a gesture with the same social connotations as a slap in the face with a duelling glove. At the door on the way out Cammy went to the trouble of telling Maureen that he wished they'd gone somewhere else. She said she wished he had too.

Maureen knew she must have done things wrong, that Leslie wouldn't treat her like a prick without justification, but she couldn't think her way through a day at work, much less six months of casual comments. She suspected that Leslie was disappointed and embarrassed by her performance at the shelter. Their friendship was dying and Maureen was too distracted by the past to make it right.

7
Driftwood

They were on the edge of the city centre, in what used to be one of the busiest docks in Britain. The area had withered, the houses were run-down and the few shops were transient and dilapidated. Leslie parked the bike around the corner, out of sight of the café so that she could drink and drive without being reported. She kicked down the stand, bending down to chain the bike to a lamp-post, leaving Maureen standing alone on the pavement.

Misty, unforgiving rain fluttered nervously around the head of the street-lights. Across the busy road stood a row of tenements with a twenty-four-hour grocer's on the corner. A huge grey concrete housing scheme loomed above the roof, the little square windows framed with cheap curtains. Designed as a series of reclining rectangles, the flats zigzagged along a straight line, joined end to end by lift shafts, like a futuristic city wall peopled by a plebiscite who could be spared in the event of an attack. The wall blocked the wild south wind from the street, and squally vortexes had formed in the vacuum, sweeping the litter back and forth. On fine summer evenings plastic bags hovered twenty feet above the tenement for hours at a time, trapped in updrafts and cross-winds. Maureen flapped the skirt of her coat open and shut, trying to shake off the worst of the weather.

'Is that a new coat?' asked Leslie.

Maureen nodded.

'Nice,' said Leslie. 'Douglas's money?'

'Yeah,' smiled Maureen. 'From rags to bigger rags.'

Leslie blanked her and put the helmets in the luggage box, clipped the padlock shut and led Maureen round the corner. They opened the door and stepped into the Driftwood restaurant, leaving the damp night behind them.

The Driftwood looked like a life-long dream swallowing a redundancy cheque. It was a tiny room with big windows on to the dirty street, little tables covered in wax cloth and candles in Perrier bottles. It served tempting fusion food but charged next to nothing because it was in exactly the wrong place. Maureen and Leslie were the only paying customers. A chef in a T-shirt and checked trousers sat at a table near the bar, reading a tabloid and eating a bowl of soup. A pretty blonde waitress fluttered across the floor, whipping the menus from behind the bar as she came towards them. 'For two?'

'Yes, please,' said Maureen.

She sat them at a table by the window. The convection heaters were blowing as hard as they could but Maureen and Leslie had to keep their coats on. The waitress apologized for the cold and promised them that the place would heat up soon. 'We're not long opened,' she explained, and took their drinks order.

Maureen looked around at the tasteful orange walls and the candle-lit tables. Behind the bright bar the waitress danced their drinks ready in a series of bunny dips and graceful swoops. 'How did ye find this place?' she asked.

'I come here with Cammy.' Leslie looked at the menu. 'The goat's cheese salad's nice.'

'I'll have that, then,' said Maureen, shutting the menu without reading it. She didn't want to eat, couldn't be arsed fighting with Leslie about it and a cheese salad seemed as good a thing to leave as anything else.

'I think I'll have a steak,' said Leslie. 'Keep my strength up.'

She smiled at Maureen, a weak and guilty smile, and Maureen thought she'd save her the bother of working around to it. 'Why are we really here?' she asked.

'Well,' Leslie looked hopefully at the waitress but the drinks weren't ready, 'it's not just for steak. It's Ann. See, her man said he didn't hit her and he didn't write to her, says he never lifted a finger.'

'Leslie,' said Maureen wearily, 'what's the fucking deal with Ann? Will you just tell me?'

'He said he didn't hit her,' repeated Leslie firmly.

They sat in silence until the waitress came over with their drinks on a rubberized tray. 'Whisky and lime for you,' she said, placing the glass in front of Maureen, 'and a vodka and soda for yourself.'

Leslie took the drink and ordered their food. Maureen watched her make eye-contact with the waitress and smile, fresh and open-faced. She hadn't seen her look like that for a long time. The waitress finished writing their order and backed off, leaving them alone together with the miles between them.

'Okay, so her man says he didn't hit her,' said Maureen, trying to kill the fractious pause. 'Suppose he's telling the truth? Could someone else have hit her? Maybe a boy-friend?'

Leslie looked incredulous. 'Fucking hell, Maureen. The men never admit to hitting these women, but that doesn't mean they don't do it.'

'No,' said Maureen, feeling slighted, 'but she'd hardly tell us a story that complicated, would she? She'd just say it was her man. If she had a boyfriend she could be with him now. Why didn't she bring her weans when she left?'

'Well, I don't know,' Leslie said sarcastically. 'Maybe

running away with four kids is more complicated than running away alone.'

And that one snide comment was enough. Maureen could be home in twenty minutes if she walked. 'What are you in a fucking nippy mood with me for?' she said.

Leslie didn't answer.

'You're always in a fucking bad mood these days,' continued Maureen. 'Ye never want to see me or talk to me or do anything.'

Leslie lit a fag and looked out of the window, her mouth slackening as if she was going to speak. Maureen took a mouthful of whisky and sat back. She waited, only half expecting an answer. Leslie scratched her nose and looked over her shoulder for the waitress.

'I think the least we can do is go and ask her man about it. He lives in the big scheme,' said Leslie, magnanimously letting Maureen's difficult mood go. 'I'd go myself but if he was hanging about the office he might have seen me.'

He could just as easily have seen Maureen at the office, but that didn't seem to have occurred to Leslie.

'Where does he live?' asked Maureen.

Leslie pointed over Maureen's shoulder. 'Over the road.'

'And you want me to go?'

'We're here now. Just don't go into the house. If he looks like trouble just run like fuck.'

'I don't like this,' said Maureen.

Leslie misunderstood and thought Maureen was telling her she was scared. She hated it when Maureen admitted to being frightened: she was letting her down, leaving the door open and letting the fear in. 'You'll be fine.' She sniggered. 'He's puny.'

'He looks beefy enough in the photo,' muttered Maureen.

Leslie looked at her. 'What photo?'

'The picture.'

Leslie was still puzzled.

'The Polaroid she left behind,' said Maureen. 'The one with the wee boy in the school playground.'

Leslie thought about it. 'Oh,' she smiled, spontaneous and honest, 'that's not him.'

They looked at each other. Leslie knew what the guy looked like but she'd never met him. She had asked for Ann as a resident when she was on a tiny budget. She let Ann get pissed and smash around the house when she'd put others out for less and she wasn't about to tell Maureen why. Maureen finished her whisky. 'You're lying to me, Leslie,' she said quietly, 'and I know you're lying. If I get my face kicked in because of it I'll never forgive you.'

Leslie could tell her the truth now but she didn't. 'He's a skinny guy,' she said, looking at the table. 'Really skinny. I promise.'

Maureen nodded. 'Anything else you can be arsed telling me?'

Leslie shook her head at the table.

'Well, give us the fucking address, then.'

'You don't need to go now, your food's coming.'

'I don't want it, you have it.'

Leslie pulled a scrap of paper out of her pocket with an address biroed on it. Maureen snatched it away, stood up and pulled on her damp scarf.

'You'll want a proper drink when you get back.' Leslie smiled hopefully. 'I'll wait in the Grove. I'll have a drink ready for ye. I'll drive ye home.'

'Do what ye like,' said Maureen, and left.

8

John

She stopped on the edge of the pavement, waiting for a break in the traffic. Fat, freezing lumps of rain began to fall, seeping through her hair to her scalp, sending a shocked chill down her spine. She felt in her pocket for her stabbing comb, a metal one with a sharpened handle that Leslie had given her to use in self-defence. She found the head and grasped it, giving it a little squeeze, pressing the teeth into her palm to comfort herself. The sharp point was making a hole in her new coat pocket but she liked to keep it with her.

The scheme loomed over the street. Brilliant spotlights beamed skyward from the high roof, alerting passing helicopters and blinding pedestrians at a glance. Maureen couldn't recall ever having heard a story about the scheme. Bad schemes had elaborate mythologies, tales of rapes and crucifixions, of vicious gangs and gangster families and neighbours dead for months behind the door. Good schemes, like good families, had no history. A giggling couple in their forties stopped further down the pavement. The woman wore a thin dress and had the man's jacket over her shoulders, as if she'd come out for a drink in June and had been caught out by the change of season. The traffic thinned and Maureen crossed over.

The entrance to the flats was down a set of stairs and across a concrete-slabbed yard. At the base of the block a row of shops sat boarded up and empty. Only the solicitor's and a cut-price fag shop were doing any business. Maureen picked her way across the uneven paving-stones, avoiding the treacherous puddles, and opened the door into a white-tiled foyer. The lift call button had been melted with a lighter. She pressed it and a distant red light signalled to her from behind the lumpy blackened plastic.

She looked at the address on the scrap of paper. Leslie had scribbled 'thanks' at the bottom, as if Maureen was a vestigial friend doing her a favour, an unhappy reminder of the grey time before Canuny and the bracing breeze in her cleavage. The lift arrived and she stepped in, pressing the button for the second floor. As the doors slid shut she was engulfed in a cloud of dried ammoniac urine. Someone had been pissing in an ambitious arch, trying and failing to reach a felt-tipped IRA slogan on the wall. A wet cloth would have wiped it off but he probably didn't have one handy in his trousers. The doors opened on the second floor and she stepped out quickly, anxious to escape the sharp smell.

A grey concrete veranda stretched away from the lift, overlooking the busy main road. The long gallery of front doors was interspersed with small bathroom windows glazed in mottled glass. One or two of the doors had been customized, painted and fitted with fancy doorbells and alarms, letting the neighbours know that it was a bought house. Number eighty-two had not been customized. The door had been painted with thin red gloss a long time ago. Time and the weather had dried it, lifting the lustre, cracking and flaking it off the wood. The bell had been ripped out of the door-frame, leaving an empty socket in the joist.

Maureen chapped lightly, glancing down the corridor and reminding herself where the stair exit was. The door opened a crack and a tall, skinny man looked out at her. His eyes were open a little too wide and underlined by dark purple hollows, lending him the look of a startled pigeon. Leslie had been right: he wasn't the robust man in the Polaroid, he was a lifeless sliver of a man. He blinked, glancing behind her to see if she was alone. 'Aye?' he said, brushing his thinning hair back from his face, tentative, expecting trouble.

Maureen smiled. 'Is Ann in?'

'She doesn't live here any more.'

'D'ye know where I could get a hold of her?'

From deep inside the house came the noise of something falling heavily on to a solid floor and a child began to wail. The grey man took a deep breath, turned back into the flat and left the door to fall open. The living room was bare, the grimy hardboard floor dotted with offcuts of carpet. The wallpaper had been ripped off, leaving papery patches on the grey plaster, and in place of a sofa stood a plastic child's stool and a worn brown armchair. The house was a testament to long-term poverty. Maureen thought of Ann and wondered how many desperate schemes had been hatched and abandoned here, how many fights about spending, how many distant relatives and lapsed friends had been considered for a tap. A blue sports bag sitting against the far wall caught her eye. The green and white sticker looped around the handle seemed familiar and troubling somehow. Intrigued, Maureen stepped into the hall, pulling the front door shut behind her.

The man was standing over two tiny boys with Ann's clashing pink skin and fluffy yellow hair. They were babies, much younger than the boy in the Polaroid, and were thin, their ribcages visible under their skin, their baby fat eaten away by need. The man had been in the middle of changing them into their nightclothes when Maureen knocked. They were standing close to each other, chewing furiously on their dummies, their little button eyes flicking nervously around the room. The older brother was three at most and knew he was in trouble. A skin-coloured Tupperware beaker lolled on the floor, the hardboard discoloured by a spill of red juice. The man grabbed the boys and slapped the back of their legs, keeping time with the blows as he shouted, 'All – fuckin' – day – ye – been – windin' – me – up.'

The boys raised their faces to the ceiling and bawled, their dummies sitting precariously in their open mouths as they found each other and held on tightly. Maureen hovered uncertainly in the doorway. 'Are ye just looking after the weans yoursel'?' she asked.

He turned and shouted at her, exasperated, 'I'm doing the best I can,' he said. 'Their fucking ma's no' here, is she?'

'D'ye know there's a nursery down the road?'

The man paused. He didn't know why she was telling him that.

'If you're not working,' she said, 'and you're looking after them on your own, you'd have a good chance of getting them places.'

Apparently unfamiliar with good news, the man looked worried.

'Ye'd get some time on your own,' she added, wondering about the blue sports bag, wary of looking straight at it.

'Aye?' he said, watching his babies as they forgot what they were crying about and began to pull at a newspaper on the floor. 'What's your name?'

'Maureen. What's yours?'

'Jimmy.'

He tried to smile at her, sliding his lips back, but his face was too tired to pull it off. He had threateningly sharp teeth, which slanted backwards into his mouth. They looked like a vicious little carnivore's, naturally selected because they slid deeper into the flesh when the victim resisted.

'I'm going fucking mad here.' He picked up an old pair of Mutant Ninja Turtle pyjamas from the cold floor. 'What d'ye want Ann for?'

'I owe her some money,' she said.

'You taking the piss out of me?' He said it as if everyone did and he was past caring.

'No.'

'You owe *her* money?'

Maureen nodded uncertainly. Jimmy knelt down and started to dress the smallest boy, tugging him into his pyjamas. The boy chewed his dummy, holding his daddy's jumper.

'Why are ye really looking for Ann?' he said.

'What makes you think I'm lying?'

Jimmy displayed his sharp little teeth again. 'Ann owes everyone on this scheme money. If ye ask me, that's why she's off. Last I heard she was living with the Place of Safety people.'

'Place of Safety?'

'Aye.' His voice dropped to a whisper. 'She telt them I'd hit her.'

It was painful to watch a man so ready to take a punch.

'Did ye hit her?' she asked.

'No,' he was adamant and Maureen was pleased, 'I never hit her. Nor anyone else.'

Maureen thought of him slapping the children, but then remembered that children don't count as people. She leaned against the wall and felt the sandy texture of plaster rubbing into her shoulder. She stepped back and propped herself against the door-frame. 'Why would Ann say you hit her if ye didn't?' She noticed herself changing her accent to speak to him, paring down her language, as if Jimmy was so thick he wouldn't understand if she spoke normally. She hated herself.

'I don't know,' said Jimmy, squeezing the child into a pair of tight pyjama bottoms. 'The police said she'd had a doing. Maybe she wanted to hide.'

'Did ye send her a Christmas card?'

'A card?'

'Yeah.'

Jimmy looked blank and Maureen guessed that he didn't have an extensive Christmas-card list.

'What are ye asking me these things for? Who are you?'

If he was going to turn nasty, now was the time to do it. Maureen was glad she was near the front door and had a five-foot start on him. She mentally rehearsed opening the door and running along the balcony to the stairs. 'I work for the Place of Safety,' she said quietly.

Jimmy looked at her and nodded softly. 'We've had hard times,' he said, 'but ... Ann knows ... I can't believe she's going about saying that about me. I'd never hit her. You won't believe me.' He turned away from her, patted his son's bottom to let him know he was finished changing him and held out his hand for the older boy to come. The children swapped places on the strip of rug.

'I do believe ye, Jimmy,' she said, and she meant it.

'Ha,' he said, as if he'd never really laughed. 'Thousands wouldn't, eh?'

He looked at her, genuinely expecting a response to an inappropriate cliché. Maureen couldn't imagine a suitably bland response. 'If you didn't hit Ann,' she said, 'can ye think of someone who would?'

'Take your pick. There's hard men up at this door every night in the fucking week looking for her. I'm left paying her debts while she's off gallivanting with the child-benefit book. They've even threatened the wee ones in the swing park,' he said, yanking his son's pink little body into worn pyjamas. 'All I know is that she left here without a mark on her.'

'When did she leave?'

Jimmy thought about it. He thought for a long time. He remembered that one of the boys' birthdays was on 15 November and Ann wasn't there for it. But Jimmy had money for presents so he figured that he'd probably had the child-benefit book that week. Ann had disappeared from Finneston around 10 or 11 November.

'That's a while back,' said Maureen. 'Did she go straight to the Place of Safety?'

'I don't know where she went.' He pulled worn sweat-shirts over the boys' pyjamas. It must get cold in the concrete flat at night. 'She came back at the start of December for Alan's birthday. I was at the shops and when I came back she'd been and gone. She telt him she hadn't been to visit because she was up and down tae London all the time. Could have been a lie, but ...' He touched the smallest boy's head. 'There's plenty on this scheme think I'm lucky because it's only the drink she's into.'

Maureen looked around the desperate room, at the filthy bare floor and the cold children and the skinny man bent over them. Jimmy was anything but lucky.

'Can I make ye a cup of tea, Jimmy?'

It had been a long time since anyone had been kind to Jimmy and he didn't know what it meant. He looked up at her, trying to work out her angle. 'There's nothing worth thieving,' he said.

'I'm just offering to make ye a cup of tea.'

He looked her up and down, licked at the dried spittle in the corner of his mouth and smothered a lascivious smile. He thought she fancied him.

'Aye, hen. A cup of tea. I'll put the weans to bed.' He hurried the children off, carrying the smallest boy on his

55

hip and holding the other one's hand, leading them out to the hall. He called back to her from the door, 'Don't use the milk, I'll need it for the night feed.'

She could hear Jimmy out in the hall encouraging the child up the stairs. She looked around the dirty flat at the broken toys and the worn clothes discarded on the floor. She went into the ragged kitchen. The bulb didn't work. Light from the street cast a dull orange glow on to the work-top. There was no kettle and no cooker, just a chipped portable grill with a single electric ring on top. Her eyes adjusted to the gloom and she saw a small scale-scarred saucepan in the sink. She filled it from the tap as the red ring came alive, livid in the darkness.

Back in the living room she crossed her arms. There was no TV in the room, no family photos, no books or ornaments or mementoes, nothing that wasn't essential and second-hand. They didn't even have a radio. Next to the armchair sat a stack of free local newspapers. Jimmy had been tearing them into strips for use as toilet paper. She could hear him through the ceiling, coaxing the children into bed, when she suddenly remembered the blue sports bag with the troubling sticker. It was green and white and looped around the handle. She looked at it. It was a British Airways luggage sticker. Liam used to have them on his bags all the time when he was dealing. She crept over to it. The bag had been from London to Glasgow and the name, in tiny print on the fold, said 'Harris'. It was dated less than a week ago. She stepped back and looked at it, trying to reason away the incongruity. Someone might have given him the bag, someone with his name, a family member, but the bag sat as if it had been emptied recently, the base flattened on the floor, the sides flapping open. The scenario made no sense. Jimmy had flown to London on an expensive airline when they were too poor to buy a kettle.

The water was spitting hot but she could only find one mug, with black rings of tea stain inside. She made tea, took it back into the living room, sat down in the chair and lit a cigarette. It was damp and cold in the room. She could hear Jimmy coming down the stairs, leaving the restless children calling for him, answering their pleas with a curt 'Shut it.' He sauntered into the living room. He had wet his hair. Maureen stood up and offered him a fag. He took it, bending over her for a light. 'You sit,' she said.

Jimmy lifted the mug and sipped, looking up at her as he sat down.

'Jimmy, why does Ann owe so much money?'

'Come on.' He smiled. 'Come on, we'll not talk about her.'

Jimmy didn't want to talk about kids or Ann or money. He wanted a quick, fumbled fuck with anyone willing and a ten-minute pause in the incessant worry. He held out his hand to her and bared his sharp, hunting teeth. Maureen pulled her coat closed. 'I want to talk about her,' she said quietly. 'That's why I came.'

Long acclimatized to disappointment, Jimmy let his outstretched hand fall to the side of the chair. 'She borrowed money for drink,' he said finally. 'Then she borrowed to pay the loan and it got worse and worse and worse. Ann's not a bad woman. It's the drink. She's different when she's not drinking. When she drinks she's a cunt.'

'Ye don't think she could be dead, do ye?'

'I know she's not. She cashed the child-benefit book on Thursday.'

'In Glasgow?'

'Dunno.' Jimmy sipped his tea despondently. 'They don't tell ye that at the post office, just that it's been cashed and I can't get it.'

'Do you think she'll come back here?'

Jimmy shook his head into his chest. 'She's not coming back.' He sipped the tea, tipping the mug back and grimacing.

'D'ye know where she is?'

'She's got a sister in London. Maybe she knows.'

'Could I phone her?'

'I dunno if she's on the phone.'

'What's her name?'

'Moe Akitza.'

Maureen wrote the sister's name on a receipt from her pocket and showed Jimmy the spelling. 'I think that's right.' He smiled at her. 'Mad name, eh? She married a big darkie.'

She knew if she pressed him he'd claim not to be prejudiced against anyone, except those grasping Pakis, of course. And the freeloading Indians. And the arrogant English. And the drunken Irish. And the suspiciously swarthy. 'Well, Jimmy, thanks very much. It was kind of ye to talk to me.'

'Aye,' he said. 'Well, I'm pressed as ye can see.'

They smiled at each other to pass the time. Maureen broke it off. 'Ye really don't know where she is, do ye?'

He looked into his empty mug and shook his head.

'D'ye miss her?' she asked.

Jimmy didn't need time to think about it. 'No,' he said, very sure and very sad.

Behind her the front door flew open, letting a cold slap of night air into the living room. Two wee boys with wet hair and filthy faces strolled into the room, their arms at forty-five-degree angles to their small bodies, strutting like miniature hard men. Their clothes were poor, even for scheme kids. Everything they were wearing had approximated to a dull grey colour, the result of overwashing in cheap soap. Jimmy warmed and smiled when he saw them and his boys grinned back. 'All right, Da?' said the oldest. 'Where's our tea?'

Jimmy cupped a gentle hand around the back of the bigger boy's head and swept him along into the dark kitchen. The younger one stayed in the living room and looked up at Maureen. He was the boy from the Polaroid photo, the boy holding the hand of the big man in the camel-hair coat, but he looked different close up: he had a little widow's peak, his eyelashes were thick and long.

He looked at her expensive overcoat. 'Are ye a social worker?' he asked, in a tiny voice.

'No, I'm a pal of your mum's.'

His face lit up. 'Mammy? 'S Mammy coming home?'

'No, John,' Jimmy shouted. 'The lady's just looking for her.'

Maureen looked into the kitchen. Jimmy was standing in the shadowy kitchen with his son, spreading cheap margarine on Supersavers white bread. She turned her back to the kitchen door, hoping Jimmy wouldn't hear her. 'Son, did you get your picture taken with a man at school recently? In the playground with a big man with short hair?'

The boy nodded.

'Who was the man?'

The boy licked at the snotters on his top lip with a deft tongue. 'It was picture for Mammy,' he said quietly, as if he didn't want Jimmy to hear either.

'Was your mum there?'

'Naw.'

'Who took the picture?'

''Nother man.'

'And did ye know that man?'

'Nut.'

'Have ye seen your mammy since your brother's birthday?'

'Nut.'

'Thanks, son,' she said, and it struck her how small he was, how thin his skin was, how it was a quarter to ten at night and he was six and had just come in from playing in the street with his brother. She wanted to wrap him in her good coat and make him warm and take him away and feed him nice food and read to him and give him the chance of a life. She wanted to cry. The wee boy sensed her pity and knew she was sorry for him, for the state he was in and for his future. He frowned at the floor. She hated herself. 'You're a good boy,' she said, and stood up, ruffling his hair like a patronizing idiot. She cleared her throat and called into the kitchen, 'I'm away, then, Jimmy.'

Jimmy didn't turn to see her go. 'Aye,' he said.

'I'll come and see ye if I find her.'

'Don't,' said Jimmy flatly, folding a slice of bread into a sandwich. 'Don't come.'

A scratched message on the back of the lift doors informed the world that AMcG sucked cocks. Maureen was glad to get out of the smelly lobby, glad to be away from Jimmy and his malnourished kids, eager to forget what she had seen. It was hard to look on poverty so all-pervasive that it even extended to his speech. She worked through the normalizing justifications: maybe Jimmy was lazy and deserved it; maybe he liked it, lots of people were poorer than him – but she had eight thousand pounds in her bank account and he had four kids and no kettle and she couldn't think of a single thing that made that all right. She felt her father following her across the yard to the street, his glassy eyes watching from every dark corner. Her muscles tensed suddenly and she broke into a run. Jimmy was right. Wherever Ann was she wouldn't come back here.

9
Fight Night

'Jimmy Harris couldn't hit a tambourine.' Maureen took a deep drink of her whisky and lime and felt the thin skin inside her top lip shrivel in the concentrated solution. 'Someone else must have beat her up.'

Leslie was sitting across the table picking at the picture on a sodden beer mat. They were in the Grove, a small pub below a block of tenements. It had been the bottom flat at one time and the layout was still discernible. The supporting walls had been knocked down and riveted cast-iron pillars stood in their place. The lights were bright and two large televisions flickered silently at either end of the fifteen-foot bar. The pub attracted a good-natured crowd of regulars, they milled around the room, talking and laughing, watching the horse-racing with one eye while they chatted to their pals. Leslie had been thinking about what Maureen had said to her in the Driftwood and had worked herself into a filthy mood. Maureen thought Cammy would be waiting for her at home and Leslie would be anxious to get back before the boil on his neck exploded.

'What did he say?' Leslie asked casually, as if she didn't really care, but Maureen could feel her fishing for something, something too private and precious to share with her.

'Nothing much.' She shrugged. 'Ann owes money to loan sharks and he doesn't think she'll ever come back. She's taken the child-benefit book and it's being cashed consistently.'

Leslie sat up. 'Is it?'

'Aye.'

Leslie thought about it. 'Does that mean she's cashing it?'

'Dunno. When did Ann turn up at the shelter?'

'December ninth,' said Leslie, without having to think about it. 'Why?'

'There's about a month-long gap between her leaving Jimmy and coming to us. She was up and down to London, seemingly.'

'Who says?'

'He says.'

'Aye.' Leslie was sceptical. 'Why would you believe anything that bastard says.'

'Look,' said Maureen, 'he's just a poor fucking soul who knows nothing. She won't go back there and he didn't hit her either.'

'You could tell that from one meeting?'

But Leslie hadn't seen the bare house, she hadn't smelt the lift, couldn't imagine the effort it must take for Jimmy to get up in the morning and manage all day. Maureen lit a cigarette, haunted by the image of Jimmy's jagged teeth. 'I think she had a boyfriend,' she said, 'and she's gone back to him and he hits her. She'll be there now, pissing it up on the child benefit while that poor bastard feeds his kids on watery bread and margarine.'

Leslie sneered at her. 'Why do you think he's telling the truth?'

'Because if he was lying,' said Maureen firmly, 'he'd give himself a better part.'

Leslie watched Maureen looking miserably around the pub, drinking quickly like she did these days, sighing heavily, as if she wanted to get away and be alone. Maureen had changed. Leslie knew she was nervous about her father being back in Glasgow but she was jumpy and moody and frightened of everything. They had been spending less and less time together and Leslie couldn't see an end to it. Maureen didn't like Cammy because he wasn't polished and hadn't been to university. They should have been closer now that they were working together but they weren't. Maureen looked freaked out half the time and bored the rest of it, and she had a new boyfriend she hadn't bothered to mention – Leslie had to hear it from Katia in the office. Leslie was beginning to think they had been too close, that it had been too intense before, with the poster campaign and Millport, and she'd seen a side of Maureen that frightened her. There was a fight brewing between them and she knew it would be a big fight. She took a drag and looked up. Maureen was watching the racing results. She was watching racing results rather than talk to her.

'What should we do now?' asked Leslie.

Maureen sipped her whisky and looked at the racing results again. 'You want to find Ann?' she said.

'Yeah,' said Leslie.

'Well, why don't you check out the pubs around the shelter? They'll have seen her.'

Leslie stared at her. She'd gone to Millport with her. She'd spent a summer in a mental hospital keeping her company, she had driven her around for weeks after Douglas was killed, and now Maureen was refusing to help her. 'You really don't give a shit what happened to Ann, do you, Maureen?'

Maureen sighed. 'Give it a fucking rest, Leslie. She's fucked off. Accept it. She fucked off and left her weans and her poor wee man to pay off her drinking debts.'

'*Her poor wee man?* I don't fucking think so.'

'I know he didn't hit her.'

'Because he seemed ordinary?' said Leslie, pulling rank.

It was a basic article of faith at the Place of Safety Shelters that any man was capable of hitting any woman, and for her to suggest that Maureen was dismissing Jimmy because he looked ordinary was as good as calling her an idiot.

'Right, Leslie. Stop it. This isn't about PSS theology.'

'Maureen, two women are murdered every week by their partner or an ex.'

'Fuck off,' shouted Maureen, losing the place. 'I know all that. I know he didn't hit her because he's passive and put-upon and he's got four kids under ten and she's fucked off and doesn't give a shit. It's just possible that she was battered by a loan shark, did that occur to you? Maybe that's why she wanted the compensation-board photos taken, so she could use them as protection if they came back for her.'

Maureen was shouting at her in a pub full of people. Leslie didn't know what to do. She couldn't walk away from another fight because she'd lost her bottle in Millport, and Maureen would never respect her if she ducked again. She leaned across the table and spoke quietly. 'Do you want to fight me?'

Maureen snorted, and shouted back at her. 'Do I want to *what*?'

'Let's go outside and have a fight and sort this out once and for all.'

'What the fuck is wrong with you?'

'I'll fight ye,' said Leslie quietly. 'Things haven't been right between us since Millport.'

'It's a pity you weren't so fucking ripe at the fucking time, isn't it?' It was wrong of Maureen to say that but there was no going back. The final thread of cautious concern snapped and she went for it. 'You've completely changed since you started seeing that prick Cammy.'

Leslie stood up. 'How have I changed?'

Maureen stood up to meet her, slamming her glass down

on the table, knocking the ashtray on to the floor. 'You're precious,' she shouted. 'And you're moody.' She jabbed a vicious finger at Leslie's shoulder. 'And why the fuck are you walking about with your tits hanging out?'

'LADIES!' The barman bolted across the floor of the pub, shouting louder than both of them. 'LADIES. Keep it friendly or go home.'

They swung round in unison, glaring at him, and he knew the fight wasn't going to end there. He held his hand towards the door. 'Good night to both of you,' he said firmly.

They gathered their jackets and helmets and stormed out of the bar into the rainy night, stopping on the pavement as the pub doors swung shut behind them. They could hear the crowd in the bar chorusing a long swooping 'woow' and laughing at them. Leslie leaned into Maureen's face. 'Give me my fucking helmet back.'

A pinprick of saliva landed on Maureen's pupil. 'Take it.' Maureen shoved the helmet at her. 'Fucking take it, then.'

Leslie snatched it from her and walked off round the corner, leaving Maureen standing alone in the spitting rain. They should have waited five minutes. They would have been crying and hugging each other within five minutes. They'd go home with a bottle and talk it out. Maureen waited on the pavement, hoping Leslie would come back.

The pub door opened behind her and a couple stepped on to the pavement. They recognized Maureen and smirked, wrapping their arms around each other and tramping off into the wind. The door swung shut, banging off the frame a couple of times, coming to rest. The street was still. One block away a motorbike fired up and roared away to the west. Leslie wasn't coming back. Maureen waited. Leslie wasn't coming back.

She walked home in the pissing rain, too tired and sad

to think. The rain was running down her face, trickling through her hair, dripping down her neck and soaking into her shirt collar. She'd reached the bottom of the steep hill to her house before she remembered Jimmy. She turned round and walked back down the road, stopping at a cash machine on the way. She withdrew two hundred and fifty quid, walked to the scheme in Finneston and took the pissy lift up to the second floor. She tiptoed along the landing and slid the money through Jimmy's letterbox, bolting for the stairs in case he came out and saw her. She knew from her own experience that nothing belittles more viciously than pity and Jimmy was small enough already.

It was only when she got down to the street that she admitted the truth: going back to give the money to Jimmy was just a pretext. She wanted to go past the pub again, to see if Leslie was there. She stopped and looked along the street to the Grove, too embarrassed to go back in. But Leslie wasn't there. And Leslie wasn't coming back.

10

Bad Day

Michael had a fever. He was scratching through the window into her bedroom, his knife-edged nails gouging through the glass. She was sweating and exhausted, and knew she couldn't take the noise any more. She leaned across to open the window and a river of blood flooded into her house. The anxious, heavy knocking woke her up. Her first thought was Leslie, Leslie had come back, but it wasn't her knock and she didn't do morning visits. She sat up and looked at her watch. It was nine thirty and the Ruchill fever tower lurked behind the bedroom curtain.

It was cold out in the hall. A lone blue envelope ached on the mat and the answerphone flashed a red message. She pulled on her overcoat over her T-shirt and knickers, kicking the letter under the telephone table for later, and looked out of the spy-hole. Detective Inspector Hugh McAskill brushed the rain from his red hair and looked back at her, his long melancholy face distorted wide by the convex glass, his blue eyes watery and tired, his cheeks flushed from the cold. Behind him stood moustachioed DI Inness, dressed for the weather in a scarf and gloves and sturdy anorak. It was a bad day for this; she felt stupid and friendless and sick. She could pretend to be out and hope they'd go away.

'We know you're in there.' McAskill spoke gently. 'We can hear you moving about.'

Maureen paused with her hand on the latch, took a deep breath and opened the door.

'Hugh.'

McAskill nodded sadly. 'Can we come in for a minute, Maureen?'

She opened the door and the policemen brushed their feet on the mat before stepping into the hall. She had left the heating on overnight, hoping to evaporate some of Douglas's money, and it was warm in the flat. They took off their scarves and gloves. 'Why has he sent ye this time?' she said.

Hugh raised his eyebrows and pressed his lips together. Chief Inspector Joe McEwan was determined to get her for the assault on Angus in Millport. He had no evidence, he couldn't place her or Leslie on the Isle of Cumbrae at the time, and Angus himself was acting mental and wouldn't tell them anything. But Joe had made it a special point of principle to question her about any detail that came up, just to remind her that he was still in the game.

''Nother line of questioning's come up,' said Hugh, 'so here we are.'

'How are you today, Miss O'Donnell?' said Inness unpleasantly. He was an officious prick with a Freddie Mercury moustache and the social skills of a horny lap-dog.

'Look,' said Maureen, praying she wouldn't cry and watching her feet as she did up the buttons on her overcoat, 'just tell me why you're here. I'll get scared and then ye can leave.'

'We have been given information,' began Inness, warming to his petty office, slapping his gloves through his palm like a TV Nazi, 'that you have been receiving letters from a certain hospital patient. We've come to pick them up.'

Maureen folded her arms. She could give him the letters, just hand them over and let them deal with it, but the letters hinted at Millport. 'Tell Joe that I know I don't have to answer anything,' she said.

'Well, why on earth would you refuse to answer us?' said Inness, feigning cheap surprise. 'Could it be that you have something to hide?'

McAskill blushed and looked at his shoes.

'I'd think you'd want to help us,' said Inness, ploughing on with an already failed ploy.

Maureen caught Hugh's eye. 'Isn't his patter woeful?' she said, in a vain attempt to cheer herself up.

Hugh raised his eyebrows again. He was always more or less silent during these visits. They had been friendly to each other during the investigation into Douglas's death. She knew he was sharper than Inness and that Joe trusted him more, but every time they came up Hugh stood by and let Inness do the talking.

'Angus Farrell has convinced the doctors that he's mental,' said Inness, glaring into the living room. He saw discarded newspapers, full ashtrays and the low sun seeping through the sheen of white dirt on the windows. He looked at Maureen, tousle-haired and half naked under her overcoat. She felt the implicit criticism of everything his eye fell on and knew he'd report every detail to Joe McEwan.

'Maybe he is mental,' said Maureen.

'Yeah,' said Inness. 'My boss thinks Farrell knows what it means if he's mental. He knows he'll get a short sentence in minimum security. Maybe he'll make a miraculous recovery in two years' time and get out. Do you think a psychologist would know that?'

Maureen shrugged. 'I don't know him that well,' she said.

'But he was your therapist.'

'Briefly,' she said. 'Only briefly.'

'The hospital told us he's writing to you. Is he?'

'No,' she said, conscious of the letter below the telephone table.

'The nurses,' said Inness forcefully, 'post the letters to

you, so you can stop lying. I'll ask again. Is he writing to you?'

'Maybe he's got the wrong address. Did ye think of that?'

'Is he threatening you?'

'I don't know what you're talking about.'

Inness ground his teeth. 'If Farrell gets a sentence in low security who do you think he'd be most anxious to see?'

Maureen began to sweat and felt an anxious prickle on her neck. She looked to Hugh for support, but he slid his eyes away from her and left her alone. Whatever she said or did was going straight back to McEwan. She took a deep breath. 'Look, Inness,' she said, 'I know Joe sends you down to do the talking because he hasn't got anything on me. He sends you because you're an idiot and you're aggravating.' She could see Inness getting annoyed. She could see him thinking through the order to come down here, thinking through the politics at the office, wondering if she was right. Hugh bit his bottom lip and stared at the ceiling. 'So just tell him from me, you're not as much of an aggravation as he thinks you are and I'm not going to confess to an offence I didn't commit to get out of your company. Will ye tell him that for me?'

Flustered, Inness raised his hand to his face, flattening his moustache. 'This place is filthy,' he said bitterly. 'Is that a feminist thing? Not cleaning up after yourself?'

Maureen mustered her threadbare dignity. 'Are you taunting me in an official capacity now?' she said, feeling the rising panic at the back of her throat, hearing Michael scratching through the glass. 'Tell Joe that this isn't Chile. He can't just send you up here whenever he feels like it. These fishing trips are illegal.'

'Who told you that?'

'My brother.'

Inness gave himself a couple of seconds to think up a

70

witty retort. 'How is your brother? Still selling drugs to schoolkids?' Evidently a couple of seconds wasn't long enough.

'Liam's retired,' she said. 'You know he's retired.'

'Aye, he's a student now. Selling drugs to other students, is he?'

She felt hot and furious, felt the heat of the blue envelope at her heels, felt Leslie's saliva on her eye, and knew that she might start bubbling at any moment. She couldn't cry in front of Inness, he'd love it, he'd tell Joe McEwan, she couldn't. She pushed past him and threw open the front door. Startled, Inness dredged through his mind for something to hit her with. 'How's your friend?' he said. 'The girl on the motorbike? Maybe she'd like to talk to us?'

'Inness,' she slapped his arm, keeping her head down to hide her tears, 'you're pathetic. You're fucking pathetic.' She was shoving him into the close and shouting at him, 'Get out.'

Inness was shocked. O'Donnell had never shown emotion before but she was crying, slapping him, pushing and shouting at him. She was genuinely upset. 'What are ye doing?' said Inness, giggling nervously, trying to wrestle her flailing hands down.

Maureen didn't know what to say so she told the truth. 'You're frightening me,' she shouted.

Inness stopped still. 'I didn't mean to,' he said stupidly.

In a TV movie they would have hugged each other, he'd have come back in and they'd have had an honest discussion about their feelings, a sun-dappled moment of tenderness with a stranger, and they'd leave, elevated and touched at their common humanity. But this was Glasgow. 'Fuck you,' shouted Maureen, and slammed the door in his face.

She turned round and found McAskill standing by the living-room doorway like a spare arse. 'Hugh,' she said, struggling for breath, 'how can you stand by?'

'Maureen—'

She threw open the door again and McAskill brushed past her, turning and muttering to her, 'It's my job.'

She slammed the door the moment he was through and stared at it, crying and listening as the two men murmured to each other and walked away down the stairs, their footsteps receding to a gentle clip-clop as they reached the ground floor and opened the door to the street. She skipped into the living room, flattened herself against the wall and looked out. They were climbing into a car. She watched as Inness wound down the window and lit a cigarette, blowing the smoke out into the street. They pulled out and drove away.

Maureen lit a cigarette. Back in the hall she leaned under the telephone table and pulled out the blue envelope. She ripped it open. Angus was writing to say he hoped the bleeding had stopped and he would like to cut her himself. The answerphone was blinking.

'I know you're there,' slurred Winnie. 'Pickup, you little shit.'

'Yeah, I'm a shit,' she murmured, taking a deep draw on her cigarette, savouring the knowledge of an early death. 'I'm a shit. I'm a shit.'

It was nine forty-five in the morning and she wanted to get drunk and stay drunk.

II

Short Drop

Maureen tramped down the rainwashed hill. Cars sped happily through deep puddles, sloshing the pavement and splashing pedestrians. She should give Angus's letters to the police, he was threatening her after all, but if she was ever done for assaulting him the letters would be evidence against her. She knew he wasn't mental but she couldn't count on Joe's continuing scepticism if he saw the letters. She'd have to explain the meanings and symbols, and that would mean admitting to Millport and telling about Michael. She imagined policemen photocopying the letters, shaking their heads at the nonsensical symbols, handing Angus a bus pass and a coat and letting him go free at weekends.

She threw her fag into the gutter and opened the thick glass door. The stairs were black with dirt and rain. She could almost smell the ruined women, Katia's smugness and Jan's dull stories. She didn't want to be here or meet Leslie but there was nowhere else for her to hide. She could sit in the house and worry about the letters, listening to Winnie on the answerphone. She could go to the shops and see Michael's face everywhere and feel guilty for buying things she didn't need. She took the stairs slowly, trying to prolong the journey.

The job-shares were handing over to each other and the office was bustling. Three downcast women waited on the hard chairs by Maureen's desk. She managed to hang up her coat before Jan spotted her.

'Hi,' said Jan, going to the trouble of getting up and coming over to her, 'how are you?'

'Oh,' said Maureen, trying to smile, 'lots of work to do.'

She sat down at her desk and took a random file out of the drawer, pretending to pore over it, trying to shake Jan off. Jan picked up her mug. 'Maureen, you look even paler today,' she said. 'Coffee?'

'That would be lovely, thanks, Jan.'

Jan offered the waiting women a cup but they refused. She went off to the coffee room. Maureen took out her fag packet and handed it to the first woman in the line, motioning to her to pass it along, and went back to pretending to read the file. She didn't watch them, she didn't want them to feel self-conscious if they were short and needed to take one. When her packet came back to her it was six fags short. She looked at the trio of women. They were smoking hard and staring at the floor.

She took a different file out of the drawer and tried to lose herself in the wording of a statutory clause. All she had to do was get through today and avoid speaking to anyone. She stared at the same sentence for fifteen minutes, thinking vaguely about all the minor disputes all over the world, and all the idiots who fell out with their friends and thought it mattered when nothing meant anything anyway. Jan came round the desk and handed her the cup of coffee before opening her fag packet and passing it to the first of the waiting women. 'The police phoned here,' she said, 'looking for your pal Leslie.'

'Who?'

'The police. They asked to talk to her.'

'But why would they phone her here? She doesn't even work here.'

'Dunno,' said Jan.

'Did they leave a name?'

74

Jan shrugged. 'Just said the police.'

'Did they ask for Leslie by name?'

'Dunno,' said Jan, reaching over and taking her fag packet back from the last woman.

'Who did they speak to?'

'Katia.'

'Cheers, Jan,' said Maureen, but Jan wasn't listening to her. She was staring at the two lonely fags left rattling about in her packet.

Katia wasn't at her desk. She was in the stationery cupboard, chatting to Alice, the funding co-ordinator. They were making arrangements to go to a nightclub at the weekend. Katia had been there loads of times and knew the doorman. She said she could get Alice and her boyfriend in for free. Alice saw Maureen standing by the door and stepped aside to include her in the conversation, but Maureen held back until they had finished talking and caught Katia on her way out. 'Can I have a word?'

'Sure,' said Katia. 'Come on over to my desk.'

Katia had done well with her space. A partition wall closed off her corner desk from the rest of the ugly room. Her filing cabinet was decorated with photos of herself looking just lovely, standing with attractive pals in a kaleidoscope of thumping venues. 'What can I do for you?' she said, settling into her chair, her suede mini-skirt riding up her perfectly geometric thighs.

'Well,' said Maureen, trying to sound casual, 'I heard the police phoned today and you spoke to them.'

'Yes,' said Katia.

'I heard they asked for Leslie.'

'Did you?'

'The thing is I've been …' she didn't know how to word it without sounding like trouble ' … I've been getting visits from a policeman.'

Katia sat forward and looked at her. Maureen spotted a spark of self-interest in her eyes, instantly smothered with treacly concern. 'Are you going out with the policeman?'

Maureen was getting annoyed now. 'No, Katia, he's been harassing me.'

'Oh,' she said. 'Have you reported him?'

'I don't want to report him. I just want to know if it was the same policeman who phoned for Leslie. Did he give a name?'

'Well, it was a woman who phoned, actually. How is he harassing you?'

'It just – it doesn't really matter.'

'No, please.' Katia reached out to take her hand and Maureen almost felt the saccharine sear. 'Would you like to talk about it? It must be very upsetting for you.'

Suddenly Maureen began to cry big belting sobs and Katia fell to pieces, standing up and knocking her seat over, banging the filing cabinet and sending a shower of flattering photos to the floor. 'Listen,' she said, scrabbling about the floor, picking up the pictures, 'shall I ... will I go and get someone? Here are some tissues.' She handed Maureen a box of pretty Hello Kitty tissues, making her cry harder.

'Would you like a cup of tea? Shall I phone Vikram?'

'God, no!' said Maureen, with such force that a bubble of snot appeared at her nostril. She wanted Katia to go away, just go away, until she got herself together. 'Just tea, hot tea.'

Katia scuttled away, leaving Maureen alone behind the partition. She managed to slow the crying and dried her eyes. Whatever she had been crying about didn't seem half as bad when Katia wasn't there. A final lovely photo of Katia left its Blu-tack moorings and fell from the filing cabinet to the floor. The filing cabinet held the CCB photos. Maureen stood up and opened a drawer quietly.

Ann's surname was Harris and she found the file in the top drawer. It was a brown envelope, stiff with photos. She shoved it up her jumper, turning it sideways, tucking it into the waistband of her jeans, and sat down again, startled by what she had done. She didn't know if she'd done it to spite Katia or for Leslie or to fuck up her job even more so she could leave.

By the time Katia came back with a mug of milky tea Maureen had stopped crying and, as well as taking the photographs, she had stolen most of the Hello Kitty tissues too.

'Better?' asked Katia.

'I'm sorry,' said Maureen, dabbing her nose with the second-to-last tissue, 'I just, I got upset.'

'Who's the policeman who's harassing you?'

'It's a guy. I met him a few months ago ...'

'He's from Glasgow?'

'Yeah.'

'Well, it was nothing to do with him, then. This phone call was from the Met in London.'

Maureen stood up. 'Right. Good,' she said, crossing her arms in front of her to cover her tummy. 'Thanks'

'That's all right. Please think about reporting him, will you?'

'Yeah. I will.'

'How's Vik?'

Maureen moved over to the edge of the partition, wanting to get away before Katia realized that she had a strange package up her jumper. 'Fine,' she said. 'He's fine.'

Katia stepped in front of her. 'Maureen, do you resent me?'

Maureen was a little surprised. 'Do I what?'

'Do you resent me because of Vik?'

Maureen looked at her blankly. 'Why would I?'

'Well,' Katia rolled her head at the floor, 'you know we went out?'

'Yeah, I knew that.' Maureen felt a pang of jealousy coming from nowhere.

'About a month ago.' Katia looked at her knowingly.

Maureen had been seeing him for a month, just over a month, and Katia knew that. Maureen wanted to say that she didn't give a shit, that she wasn't even fucking sure she was going to live through the afternoon. 'I need to go now,' she said.

Katia held the cup towards her as a peace-offering. 'Won't you drink your tea?'

'I don't take milk,' said Maureen, and walked straight out of the office, picking up her coat and fags on the way out, leaving her files scattered on the desk. She was never going back there.

The rain was coming down sideways, cascading down the sandstone buildings, running in small ardent rivers in the road and pooling around the drains. Pedestrians pulled their hoods up and ran to get out of the weather, clustering together for shelter in the doorways, watching out of shop windows, waiting for the storm to pass. Maureen felt an unaccustomed creamy calm. She had the whisky and she had decided. She was never going back to the Place of Safety.

Her boots squelched noisily. She jack-knifed as she climbed the steep hill, staring at her feet, watching the rain bubble up through the lace-holes. The close smelt damp and crumbling. Heat from the lower flats crept under front doors, warming the upper flights, making her numb ears tingle.

The answerphone had tales to tell: it blinked nervously, full of Winnie's venom. Maureen took her boots off in the kitchen and emptied them carefully into the sink, peeled the stolen envelope of CCB photos from her damp belly and left them on the table. She dried her wrinkled white feet with a towel, rubbing hard to get the feeling back. The whisky bottle was sitting in the plastic bag. She lifted it out, enjoying the clak-clak-clak as the lid came off, and filled a half-pint tumbler. The brimming glass sat on the table, distilling the grey light from the window, turning it amber. She watched the drink out of the corner of her eye, flirting with it. Whatever happened in the next few hours she had all of that whisky to deaden it, a Scottish *petit wort*. If only she could feel this way all the time, the anticipation of comfort excluding other thoughts. She drank, gulping three big mouthfuls before stopping for breath. She lit a fag and inhaled, sucking the smoke deep into her lungs and then drank again, more slowly this time.

The answerphone was winking at her. She wandered out to the hall, pressed 'play' and closed her eyes, feeling the alcohol seep through her, lining her head, softening everything. Winnie cried pitifully and reminded Maureen that she had given her life. 'I am thinking of you and missing you ... I love you.' She hung up slowly. Past the bleep she'd called again, drunk and angry, to tell Maureen that she was a wee shite. The machine beep-beeped and rewound. The thought of Jimmy's carnivorous teeth floated into her mind. She took another drink and watched the machine, until the memory of the big bottle in the kitchen brought her round.

Far below the kitchen window the traffic was moving slowly on the motorway, wriggling out of the brutal hole of the city. She looked across to the north side and saw the jagged tower of the Ruchill fever hospital stabbing at the sky. It was watching her, looking into her house. She hugged the bottle like a new best friend and picked up the glass and her fags. As she passed the answerphone in the hall she swung her free fist, punching the machine hard, knocking it noisily to the floor. The blow tingled deliciously on her knuckles.

It was dark in the living room, dark enough for the bloodstains on the wooden floor to melt into greasy shadows. Maureen sat still on the settee and thought about her dream the night before. The flat had seen a lot of blood. Douglas's stains were still on the floorboards, dark discolorations like patches of itchy varnish. She couldn't bring herself to paint over them. It would be like saying he'd never been there. Douglas's death had hit her hard. The aftermath of a violent death is different from normal grief. There is none of the usual tidying up, pumping the veins full of glue, dressing the corpse for a dinner dance, pretending that it all makes perfect sense and God will care for them now. There's blood and shit and matter everywhere, faces ripped off, limbs missing and the realization that life is brutal and meaningless, that everyone is only a split skin from spilling into death.

She lit another cigarette, finished her drink, and watched the rain slow outside the window. It had almost stopped. She refilled her glass and walked across the room, opened the window wide to the wall and sat down on the windy sill. The rain fell softly on to her face, and the wind whipped her hair. The few people in the street below were oblivious to her.

She swung her leg over the ledge into the void, smoking hard and listening to the purr of the city below. She couldn't see Ruchill from here and no-one in Ruchill could see her. Ash fell from her fag into the air, disintegrating in the high wind. She swung her bare foot through the air, banging it against the outside of the building. A small shard of sandstone crumbled off the wall and tumbled through the air, spinning slowly as it fell the five storeys to the pavement below. It shattered with a light clack and the noise bounced away down the narrow street, echoing off the facing block of flats. The phone rang out in the hall and the battered answerphone intercepted it. Winnie sobbed and told her some fucking thing or other, I love you / you're a shit, come and see me / I'll never see you.

The rain came on again, splattering against her leg, pattering against the floorboards in the living room. She'd known a lot of people and didn't remember liking any of them. She looked down. It was just a short drop. But Jimmy had nothing, and she had thousands of Douglas's pounds left. She could leave a note in the living room, tell them to give Jimmy everything, but Winnie would rip it up. The banks were still open: she could take it all out and drop it through his door. But she might not come back to this point, this part of the windowsill. She dropped the rest of her cigarette out of the window and watched it spiral slowly as it fell. The whisky was making her warm.

It was nice out here with the wind and the rain, and Maureen closed her eyes. She saw Pauline Doyle sitting in a big chair, arms outstretched, inviting her to a break in the tedium of coping and Maureen slid softly to her. She was falling forward, slipping into space, her limp body yielding to the air but then Pauline turned into Ann Harris, reaching out to her, grabbing her by the hair, her grin splitting the scab on her swollen lip, the flesh red and raw beneath it. Maureen sat up suddenly, grabbing hold of the window-frame, and shoved herself back into the living room.

She landed on the base of her spine and stood up unsteadily, rubbing her bruised coccyx, grunting and panting with the pain. She stopped and looked around the living room, sniggering nervously, feeling as if everyone she'd ever known had been watching her. Blushing and ashamed, she shut the window tight and went into the hall to phone Liam.

12

Not Best Pleased

Arthur Williams liked her. He didn't *like her* like her, he knew she was married, knew she had a kid. He just thought she was a nice person. Even-tempered. Didn't make jokes about him being Scottish all the time, which was a miracle for a Met copper, and he was glad they were working together on the mattress thing.

'This is a great opportunity for you, Bunyan. You'll be working with one of the greats. Best interview technique I've ever seen.' Detective Superintendent Dakar couldn't just compliment his work, he had to work in a codicil. 'Even if he is of the Scottish persuasion.'

Williams smiled like a good guy would, and sipped his tea. He looked at Dakar, watched him wittering on about caseloads and the Home Office report about the clear-up rates. Dakar was uncomfortable with Bunyan because she was a woman. Couldn't look her in the eye. Kept thinking about her tits, Williams could tell. Just shut up now, Dakar, shut up and go. Go away. Go, go, go, Williams sang inside his head, until Dakar stood up.

'Well, I'll leave you to it. Should be straightforward; we've got an ID, a sister in Streatham and a family up north. We've put a request for background information in to the Serious Crime Squad in Scotland and the local police are looking into it as well. You'll want to chase that up.' He walked away, holding his belly in until he got behind Runyan.

Bunyan looked at Williams and raised her eyebrows. 'Brixton first, then?' she said.

'Yeah, we should phone her sister and check she's in.'

'Already done it, sir,' she said. 'Mrs Akitza's in and she'll be staying in for the next two hours. She's expecting us.'

Williams tipped his head appreciatively and nodded at her. 'Very good,' he said, picking up his jacket. 'You keep doing that sort of thing and I'm going to enjoy this.'

It took them half an hour to drive the eight miles to Brixton, and Bunyan directed him down several short-cuts. Her family had lived here, she said, until they moved out to Kent when she was ten. He noticed how small she actually was when he saw her sitting in the passenger seat. He was used to seeing Hellian sitting there, his big legs smashed up against the dash. She could have fitted in three times she was so wee. Tiny, she was.

'How tall are you?' he asked, as he drew into the circle of Dumbarton Court.

'Tall enough,' she said, sounding pissed off and throwing her fag butt out of the car window.

Williams laughed. 'Get a lot of stick for being wee, do ye?'

'Yeah, I get stick for "bein' wee".' She mimicked his accent as badly as a London girl could. 'And for the rest.'

Williams parked. 'Can't be easy,' he said, cranking the handbrake on without depressing the button. He saw her out of the corner of his eye, cringing at the ratchet noise.

'You'll ruin the car doing that, you know. Wear down the sprocket and lose grip on it.' She saw him looking at her. 'I come from a family of mechanics.'

Williams leaned into the back seat for his jacket. 'That's handy,' he said, 'because my handbrake keeps going.'

Bunyan smiled and he was pleased. He wanted her to do well, wanted to get on well with her.

Moe Akitza opened the door and looked out at them. Her eyes were very swollen and her blonde hair was very dirty. The house behind her was dark, and as she let them in they noticed that she hobbled when she walked and was badly short of breath. Bunyan lent her an arm and helped her into a chair in the living room. She sat down opposite Moe, leaning across the arm, looking sympathetic and concerned. 'Are you ill, Mrs Akitza?'

'Yes.' Moe Akitza looked up at them and clutched her chest, opening her eyes wide, choking slightly.

Bunyan was on her feet. 'Can I get you something?' she said. 'Is there some medicine somewhere?'

Moe shook her head and caught her breath, patting at her chest and sitting back in the chair. Bunyan looked at him and Williams nodded to her to sit again. He waited by the door, taking in the house and watching her. 'We won't be long.' Bunyan spoke slow and loud, as if Mrs Akitza was deaf. 'I know this must be distressing for you but we wanted to ask you a few short questions about your sister. Okay?'

Moe was panting and shutting her eyes.

Bunyan took out her notebook and unsheathed her pencil. 'Now, first of all, before we ask our questions, is there anything you'd like to ask us?'

Moe sat forward, wincing at her chest. 'Bracelet,' she murmured, 'was my mother's.' And she fell back into the chair.

'Once the case is cleared up.' Bunyan nodded at her to see if she understood. Moe nodded back. 'You'll get it back then.'

Pleased by this news Moe smiled a little to herself. 'Hah,' she said. 'Her husband. Battered her.'

'That's right,' said Bunyan. 'We know that. You told us that in the missing-person report. She was hiding from him in a shelter, wasn't she?'

'Leslie,' said Moe, with great effort, 'hah, Fin-hah?'

'Leslie Findlay at the Place of Safety Shelters in Glasgow.' Bunyan nodded. 'That's right, we've been in touch with them.'

'Hah, photographs, hah, of Ann?'

Bunyan didn't understand. 'Do you have photographs you'd like to show us?'

Moe Akitza raised her hand off the arm-rest to point into her lap.

'Shelter?' she said finally.

'Oh, yes,' said Bunyan, looking at her notes. 'The shelter photographs?' Moe nodded. 'Unfortunately, they seem to have been misplaced. You must be quite anxious for a case to be brought against your brother-in-law for that assault?'

Moe shut her eyes and nodded again.

'Well,' Bunyan continued, 'I'm afraid that's not our jurisdiction. The assault case happened in Scotland and would be dealt with by the legal authorities up there.'

Moe Akitza stopped dying and opened her eyes wide with annoyance. Williams stepped forward. 'It's a separate legal system up there, Mrs Akitza,' he said. 'I'm very sorry. Because Ann has passed on the assault case will probably be dropped. Unless there were other witnesses?'

Moe Akitza shook her head. 'No case?' she said. 'He's ... not charged? At all?'

'Well,' said Williams, 'if the assault is relevant to the murder case it may be mentioned tangentially but I'm afraid it won't be dealt with by an English court.'

Moe Akitza was not best pleased. She was not pleased at all.

13
Ten-Gallon Hat

Liam hadn't seen her this drunk since the experimental drinking days of teenage parties. She was sitting on the floor, slumped against the settee with her eyes half shut, ash all down her front and what appeared to be cheese on her sleeve. Despite being well supported by the settee she was still managing to sway. She had sounded progressively more and more tipsy on his answer-machine but he hadn't been ready for this.

Maureen had everything she needed here, fags, whisky, water, ashtray, but she felt so sick. She had half the bottle of whisky inside her and it was a big bottle. At some point she'd realized that she'd be sick if she didn't eat, so she had something she found in the fridge, cheese probably, but it wasn't sitting well at all. And there was Liam in front of her, dear Liam, who'd come an entire mile from Hillhead to see her. He was so kind. She started to cry.

'Fuckin' hell,' said Liam, taking his jacket off. 'What brought this on?'

She nodded – at least, she meant to nod. She threw her head around in uneven circles and Liam watched her for a while, mesmerized and enchanted by her lack of co-ordination. 'Mauri,' he said, in awe, 'you're utterly fucking bloothered.'

She wiped her face on her sleeve, rubbing ready-grated Cheddar into her hair. 'I'm unhappy,' she said indignantly.

'Well,' said Liam, serenely, 'that makes you very special.'

He sat back in the horsehair armchair and watched her trying to pick up a cigarette from the floor with rubber fingers. 'Why are you so drunk?'

Maureen gave up on the fags and shrugged at him for an age. 'Life's shite,' she havered, drunk and guileless. 'Leslie's ... spit on my eyes.'

Liam stood up. 'Oh, God, Mauri, I'm sorry, I can't stand this.'

He left the room and Maureen waited, forgetting that he was in the house and then remembering and then forgetting. When he came back into the living room it was a delightful surprise and she started crying again Liam made her drink the coffee and the coffee made her very sick.

He stroked warm water through her hair, holding the showerhead too far back on her neck, letting the water run over her jaw and up her nose. She was bent over the bath, trying to stay up, but her legs weren't working very well and she kept tottering forward.

'Oh. Fuck. I'm sick.' Her bleary voice echoed around the white ceramic valley.

'You've spewed up everywhere.'

'That's enough.' She tried to stand up but Liam was holding her shoulder down and she staggered back and forth.

'Mauri, there's vomited cheese in your hair. Stay still for fucksake.'

He rubbed the shampoo into the nape of her neck and washed it out slowly, wrapped a fresh towel around her neck and gathered her hair into it. Maureen stood up and staggered into the wall, leaning on it, testing her head. Through the curious alchemy of alcohol, her wet hair made her feel close to sober. 'Oh, fucking hell,' she said.

Liam perched on the side of the bath, feeling responsible

because he'd given her the coffee. 'D'ye feel any better?'

She patted her towel turban. 'Aye.'

Liam didn't look convinced.

'Honest,' she said. 'You throw up and I'll do it to you.'

They went back into the living room and Maureen arranged herself in a small bundle on the settee. The debris of a drunken afternoon was all over the floor. Her packet of cigarettes had spilled everywhere and more than half of the contents of the bottle of whisky had evaporated. A photograph of Winnie was propped up against the leg of the easy chair, facing her encampment. She looked at the window and thought back to the cold wind wrapped around her and her bare foot swinging over the void. Liam would be so horrified if he knew.

'God,' she said, feeling guilty and trying to change the subject in her head, 'that was very good of you.'

'Greater love hath no man,' said Liam, lighting a spliff.

'I'm not even tired.'

'It's only seven thirty. Why were you so drunk?'

She frowned and sipped a glass of water, trying it to see if she would be sick again. Her extremities felt shaky but her stomach felt fine.

'You always get drunk with Leslie,' said Liam. 'Where is she?'

Maureen owned up. 'We've fallen out. It's since that Cammy guy. She's dropped me like a sack of hot shit and I'm sick of being nice about it.'

'But she's fallen in love for the first time. She's going to disappear for three months.'

Maureen watching him, puzzled.

'You wouldn't know about it,' said Liam, 'because Douglas was married. When ye first fall in love ye spend all your time together for three months and then you come out the other side wondering what that was all about, looking for your old pals. That's what's happening with Leslie. I bet she's never been in love before, has she?'

'It's more than that, Liam, she's changed. You've seen the way she dresses now.'

He smiled indulgently. 'She's trying to please him,' he said. 'He'll be doing the same for her too.'

'You mean, she wants him to dress like that?'

Liam frowned as he thought back to the straight-leg jeans and Celtic top Cammy had worn to the Hogmanay party. 'We don't know what he was wearing before he met her,' he said. 'Could've been a flying-suit with zips everywhere.'

'And platforms,' Maureen said weakly.

'With spurs.'

'And a ten-gallon hat.'

'Could have been,' said Liam. 'Don't fall out with her now – you'll spoil it for her.'

He picked up a book and started arranging Rizlas on the back of it. He had brought a huge lump of black with him. The lamp on the floor shone on the Cellophane, turning it into a cube of water. She gestured to it. 'Where did you get that, anyway? I thought there was a dry on?'

'Got lucky.' He smiled at his origami. 'Is Leslie all that's bothering ye?'

Maureen slumped. Winnie came to see me. I miss her. I know I slag her but I miss her, and when I saw her she said George won't talk to her. They won't split up, will they? We'll never see him again if they do.'

'No, wee hen, they won't split up. He's just letting her know it's not on, her having Michael over to the house.'

'I miss George.'

'He misses you as well.' Liam smiled at her. They never discussed it but all four of the children loved their stepfather. George never spoke to them or gave them guidance. He

89

wasn't even in the house very much. He drank like Winnie, but instead of starting fights or trying to involve them in fictional dramas, George sang a lot and recited sentimental poetry. Winnie fought with him, as she had fought with Michael, vicious and loud and relentless. George listened to her until he couldn't be bothered any more and then he went out to visit his pals. He was the closest thing the children had ever had to a benign parent.

'She told me Michael's staying in Glasgow.' Maureen looked at Liam, but he was licking a cigarette down the seam and pulling the paper away. 'Well,' she said, 'is he?'

'He doesn't have anyone to drink with,' he said dismissively. 'He won't stay long.'

Maureen sighed heavily into her chest. It had been a long day.

'I walked out on my job. I hate it. Leslie got me that fucking job. She'll never speak to me again if I don't go.'

'Ah, she would so.'

Maureen watched Liam busily keeping himself replete with spliffs, rolling as he smoked, acting casual as if it didn't really matter but working hard. She was like that with drink. It looked casual on the surface but underneath she was frantic about her intake, desperate not to slow down or lose the level.

'Look at you and your wee spliff factory,' she said unkindly.

He looked up at her, resenting the intrusion. 'Look at you and your wee vomit factory,' he said, and went back to work.

'I worry about drinking,' said Maureen. 'I worry about turning into Winnie.'

'I worry about it too. Before Christmas there I was very worried. Alcoholism's supposed to be genetic so I've decided to cheat fate and just take hundreds of drugs.' He giggled, glancing at her feet. The cheer snowballed in his belly and he laughed loud, coughing when the laugh went deep into his lungs. He sat laughing and coughing like a jolly consumptive, and Maureen smiled sadly and watched him. Liam used to be angry all the time; he had mellowed so much since he retired – it was like watching him regress back to the hopeful wee guy he'd been as a kid. If she'd died she'd be missing this. A polite rap on the front door stopped Liam dead. Startled, Maureen sat up straight and they stared at each other, sitting still in case they were heard. Liam giggled silently. 'Why are we ...?' he whispered, holding his nose to abort a guffaw. 'We're not in trouble.'

The caller chapped again.

'Go,' mouthed Liam, waving her to the door as he shoved the lump of black under the sofa. 'Go on, get it.'

'Throw that out of the window if it's the police,' she whispered, pointing to where he had stuffed the hash as she tiptoed out to the hall. She peered out of the spy-hole.

Vik was standing on the landing, holding a bottle of white wine and a small bunch of flowers, his handsome face shiny and hopeful, watching the crack of the door, waiting for her to appear. She felt instantly wicked and guilty and angry about Katia. She should open the door and tell him to go away, that was the honest thing to do. Maureen and Liam had always looked alike, they had the same square jaw, the same dark curly hair and pale blue eyes, but Vik might not notice the family resemblance. He'd think she had another man in and she wasn't well enough to explain why she could let her brother in but not him She leaned her forehead on the door, less than a foot away from Vik's shoulder, and listened as he knocked and shuffled his feet impatiently. The door pressed towards her, he was leaning on it, scratching lightly or something. She heard the chink of the bottle on stone and cringed as he walked away alone, his feet falling heavily on the stone steps. The close door slammed shut in the high wind and she listened to the stillness for a while, just to be sure. She opened the door. Vik had left the note under the bottle and the flowers. His writing was big and round and cheery. He said, Hi! He'd just popped up for a visit! Phone him soon! She was starting to hate him.

She sloped back into the room with the bottle of guilt and the wreath.

'Not the police, then?' said Liam.

She fell into the settee. The flowers were pale pink roses, already open, tinged brown on the petal tips.

'They're nice,' said Liam.

'I've been kind of seeing someone.'

'It must be going well if ye won't even open the door to him.'

'He's nice.' They didn't usually talk about certain things but she didn't have anyone else to tell. 'The sex is great.'

'Yeah, that's tricky.' Liam didn't seem to mind. 'Maggie and I had great sex but that was it for me. You can stay in a relationship like that for years waiting till after the next shag.' He glanced at her. 'Ye did the right thing.'

But Maureen knew she hadn't. She pulled her legs up to her chest as a sudden burst of rain smattered against the window. They fell silent and she looked up to find Liam red-eyed and watching her. He was smiling, as smug as Yoda, and nodded towards the hall. 'Phone Leslie,' he said.

Maureen's stomach tightened at the mention of her name. 'You don't understand,' she said. 'She doesn't want me to phone her. She lies to me about things. It's like she doesn't trust me.'

'Phone and ask her why she's lying.'

'I've already asked her and she won't tell me.'

'Mauri, Leslie doesn't owe you every thought in her head. Phone her anyway.'

'No.'

'Ah, go on.'

'Nah, fuck off, Liam, ye don't know anything about it.'

'But she's been such a good pal to ye. She won't mind if you leave the job. Just tell her. She's very loyal to you.'

Liam was right. Leslie had stood by her in hospital; it was Leslie who'd helped her after Douglas died, Leslie who'd come after Angus with her, even though she was terrified and wanted to run away. She'd compensated for Maureen a hundred times and, now it came to it, Maureen wasn't reciprocating. She was a graceless shit.

'Fuck, no.' She tucked her head between her knees. 'I'm wrong again.'

She looked up, wanting reassurance, but Liam was nodding at her. She rolled off the settee and tramped out to the hall, putting on the light and dialling Leslie's number. Liam followed her, bringing the ashtray to smoke his spliff over. The phone rang out at the other end. It rang eight times. Maureen knew Leslie's small flat intimately. No corner of the flat was eight rings away. Deflated, she was hanging up when Leslie picked up the phone. 'Hello?'

Maureen whipped the receiver back to her ear. 'Leslie?'

'Yes?' She sounded very serious.

Maureen didn't know what to say. 'Leslie? Are ye okay?'

Leslie sighed a long slow crackle into the receiver.

'I'm sorry for phoning,' said Maureen, bracing herself for a knock-back. She felt like Vik on the stairs. She looked helplessly at Liam, who winked and gave her a happy thumbs-up. He was off his tits, he wasn't picking up on anything.

'Mauri, listen,' began Leslie. 'Tonight was ... Ann's dead.'

93

Maureen faltered. 'Ann's what?'

'She's dead,' said Leslie, choking on the words, and Maureen suddenly realized that Leslie sounded strange because she had been crying. 'She was found in London, in the river.'

Maureen thought of Jimmy's BA sticker. Not Jimmy, it couldn't be Jimmy. 'Do they suspect foul play?' she said. Liam giggled and fell against the wall.

'Who's that laughing in the background?' said Leslie suspiciously.

'It's Liam,' said Maureen, kicking him gently in the shin and turning away. 'He's been smoking. And I'm a bit pissed. Leslie, I'm sorry for what I said. I'm a bad friend.'

'Yeah. Never mind . . . Go to sleep, Mauri—'

'I'm sorry,' said Mauri.

'We'll talk about it later.' Leslie sniffed.

'What happened to Ann? Did she kill herself?'

'Lots of things happened to her. She was tortured and killed, put in a mattress and flung in the river.'

'Fucking hell,' said Maureen.

They paused. Maureen tried to clear her mind and think of something appropriate to say. 'Was it the loan sharks from Finneston?' she asked.

'I really don't think so.'

They paused again.

'Leslie, what is Ann to you?'

Leslie sniffed again. 'Jimmy's . . .' she began to cry '. . . he's my cousin,' she said, and Maureen suddenly understood. Leslie had asked for Ann in her shelter because she felt responsible. She must have known it would be safe for Maureen to go and talk to Jimmy, and after years of picking through the rubble of other men's transgressions, she would be far too ashamed to admit that he was family.

'Leslie, I don't think he hit her.'

94

Leslie was sobbing into the receiver. 'I was gonnae tell ye,' she said, gasping for breath. 'I don't want to fight ye, Mauri—'

Maureen interrupted her. 'Leslie, don't be alone,' she said. 'Come over here. We've got loads of whisky and Liam's got a lump of black the size of his foot.'

Leslie sniffed a long hard rumble. 'I'll ... I'll be there in half an hour,' she said, and hung up.

14

Tower

Leslie sat cross-legged on the floor, holding a bundle of Katia's stolen Hello Kitty tissues in one hand and a whisky in the other. She wiped her nose. 'Did ye see the CCB photos?'

Maureen shook her head.

'God,' whispered Leslie, 'her fanny was kicked in.'

'Listen, listen.' Excited by something, Liam waved them quiet and looked from one to the other, blinking slowly like a red-eyed idiot, 'Listen. Brilliant idea. Who's up for a curry?'

'God,' said Leslie. 'Can ye shut him up?'

They put on the television to distract him and Liam watched *Newsnight*, tilting his head left and right, trying to make something interesting out of powerful men haranguing each other.

'When I deal with this every day,' continued Leslie, 'I'm always looking for someone to blame, just to make sense of it, so it could be avoided, so it didn't need to happen, and I always come back to the families. Their families could have done some fucking thing. And then it's my own family and we weren't even in touch with the guy. Isa would die if she knew she'd been murdered.'

'You two know someone else who was killed?' smiled Liam, spliffed and swinging randomly in and out of the conversation. They looked at him. 'I'm staying away from you two. You're jinxed.'

Leslie sniffed hard and frowned at him. Maureen touched her arm. 'How can you be sure it wasn't the hard men from the scheme?'

'Come on, Mauri, London's full of Glaswegians running away from trouble here. She owed a bit of money, that's all.'

'Maybe she owed more than we think.'

'Yeah. Maybe. Maybe.' Leslie took a long drink of whisky and sighed at its harsh comfort. 'The police'll be so hard on Jimmy. God, I'll be surprised if he gets out of an interview alive.'

'Why?' said Maureen.

'You haven't seen the photos. She was battered shitless.' She slumped against the settee.

Maureen sat quietly, ashamed of herself, unsure whether to tell. 'I've got them,' she said suddenly.

'You've what?'

'I've got the photos.'

'Why?'

'Stole them,' she muttered.

Leslie sat upright. 'To protect Jimmy? Maureen, if he did beat her up he needs to be put away.'

'But he didn't hit her. Are they sure she was killed yesterday?'

'They said she'd been in the water for a week.'

Maureen didn't want to tell her about the week-old BA sticker. They were sitting cosy in the nice warm flat, drinking and smoking together, and she didn't want to tell her. 'He didn't do it,' she said, damning herself. 'I promise he didn't.'

'How do you know?'

'I just know,' she said. 'I know it wasn't him.'

'You knew she wasn't dead as well. Hoping isn't the same as knowing, Mauri.' Leslie cradled her head in her hands.

'God, if he goes to prison Isa'll try and take the kids. She's not fit, it'll kill her.'

'Can't you just tell her not to?'

Leslie tutted and rolled her bloodshot eyes. 'Can you tell your mum to do anything? Anyway, Isa's got this thing about Jimmy. She won't let him down this time.'

'Leslie, I walked out of the Place of Safety today. I don't want to go back.' She saw the dismay on Leslie's face and added, 'For a while. Are ye angry?'

'Naw, I understand. It's just an office job for you. At least I'm on the ground.' She cupped Maureen's elbow in her hand and squeezed, just a little, before letting go. 'Listen, I'm not working for a couple of days, do ye want to kick about together and ask about Ann? See what we can come up with?'

'Okay,' smiled Maureen.

'And you can have a think about your job,' said Leslie, 'and decide what you want to do.'

Maureen bit her lip and played with the edge of the cushion.

Michael was scratching at the bedroom window again. She sat up to see him, to know what he looked like, so she could be ready for him, but he opened his mouth and breathed, splattering specks of blood and liver on to the glass.

Leslie was giggling in her sleep. Maureen turned her head on the pillow and looked at her, Her cheek was folded under her eye, her long dark lashes lying on the pillow. Maureen had been mistaken when she thought herself sober the night before. Her throat felt like a raw scab and the back of her head throbbed viciously. She tried to get out of bed but her head was bursting and her stomach hurt so much she couldn't sit up. The hangover was threatening to wash over the top of her skull and attack her eyes. She lay down again and rolled sideways out of the bed, holding the duvet down to keep the warm in for Leslie, and stood up very slowly. She needed some nicotine but didn't think her throat would tolerate a cigarette.

The postie had left some bills but that was all. She went into the kitchen, put the kettle on and sat down at the table. It was dry and crisp outside. Grey frost mingled with the black dirt on the window, framing the view of the motorway like an ill-conceived Christmas card. She saw the Ruchill tower and scratched her head with both hands, digging the nails deep into her scalp. Her hair felt lank and heavy. She got up, averting her eyes from the window, and tripped down the hall to the bathroom.

The sill was crammed with expensive bottles of cosmetics, sachets and applicators and miracle creams. She thought of Jimmy, a man too poor to buy toilet paper who'd flown to London on BA. It didn't make any sense. There were lots of budget carriers he could have gone on for less than half the price of a BA flight. If Leslie knew, she would be convinced he was guilty, and she'd insist that they give the police the photos of Ann. They'd crucify him.

She washed her face and wondered if she could be right. Jimmy just wasn't the sort of man who would kill a defiant wife. He wasn't in control of anything when she saw him and he didn't even try to defend himself when he thought she was lying to him. The only thing he vigorously denied was hitting his wife. She played with the possibility that he had been to London and killed Ann, but the mattress troubled her. It suggested a house and a bed and privacy and a van to get her to the river. He'd have to know people in London. She scratched her heavy hair again and looked over to the bath. A small blue glass bottle lay on its side with the lid off and a final portion of lavender-scented hydrolyzed collagen trickled on to the ceramic ledge. Liam had washed her hair in industrial-strength conditioner.

Back in the kitchen she made herself a coffee, sensing the eyes of the fever hospital tower on her body. She sat down, ignoring it, and lit a cigarette, breathing in deeply. It felt like breathing in sand, and the pain brought her back to the present. She heard the thud of feet on the floor in the bedroom. Leslie padded to the kitchen door dressed in a T-shirt and knickers. Her black pubic hair extended an inch below the elastic on either side. 'Fuck, it's parky. Get us a coffee, will ye, Mauri?' She turned and trotted down the hall to the loo, picking the gathered underpants out of the crack of her arse.

Maureen got up and made two cups. She wouldn't tell Leslie about the London ticket, she'd ask Jimmy about it first. She was sure it wasn't him, deep in her gut she was sure.

The toilet flushed at the far end of the hall and Leslie came back down. 'God,' she said, 'you've got some amount of stuff in there.' She nipped into the bedroom, pulled on some jumpers and her leather trousers before coming back to the table for her coffee. She noticed Maureen glancing out of the window and saw her looking away quickly, smoking anxiously. Leslie looked out, across to the three high-rise blocks at George's Cross and the snow-capped hills beyond. Thick custard clouds skimmed by, letting the sun wink through at them.

'What are you looking at out there?' she said, and pointed to the grey sky.

'I hate that tower,' said Maureen, embarrassed that Leslie had seen her. 'It does my head in.'

Nonplussed, Leslie looked at the jagged Ruchill tower peering over the hill. 'Why?'

Maureen shrugged. 'It's so ugly,' she said. She couldn't make herself look at it.

Leslie wondered if it was because it was a hospital – maybe it reminded Maureen of being in hospital herself. 'The hospital's shut now,' said Leslie. 'It's been sold off for housing.'

Maureen looked up at it. 'What, the land's been sold?'

'No, the buildings are listed. They have to keep them.'

'Are they houses now?' Maureen sounded so tense and Leslie felt sure she'd helped her.

'Dunno,' she said, 'but it's not a hospital any more.'

Maureen stood up and lifted her makeup bag from the worktop. She used a magnified mirror so she wouldn't have to look at her face and rubbed foundation over her nose. Leslie knew she didn't like to remember the hospital.

'See about Ann?' she said, trying to bring Maureen back to the moment. 'We might as well face it, Jimmy's the most likely candidate, isn't he?'

'Jimmy's the only candidate so far,' said Maureen. 'He's the only person connected with Ann that we know about.'

Leslie looked into her cup. 'To be honest it's not exactly a surprise that he turned out violent.'

Maureen picked up her mascara, making sure she had the waterproof one. 'Is he violent?' she asked.

'His background's very violent.'

'But Jimmy isn't violent?'

'No,' said Leslie, 'but it runs in families, doesn't it?'

'Well, it's your family too and you're not violent.' It sounded like a reproach but she hadn't meant it that way.

Leslie let it pass. 'We didn't see that side of the family, really. I haven't seen Jimmy since I was wee.'

Maureen plunged the mascara brush back into the holder and screwed it shut. 'Why not?' she asked. 'The rest of ye are awful close.'

'Yeah,' said Leslie. 'You know how it is, families stay together through the women. We're nature's diplomats.'

Maureen smiled. Leslie was the rudest person she'd ever met. 'Are you one of nature's diplomats, Leslie?'

Leslie grinned fondly back at her. 'No, but I'm a throwback,' she said. 'A warning from nature. Anyway,' she said, serious again, 'wherever it comes from, women are the ones who say sorry and negotiate families. We're the ones who keep in touch and look after each other. Jimmy never phoned anyone, or looked after anyone's weans, or invited anyone to anything, and we just sort of, I dunno, lost him.' She took a deep breath and looked out of the window, her eyes darting over the city. She looked suddenly haggard and old. 'This is going to kill Isa.'

'The social worker won't let her take the kids, Leslie, she doesn't even know them.'

'It's not just about taking the kids … It's a long story. Mauri, will ye come with me? She won't cry if you're there and you can comfort her better than me, I'm not very good with her.'

Maureen pulled the zip shut on her makeup bag. 'Let's go and see your mammy.'

15
Isa

Leslie couldn't see a way around it. Her mum had a heart condition and she didn't want to worry her but if they lied to her and Isa found out she'd worry all the more. Leslie adored her mum. When she talked about Isa she became almost tearful with awe and frustration because her mother was a deeply good person, not just kind but a woman who had tended and cared for other people all her life. Isa was beyond selfless, she was almost invisible, one of a breed of women left penniless and aching from a lifetime of chores and caring, women who spent their lives waiting for the work to be done. It never was: there was always another potato to peel, another child to wash, another dirty floor. Leslie didn't talk about it but it was glaringly obvious how pivotal meek Isa was to Leslie's pathological bolshiness. Isa wanted little for herself: her idea of a high old time was sugary food, her family around her and a wee chant at the old songs.

It must have been devastating for little Leslie to grow up seeing her mother never off her feet, never asking for anything for herself, just shutting up and taking the blows. Her father was absent most of the time and a pest the rest of it so there was no alternative. Isa's life said be this or be nothing, reduce yourself to a shadow, deny anything you've ever wanted and never, ever dream of more.

Leslie's extended family all lived in Drumchapel. It was a matriarchal guddle of hard-working women and strangely feral children. Traditionally, the men fathered the children then hung about for a couple of years, competing with the babies for attention and resenting the responsibility before pissing off. They floated away into the ethereal world of orphaned men, propping up bars, wasting their child support on take-away dinners and taxis home while the women struggled bravely on. Isa had already raised two generations on a dinner lady's salary. Born the oldest in a family of five she stayed and raised her brothers and sister after her mother died. She waited until the children left home before getting married herself and starting the whole chore again.

She was in her fifties and looked eighty, with a little barrel body and skinny legs. The fat accumulated near her heart making her a candidate for a Scottish death, face down on the floor, choking on her own spittle while her heart exploded. She dressed plainly, in nylon skirts and blouses, and always wore a flowery pinny when she was in the house to keep her clothes good. Her house was spotlessly clean and orderly, the furnishings plain. Any ornamentation was contained within a teak wall unit in the living room; framed photographs of the family wearing stiff clothes at weddings and christenings, a mock crystal vase sitting on a doily and a grey ceramic model of a rabbit.

Isa wouldn't sit down at the kitchen table. She couldn't seem to understand that Leslie and Maureen had come to speak to her, not to see how many gammon rolls they could eat in an hour.

'Mum, for fuck's sake come and sit down.'

Isa bit her lip when Leslie swore. 'Oh,' she said to Maureen, 'I hope she doesn't use language like that all the time.' The question was rhetorical because Isa knew she did. She put another plate of home-made fruit scones on the table and scurried back to the worktop.

'Come on, Isa,' said Maureen, sounding casual to avoid frightening her, 'sit down and give us your chat.'

'I'll just get a drop more tea,' said Isa, topping up the stainless-steel pot from the kettle.

The sad thing about Isa's shaming hospitality was that nothing was very nice. The tea was stewed, the gammon rolls were tasteless and even the biscuits were a bit plain. It was as if the endless repetition of the caring task had made her forget the purpose. Leslie said it was because of her Calvinist upbringing: Isa associated enjoyment of any kind with terrible moral danger and thought that a tasty roll might result in a massive sensual overload, driving the recipient off the rails into the hands of bookies, bakers and white-slave traders. Isa put the tea-pot on the table and looked at Maureen. 'D'ye want a wee bit fish in milk?'

'Mu-um!' wailed Leslie.

'No,' said Isa, defensive and embarrassed. 'I'm asking because Maureen looks a bit peaky.'

The thought of fish in milk made Maureen feel distinctly unwell. They could go on all day like this, with Isa bringing more and more food until the swing-leg table collapsed. 'Isa, please,' said Maureen. 'We came to speak to you. It's about Jimmy Harris.'

Isa turned and looked at her. She set her face for a harsh wind, sat down and picked at a mark on the table. 'What about him?' she said.

Maureen wasn't prepared for such a sinister response. 'He's had a bit of trouble,' she said quietly.

'What sort of trouble?'

Maureen looked at Leslie but Leslie gestured to her to tell it. 'D'you know his wife, Ann?'

Isa nodded.

'Well,' said Maureen gently, 'I'm afraid she died.'

'Oh,' exclaimed Isa, 'but she's very young to die.'

Maureen and Leslie looked at each other and Leslie took a breath. 'She was murdered, Mum.'

'Oh.' Isa covered her mouth and shut her eyes tight. 'Dear Lord.'

Maureen didn't know whether to go on but Leslie nodded encouragingly. 'Before she died she came to us at the shelter. She was badly bruised and said that Jimmy had beaten her—'

'Well, I just don't believe that,' said Isa, tearful at having to state an opinion.

Leslie took her mum's hand. 'Mum, he might have hit her.'

But Isa brushed Leslie's hand away and clutched her teacup. 'Leslie,' she said, shocked and shaken, 'I knew James Harris as a child and I'll tell you this: he couldn't have beaten her.'

Leslie pointed at Maureen. 'That's what she says.'

'She's right.' Isa turned to her. 'How do you know?'

Maureen felt less sure than she had been. 'I went up to see him. I just don't think he's the type.'

'See?' said Isa to Leslie.

Maureen looked back and forth at them. She didn't know what else she was allowed to say and it might be a disaster if she got it wrong.

Leslie took over. 'Well, she was killed anyway.'

'He didn't do it,' said Isa.

'Mum, how do you know? Plenty of men who batter women seem put upon to outsiders. You of all people should know that.'

Isa took a deep, warning breath and raised an eyebrow at her. Leslie had said exactly the wrong thing.

'And there's his da and everything,' added Leslie, compounding the felony.

Isa sat up, bewildered by her daughter's shameless nature. 'Well,' she said, 'I don't see what—'

'Mum,' sighed Leslie, 'tell Maureen.'

Isa was mortified. She didn't want to insult Maureen but family secrets were private business and Leslie had broken the rules without even asking. She stood up and the girls looked at her. 'I'll put the kettle on,' she said tearfully.

'Mum, come and sit down.'

Isa filled the kettle and plugged it in. She'd run out of things to do so she picked up a damp cloth from the windowsill and rubbed the immaculate worktop even cleaner.

'Mum, please come and sit down.'

But Isa was weeping softly. Leslie got up and went over to her, wrapping her arm around her mum's shoulders, taking the cloth from her hand and setting it down. 'Mum,' she said softly, 'why are you still ashamed for Billy? He hadn't the decency to be ashamed of himself.' Isa shook her head. 'Come and sit down.'

'I don't want tae,' whispered Isa.

'Mum, if we don't come up with a plan Jimmy's going to prison and his four wee bits of weans'll be going into care.'

'I'll take them,' said Isa, too loudly.

'Ye wouldn't get them,' insisted Leslie. 'You're not fit and they don't even know ye. They can go to her family.'

'I'll take them.'

'Mum, come and sit down and tell Maureen the story. She's good at this, she'll try and sort it out.'

'Isa,' called Maureen, from the table, 'come over. I don't think it was Jimmy either.'

Isa blew her nose on a cotton hankie from her sleeve. 'Why don't you think he did it?'

'He's so mild. He makes you look like Ian Paisley.'

*

They were smoking Leslie's cigarettes and sitting around the table, intimate and close, and Isa was telling them about Jimmy's dad and all the wrong he did. She balked sometimes, straining to overcome a lifelong habit of secrecy, mentioning herself occasionally, minimizing her kindness.

Jimmy's father, Billy, was Isa's cousin and a gangster of the old school. It was in the fifties and Billy Harris didn't bother organizing himself to rob banks or anything, he just bullied the other men and had street fights, getting a reputation as a hard man in the Carlton, the roughest part of a wild city. He was friends with all the gangsters at that time and she reeled off a string of threatening names, hollow echoes of the past. Billy was terribly handsome. He would have had his pick of the girls if he hadn't been such a fighter. He had a lot of scars by the time he was seventeen and the nice girls were afraid of him. They'd give him one dance and leave the hall if he asked again. Isa's brothers and sister avoided him at the dancing, ashamed that he belonged to them. He married Monica Beatty when she was expecting, which was shameful in those days, not like now, and Monica looked like a movie star. She had platinum hair, red lips. Billy first beat her on their wedding night; he put the head on her for smiling at the photographer. There were no shelters in those days. Pregnant Monica had to leave the house when Billy came home drunk. She'd waddle around the dark Bridgeton streets waiting until he was asleep before creeping back into the house. No-one questioned it. You married a man and if he beat ye that was just your luck. Isa said that in those days there was a time of night, about an hour after closing time, when the only people in the streets of Glasgow were women and children.

The moment Jimmy was born it was clear that he wasn't Billy's. He took after him in nothing, neither in looks nor temperament. Jimmy was always gentle, always fearful, there was never a drop of Billy in him.

Billy worked the boats. The last time he came home on leave he brought wee Jimmy over to Isa's to stay for a couple of days. Isa took the child, she had no idea, she honestly had no idea. Jimmy had stayed before, when Monica brought him. He'd stayed for days sometimes, but Isa was glad of his company. He was a nice wee thing, always laughing, and Isa's brothers and sister were out at work all day and the dancing at night, so having the bairn was like being a real mother. Billy left the child and went looking for his wife. He had heard about Monica. She'd been running with a crowd from the Gorbals, leaving the child alone and going with other men. He found her in a rough pub by the docks and took her outside. He broke her arms and, Isa paused and stared at the table, he took one of her eyes out. The men in the pub heard the screaming. When they found what he'd done they beat him. He hanged himself in the cells at the Marine. Monica died a few months later, got an infection, Isa pointed to her eye and winced. She thought something bad must have happened to him on the boats, and it must have been something terrible to make him so vicious.

'Maybe he was just like that?' suggested Leslie.

'*He took her eye*,' said Isa.

'Mum, I hear about things like that all the time and there aren't any boats for the bastards to go on any more. They're just like that.'

'Oof.' Isa turned away as if she'd been slapped. She smiled hopelessly at Maureen. 'I hope she doesn't use language like that all the time.'

Maureen patted her hand. 'What happened to wee Jimmy, Isa?'

'Monica's sister came,' she hung her head, 'and took him

109

away. She thought I knew what Billy was going to do but I didn't. I wouldn't think of such a thing, I was just a girl myself. But he was my cousin and he was dead and I got the blame. She wasn't very nice to me.'

'And did ye see wee Jimmy after that?' asked Maureen.

'Not for a long time. Then about ten years ago I bumped into him at the Barras.' She flushed. 'He was all grown-up and he knew me, came running over and kissed me in the street, in front of everyone. I was that pleased. I thought his auntie would've turned him against me but, to her credit, she hadn't. She died before he married. We kept in touch, he came to our Maisie's wedding,' she nodded at Leslie, 'and he brought his new wife, Ann. It was nice, us all being together, but then he just drifted away. He wouldn't hit his wife . . .'

Isa trailed off and Leslie sat forward. 'I think he did it,' she said certainly.

'Rubbish,' said Isa flatly, and Leslie opened her mouth to start a fight—

'I don't think he'd hit anyone,' interrupted Maureen, 'not coming from a background like that.'

'He's *more* likely to hit someone coming from that,' insisted Leslie.

'No, he isn't,' said Isa.

'No,' said Maureen. 'If ye come from that ye can't lie and pretend it doesn't matter. If ye come from that ye'd be acutely aware of what it meant and what it could lead to.'

'I still think he did,' said Leslie stubbornly.

Isa poured more tea for Maureen. She tried to make her take a gammon roll or at least a biscuit, have a wee biscuit. Maureen took a teacake just to be nice.

'What d'yees think'll happen to him?' whispered Isa. Leslie looked at Maureen but Maureen's mouth was full.

'The police'll do him for murder when they see the shelter photos,' said Leslie.

'What if they don't see the photos?' said Maureen, struggling to speak through a mouthful of mallow and cooking chocolate.

'But they're going to see the photos,' said Leslie firmly.

'Could you hide the photos?' whispered Isa.

'Mother,' said Leslie, 'what are you suggesting?'

Isa quietly rearranged the plate of biscuits. 'Ye might misplace them,' she said quietly.

'Mum, for God's sake—'

'I've stolen them,' said Maureen to Isa. 'They're in my bag.'

'Oh,' beamed Isa, 'that's wrong.'

'I'm a bad lot,' said Maureen. Isa made her take another biscuit. 'I think Ann had a boyfriend,' said Maureen, basking in Isa's approval. 'He could have beat her, she could have followed him to London and he might have killed her there. We should look for a boyfriend.'

'Yes,' said Leslie, nodding at Maureen as if she was prompting her a line. 'But we need to wait and see what the police make of it.'

Isa sighed heavily. 'I'll go and see Jimmy and get to know the children,' she said. 'Every time something terrible happens to that family I turn up like typhoid Mary.'

'Mum, if it wasn't for you Billy might have killed the wean as well.'

The doorbell rang three times in rapid succession. Isa sighed and stood up, straightening her pinny and narrowing her lips. 'I bet that's that bloody Sheila McGregor,' she said.

'Oof,' said Maureen to Leslie. 'I hope she doesn't use language like that all the time.'

Isa teeheed and disappeared into the hall. They heard

two oscillating lady voices greeting each other with offers of tea and cake.

'You were brilliant,' said Leslie. 'She'd have been gutted if I'd told her.'

'No bother.' Maureen gestured out to the hall. 'Who's this?'

'Hungry neighbour. Catches the smell when the lid comes off the biscuits.'

Mrs McGregor's shopping bags filled the doorway. She humphed them on to the kitchen floor and stood up, blinded by the condensation on her glasses. She was dressed in a thick green tweed coat and stood less than five foot tall on bandy cowboy legs. Isa came back into the kitchen and put the kettle on again.

'Oh, my,' said Mrs McGregor, pulling out a chair and sitting herself down, 'but it's wild out there the day. Is that you, Leslie, pet?'

Leslie looked as sullen as she ever had. 'Aye, hello, Mrs McGregor. How ye keeping, all right?'

Mrs McGregor helped herself to a shortbread biscuit and looked at Maureen. 'And who's this?' she said, looking her up and down. 'Is this your life-partner, Leslie?'

'Stop trying to be modern, Mrs McGregor. She's my pal.'

'Very good,' said Mrs McGregor, taking a half-cup of weak tea from Isa and filling it to the brim with milk. 'Your mother says I can't stay long because you've had a death in the family.'

'That's right,' said Leslie.

'Aw, well,' said Mrs McGregor, opening her mouth, letting shortbread crumbs fall willy-nilly on to her coat. 'And just after Christmas as well.' She wrinkled her nose at Maureen. 'No time for turmoil.'

They had to wait until Mrs McGregor left because Leslie wouldn't leave Isa alone with her. 'McGregor bullies her,' said Leslie, unchaining the bike from a lamp-post. 'She'd be staying for her tea if we hadn't seen her out.'

'You're very abrupt with her,' said Maureen. 'Who is she?'

'She's a misery magnet, that woman,' said Leslie. 'Every time there's a tragedy on this scheme that woman turns up for the purvey.'

Maureen put her helmet on and did up her coat, watching while Leslie jump-started the bike.

'Why did she think I was your girlfriend?'

'She's been saying I'm gay since I was wee. And then the bike, ye know.'

'Oh, yeah, sure sign. Ye should tell her that a bipolar conception of gender is widely discredited now.'

Leslie threw back her head and laughed a wide-mouthed dirty laugh, baring black fillings and coffee stains. And Maureen wanted her to keep laughing so she could watch.

16

Baps

'So far nothing, then?'

'Yes, sir. So far fuck all,' said Williams.

Dakar shook his head and stood up. He remembered himself, remembered what he would look like to Bunyan, and held in his belly until he got to the window and had his back to her. 'It's a mattress, for Pete's sake. Thames Division say an object that big doesn't move far so it had to go in near the Chelsea Wharf. They're not even sure it could have made it across the river so it had to go in at that side of the river. Someone must have seen something.'

'I'm sure someone did,' said Williams, between bites of chicken bap, 'but they're either keeping quiet about it or they didn't realize it was suspicious.'

Bunyan sat forward, pressing her waist against the edge of the desk, pulling her blouse tight. Williams saw Dakar being careful not to look. 'If,' she said, 'they dumped the mattress at four in the morning, that road could have been completely empty. Maybe no-one saw anything.'

'Possible,' agreed Dakar. 'Quite, quite possible. The husband's the only thing we've got to go on, isn't he?'

Bunyan nodded. 'Can't place him in London until we talk to him, though.'

Williams swung back in his chair and thought about home. They'd have to go to Glasgow and interview the husband. He hadn't been back for years, not since his dad's funeral.

'... Glasgow,' finished Dakar and looked expectantly at Williams.

Bunyan was looking at him too. 'We have to go to Glasgow,' she said.

'Oh, right,' said Williams. 'Obviously.'

Dakar pointed at him. 'I'll approach Liaison about a spot on *Crimewatch*. She's a mother of four, for Godsake. Someone must have seen something.'

17
The Big Picture

Maureen had never seen CCB photographs before. The glossy pictures were spread over the floor, a patchwork of angles and body parts lit by a harsh white light. 'Are they always like this?' she whispered reverently.

'No.' Leslie sat down next to Maureen and looked out over the sea of photographs. 'They're not usually this bad. These are the worst I've seen.'

Ann was standing against a white wall wearing nothing but her tired underwear. She looked into the camera, vacant and resigned, her mouth hanging open with Hindleyesque apathy. Full-length shots of her front, side and back established the scale and then the pictures homed in on her injuries, slicing her body into digestible pieces. She was seriously underweight; her arms were pencil thin and her pelvic bone jutted out of her back. There was a two-inch chasm between her bony thighs. A whispering silver road map sprawled across her withered belly and spent breasts. Someone had kicked the shit out of her.

A punch to her jaw had split her lip and left it grotesquely swollen. Black and yellow bruises were clustered on her back, creeping around her torso to her chest, slipping under her grey bra. One series of shots concentrated on the injury to her groin. The pictures centred on the modest bridge of her pants, a patch of white cotton in a sea of blackened skin that extended all the way down to her knees.

'See there?' Leslie leaned forward and pointed to an oval

bruise on the back of Ann's neck, gesturing with her pinkie as if reluctant to touch it. 'That's a stamp mark, from a shoe.'

'Jesus,' whispered Maureen, 'she must have fought like a bastard.'

'No,' said Leslie, picking up a full-length shot and pointing to the back of Ann's hands. 'Look at that. There's not a mark on the back of her hands or her arms.'

Maureen didn't get it. 'What does that mean?'

'This is what ye do when you're being hit,' Leslie crossed her hands over her head and rounded her back, 'but Ann didn't. See that big bruise?' She traced a big diagonal one on her chest. 'She wasn't defending herself at all. She was probably unconscious.'

'She might have been steaming,' said Maureen, pointing to Ann's legs in the full-length shot. Cuts and bruises of various ages were slashed across the knife-edge bone on her skinny shin. Ann had a habit of falling down. She'd been falling for a long time. Maureen looked at Ann's tired eyes. 'She looks dead already.'

They sat for a moment looking at the pictures, frowning and sick and sad. Maureen tried to imagine how angry someone would have to be to do that to a limp body. The clouds parted outside the window, and for a brief moment Leslie's living room was full of brilliant yellow sunshine.

It was a small flat in a good, low-level block in Drum-chapel. Leslie was lucky with her neighbours. They were elderly and watchful of one another, and they kept the close clean and tidy. The houses were small and neat with low ceilings, little square rooms and a veranda through the door at the back of the kitchen. Leslie's favourite thing was to eat hot food outside, she said it made her feel privileged, and on milder nights they used to sit on the veranda, watching the wasteground around the back, and eat dinner together. Maureen supposed that Cammy sat with her now – his presence was evident everywhere else in the house. His jacket was hanging up in the hall, his shaving foam was in the bathroom and, judging by the Celtic mugs in the kitchen and the bad oil painting of Jock Stein, he had brought his most treasured possessions over to the house so that he could be near them. Maureen berated herself. She should wish Leslie well, she was her friend, after all, and they seemed happy together, the house felt comfortable. She looked down at Ann again and sat back on the settee to distance herself from the pictures.

'Did Ann know you were Jimmy's cousin?' she asked.

'No,' said Leslie. 'I didn't recognize the name but I knew her when I saw her face. Mum's got photos of a cousin's wedding a few years ago and Ann and Jimmy were there. I kept my distance.'

'Did ye tell the committee you knew her?'

'No, well, I wasn't sure it was her. I can't tell ye how pleased I was when you said ye didn't think it was him.'

'You didn't act pleased.'

'I wanted it to be true,' said Leslie. 'It felt like a cop-out.'

'Jimmy's awful spent. Ann looks like a weight-lifter next to him.'

'Yeah.' Leslie rubbed her face with an open hand and looked at the pictures. 'But how fit do ye need to be to stamp on the back of someone's neck, Mauri?' She started picking up the photographs from the floor, shuffling them together into a tidy pile.

Maureen thought of the tiny hard men coming home to a dinner of bread and marg. 'Leslie? Do we need to take these back?'

Leslie thought about it, her fingers trailing on the edges of the pictures. 'Do you want to take the chance, Mauri? What if he did do it?'

'Come and meet him,' said Maureen.

'I don't want to.'

'You'll have to sometime. Can we keep the pictures until after you've met him?'

'I don't want to meet him.' Leslie gathered the pictures together, tapping the edges on the coffee table and looking perplexed. 'Why have you got these, anyway?'

Maureen drew hard on her cigarette. 'I just ... I dunno, wanted to see them.'

'Yeah.' Leslie sounded as if she understood. 'Ann was a poor soul, wasn't she?'

Maureen was eager to move the conversation on. 'If she was popping out to the shops and coming back drunk she must have been drinking nearby. We can photocopy her face from the big picture and ask about her in the pubs near the shelter. We could do it tonight if you're not busy.'

'No,' smiled Leslie. 'No, I'm not busy.'

Maureen felt inside her jeans pocket and found the bit of paper with Ann's sister's name on it. She was going to tell Leslie what Jimmy had said about Mr Akitza being a big darkie but Leslie hated him enough as it was already and she hadn't even met him. She gave the name to Leslie, told her it was in Streatham somewhere, and Leslie dialled for directory inquiries, waited for a long while and then asked the operator, 'Why not?' a couple of times. She got pissed off and hung up. The operator wouldn't give her the number unless she had the postcode. Leslie said she didn't know her own fucking postcode but they could probably get the number at the Mitchell library.

They drank their coffee in the living room and Leslie added a little drop of whisky to ease Maureen's hangover and give herself a treat. They sipped and smoked and tried to work out how they could find out what was in the letter Ann got before she left.

Ann had a friend at the shelter called Senga. She had stayed in over Christmas and there was just the slightest possibility that Ann would have shown her the contents of the envelope. Leslie said that she could get Senga's new address from the office and they could go and talk to her. The more plans they made together the more excited they became and it began to feel like old times, but Maureen knew it wasn't the same. The tension between them remained unexplained and would probably never be sorted out. She watched Leslie stub out her fag, rubbing the doubt into the blue glass ashtray. It couldn't be patched up. They'd never have that crystal confidence between them again. Her mutinous eyes welled up again and she stood up, excusing herself, saying she needed a piss. She sat on the side of the bath and pulled herself together with deep breaths and scathing self-reproach.

'Mauri,' Leslie called up to her as she came down the hall, and Maureen thought for a moment that Leslie had seen her tears, 'what can we do if we find anything out?'

'Tell the police?'

'You can't go to the police, they're still hassling you for what you did to Angus in Millport.'

'*Some* of the police are hassling me for that,' said Maureen.

'What are the rest of the police hassling ye for?'

Maureen sat down and sipped her whisky coffee and wondered. She picked up the phone book and found the listing for the Stewart Street police station, dialled the main switchboard and asked for Hugh McAskill.

Hugh picked up the phone before it rang out. 'Hello?'

'Oh, Hugh?'

'Yes, this is Hugh McAskill. Can I help you?'

'Hugh, it's Maureen O'Donnell.'

'Maureen,' she could hear him smiling, 'are ye all right?'

'I'm fine. I got a bit upset.' She felt angry with him but knew she had no right.

'Maureen, about the other day, I'm sorry—'

'It's okay.'

'—but it's my job. Going to see people and asking about unsolved crimes is my job. I can't refuse to do it because I like you.'

'I know,' she said. 'I was having a bad day.'

'Aye,' he said. He seemed to be looking around the room and then huddled into the receiver. 'Fine, fine. Ye never came back to see me.'

Maureen imagined herself standing in front of a trestle table of angry policemen in elaborate uniforms. Leslie was watching her expectantly from the sofa. 'I was going to,' she said uncertainly.

'I thought I'd've seen you at the meeting.'

Hugh attended an incest survivors' meeting on Thursdays and he had outed himself to Maureen so that he could invite her. She had been once, only staying long enough to have a cup of tea and see Hugh, but an annoying man had come in and she couldn't face the whole meeting. She thought she might have to give them a talk about herself and her family and she couldn't face it.

'I kept meaning to come . . . Hugh, I was phoning because . . . if I had some information about a crime, would you be able to take it?'

'We're always looking for information,' said Hugh, without hesitation. 'Is it something that happened in Glasgow?'

'No, it was in London.'

'It's not our jurisdiction but we can pass it on. Listen, don't go getting involved in anything.'

'I'm not going to do that, Hugh.'

'Maureen, this assault in Millport, Joe isn't going to let it go. He's convinced Farrell's at it to get a lighter sentence.'

'I think he's right.'

'He's determined to get you for it. The worst thing you can do is get involved in something else.'

'I'm not getting involved.'

'Listen,' Hugh lowered his voice even further, 'I'm going to ask you again: is Farrell writing to you?'

Maureen looked at Leslie. 'No.' It was a cheap lie and Hugh was a nice man who had gone out of his way to help her. He deserved better and she felt low for lying to him.

'The hospital said he was,' insisted Hugh.

'Maybe he's writing to the wrong address.'

'They've checked, he's writing to your address.'

'Well, I'm not getting any letters so I don't know what's happening there.'

Leslie was watching her from the settee, making questioning faces at the mention of letters.

'Okay, pal,' said Maureen briskly. 'Listen, I'll be in touch then.'

'Will I hear from ye soon?'

'Ye will. Cherrio.' She hung up. Leslie was staring at her intently.

'Was he asking about the letters from Angus Farrell?' asked Leslie.

'Yeah, the nurses told them he was writing to me.' She sat down next to Leslie on the settee. 'They want to see them but I can't – God, they mention Millport and everything. If they ever do me for the assault they could get the whole story from them.'

'You don't think he could be writing to Siobhain, do you? He definitely knows where she lives.'

'I don't know,' said Maureen. 'I haven't seen her since before Christmas.'

'We should go and see her.'

Like most of the women on her ward, Siobhain had

been viciously raped by Angus. She was the only surviving witness to what he had done, or at least the only one who could still speak in full sentences, and if he was coming for anyone he would be coming for her.

'His writing's getting smaller,' said Maureen quietly. 'I think he's getting better.'

'He's still mental, though, isn't he?' said Leslie.

'The letters sound mental but it's put on. I know it's put on.'

'How do you know that?'

Maureen shook her head. 'It's too set,' she said. 'It's not random enough. I don't know. It's difficult to explain. Joe McEwan thinks he's at it. He says that Angus'll get a short sentence and get out. You don't think he'll come after me, do you?'

'I don't know.'

Maureen desperately wanted some bluster and comfort. 'You don't think I'm in danger, do you?' she said, trying to prompt a response.

'Bollocks,' said Leslie, sniggering uncertainly. 'Think about it rationally. If he was coming to get you why would he write and warn you? That's evidence against him if he does.'

Maureen wanted her to be right, but Angus was bright, probably brighter than both of them, and everything he did had a purpose.

They drove through the town to the Mitchell library, an imposing Victorian building sitting precariously on the verge of an open-cast motorway underpass. The building was deceptively big, housing a large library, a café and a theatre. An obese porter was sitting at the reception desk, panting at the effort of keeping still. He directed them to the fourth floor.

The Business Information Centre was a quiet room with three scruffy clients sitting equidistant from one another at a long table. The lights were soft and relaxing and the guy behind the desk smiled cheerfully as they walked over to him. 'Yes, ladies, can I help you today?' he said, his eager eyes wet with the desire to serve.

'We need to use a photocopier, colour if you've got it,' Maureen tried not to smile, 'and a set of phone books for London.'

'Our colour photocopier is over there,' he flicked a finger at the far wall, 'and costs fifty pence per copy. Now, London, north or south?'

They didn't really know.

'I have a map here,' said the nice man, pulling out a small diagram of the London postal regions and holding it up over his face. 'Please, take your time.'

Bewildered by the man's courtesy, Leslie walked off to the colour copier. After a while Maureen spotted Streatham on the map, south of the river, right next to Brixton. His arms must be getting sore by now. 'South,' she said, lowering the map to look at him. 'I think it's in the south.'

'This place is like a weirdos' convention,' said Leslie adamantly, once they were safely in the lift.

'He was just being helpful,' said Maureen.

'Did ye get the number?'

'Aye. It's the only Akitza in the book. I checked the north as well, just to be sure, but there was only one and it was in Middlesex somewhere.'

Maureen looked up. Leslie had turned to her and was standing formally on both feet. She seemed to be trembling. 'I'm sorry I tried to fight ye, Mauri,' she said and looked like she might cry.

'I'm sorry for being a wee shite,' said Maureen. 'About Cammy, Leslie, I'm pleased for you.'

Leslie looked away and her breathing returned to normal. She paused for a moment and looked at her feet. 'Do you mind doing this for Ann?' she asked.

'No,' said Maureen, but they both knew why she was doing it, and they both knew she wasn't doing it for Ann.

18

Interested

The low winter sun was a blistering horizontal beam slicing through the city's grid system, leaving patches of ragged frost and frozen puddles on the cross. Pedestrians dragged fifteen-foot-long shadows after them and the high Victorian buildings of the city centre melted into the earth. Leslie turned the corner, slowing down as she drove towards the light.

Maureen sat tall on the pillion, her coat tails brushing the passing cars and her hair snapping at her neck. She took herself back to yesterday, to the deep calm and the vortex of welcoming air at the windowsill. She was still alive and having another day, losing herself in the problems of Jimmy and Ann and feeling all right sometimes. She looked at the people on the street and realized that the world must be busy with people who tried to kill themselves last night, people who woke up this morning, nauseous and disappointed, and had to go to work, living the afterwards. She thought of Pauline, and it struck her that suicide was never the definitive statement; it was an impulse, a comma, not a stop. If she had jumped from the window the comma would have gone on for ever, like Pauline, a breathless hush hanging for infinity without the possibility of resolution.

She thought of Winnie's little hand and there it was again. She was crying under her helmet, as sentimental as a recent divorcee at New Year. And then, for one clear, shining moment, she saw how it would be if only she were wrong about everything. Michael would be a prodigal father, all the more welcome for his long absence. Una and Marie would be her patient sisters, waiting for her to be a sister to them. And Winnie, the kind mother, fighting for her disturbed daughter's affection despite a thousand rejections. It was simple from the other side.

The bike stopped at a set of lights on Woodlands Road and Maureen looked up. An abandoned shop had two of their shelter campaign posters plastered to the window. Maureen and Leslie nudged each other, remembering six thirty in the morning, their hands sticky from a night brushing paste, as the dawn wind gathered and the sleepy shift workers waited at the bus stop. The lights changed and Leslie pulled off into the road.

Siobhain's close smelt of cats and bleach and hot food. A squawking television in the flat opposite sounded urgent and foreign. Leslie knocked and stepped back to wait. The door opened on the chain and Siobhain looked out at them through the two-inch crack. She was beautiful. Her skin was lunar white, her lips salmon pink, even the streaks of white through her thick black hair looked like sheen. 'I am watching television,' she said, her hootie-shush-teuchter accent sounding like an order to slow down.

'Can we come in anyway?' said Maureen. 'We've come all the way over to see you.'

'But it's *Quincy*.'

Along the hall they could hear the monolithic television twittering as Quincy made a bunch of brand-new close friends, solved all their problems then never had to see them again. Douglas had given Siobhain a wad of cash before he died and she spent it sporadically on big things. The giant television was Siobhain's delight. She talked about it like a new horse, how well it worked, how sleek it was, how she didn't know of anyone else with one as good as that.

Occasionally, when she and Maureen were sitting watching telly, she'd turn to Maureen smiling and say, listen to that sound, look at the colour, wasn't it great? She'd joined a video club as well and had taken to watching wet romances and schlock horrors night after night. Running seriously short of things to say on her fortnightly visits, Maureen had mentioned Liam's films. They weren't very good and there was no story but she thought it might be nice for her to see a film and meet the person who'd made it. Siobhain hated them. Liam sat on the beige sofa at the end of his twenty-minute video and Siobhain turned to him and asked him sincerely why he had bothered.

Leslie pushed in front of Maureen. 'Look, Siobhain, we're only here to see if you're okay.'

Siobhain pursed her pretty mouth. 'You should telephone me before you come here,' she said. 'This is not a tea room.'

'We tried to phone,' lied Leslie, 'but you've turned your mobile off again.'

Like everyone else with a bit of spare cash in Britain that Christmas, Siobhain had felt the need to have a phone in her pocket at all times and had bought a mobile, but she couldn't stand the noise it made. She would forget to re-charge it and kept it in a drawer in the kitchen so that if it ever rang out she wouldn't hear it.

'Oh, I suppose I have.' Siobhain shut the door, undid the chain and let them into the hall, closing the door carefully after them and sliding the chain back on. She smiled a pleased, secretive smirk, as if she was walking about with no knickers on, and pointed them into the living room.

Siobhain didn't care about her appearance. She generally wore whatever was clean and came to hand. Today she was modelling a red golfing jersey, gathered tight at the waist, and orange nylon tracksuit bottoms that swish-swished when she walked. She had worked hard to put on as much weight as possible after she was discharged from psychiatric hospital. They'd watched her eat breakfast once, half a loaf washed down with full-fat milk. She didn't care much about her surroundings either. Well-meaning social workers had decorated the house, and every room was painted cleanable beige with a beige carpet throughout and predominantly beige furniture. Maureen didn't usually buy into the spiritual significance of home decor but Siobhain's house made her soul wither. The only thing of any interest in the living room was the painting. She had used Douglas's money to have a photograph of her dead brother reproduced as an oil painting and hung it over the gas fire. It looked exactly like a painting of a photograph, the little boy's spontaneous gestures, a pointed finger, a half-wink, suddenly invested with elusive meaning. The little boy stood smiling sadly into the camera, his little knees pink under his shorts, his red wellies trimmed with black mud.

She led them into the living room and sat Leslie in the armchair and Maureen on the settee by the door so that Siobhain herself could be nearer the television and wouldn't have to miss anything Quincy said. Leslie crossed her legs, resting her leather biker boot on the arm of the chair. Siobhain pointed at her. 'Get your feet off the furniture,' she ordered. 'Please.'

Leslie tutted and moved her leg. They sat silently, listening as Quincy summed up the case to his idiot sidekick. Siobhain leaned down to the side of the sofa and pulled two blue plastic photo albums on to her lap. She sat with them on her knee, patting them occasionally, smirking to herself when Quincy made a joke. The ads started.

'Have you brought something for us to eat together?' she asked Maureen.

'I think I've got some chewing-gum.' Maureen pulled a battered packet out of her back pocket. Siobhain held out her hand while Maureen squeezed two shiny rectangles of gum out of the tight wrapper and took one for herself. Leslie refused. They sat chewing and watching the ads until Siobhain turned to Maureen, put one album in her lap then stood up slowly, walked over to Leslie and handed her the other. 'Have a look,' she said, and sat back down.

Maureen opened the first page. Below the sticky Cellophane a cacophony of colour shrieked across the page. The pictures were cut out of magazines, printed on flimsy paper. They were pictures of babies, of models and members of the public, photographs of toothpaste tubes and ketchup bottles and houses and new cars and competition prizes. Each picture had been cut out very carefully, no detail too insignificant to be missed. They were perfect. Over the page another riot was in progress, and over another and over another. It must have taken her hours. Siobhain was delighted at their surprise. 'See?' she said, grinning at them.

'See what?' asked Leslie.

'See my pictures?' said Siobhain.

Maureen knew that Siobhain took her medication religiously and she knew that she was treated for depression but she didn't know what to make of this. 'Are they your pictures?' she asked.

'Yes,' said Siobhain. 'They are by me and for me. Do you like them?'

Maureen smiled uncomfortably. 'Yeah, but what are they for?'

'They're about my people,' said Siobhain, 'about when I was young and the martyrs.'

Leslie pointed at a picture of a baby in a bath, wearing a pointy hat of soapy foam. 'Is this one about martyrs?'

'It's about my mother bathing children in Sutherland.' She stopped.

'Should you be doing this, Siobhain?' said Leslie, turning

the page and staring down at a tourist-brochure photograph of Majorca.

'Yes, yes, they're from my books,' said Siobhain, nodding over to a mutilated pile of true-life magazines behind the television. 'They gave them to me at the day centre. I can do what I like with them.' She pointed to the picture Leslie was looking at. 'Shangri-La.'

'How long did it take you to do it all?' asked Maureen.

'All of yesterday evening and this morning,' she said solemnly, as if she had achieved a long-held goal. She pointed to Leslie's lap. 'Go forward a wee bit, there, there, look at that one.'

It was a picture of a car. Maureen watched her. Siobhain didn't seem volatile or changeable but she was quite high and the pictures were bizarre. She might be getting letters from Angus, she might have upped her medication if they bothered her, that might explain how high she was. Siobhain smiled at her, not the sleepy smile Maureen knew her for but a big wide-awake grin. 'Do you like them?' she said hopefully.

'I don't understand them, to be honest,' Maureen answered.

Siobhain nodded. 'No,' she said quietly, 'I know. They are a story you haven't heard, about my home and my people.'

Maureen was stumped. 'Are you thinking about going home?' she asked.

'No. My home is gone.' She patted the album on Maureen's knee. 'It's in here now.'

Leslie put her album down on the floor and stood up. 'I need the loo,' she said, and walked out to the dark hall.

'If you forget where you're from,' said Siobhain, when Leslie was out of the room, 'if you forget your people, it's a kind of betrayal, isn't it?'

Maureen cleared her throat. 'Do you get a lot of post, Siobhain?'

'No,' she said, and turned back to the album on Maureen's lap. 'How do you like this one?'

'Nice,' said Maureen. 'So, what else have you been up to? Have you been going to the day centre?'

'Yes.'

Maureen scratched her arm. 'How's Tanya?' she said.

'Fine.'

Maureen didn't know how to ask about Angus without frightening her.

'D'you understand now?' asked Siobhain.

'A wee bit. Do you get post?'

'Not much.' Siobhain chewed her gum for a moment, looking out into the hallway for Leslie. 'What's taking her so long? I hope she's not rummaging in there.'

'You haven't had a letter recently?'

Siobhain sighed and looked at Maureen insolently. 'No. No post. No,' she said spitefully. 'Stop going on about it.'

'Are you sure?'

'Look,' said Siobhain, snide and quiet, like a bullying babysitter having a dig while the parents were out of the room, 'I'm not your patient. You cannot come to my house in the middle of the day and ask me questions over and over.'

'I'm sorry,' said Maureen, feeling tearful again. 'I just – I don't understand the pictures.'

Siobhain looked into the hall again. 'I know you don't understand,' she whispered. 'It doesn't mean I'm wrong, does it?'

Maureen looked at her. The colour had risen in Siobhain's face, her chubby cheeks were flushed. She touched her hair, tucking it behind her ear. She seemed so different, like someone Maureen would know, someone she'd be friends with, like a girl of her own age and time. 'Siobhain, I've never seen you like this.'

'It's a long time since I felt like this.'

'Like what?'

Siobhain patted the album on Maureen's lap and looked her in the eye. 'Interested in something.'

They heard a flush down the hall and the bathroom door opened, amplifying the noise. Siobhain waited until Leslie sat back down and arranged herself in her chair before telling them it was time they left because her favourite soap was coming on.

A damp sheen coated the close, making the stone stairs slippery.

'Do you think we should phone the doctor?' said Maureen, as they stepped out into the blinding sunshine.

'I don't know, she's pretty strange most of the time.'

'She's high, though. Depressives don't get high unless something's going on.'

'Did you ask her about the letters?'

'He's not writing to her,' said Maureen.

'He's just writing to you, then?'

'Yeah.'

'Well, she's got more on him than you have. If it was a real threat he'd be writing to her too.'

'But if it's not a threat,' said Maureen, 'then what is it?'

Duke Street was busy and clogged with cumbersome buses easing their way around the pedestrians. The scathing sunshine beamed directly down the busy street, blinding everyone facing west, catching the drivers heading east in their rear-view mirrors. Leslie nipped through the line of traffic, cutting up the taxis and driving along the central line, keeping her head tipped down so that her visor afforded some shade. They crossed a junction and followed the hill to the town, passing the abattoir and the brewery. They stopped at the lights outside the Model Lodging House Hotel, a crumbling homeless shelter built in the shadow of the Necropolis. Behind a protective pedestrian barrier dirty-faced men of indeterminate age squatted on the steps, drinking lager out of cans and smoking rollies, watching up and down the road.

Leslie parked across the street from the office and left Maureen with the bike while she ran in. Katia and Jan were standing in the doorway of the baker's vent, warming their heads against the jet of warm air and having a stilted chat. They hadn't spotted Maureen. She sat down on the bike with her back to them, keeping the helmet on. If it was something in her maybe she was sick. Maybe she'd been wrong to think she didn't need to see a psychiatrist any more. Maybe her family were right about her, maybe she was mental. She toyed with the idea, enjoying the possibility, running it through her mind like sun-warmed sand through her fingers. There was nothing wrong with her. He had done it and the family was siding with him and the world was a dark and despairing place.

Leslie was at her side, panting with excitement. 'The police have phoned a couple of times but haven't been yet, and Senga said we can go and see her tomorrow.'

19

Veranda

They had a couple of hours to spare and Leslie was hungry for a supper. She said that a Frattelli supper was the only decent supper in Glasgow and insisted that they go back to Drumchapel. Maureen didn't want to go back to Leslie's house. She had a suspicion that Cammy was living there and couldn't be sure that the Frattelli line wasn't just a cover for Leslie to go back and see him. She had never mentioned Frattelli's before. But Leslie shamed her into agreeing and they drove back along the Great Western Road into a golden sunset.

The tea-time queue was already forming in Frattelli's. Dads bought five portions of chips on the way home from their work and singletons came looking for a hot meal. Maureen was relieved when Leslie ordered a fish supper for each of them and nothing for Cammy. She ordered a glass bottle of Bru as well and a Chomp bar each for their pudding. Maureen insisted on paying.

'Don't be daft,' said Leslie. 'It was my idea.'

But Maureen muscled in front of her and handed over a tenner. They put the flimsy plastic bag in the box and Leslie drove like a bastard up the hill to get home before the chips went soggy. Cammy wasn't in and the house was dark, but he had left a scribbled note in the kitchen and Leslie read it, chuckled indulgently to herself, and looked up at Maureen as if she was surprised to see her. 'He's at football,' she said.

'Are you two living together, then?' asked Maureen, taking two scratched Barbie dinner plates down from the cupboard to sit the paper parcels on.

'Kind of. He lives with his folks but he spends a lot of time over here.'

'Have ye given him his own key?'

Leslie glowered at her. She had always sworn she would never give a man a key to her house because she saw what happened to the women in the shelter. It was a routine trap. The women met a nice man, fell for him and he gradually insinuated himself into their homes. They gave him a key for convenience and when he beat them the only practical solution was for the woman to run away and leave him with the house.

'Nah,' she said, unwrapping her supper and arranging the paper over the edge of the plate. 'Mrs Gallagher across the landing lets him in.' She blushed and got two Barbie glasses out of the cupboard, unscrewed the lid of the ginger and meticulously poured them a glass each as Maureen watched.

'You gave him a key, didn't ye?'

'Yes,' said Leslie, slamming the bottle down on the side. 'I gave him a key. Happy?'

Maureen grinned at her. 'I don't make up your fucking crazy rules, Leslie, don't get pissed off with me.'

'Well, what are you having a go at me for?'

'Leslie,' said Maureen, teasing her, 'you're having a go at yourself.'

Leslie huffed at her dinner. 'I don't know. You give out all this advice for years and then when it happens to you, I don't know, I just feel so out of control around him.'

'Yeah,' said Maureen, unwrapping her parcel, 'I know.'

Leslie looked out of the window and crossed her arms. She looked terrified. 'Sometimes,' her voice had dropped and she could hardly bring herself to say it, 'I make his dinner for him coming home.'

'Ooh,' said Maureen, 'that's a very bad sign. You'll be dead in a month.'

'Is it a bad sign?' said Leslie anxiously.

Maureen saw she wasn't joking. 'You've just fallen for someone. Enjoy yourself.'

'But I don't feel like myself.'

'That's what falling in love is. You lose control and you don't feel like yourself. It's supposed to be nice. Isn't it nice?'

'Did you feel this way about Douglas?'

Maureen picked out the brownest chips from her dinner, the withered twice-fried ones that tasted of caramel, and thought about it. She couldn't remember the relationship very well, all the softness and the fond good times were lost in the violent end, but she supposed she must have felt that way, and her behaviour must have been just as confusing to Leslie. Douglas was married and old and a bit predatory. When she thought about it she could see how angry it must have made Leslie and she began to soften towards Cammy but then she remembered that Leslie hadn't liked Douglas and had never been even passingly pleasant to him. 'I suppose I did,' she said, picking up her plate and glass and wrapping her pinkie around the neck of the sauce bottle. 'My supper's getting cold.'

Out on the veranda they climbed over the dead pot plants and sat on stained deckchairs, resting their plates on their knees and eating with their fingers. Small clouds of fragrant steam rose as they each broke into the battered fish, filling the veranda with the tantalizing smell of vinegar.

The veranda looked out on to a wide stretch of wasteland. Children from the scheme gathered there; the older ones stood talking to each other, watching over their younger siblings as they took turns at riding someone's mountain bike over and around the hillocks and splashing through the muddy puddles. Leslie was right about Frattelli's suppers. The fish was fresh and firm and the chips were crunchy.

'Good, isn't it?' asked Leslie, sinking her teeth through crisp batter to the soft and subtle fish.

'Lovely,' said Maureen.

The light was failing. The burnished yellow sky was smeared with streaks of orange and thin cloud. Heavy black rainclouds conspired on the horizon. Maureen sat back and sighed at her dinner. 'God, I don't know if I can eat all this.'

'You'd better or you won't get your Chomp bar.'

Maureen smiled out at the muddy hillocks and the big sky.

'Ye left that cheese salad the other night as well,' said Leslie quietly. 'Are ye eating?'

Maureen's eating habits were always a good measure of her mental state. She could never swallow properly when she got upset because her throat closed up. When she had had her breakdown she lost three stone and had had to be fed soft food in hospital. 'I'm eating fine,' she said.

'How ye feeling, though?'

Maureen took out her cigarettes. 'Sad. I feel very sad. I'm not angry or upset or anything, just very sad.'

'Maybe you're grieving for Douglas.'

'I feel as if I'm grieving for everything.' She held out the packet to Leslie. 'I keep fucking crying. I can't control it and it always happens at awkward moments like in the middle of a fight or in a shop or something.'

Leslie took a fag from her and set her plate down on the floor, pulling up the collar of her biker's jacket to keep her warm. 'If it's grief that's good,' she said.

'Why?'

'It's healing and grief isn't infinite.'

'Feels infinite.'

Downstairs a rogue child sprinted across the ground, jumped on the mountain bike and cycled away from the waiting crowd, pedalling fast over the far hills. The angry mob of small kids ran after him, shouting at him and calling to their brothers and sisters to get him. The older children looked on, their arms folded, and did nothing.

'Hey,' said Maureen, sitting up, 'that wee bastard's just stolen the bike.'

'It's his bike,' said Leslie. 'He got it for Christmas. The tiny team keep taking it from round the back of his house. He has to steal it back at night.'

Maureen sat back. 'Have ye got that Polaroid of Ann's on ye?'

'Yeah,' said Leslie, and pulled it out of her inside pocket.

Maureen looked at it in the light from the kitchen window. 'Look,' she said, and pointed to the wee boy's hand, 'see the Christmas card he's holding? Could that be the card she got in the post?'

'I dunno, it's bigger than the envelope.'

'He's only a wee boy, though. Maybe it looks big in his hand?'

Leslie squinted at it, flicking her ash on the floor. 'Yeah, still bigger and it's got cotton wool on the front. Ann's card felt smooth and thin, it wasn't spongy. It was square.'

'How square?'

She was explaining that the letter was only about as square as the Polaroid and weighed about the same as the Polaroid when she stopped and stared at it.

'Hmm,' said Maureen. 'What could it have been?'

Leslie smiled faintly and looked at the picture.

'But why would someone send her a photo of one boy?' said Maureen.

'Maybe he was her favourite?' said Leslie.

139

'Shut your eyes and feel it again.'

Leslie did and felt sure it was the right size. 'And it felt slippy inside,' she said. 'Like a glossy card.'

'So it could have been this?'

'Could have been.'

Maureen pointed down to her plate. 'I've eaten enough to get a Chomp, though?'

Leslie looked at it carefully. 'Oh,' she said grudgingly, 'okay,' and handed her one from her pocket.

They sat chewing their toffee bars, smoking and watching the black stormclouds steal across the sky and swallow the sunset. The children below began to disperse and they could hear rain approaching in the distance. Maureen thought about what Liam had said, that she shouldn't spoil things for Leslie. 'Are you happy with Cammy?' she asked, watching the horizon.

Leslie looked at her. 'Yeah,' she said, 'I am.'

'I'm sorry for what I said in the Grove,' said Maureen quietly. 'I'm a bit wrapped up in myself just now. I do want ye to be happy, Leslie, you're the nicest person I know.' The words were hardly out of her mouth when her eyes overflowed. She slapped her forehead impatiently and looked at Leslie. 'See?' she said, pointing at her wet eyes. 'They're fucking doing it again.'

But Leslie was crying too, watching a heavy wall of rain wash across the dirty yard. 'I got a fright in Millport,' she said, her voice trembling, 'Mauri, I got a fright and I was disappointed in myself because I couldn't do it, I just couldn't do it.'

Maureen leaned over and touched Leslie's cheek, lifting the little fat tears with her fingertips. 'Auch, wee hen,' she said softly, 'I think Jimmy's the same. I don't think he could either.'

They sat together for a while, sniffing, their heads inclined together, sniffing and thinking.

'I understand how ye felt at the time,' said Maureen quietly. 'Right now I want to pack up and fuck off and never come back here.'

'Really?' Leslie looked at her. 'I always think you're fearless.'

Maureen shook her head. 'Just want to get the fuck out, away from Winnie and Una. My flat doesn't even feel comfortable any more.'

Leslie had never imagined either of them moving away. She'd always assumed they'd have their kids together, be single mums together, rubbing along and managing somehow. 'What would running away solve, though?' she said.

'Don't know, but I can't just keep on fighting everyone all the time, can I? That's no life for anyone.'

'You're not fighting everyone all the time.'

Maureen sighed into her chest and looked up. 'Feels as if I am.'

'Ye can't just stop fighting and walk away. You're not the sort of person who can just opt not to give a shit just because you live somewhere else. D'ye think what ye did to him in Millport affected ye?'

'Dunno.' Maureen shrugged. 'I suppose. Violence corrupts.'

'Does it, though?'

'It has to. Ye have to lose empathy before ye can deliberately hurt someone, don't ye? Or else ye'd feel it yourself and ye couldn't do it.'

Leslie thought about it and hesitated before she spoke. 'Does it need to corrupt? Can't ye lose empathy selectively?'

Maureen snorted. 'And just attack the bad guys?'

'Yeah.'

'In theory, maybe. Those distinctions are hard close up.

141

the good guys from the bad it's easy, but distinctions always blur close up, don't they?' She sighed and took a draw. 'It corrupts ye. Blood will have blood.'

'Yeah, close-ups are tricky,' said Leslie, looking at her lap. 'I've been talking like a psycho for years and I can't even slap a wean's hand. I've been telling women at the shelter not to give their keys out and then I meet someone and within two months I'm asking him to take it.'

Maureen wanted to let the doubts about Cammy lie and fester but she couldn't. 'I'm not very taken with Cammy but I think he's quite safe.'

Leslie sat forward and stared at her intently, the warm kitchen light reflecting off her leather collar. 'Do ye?' she said.

Maureen nodded.

'How can ye tell?' asked Leslie, and waited anxiously for a reply.

Maureen stared at her. 'Do you honestly not know whether he'd hit ye?'

'No, I don't. I don't know how to tell them apart, the ones that will and the ones that won't.'

'Then what the fuck are ye doing letting him into your house?'

Leslie shook her head and looked away. The rain was falling hard, pattering on to the veranda and wetting the toes of their shoes. They could see the water sheets wafting across the wasteground. The few remaining children huddled in dry close mouths waiting for it to finish.

Leslie leaned heavily on her knees, letting her head hang as she took a draw. 'D'ye remember when they were looking for the Yorkshire Ripper?' she said. 'One of the things that held them back was so many women suspected their partners and reported them and they had to investigate every one of them. I thought that was ridiculous at the time.'

Maureen patted her hand. 'I don't think Cammy's the Yorkshire Ripper, Leslie.'

'I know. But ye think ye know things about yourself, think ye have principles, and then things happen and ye find out ye weren't who ye thought ye were at all.'

'That's just growing up.'

'Well, it's scary.' Leslie sat back and exhaled a grey cloud. 'I don't like it.'

'Me neither.'

20

Malki the Alki

Night came quickly and dark clouds continued to roll in from the north. The pavement glistened black smeared with orange from the street-lights. Leslie walked the bike down the gravel alleyway at the side of the house and chained it to the railings, taking care to tuck it in the shadows, out of view from the street. Maureen left her to it, wandering out into the empty road. Rain fell hard, bouncing off the pavement, and she was glad of her big coat. She stood and looked up and down the street, trying to imagine how Ann would have felt standing here, fresh to the shelter with a bruised, bony body and four absent children, looking for somewhere to drink.

It was a broad road, wide enough for two carriages to pass each other comfortably, and long-established trees grew out of the generous pavement. Maureen pulled up her collar and looked at the detached Victorian house behind her. It was built from huge blocks of red sandstone and stood three storeys high with a coy attic for the servants' rooms. The neighbouring houses were equally imposing, set back from the road by small gravel forecourts and low walls. It was obvious to the most casual observer that the shelter was poorer than the others. There were no cars outside, the narrow front garden was overgrown and lights shone from every window in the house. Leslie came out of the shadows and walked across the road to Maureen. They looked up at the shelter, listening as a radio blared through a frosted bathroom window. The DJ whinnied and played a thump-thump dance record.

'We've ruined that house, haven't we?' said Leslie.

'We haven't done anything that couldn't be fixed,' said Maureen, looking down the road. 'Did Ann know this area before she came to stay here?'

'No,' said Leslie. 'She needed to be told where to get the bus into town.'

'Okay.' Maureen nodded. 'She probably just followed the biggest road, then?'

Leslie shrugged. A hundred yards further up a yellow-lit junction glistened like a jewel in the inky darkness. They walked slowly towards it, passing big houses with expensive cars parked outside. The curtains were open in one house and an elegantly greying couple were sitting on an oversized white leather settee, watching a large television. Their slim teenage daughter came into the room and moved her mouth at them. She looked pissed off. Her blonde hair reached down beyond her waist, so thick and wavy and young it would have made an old man cry. The mother said something and the young blonde slapped her thigh petulantly with her fist and left the room in a huff. They looked warm and satisfied and Maureen wished she were the girl, a cherished member of a comfortable family, with parents steady enough to kick against. 'Nice life,' she said, wiping the rain from her forehead.

'Aye,' said Leslie. 'The girl's learning to drive. I see her going up and down the road at three miles an hour in the Merc.'

'She's learning to drive in a Merc?'

Leslie nodded.

'God.' Maureen looked back to the warmth and lack of want, covetous and wondering. 'Nice life.'

Cars and lorries hurtled across the bright junction. They

stopped and looked and Leslie pointed to the right. They walked down a few hundred yards and came to a row of white pub lights glistening through the rain. It was a free-standing house, broader and older than the shelter, white-washed, with an illuminated plastic sign in garish red and gold. Flower-boxes of plastic greenery lined the inside of the windows. A Jeep and a Jag were parked in the forecourt.

'No way she drank there,' said Maureen. 'She couldn't have seen it from the junction and, anyway, it's a brewery pub and they're always pricy. She wouldn't have enough money for a lot of drinks and I can't imagine anyone else buying for her.'

'Yeah,' said Leslie. 'It's handy, though.'

'If you were covered in bruises and feeling like a good bevy, would you go in there?'

Leslie looked at the pub façade. 'No,' she said.

They retraced their steps to the junction and walked to the left this time. They could just make out a dingy shop-front further on. It was a pub called the Lismore, ill-lit and set up against the road without a gable sign.

'There,' said Maureen, and walked towards it.

The Lismore was pleasant inside. The varnish on the floor had been worn away from years of shuffling punters; a strip of worn and softened wood led around the bar like the suggested route in a department store. More striking was the absence of music; the only sounds were the un-dulating murmur of voices and the chink of glasses being washed behind the bar. A lone table of elderly men huddled over their half-and-halfs, chatting to each other. The barman smiled automatically as they came in and put down the glass he was polishing. 'Good evening, ladies. What can I get ye?'

'Two whiskies, please,' said Maureen, brushing the rain from her hair.

They pulled up two bar stools and looked around the room as the barman relieved the whisky optic of its contents. He put the drinks in front of them, sliding a fresh beer mat under each glass and pulling an ashtray over for them.

'I wonder if you could help us,' said Maureen, counting out the right money for the drinks. 'A pal of ours is missing and we're worried about her. We wondered whether you might have seen her.'

The barman took the money and looked uneasy. 'Depends,' he said.

Leslie pulled the photocopy out of her pocket. She hadn't done her job very well. She'd enlarged the full-length shot by two hundred per cent, getting Ann from the waist up. They had to fold the photocopy over in the middle so that her bra and battered tits were hidden, and the colour on the photocopier had been wrongly set: Ann's face was high orange, her irises deep black. She looked as if she'd been coloured in by a child.

'Oh, aye, Ann, is she missing, then?' The barman paused and looked at them sternly. 'You're not here on behalf of her man, are ye? Because I know he hit her.'

'No,' said Leslie quickly. 'We're trying to make sure she didn't fall back in with him.'

'We don't even want to find her, really,' added Maureen. 'We just want to know if you've seen her.'

'Right.' He thought about it. 'Right, no, I don't know where she is. She came in here for a while, a couple of weeks, she'd a burst lip. She was a favourite with the old fellas over there. She used to listen to their stories and flirt with them and that. Aye, she was a big favourite.'

'When did she stop coming in?' asked Maureen.

''Bout a month ago. 'Fore Hogmanay. She came in Boxing Day but I put her out. She was begging people, not even tapping; but begging for drink.'

Leslie leaned across the bar eagerly, letting her hands fall over the far edge. 'Ye put her out?'

'Aye.' He pointed to an old-fashioned black-on-white enamel sign hanging on the wall:

> No Football Colours.
> No Spitting.
> No Hawkers.

'Don't need it,' he said, wiping the bar closer and closer to Leslie's arm, reclaiming his space.

Leslie sat back.

'She can't have been disrupting ye, surely?' asked Maureen.

'See those old swines over there?' He gestured to his only customers. The old men heard him and their chat fell silent. The barman raised his voice. 'They were asking what they would get for their money. Auld swines, playing on the lassie's weakness for the drink.' He lowered his voice. 'That's pensioners for ye, they can smell a bargain a mile off,' he muttered, as if the bargain-hunting skill of the elderly was an unspoken universal truth.

Maureen turned back to the bar. 'So, she was bothering ye?'

'She wasn't bothering me, hen, but I'm a publican, not a vulture, and if ye need a drink that badly you won't get it here.'

'Where would ye get it?' asked Maureen.

'The Clansman. It's a couple of blocks down.' He pointed over his left shoulder. 'I heard she was drinking in there. It's a hole.'

Maureen finished her whisky. 'Right,' she said. 'Thanks very much for your help.'

'No bother, ladies. Call again.'

The wind had risen and Maureen had to peel her wet hair from her face as they walked. They headed away from the main road, following the barman's directions, passing progressively meaner tenements with smaller and smaller windows. The area deteriorated quickly, the blocks of flats got higher and less cared-for. Pseudo-tenements, built in the fifties and sixties from prefab concrete slabs, stood in the holes left by German bombs. Three streets down from the Lismore they reached a desolate block of burnt-out and boarded-up flats. The Clansman was on the far corner. A very drunk man was standing outside, holding on to a street-light, his hips swaying softly from side to side as if his knees were full of mercury. Frosted windows sat high on the wall, an old pub device to stop women and children from seeing in. The front door heaved against the press of men, opening slightly, and the sweet smell of drink wafted into the street, as subtly enticing as a pheromone signal. Leslie pulled open the door, pushed her way through the crowd and Maureen followed in her wake.

The bar was filthy but still looked too classy for the dead-eyed men drinking wine and smoking ten-packs of Club. The carpet was as shiny as linoleum. Candle-shaped electric wall lights were dim beacons through the layered smoke, and empty glasses sat abandoned on every surface. The drinking men were shouting to each other and laughing, some the entertainers, some the entertained, a distinction determined by who was holding the money that night. Hard men jostled with cardboard gangsters, the lesser mortals who fed off their detritus, mimicking their language and stealing their stories. Maureen could see Ann drinking in a pub like this. There were no other women in the bar and Ann wouldn't have been stuck for hopeful beaux, keen to buy her a drink and see what they got in return. Maureen and Leslie squeezed their way through to the bar.

'You get the drinks and I'll ask around,' Maureen shouted, over the noise.

'I don't like this,' said Leslie, looking furious because she was scared.

'Hey, you.' The voice was deep and husky. 'The women, there.'

They looked over their shoulders but couldn't find the speaker until a tiny man wriggled in between them. He had a large head of greasy black hair, a protruding lower jaw and lopsided shoulders, the result of a jaunty wave to his spine. He was drinking a tumbler of purple wine and grinning up at them. 'I'm Malki,' he shouted, staring at Leslie's leathers, holding his hand up to her face for a shake. Leslie looked at his hand and declined, but Malki took the snub in his stride and grinned at her again. 'Are ye a polis wummin?'

Maureen leaned into Leslie's ear. 'Leslie,' she muttered, 'gonnae go and sit down? No-one's going to talk to us.' Leslie nodded reluctantly and turned away from the bar. Maureen went for the double. 'And stop looking so angry,' she said. 'They'll think we're trouble.'

'I'm not looking angry,' snapped Leslie. 'It's the way my face falls.'

'Are ye, though?' Malki was staring at Leslie's back. 'Are ye a polis? I like polis, especially the wummen.' He hacked a laugh, looking from Maureen to Leslie. He saw that they weren't joining in. Unperturbed, he stopped laughing abruptly and took a sip.

'I'll go,' said Leslie, pointing to an empty table at the back of the room.

'Aye,' agreed Maureen, 'you go.'

Leslie sloped off and Maureen slid into her place at the bar. 'Hey, Malki,' she said, 'listen, do you come in here a lot?'

'Aye, how?'

'We're looking for a lassie called Ann, ye seen her?'

Malki's eyes shifted from side to side. 'Naw,' he said, and turned to the bar.

Maureen leaned over to him and smiled. 'How d'ye know ye haven't seen her?'

Malki looked around the bar for someone.

'Will ye let me buy ye a drink?' she said, waving a tenner under his nose.

Malki relaxed a little. 'Aye,' he said, toasting her with his glass. 'Large red.'

She leaned over the bar, showing her tenner and trying to catch the attention of one of the staff. They were running around at the far end of the bar, handing drinks and taking money, waiting for their turn at the till. Impatient for his free drink, Malki stood up on the foot rail. 'Service!' he screamed, louder than anyone should in an enclosed space. 'Service!'

A young barman walked over to them, his heavy hooded eyes looking tired and pissed off. He tipped his chin at Malki.

'More wine,' shouted Malki, and pointed to Maureen's tenner. The barman looked from the money to Maureen.

'And two whiskies,' yelled Maureen.

The barman hesitated, looking at her, wondering what the fuck she was doing in here. He decided it didn't matter anyway and went to get their drinks. Malki was pleased to be seen at the bar with a woman and a tenner. He smiled at her.

'How are ye fixed?' asked Maureen.

Malki frowned at her. 'I'll get ye one back,' he said, unconvincingly.

'I don't want one back,' said Maureen. 'I just thought – if you're a bit stuck.'

She was leaning into him, shouting intimately, when the

crowd parted behind them and a shaft of light hit the side of Malki's head. Maureen looked into the flat plane of his ear and found herself inches from a nest of the biggest, ripest blackheads she had ever seen. Reeling with nausea, she caught herself and shouted again, looking over his shoulder this time, 'I thought, since I want information about my pal, you might find a use for a fiver or so?'

Malki looked up at her, a greedy glimmer in his eye. He stopped himself and looked around the bar again. Whoever he was looking for wasn't there. Malki turned back to her. 'We'll sit down,' he said, pointing at the barman coming back with their drinks.

Maureen paid, and they carried the greasy glasses over to Leslie. She was sitting alone at a table on a raised platform two steps up from the floor of the pub, glaring and daring anyone to speak to her. No-one had tried. They sat down and arranged the drinks on the dirty table. Maureen offered Malki a fag and he took it. 'So, do ye want a fiver?' she asked, as she lit it for him.

'No,' he said. 'But I want a tenner.' He grinned, screwing up his eyes; it was less of a smile than a disguise.

Maureen hesitated, trying to look reluctant so he wouldn't push the price up again. 'Well, okay,' she said finally. 'But answer everything, okay?'

Malki looked at his full glass of wine. 'Give us it now,' he said.

Maureen shook her head. 'After,' she said, wishing any fucker had approached them but this wee bastard.

'Now.'

She sat back. 'Forget it, then,' she said.

It took less than thirty seconds for Malki to tug her sleeve.

'Okay, okay,' he said. 'After.'

Maureen took out the folded photocopy, sliding it under

the table to Malki's lap. He looked down at it. 'Recognize her?'

Malki nodded vigorously, looking at his drink, imagining the glass full again.

'When was she in here?'

'Weeks ago, haven't seen her since.'

'Where did she go?'

'Dunno. She just doesn't come in any more.'

'Did you speak to her?'

'I tried,' Malki smiled a horny smile, 'I always try.'

'Who did she hang about with?'

This was clearly the question Malki was afraid of. He glanced around the faces in the bar. 'Everyone, everyone,' he said. 'We're all pals.'

'You can tell me,' said Maureen, flirting with him. 'She's a friend of mine.'

But Malki wasn't playing. He drank some wine and puffed his fag nervously, looking to the left and correcting his gaze so suddenly that Maureen knew he'd seen something. 'Was she hanging around with someone in particular?'

He crumpled his face into a smile again. 'Are yees polis?'

'No,' said Maureen, leaning across the table to him, closing the circle, making it just the two of them. 'See, Malki, her man was hitting her. We want to make sure she's not gone back to him.'

Still grinning, Malki shook his outsized head at her. 'She's not with her man,' he muttered.

'Is she with another man?'

Malki was about to answer. He teetered on the edge of indiscretion, swaying at the precipice, looking down and making himself dizzy. Leslie sat forward to increase the pressure and shoved him back on to safe ground. He looked at her. 'You've got a lovely big arse, you,' he said loudly.

Leslie wanted to hit him and Malki felt it. 'Gae us my money,' he said.

Maureen was dismayed. 'But ye never answered me.'

'I did so answer ye,' said Malki, ready to make a scene if he didn't get his cash.

'Malki, here's the thing,' said Maureen, thinking on her feet. 'Leave your drink here. Go to the toilet and come back and I'll give ye the tenner. Okay?'

He looked bemused.

'I know he's in here,' said Maureen. 'I know ye've just looked up and seen him. So, you go to the toilet and on your way past him you scratch your head and I'll know. That way you're not telling me and I'm paying ye anyway, okay?'

Malki hovered, reluctant to leave a drink but more reluctant to walk away from someone holding his tenner.

'It's the only way ye'll get the money,' she said.

He paused and looked at his glass. 'I think I'll take my drink with me,' he said and stood up. 'That way I'll have something anyway.'

'Ye can buy ten glasses of wine with a tenner, Malki. Make a night of it, eh?'

Malki shuffled away into the crowd. A third of the way round the bar he raised his hand high and scratched his head. He was standing in a milling crowd of drunk men and it could have been any one of them, but Maureen knew immediately who he meant. He was fatter now, his face bloated and watery, pink with drink, but she knew him. He was a head taller than the short drunk men around him, wearing a rain-warped donkey jacket and drinking a half-pint of red wine. He was looking at her and he recognized her too. He put out a hand, pushed the men in front of him aside, and made his way over to their table.

'Mother of God,' said Maureen, shrinking into the table, 'Mark Doyle.'

'What?' asked Leslie.

'Mark Doyle. Pauline's brother,' whispered Maureen.

Leslie hadn't heard her and he was standing by their table before she had the chance to say it again.

'How are ye?' said Maureen.

'Aye, what're yees doing in here?' His diction was drawled, like a tough guy used to getting fat lips in fights. He stood by the table, looking them over.

'We're trying to find a pal of ours,' said Maureen.

He nodded slowly and looked at Maureen. He had very bad eczema – his skin was flaking and painfully dry. A raw patch under his left eye was oozing clear fluid, and lumps of scalp were falling away under his thick hair.

'What's your pal's name?' he said.

'Ann,' said Leslie, squaring up to him. 'Her name's Ann.'

Mark Doyle slid into Malki's vacant chair, putting his drink on the table and reaching down to his ankle. For a moment Maureen thought he might have a knife in his sock and she flinched before realizing that he was only scratching his leg. She fumbled a cigarette out of her packet and lit it. His big, scalded hand sat on the table. He finished scratching and looked up, curious and blinking slowly as if he was drunk or on medication.

'I know you from somewhere,' he said to Maureen. 'Where do I know ye from?'

'I think,' Maureen was terrified, 'I knew your sister.'

'Pauline?' he said wistfully. 'You knew Pauline?' He stared at the table and Maureen watched him. He looked up. 'Did ye know her well?' He was watching Maureen's face, trying to see what she knew.

Maureen took a draw on her cigarette. He was still looking at her, waiting for an answer to the unspoken

155

question, his eyes tired and old with a knife threat beneath them. 'No,' she said, 'not very well. I was at her funeral because of my pal ...'

Shaking slightly, he managed to breathe in, expanding his chest to fill his crumpled shirt.

'Do you know Ann?' she said, changing the subject before it started again.

He shrugged carelessly. Maureen took out the photocopy, laying it on the dirty table in front of him. Ann's black eyes looked up at him. 'She was here, aye. Hasnae been in for a while. I seen her in London.'

Leslie shot forward in her chair. 'In London?'

He turned to her. 'Aye, hen. In Brixton. In a pub called the Coach and Horses. Lot of Glasgow folk drink there.'

'Whenabouts did ye see her?' asked Maureen.

'Month mibi.' He stopped and gazed at his hands. 'She was keeping rough company. That's a bad thing for a woman to do. I warned her.'

He looked at Maureen, his eyes bright and open, telling her something she didn't understand. She felt cold to the core. As she folded the photocopy with tremorous hands Mark Doyle stood up and straightened his coat. She shouldn't be sitting here, peaceful in his company. Out of respect for Pauline she should at least have insulted him.

'How's your brother?' she asked.

He was dumbfounded. ''M' brother's dead'n'all,' he said simply, and swaggered away across the smoke-filled pub.

Maureen watched him. He was tall and broad across the shoulders, a powerful man with a shadow for a conscience.

Malki arrived back, clutching an empty glass. He didn't move to sit down but stood at Maureen's elbow, blocking the sight of her hands from the pub floor.

'Who did ye mean?' asked Leslie, leaning on the filthy table and pointing at him. 'The big tall guy, scabby hands?'

Malki nodded.

'Cheers, Malki.' Maureen slipped him a tenner.

The moment the money touched the inside of Malki's pocket they ceased to exist for him. He turned and walked away without a word.

'Let's get the fuck out of here,' said Maureen.

They left, parting the crowd on their way out, and Mark Doyle's hungry eyes watched them go, remembering their faces. Maureen walked so fast she was panting by the time they got back to the shelter.

21

Herb Alpert

Leslie drove carefully through the glistening city to Maureen's house. Maureen didn't want to go home, she didn't feel comfortable in her flat, but she couldn't stay out indefinitely and Mark Doyle had freaked her. Leslie stopped the bike outside her close and Maureen climbed off, opened the box and put in her helmet. 'I'll see ye in the morning,' said Leslie. 'We'll go and see Senga, see what she says.'

'Can we go and see Jimmy as well?'

'We'll see.'

Vik had been sitting in his car for over forty minutes listening to Glen Campbell, smoking and wiping the mist from the window. He saw Maureen climbing off the bike and waited until the biker drove away before opening the door and getting out. He called to her and ran over as she was opening the outside door. 'Hiya,' he said, smiling and panting from the exertion of jogging a hundred yards with lungs full of smoke. 'How ye keeping?'

'Not bad.' She nodded and found her neck shaky and unsteady. Her shoulders were aching with tension.

'You don't look well. Have ye been ill?'

'No,' said Maureen, opening the close door. 'I've just had a strange night.'

She walked into the close, assuming he was coming up, but Vik waited, his black hair glistening with drizzle. 'Are ye not coming up?'

He shook his head uncertainly. 'D'ye want me to?'

She hesitated, not knowing what he wanted from her. 'Well, yeah.'

Vik shrugged at her, his black eyelashes gummed together, the rain dripping from his chin.

'Vik,' she said, 'why did ye come to see me if ye don't want to come upstairs?'

Vik's hair gel was emulsifying in the rain, running in little white rivulets down his jaw and neck. 'I came to chuck ye,' he said gently. He wasn't angry and he wasn't playing a game, he was standing up for himself.

Maureen let the door fall shut. 'Chuck me?'

'You don't return my calls, when I chap the door you stand behind it and won't answer.' She cowered. 'Yeah, I could hear you behind the door. I felt ye looking at me—'

'Vik, I'd just been really sick and my brother was in—'

'Why can't you introduce me to your brother?'

'I didn't want to—'

'Is it because I'm black?'

She smiled and tried to look up at him, but the rain was heavy and he was standing with a street-light behind his head. 'You'd have to know Liam to know how ridiculous that is.' She squinted hard and saw him He wasn't smiling back.

'Maureen,' he said, digging his hands into his pockets, 'you don't introduce me to your friends or your family, you leave me standing behind the door. You treat me like a twat.' She thought back over the month and she knew he was right. When Vik's cousin Shan had introduced them to each other in the Variety bar Maureen couldn't believe her luck. Vik was tall and slim, his hair as black as Guinness, his eyes deep brown and adoring. That first night they'd got drunk and giggly together and fell back up the hill to her flat at closing time. Alone in the quiet living room, they found that they had nothing to say to each other. Vik was a quiet man. He only spoke when he had something to say and Maureen was too drunk to chat. Through a drink-sodden blur they mistook the heavy silence for sexual tension and started kissing. Twenty minutes later they were sweating and naked and panting on the bed, holding hands and staring at the ceiling, sobered by surprise. In the month they had been seeing each other they hadn't talked about much – they went out with his friends to bars and listened to music or stayed in bed but they didn't exchange romantic histories or talk about anything. The relationship felt comforting but meaningless to Maureen. She opened her mouth to apologize but nothing came out.

'Yeah.' Vik stepped away from her. 'G'night anyway.' He turned and walked to his car.

'Vik, please.' She followed him and found herself panicking. 'My head's full of battered shite, I don't know what I'm doing half the time and then Katia said that she was seeing ye—'

'That was ages ago.'

'She said it was a month ago, when we started seeing each other.' She stopped and looked at her feet. 'I felt funny about it.'

'Katia was two months ago,' he said, insulted. 'And I only saw her for three days.' His hand was on the car-door handle and he was leaving.

'Please.' She looked away, not wanting to watch his face while she said it. 'Come up and have that bottle of wine with me, let me explain. At least let me explain. I don't want ye to go away feeling bad.'

He hesitated and she saw his thumb pressing on the handle button. 'I'm not a complete tit, ye know. I see what's going on around me.'

'I know, I know that.'

He let go of the car door and stood up, looking down at her. 'What d'ye mean, your head's full of battered shite?'

She tried to smile but it didn't work and she let it slide.

'What are ye thinking?' he asked.

She looked away to Ruchill, remembering blood splattering on to the window and nails scratching through the glass. 'Sometimes,' she said, and stopped. 'Vik, d'ye think life's fair?'

'What the fuck are you on about?'

'D'ye believe that good things happen to good people? D'ye think your life is the one you deserve or something?'

Vik smiled nervously. 'No,' he said. 'Not really.'

'Sometimes I just feel all this striving and trying, it's pointless. Life's just a series of dispiriting humiliations and why bother.' She looked at him. 'D'you never feel that?'

'See this?' He wagged his finger at her. 'This is exactly why I don't think we should go out any more.'

'What?'

'This. You're stuck in the big questions, Maureen. All you talk about is politics and truth and beauty and justice.' He hooked his finger into a big curl of hair on her cheek and lifted it to behind her ear. 'You're only twenty-four, lighten up, for fuck's sake. Get a hobby or something.'

'Right,' she said indignantly, feeling that he hadn't been listening at all. 'And all you like to do is drink and play music in smelly wee clubs—'

'And what do you like?'

She opened her mouth to speak. She shut it again. It was a show-stopping question. She liked whisky. And being in her house, alone. And fried food. She used to like art.

'See? Ye don't like anything.' A fat drop of milky rain fell from Vik's hair and landed on her forehead. He smelt nice, fresh, like oranges or something. She looked up and saw his dark eyes smiling into the distance, his jowls dripping milk on to the lapels of his good leather.

'Thanks for the flowers and the wine.'

His kind face split into an easy grin. 'Aw, that's all right.'

'Gonnae come up?'

He looked into Mr Padda's dark shop and thought about it. 'Aye, all right.'

Vik locked the car and they climbed the stairs to the top floor, giggling and shoving each other off the top step because it was late and they should have kept the noise down. Maureen was sorting through her keys and fighting Vik off when the door across the landing opened. Her neighbour, Jim Maliano, was standing in his doorway with his peculiar hairdo, wearing an imperial purple dressing-gown and burgundy slippers with embroidered monograms on the toe. Maliano routinely backcombed the top of his hair over his crown. It was a vain man's device to disguise a bald patch but Maliano wasn't balding and the reasoning for his hairdo was the source of intermittent speculation for Maureen. He had clearly been lying in bed when he heard them on the stairs and his strange mini-bouffant had separated against the pillow. Three indignant shafts of hair, sticking straight up like show plumage, trembled as he spoke.

'Will you keep the noise down?' he said, whispering loudly. 'There are elderly people living in this close, sick people.'

'I'm sorry, Jim,' said Maureen, trying not to laugh.

Jim looked at Vik, waiting for an introduction, but Maureen wasn't in the mood to humour him. 'Good night, then, Jim.'

Jim looked at her again and slowly shut the door.

'Good night, then, Jim,' said Maureen, addressing his front door.

They heard him tiptoe away down the hall.

The living room was a terrible mess and smelt of hash and stale cigarettes. Vik opened the bottle of wine he'd left the night before but Maureen wasn't up for it and made a mug of tea. They sat in the living room and Vik used the window of honesty to look through her records, slagging off the worst albums and nodding appreciatively at the good ones. Maureen had never understood the male obsession with music and record-collecting. Liam had gone through it when he was a teenager, collecting the most obscure dance records he could find, listening to them once then boasting about them at parties. She liked a good tune but listened to the same things over and over until the novelty wore off, and could barely remember the names of three pop stars.

She was sitting on the settee, watching him flick through the vinyl singles, trying to push aside thoughts of Mark Doyle, when she spotted a pea-sized bit of black on the floor. Vic followed her eye to the lump.

'Where the fuck did ye get that?' asked Vik. 'I can't get a deal anywhere.'

'My brother left it by mistake. Will I roll a wee one?'

'You'd better not, he'll be back looking for it. It's like gold dust just now.'

'Naw, he's got a big lump.'

Vik couldn't have been more impressed if Maureen's brother had been Howard Marks. He was crouched on the floor, smelling the lump to make sure it wasn't an oxo cube, when she suddenly saw Mark Doyle wanking on to dead Pauline's back. She frowned hard, closing her eyes and rubbing them to bring herself back round.

'Yeah, go on,' said Vik, handing the black to her with his band lighter. 'Roll it up.'

Vik's band had chipped together and given him a flat- tened oval chrome lighter for his birthday. It was a pleasing shape and sat comfortably in the palm. The band had spoiled the look by having 'let's get the rock out of here' engraved on it in reference to a dodgy album they'd found in Vik's collection.

The heating had been off all day so Maureen brought out the duvet from the bedroom and they sat at opposite ends of the settee, facing each other with their legs tangled, keeping cosy, smoking gold dust and listening to Herb Alpert and the Tijuana Brass. She watched Vik sipping his drink and willed the wine into his mouth, knowing that by the second glass he would have had too much to drive and he'd be staying over.

'Did ye really think I'd been unfaithful to ye with Katia?'

'She said it had been a month.'

'Katia's a wanker. She wants to go out with me because I'm Asian and I'm in a band. She went out with the bass player for a couple of weeks. When he chucked her she kept coming to the gigs and pestering me.' He handed her the spliff.

She took a draw and felt the ticklish scratch in her throat, the warm sensation in her belly and the drowsy aftermath. 'You must have encouraged her a bit,' she said. 'You went out with her.'

'It was just one or two nights. I was pissed and to be honest I just thought, If she wants it that much I'll give it to her.'

Maureen didn't like the explanation – it made him sound nasty and careless. She couldn't imagine herself shagging someone because they were pestering her. 'I don't think that's very nice,' she said.

'Maureen,' he said, 'I don't think you can pull me up about being nice.'

She tried to smile but she didn't really feel sorry. She didn't want Vik. As she looked across the settee at him his geometric cheekbones caught the light and she knew she wanted Douglas back, or to go back to that time, or for it not to be now. The yearning caught in her throat and she had to cough to shift it.

'What you said about life being fair,' said Vik. 'It's an interesting question.'

'Don't ye have some wisdom from the East to help me out?'

'Don't ask me, hen, I'm frae Wishaw.' He sipped his wine. 'Life isn't fair.'

'I know that,' said Maureen. 'But if it's not fair, what's the point? What's the point in working hard if you'll get run down by a bus or die of cancer or have rotten kids? Why be kind or holy or help people? Like, you're kind to me and I'm not kind to you, what's the point in you being nice to me?' She took a draw and held her breath as long as she could, ingesting the goodness.

'I'm nice to you because I'm a nice guy and I like your bum.'

Maureen smiled as she exhaled and Vik giggled. 'Nah,' he said, reaching over for the spliff. 'What's the point of life? Well, little Maureen, it isn't truth and beauty and justice, that's for fucking sure. The point of life,' he held the spliff aloft, toasting her, 'is to have a laugh with your pals,' he raised an eyebrow, 'and take care of your mum. I have to say that or she'll slap my legs.'

Maureen thought of Leslie sitting on the bike outside Isa's, laughing with her fillings showing, and Liam coughing and snorting on the floor.

'I know ye have nightmares,' he said, taking a draw and looking at her. 'I hear ye crying at night. What's that about?'

She looked out at the black sky beyond the window and the white glow of the city, brimming at the sill like a vaporous tear. 'When I was young,' she said, noticing that

165

her voice had dropped, 'I had a bit of, um, trouble.'

'Shan said you were in a mental hospital.'

He looked at her and his face hadn't moved, his eyes hadn't changed and he didn't seem uncomfortable. He handed her the spliff again, minding his manners and sharing the joy.

'Yeah, I had a bit of a breakdown. Now, I'm not going to tell you any more,' she said quickly, 'because I hate telling that story.' She took another draw and held it in, inadvertently catching his eye as she exhaled.

Under the duvet his free hand found hers and he caressed the inside of her wrist with his fingertips. 'Have a laugh with me, Maureen,' he said quietly.

'I've been a bit low,' she said, in a small voice.

'I know,' said Vik. 'I can tell.' And his fingertips hardly touched her skin as he soothed her.

Vik slid across the bed towards her and gathered her, still paralysed and limp with sleep, pressing her face into his warm hairy chest. It was morning and she had slept right through. It took her a couple of minutes even to remember Michael. She wriggled out of his grip, threw the duvet back and sat up.

'Why are you getting up?' he asked grumpily.

'I need to get going.'

'You always need to get up in the morning. Why can't we just lie around for a bit?'

She pulled on her dressing-gown and went to the bathroom, filled the sink and thought of the weeping sore on Mark Doyle's cheek and the Clansman pub. She threw cold water on her face and leaned heavily on the basin, her hands straddling the bowl, letting her face drip into the water. Michael was behind her, fifteen feet tall, and his hand was raised to hit her. She froze for a moment and plunged her face forward into the cold water, covering her ears. She came back up for air and he was gone. Michael would drink in the machine-gun nest pub in Ruchill. He'd drink in there and know Mark Doyle and they'd meet Ann and hurt her and Pauline dead under a tree in the warm summer with spunk drying on her back. She didn't know Vik was behind her until his hand cupped her buttock.

'Fuck off!' She swung around, her elbow jabbing him hard in the stomach.

Vik toppled backwards, grabbing the side of the basin to stop himself falling. He sat on the bath rim, holding his side, groaning at the pain. 'You total fucking cow,' he said, and hobbled out of the bathroom and down the hall, holding on to the wall to steady himself.

Maureen sat down on the toilet lid. She couldn't go and explain. It would take four fucking days to explain. She wanted a cigarette. She held out for as long as she could. When she finally went out to the hall she found Vik fully dressed and ready to leave.

'Vikram—'

'Just fuck off.'

He stomped into the living room and found his leather jacket at the side of the settee. Maureen leaned against the door-frame and found that, for the first time, she desperately didn't want him to leave her. 'I'm really sorry.'

Vik looked at her as he slipped on his jacket and pocketed his battered packet of fags. 'I've never taken shit like this from anyone,' he said, shaking his head, making his black hair fall over his eyes. 'You can't treat people like that.'

'I got a fright—' she said.

'*You* got a fright?'

'I didn't realize it was you—'

'Maureen, if you're such a cripple that you don't know

who's in the house with ye, then you don't want to go out with me. Are ye that much of a cripple?'

Behind his head she saw the fever tower shift on the horizon and she hesitated. Vik glared at her. 'This isn't what I want for myself,' he said. 'Either we're nice to each other and we have a laugh or it's over. Your choice.'

'That's what I want too,' she said weakly.

He rubbed his side. 'You don't act as if that's what you want. The world's full of men happy to take that sort of shit from women. Go out with them, leave me alone.'

'It's not as simple as that.'

'Yes, it is, you choose. But I'm not settling for less than I give out. I want more for myself.' He tried to pass her to the front door but she stepped out to block him.

'Move,' he said.

She didn't. Vik slipped behind her, opened the front door and left without a backward glance.

22

Disco Monkey

They were deep in the east end, in a sprawling grid system of grey concrete semi-detached houses. Each house held four small flats and had a long, bare front garden. Built in the sixties to house the slum clearances, the houses were bordered every few blocks by broad roads, designed to make it easy for the workers to drive into town. The few cars didn't look as if they'd make it the eight miles.

There were no cars parked outside Senga Brolly's house. The spindly metal railings along the foot of the garden were pitted with rust, the steep garden steps were eroded and crumbling.

Senga's nose was flattened and her teeth were framed with black decay like stained-glass windows. Her hairdo was twenty years too young for her face: midnight black with a stern fringe, pulled back into a ponytail around the crown with the bulk of it hanging down, hair-sprayed firmly at the sides to hang like a heavy curtain over her chewed-up ears. She was so quiet she was almost a voluntary mute. She signalled rather than spoke, and stared resolutely at the floor whatever they asked her. She was pals with Ann, wasn't she? Nod. Did they talk a lot? Nod. Did she know where Ann went when she left the shelter? Shrug. Did Ann show her an envelope? Shrug. They showed her the Polaroid: did she know this man? Shrug. A couple of times Maureen thought she saw the beginnings of a sly smile but Senga caught herself.

Leslie asked the questions, leaving Maureen alone, haunted with thoughts of Vik. She wanted a nice boyfriend, she wanted kindness and respect and decency. She didn't want to spend her life with people she was suited to, she wanted to be with people like him. A spark of honour told her she should let him go if she genuinely cared about his happiness, but she didn't want to. Senga was nodding again but even that response seemed to be fading away. But she did talk to Ann, didn't she? Nod. Did Ann talk about her kids a lot? Shrug. Any kid in particular? Shrug. Maureen excused herself and Senga managed to direct her to the loo without saying more than two words. 'Right,' she murmured, gesturing with her hands. 'Left.'

The bathroom was furnished in burgundy plastic with indelible toothpaste stains on the bowl and bleach burns inside the loo. Maureen washed her hands and dried them on a crunchy grey hand towel. When she got back to the living room Leslie and Senga were on their feet. Leslie pulled her in for a hug and Senga stood awkward and rigid, letting Leslie be affectionate on her. 'We're off, then,' said Leslie, letting go. 'Thanks, wee hen.'

Senga smiled shyly at the floor and saw them to the door. The garden steps were so crumbly that they had to walk down them sideways.

'She never shuts up,' said Maureen, when they reached the pavement. 'Did ye get anything out of her?'

'Yeah,' said Leslie. 'She's quite talkative on a one to one.'

Maureen looked sceptical. 'Really?' She glanced back up the steep path to the grey house. Senga was standing half behind the curtain, peeking out of the shadows, looking like a skull in a wig. She lifted her hand. Maureen waved back.

'Yeah. She says they were close,' said Leslie, 'but Ann fell out with her and left a few days later. She said they didn't have an argument, they were just looking at the paper one day and Ann recognized a picture of a guy, said she knew him. Senga said she knew the woman with him, she'd been at school with her, and Ann went funny with her after that. I asked her about the card and she said anyone could have sent it. She says everyone knows where the shelter houses are.'

Maureen pulled on her helmet. 'That's shite.'

'I know,' said Leslie, looking back up to the house and waving. 'I don't know why she'd say that.'

'Who were the couple in the paper?'

'Neil Hutton and his girlfriend. She says he was up for dealing,' said Leslie, doing up the strap on her helmet, 'and she was with him at the court.'

'How would Ann get to know a drug-dealer? She didn't get into drugs, did she?'

Leslie looked out of her helmet, a strip of eyes blinking slowly like Maureen's memory of Douglas. 'Naw, she was a drinker. She might know him from the scheme in Finneston. Anyway, Senga says the woman works at Fraser's in the makeup department.'

'We could go and ask Liam about it,' said Maureen. 'He'll know the guy if he's a dealer.'

'Can we go and see the woman first?'

'Are you asking me to visit a two-hundred-square-foot makeup counter?'

'Oh, yes.'

'I accept that invitation.'

The entire lower floor of the Victorian galleria was given over to the business of makeup and perfume. Fraudulent women in white coats stood sentry by their counters, chatting to each other and picking their nails, ignoring the ugly, rain-sodden customers who wandered by cooing at the price tags. The shop was five storeys high, with the different departments spread around a series of wooden balconies. A glass ceiling opened up the floors to natural sunlight, a benefit ignored by subsequent store designers who had inserted dazzling track lighting everywhere. The makeup was on the ground floor, a vast bazaar a-glitter with tatty perfume promotions and giant photographs of airbrushed teenagers.

They had asked for her at several counters and Maureen noticed the counter women tipping Maxine off, catching her eye and pointing them out. They weren't hard to spot: Maureen's coat looked expensive but she was wearing her battered boots and her curly hair could never be tidied anyway. Leslie's leathers and dirty hair would be chic in a biker bar but in the glittery galleria she looked as seemly as a dead toenail in a pair of strappy sandals.

Maxine was hard-faced, with thin lips and a determined chin. She was dressed in a powder pink two-piece suit and stood behind a counter piled high with black and gold boxes. Between her and the shelves at the back was a white leatherette chair with an arm attachment bearing a selection of samples. She wore far too much makeup which, although skilfully applied, made her look like a burns victim who was covering up very well. Her short blonde hair had been tortured into a big puff at the back and smeared into a parting at the fringe, held firm on either side of her face with diamanté clips like ornamental staples. She was well practised at not letting on. She slid across the floor to them, apparently innocent of their interest in her. 'Good afternoon. Can I help you?'

'Yeah,' said Leslie, leaning through the access gap in the counter. 'We're here to ask you some questions. I think you know a friend of ours?'

Maxine looked wary. 'Look,' she said, under her breath,

her accent dropping two social strata, her eyes watching behind them, 'I'm at my work here, leave us alone, will ye?'

'In a minute.' Leslie smiled, certain she had the upper hand. 'Our friend was called Ann Harris. Maybe ye'd know her from this.' She produced the photocopy from her jacket and showed it to her.

Maxine kept her eyes on the horizon, watching for someone. She took the time to glance at the picture but something about it caught her eye and she looked back. 'God,' she said, staring at the photo.

'D'ye know her?' asked Maureen, muscling in through the narrow gap, standing in front of Leslie.

'What's that on her lip?' Maxine pointed at the picture and cringed. 'Fuck.'

'How do ye know her?' said Leslie.

Maxine roused herself and looked at Leslie angrily. 'I never said I did know her, did I?'

But Maxine did know her. She looked at them, challenging them to contradict her. Maureen took out the Polaroid of wee John and the big man in the camel-hair coat. 'What about this guy, d'ye know him?'

But Maxine was looking over Maureen's shoulder into the body of the shop. 'The manager's in,' she said, out of the side of her mouth, 'I cannae just chat, one of yees'll need tae sit down.'

Leslie pushed Maureen into the white chair and she found herself staring straight into a halogen spotlight embedded on the underside of a shelf. Maxine tipped back the seat with a foot pedal and followed the manager out of the corner of her eye, watching him float around the shop floor. She tucked a couple of tissues into Maureen's collar to protect her coat and began to move her hands over Maureen's face. 'The manager in here's a right prick,' she said, tracing lines over Maureen's eyes and lips, drawing circles on her cheeks. 'That lassie you're looking for, I don't know her.'

Maureen decided not to push it. 'D'ye know the guy in the Polaroid?' she asked, trying to sit up.

Maxine's thin lips atrophied with annoyance. 'Sit back,' she said.

Maureen did as she was told and Maxine pulled out a white bottle from under the counter. She began rubbing oily cream on Maureen's forehead and cheeks, wiping it off with tissues as she leaned over Maureen and muttered aggressively, 'Get me intae trouble here and I'll lose the place, right?'

Maureen was afraid to have Maxine near her eyes.

A pockmarked young man in a dark suit leaned across the counter. He was about twenty, the same age as Maxine. 'Hello, ladies,' he said, his accent a twanging Edinburgh slur. 'Are you having a makeover?'

'Yeah,' said Leslie.

'Are you enjoying that experience?'

'Yeah,' said Maureen. 'Very much.'

'Good girl, Maxine, good girl.'

He straightened up and sauntered off, watching left and right, playing with the fist of keys at his belt.

'What an arsehole,' said Leslie.

Maxine sighed. 'I could have him killed, ye know.' She said it casually as she wiped the cream from Maureen's neck. Maureen and Leslie were too frightened to ask her what she meant.

'Where do ye learn to do this?' asked Maureen, her eyes straining against the bright light above her. 'You're very good.'

'They send ye on a course for a week and ye learn all the secrets.'

'Is it a good job?'

'It's a good job for me,' said Maxine, 'I'm expecting again and I can come and go. There's always these jobs if you're reliable.'

'Oh,' said Leslie. 'Are ye expecting? Congratulations.'

For some reason Maxine had taken very much against Leslie. She was offended by Leslie's good wishes and stopped cleansing Maureen to plant her tongue in her cheek and stare Leslie out. Maureen was being slowly blinded by the track lighting and the sight of Maxine's flared nostrils was interspersed with dazzling white blotches.

'That cream I've just put on ye,' Maxine said, when she turned back to Maureen, 'has a special ingredient which opens the pores and lets them breathe,' she illustrated the effect, rolling her hands outwards, 'and then contracts the skin,' hands rolling inward, 'to protect against pollution.'

'Feels smashing,' said Maureen, wanting to be nice to any woman who could get her boss killed for being a squeaky annoyance.

'It is quite expensive,' warned Maxine, holding bottles of foundation up to Maureen's face to get a colour match

'Much is it?' said Maureen, who had a weakness for cosmetic products promising voodoo benefits.

'Thirty-two pounds.'

'Well, I'm sold, leave us out a bottle.'

'Okay,' said Maxine, excitedly, letting on that the job was commission. She turned to take a bottle off the shelf and Leslie made a frightened face behind her back. Maxine put the bottle into a bag and left it on the counter to embarrass Maureen into buying it even if she did change her mind. She had decided that Maureen was a mug with money and she wouldn't stop talking about the products.

'It's creamy, creamy, creamy, and will last from first thing in the morning to last thing at night *without another application*. That's the amazing thing about this foundation.' She smeared thick tinted cream over Maureen's face with a sponge, patting it under her chin. 'It's the most common mistake women make when applying foundation. They don't blend it in at the neck, giving the face a mask-like appearance.' She smirked. 'We've all seen those women.'

Maxine accompanied her drug-dealer boyfriend to court and could have her boss killed, but everyone has standards and she would not tolerate the crime of badly applied slap. Maureen squinted hard, trying to look up at her. 'D'you know Senga, Maxine?'

'Aye, I know a Senga. Flat nose?'

Maureen nodded.

'Aye,' said Maxine. 'Poor wee Senga, she used to be no' bad-looking as well. She was in my sister's class at school. Comes in here sometimes. Shameful what he done to her face.'

Leslie shifted to the other foot. 'Who's the guy in the Polaroid?' she said. 'Is he Ann's boyfriend?'

Maxine turned her attention to Maureen's eyes, checking her eyelids for makeup. 'Anyone'll tell ye, his name's Frank Toner. He's a hard man. Lives in London. Have you got mascara on already?'

'Yeah.'

'I'll take it off and let you try ours. It actually *curls* the lashes. Ye've got lovely blue eyes, so I'm going to use this,' she held up a loud, glittery blue eye-shadow, 'to pick out the colour and highlight it. Your eyes really are your best feature. You should make more of them.'

Leslie leaned in, pretending to look at Maureen's face. 'Was Toner Ann's boyfriend?' she repeated.

Maxine began to brush on the chewy black mascara and Maureen's eyelashes felt as if they were being pulled over the top of her head. She let out a little squeal and blinked in panic.

'Takes a wee bit of getting used to,' counselled Maxine. 'I don't think he is her boyfriend, no. But then,' she paused and looked at her eye-shadow box, 'maybe he is. Can't see it, really.'

'Does he come up to Glasgow often?'

'How would I know?'

'Does he, though?'

'Don't think so.'

Maxine pencilled in Maureen's eyebrows and applied the eye-shadow, smudging it onto the skin with a brush.

They were huddled over Maureen's face in a makeup scrum, drawing on her as she went blind. She felt she had been patient enough. 'Who does he run with?'

Maxine didn't like the question at all. She went away to the counter and fiddled with her brushes. When she came back she seemed very annoyed.

'Maxine,' said Maureen, 'Ann's dead.'

'Aye, and you're the polis,' said Maxine.

'No.' Maureen tried to sit up but Maxine pushed her back with a firm hand on her chin. 'We work at the Place of Safety Shelters. Ann was in there after she had the picture taken. She said she'd been beaten up by her man.'

Maxine harrumphed. 'You work for them, do ye? The women's shelters?'

'Aye.' Maureen tried to nod but Maxine held tightly on to her chin as if she was taking her head hostage.

'Both of yees?'

'Yeah,' said Leslie.

'Aye,' said Maureen, wishing to fuck she'd let go.

'Good,' Maxine said, freeing Maureen's chin. 'Good work. Need them. The shelters.' She stopped and put her brush down, picked up a pencil. 'Her man never beat her up.'

'Was it Toner?'

'In a manner of speaking.' She stopped and ground her jaw. 'No,' she said. 'It wasn't Toner but it wasnae her man either.'

'How do you know that?' asked Leslie.

'Hear things around, ye know.'

'Thing is,' said Maureen, 'the police'll arrest her man. He's bringing up four weans himself and they'll have to go into care if he gets done.'

Maxine started drawing lips on Maureen with a dry pencil. 'There's worse things than growing up in care,' she said quietly, being rough, poking Maureen hard. She put down the pencil and recomposed herself, picked up a lipstick and held it in front of Maureen's face. 'I'm using "Peach Party" because of your colouring.' She said it like a threat. 'It will match the blue of your eyes and still accentuate the mouth.'

'We're not trying to do ye any harm,' said Leslie. 'It's just a shame if he goes to prison . . .'

Maxine slid her eyes to Leslie, glaring at her and shutting her up. Maureen had never seen anyone do that. She finished painting Maureen's lips with the Peach Party and stepped back without offering her a mirror. 'Still want the maximizing cleanser?'

'Yeah,' said Maureen timidly. 'Ye said ye hear things, do folk know where the shelter houses are?'

Maxine thought about it. 'Some people, yeah.'

'Do you know?'

'How would I know?'

It was so obvious that she might have heard the address from Senga that neither Leslie nor Maureen bothered to contradict her. Maxine frowned at the bar code on the cream, looking guilty and pissed off. She tilled up and took Maureen's credit card. 'That Polaroid,' she said, staring at the screen on the till, waiting for credit clearance. 'Burn it or something. Don't show it around.'

'Why?' asked Maureen.

'Just don't.'

A *Big Issue* seller shot Maureen a pitying look as they came out of the doors.

'How do I look?' asked Maureen.

'Like an angry monkey going to a disco,' said Leslie. 'No, don't wipe it off, keep it on, give Liam a laugh.'

23
Perfectly

Liam looked down from the upstairs window as cold rain ran off their shoulders and dripped through their hair. He made a pretence of not quite recognizing them and turned back into the room to laugh at his stupid joke with someone else before disappearing. They saw him through the glass door, trotting down the stairs and padding towards them. He opened it and took the cigarette out of his mouth. 'My God,' he said, staring at Maureen's face. 'What happened to you?'

'She fell into a makeup counter,' said Leslie.

Liam hung their wet coats on hooks, leaving them to drip on to the floor. It was cold in the hall; he couldn't afford to have central heating installed, and removing the partition from the bottom of the stairs had created a shaft of draughty breezes cutting through the heart of the house. 'Right,' he said. 'Upstairs for towels and jerseys. There's tea made already. Mauri, you get a couple of cups from the kitchen.'

'Will I bring biscuits?' she said, hopefully.

Liam rolled his eyes. 'Okay.'

Maureen trotted off to the kitchen as Leslie followed Liam up the stairs. Liam was the only man Maureen had ever met who kept nice biscuits in his house. They were lovely sugar-coated ginger sponges with jam in the middle, made under a German name in Lowestoft. And he was the only human she had ever met who could have such lovely biscuits in his house until they went stale. Concerned by this potential wastefulness she made it her business to finish the packet whenever she was in his house.

The kitchen was small and bare with a rattly window looking out on to a long, thin, scrubby garden. Liam had done nothing to the kitchen apart from washing it down with sugar soap. The fridge was very old and the motor so emphatic that it made the floor vibrate. Anything left on the worktop or the table overnight would intermittently jig its way to the edge and throw itself on to the floor. Maureen washed her face in the sink, watching the orange milky water swirl and retreat in the chipped Belfast sink. She wished she was going home to Vik this evening, that things were all right between them and that he hadn't made her face her future. She dabbed her face dry, picked up two cups and took the biscuits from the cupboard before making her way upstairs.

The front room had been Liam's retreat while he was dealing. It was tall with two floor-length sash windows, wooden floorboards and pale blue walls. He had kept it sparse in the old days but now it was cluttered with his desk, a dresser, his two favourite chairs and the Corbusier lounger. It was colder inside the room than out and Liam kept a box of second-hand jumpers for anyone who wanted to sit in there during the winter. Liam and Leslie were laughing loudly and a familiar voice shouted over them, 'And he had a bulldozer with a picture of Tammy Wynette painted on it.'

Maureen walked through the door and saw who was telling the story. Lynn was sitting in a tiny emerald green armchair under the window with a small red woolly jumper pulled over her clothes. 'Lynn!'

'Mauri.' Lynn grinned and stood up, doing a silly high-legged run across the room to give her a kiss. 'How are ye?'

'Not bad,' said Maureen, catching the brown jumper

Liam threw at her. 'You're not in tow with this balloon again, are ye?'

'Well,' Lynn lowered her lids and smiled coquettishly in Liam's direction, 'mibi.' She sauntered back to the chair, enjoying Liam's eyes on her tidy little body.

Embarrassed at witnessing such a graphic intimacy, Maureen pulled the jumper over her head and Leslie busied herself, pouring two cups of tea from the pot on the floor. They sat sideways in the dip in the Corbusier lounger, smashed into each other, sharing opposite ends of a towel to dry their hair.

'What possessed ye?' said Maureen, rubbing her hair with the towel.

'Well, Mauri,' Lynn slipped back into her chair, 'I'm an old-fashioned Scottish girl and I think pity and fear are a healthy basis for a relationship.'

She grinned and Liam looked as offended as a novice nun in Amsterdam. 'Don't poke fun at our love,' he said solemnly, and Lynn cackled in the corner.

Lynn was the first girl Liam had ever gone out with. They had met at the Hillhead comprehensive Christmas disco when they were fourteen. Lynn came from a rough part of Shettleston, she wasn't even at the school: she was only at the dance to stop her cross-eyed cousin, Mary Ann McGuire, from being bullied. Lynn had glided into the hall wearing eight-hole DMs, her shiny black bob swaying at the shoulders of her green silk mini dress. Terrified that anyone else would nab her, Liam had run over to her and forgotten his lines. He stood in front of her, startled by her opalescent skin and black eyes, gubbing like a drowning fish. Had she been any other girl she might have laughed and broken his heart, but Lynn took Liam's hand and led him on to the floor, holding it gently as they swayed to and fro, together, apart, together, apart, transfixed by one another. Kylie and Jason sang 'Especially For You' and the assembled boys cursed Liam O'Donnell for the jammy wee shite that he was. Mary Ann McGuire was never bullied again. They were together for nine years but Lynn didn't like the dealing and she couldn't cope with his anger. She said she was young and she wanted to have a laugh and watch television without a man shouting over the fucking news. It had been two years since Lynn had chucked him and a year and half since Liam had started seeing poor, dull Maggie with the perfect bottom and the whispery Monroe voice that made men want to kiss her and women want to punch her.

'What are you two doing here, anyway?' asked Liam.

Maureen put her hand into the bag of biscuits, taking as many as she could in a oner. 'We need to ask you about someone,' she said, eating a little ginger heart whole. 'Do you know a guy called Neil Hutton?'

Liam stared at her. 'I don't know him, but I know of him. Why are you looking for him?'

'We're not looking for him, he's just come up in conversation, that's all.'

'Yeah, well, stay the fuck away from him, he's mental. His nickname is Neil "Bananas" Hutton.'

Maureen wrapped her cold hands around the hot cup and sipped her tea, feeling the heat seep through to the small bones in her hand. 'And he's a dealer?'

Liam nodded reluctantly. 'Yeah,' he said. 'Out the east end. Why?'

'Oh, it's the east,' said Leslie, holding the warm cup to her cheek. 'She doesn't know him from the scheme, then.'

'Why?' repeated Liam.

Leslie thought the quickest way around Liam's uneasiness would be to tell him the truth, so she sketched Maxine and the news report Senga had told them about and said that

Ann had disappeared shortly afterwards. Maureen added that Senga used to visit Fraser's and Leslie fiddled uncomfortably with the sleeve of her jumper.

'Doesn't mean Senga told her where Ann was, though,' she said.

'Well, she'd probably tell,' said Maureen. 'And that's why she said everyone knew where the shelters were, to take the bad look off herself. But why would it matter whether Hutton knew where she was?'

'Did she owe him money on a deal or something?' asked Liam.

'No,' said Maureen. 'She was a drunk, not a user. Would Hutton beat her up himself?'

'Definitely.' He pursed his mouth with disgust. 'Hutton likes it. Likes the rough stuff, specially if he knows he can win.'

'What else is he like,' she said, 'apart from mental?'

Liam thought about it. 'He's ambitious and he's not a real dealer. He's actually a gangster who deals.'

'What's the difference?'

Liam ambled over to Lynn's chair and looked out of the window. 'Well, I'll tell you a story about Hutton. He nearly started a war two years ago moving in on another guy. He torched the guy's house, didn't even go in and take the stash first. He wasn't content with taking the patch over, he was obliterating the guy, wiping him out. No dealer would ever do that, it's far, far too angry and it's not profitable. See, Hutton isn't feeding a habit or in it for the money, like the rest of us. He's got a lot more to prove.' Liam slid the back of his hand against Lynn's face, lifting the cigarette from her mouth, took a draw and put it back.

Even Lynn was embarrassed by the gesture. She leaned forward to get away from Liam, tapping her fag into an ashtray. 'If she wasn't a user,' she said, 'she might be frightened of him for some other reason. Maybe it was personal or maybe she was a courier for him?'

'Nah.' Maureen shook her head. 'She's got four kids and she certainly wouldn't courier. She was really underweight and poor-looking. She'd be very conspicuous on a plane.'

'Not all couriers travel on aeroplanes,' said Liam. 'If it was up and down to London she might just have driven.'

'Actually, she was found in London,' said Maureen. 'She's got a sister in London and she was up and down for a month before Christmas.'

'She couldn't drive, though,' said Leslie. 'Would someone else have driven her?'

'Why pay a driver and a courier?' said Liam

'What about the train?' said Lynn.

'Well, not just now,' said Liam. 'The police have been all over the docks and they were crawling all over the trains in November and December. That's why there's a dry on. No-one's using the trains. What about the bus?'

'I don't think she would courier,' said Leslie. 'No offence, Liam, but she wasn't that sort of person.'

'What? Not an evil person like me?'

'I didn't mean that, but she wasn't involved with criminal people and she was just a drinker.'

'Did she owe loan sharks?'

Leslie didn't answer.

'She did,' said Maureen. 'She owed them shitloads.'

'There ye are, then,' said Liam. 'About five hundred quid would make her evil enough to do a couple of runs and pay them off.'

'But that's ludicrous,' said Maureen. 'Why would they entrust a package of drugs to a nervous, tipsy housewife?'

'Could have been a dummy run,' said Liam, 'to test and see if it was safe. The police've been picking up everyone. They might have used her because she was a complete outsider, knew nothing about anyone and it wouldn't really matter if she got nicked.'

'But the money's not paid off,' said Leslie sullenly. 'Maureen said there were sharks up at the door every night in the week.'

They all looked at Liam for clarification. He frowned. 'Maybe she owed different people.' He looked at Leslie's miserable face and suddenly smiled. 'Why am I arguing with ye? I don't fucking know.'

Lynn sat forward. 'Would Ann fit in on the bus to London?'

'Perfectly,' said Maureen, and looked at Leslie.

'Perfectly,' said Leslie.

Liam and Lynn went downstairs, ostensibly to make more tea but obviously to have a snog. Maureen had never known them so demonstrative. It might have been her own lovelorn perspective but their intensity felt desperate, as if they knew it couldn't last and kept having to touch each other to know it wasn't over yet. The muffled chat downstairs slowed to a trickle and Leslie stood up and walked to the window. 'God,' she muttered, 'this is a beautiful house.'

'He's done it up nicely, hasn't he?'

Leslie was looking out of the window with her hands behind her back. 'Are you ready to go back to your job yet?'

Maureen wanted to tell her she wasn't going back, but they had spent such a nice couple of days together and she couldn't cope with another fight just now. 'But we haven't even started finding out about Ann yet,' she said. 'We've got to go to London.'

Leslie wasn't sure. She said she couldn't leave work with the funding review coming up again and it wouldn't be safe for Maureen to go on her own. But Maureen wanted to go, she wanted to get out of Glasgow, get away from Ruchill and the bedroom window, away from Vik and the PSS and

Winnie's calls. She made a good case for it: she could check out the pub Mark Doyle had mentioned and visit the sister in Streatham. Maxine said the man in the Polaroid lived down there and she could ask Ann's sister if she knew him. It would be fine, she said, she'd be safe, she could stay with an old friend from her art-history class and, anyway, Ann had been running away from Glasgow so this must be where the threat was. She sounded quite plausible.

Leslie chewed her cheek and thought about it. 'But Ann was murdered in London,' she said. 'That's exactly where it isn't safe.'

'I want to do it, Leslie.'

'For me?'

'For you,' she lied. 'And for Jimmy.'

'Why for him?'

'He so poor, Leslie, no-one's going to give a fuck but us.'

Lynn and Liam came back upstairs, giggling and touching hands as they came into the room.

'I'm going to London,' said Maureen.

'If this has anything to do with Hutton I'd leave it,' said Liam.

'It doesn't,' she said, less sure than she sounded. 'I'm just going to see the woman's sister. She's related to Leslie.'

'You could stay with Marie,' said Liam tartly. Their eldest sister, Marie, wouldn't have Liam or Maureen in her house. Marie found herself in greatly reduced circumstances. She had gone to London straight from school to get away from Winnie and live the Thatcherite dream. She and her husband, Robert, made fortunes as merchant bankers and they had almost made it to a fully detached Holborn townhouse when the collapse of their Lloyd's syndicate forced them into bankruptcy, a rented studio flat and all of the indignities they had been foisting on the rest of the country for a decade. She thought they would gloat if they saw the flat and, to be fair, she was right. 'I know some other people,' said Liam, 'but you wouldn't want to stay with them either.'

'Druggie pals,' chided Lynn.

'I'll phone Sarah Simmons,' said Maureen. 'I'll stay with her. I could go down tonight and come back on Sunday, it'll be a wee holiday.'

Maureen thought of Sarah, and the name and the cold took her back years, to a long-ago winter when she felt much younger and was never without Vasari, when Otto Dix was her hero and the night terrors and sweating flashbacks were still a shameful secret that she just couldn't seem to shake. Sarah and Maureen used to study together. They were interested in the same areas and swapped notes and did complementary study tasks: one studying one part of a subject, the other studying the rest, then pooling the information. They didn't have much in common but it was a long and prosperous bond, and Maureen felt sure she could stay with her for a few days. Everything had been so much clearer then, hopeful and resonant, when she didn't know about the blood or the cupboard, and Michael was still a distant memory.

'I hate London,' Lynn was saying. 'It's so dirty.'

'The people are pig ignorant,' said Liam, because Lynn didn't like London. 'And they hate us, they hate the Scots. Glaswegians, especially.'

'How dare they,' said Leslie, smiling at Maureen. 'Those racist pricks.'

Leslie parked in front of Maureen's house and they ran upstairs to look for Sarah Simmons's phone number. They were in the bedroom, searching for her address book, when Maureen turned and saw Leslie looking at the used condoms on the floor. Maureen didn't explain, she didn't want to talk about Vik or her bad behaviour, but she noticed a delicious, spiteful thrill tickle her belly because she was holding back information too.

They found the address book and sat on the settee in the living room, working their way through the bits of loose paper that Maureen kept tucked into the fold in the cover. The bundle of scraps was so thick that the cover of the fake Filofax sat open at forty-five degrees. There were work numbers, changes of address, short-term friends she'd promised never, ever to lose touch with, and some mysterious bald numbers without title or provenance, written in her own hand a long time ago. They had found one Sara but it was a Glasgow number and Sarah had always been particular about the spelling. Finally, Maureen found the number under S, written as the second entry.

Sarah said it would be super to see Maureen again but she was very busy at work and had a lot of other commitments in the evening so she might not be free to spend a lot of time with her. Maureen assured her that she just wanted a place to crash and said she was surprised that Sarah was still at the same number. Sarah said she'd probably be at the number until she died. It was a family house, she said, assuming Maureen would understand what that meant, but she didn't. She gave Maureen directions from King's Cross and said she'd see her in the morning.

Maureen was shoving the mysterious bits of paper back into the sleeve of the Filofax when a glint of sharp sunlight caught her eye from under the settee. It was Vik's precious band lighter. She was sure he wouldn't have left it by mistake. She picked up the chrome oval and Leslie watched her stroke the dust off it. 'That's a nice thing,' she said.

Maureen stood up and slipped it into her pocket. 'Yeah,' she said. 'It is.'

24

Arthur Williams

It was rush-hour as Arthur Williams drove through the outskirts of Glasgow. The four-lane motorway slid downhill into the city, past a blackened Gothic Albert hospital. They had been on the road for seven hours, seven hours of listening to Phil Collins's greatest hits because Bunyan liked it. Bunyan was delighted by the trip up north, and she was pleased that Williams had insisted they drive because it would take longer in the car than it would on a plane. Bunyan would be getting overtime for the tour and Williams was looking at one day in lieu, day and a half tops. It had been Williams's idea to bring the car. They would need it if they arrested Harris. They couldn't interview him in a Scottish police station because of the Police and Criminal Evidence Act and would need to get him to Carlisle. But Harris didn't look like a very likely suspect. The husband of murdered woman number 14/2000 had no record, no connections and lived on a safe estate.

They had been told to come off the M8 at junction sixteen and take a couple of rights for Stewart Street. They didn't want to go there first, they had all the local intelligence they needed, but it was a courtesy and Williams knew from experience that they might find themselves looking for follow-up information later on.

'Yeah,' said Bunyan. 'And another right. Should be here.'

Stewart Street police station was at the tail of a dead end. It was a large, glass-fronted building, two minutes' walk from the city centre. Behind the building the heavy traffic lumbered past on the motorway flyover. The cars outside were coppers' cars, all good nick and thick tread, all taxed, some with flash extras. Williams pulled the car to the kerb and cranked up the handbrake.

'God,' sighed Bunyan. 'Do you have to?'

Williams smiled at her. 'Picky, picky, picky,' he said, and she smiled back at him.

'That's not how you drive a car,' she said.

'You're wrong, DC Bunyan. That is how *I* drive a car.'

They stepped out and pulled their worn clothes straight. It was a dry, cold night. In the distance they could hear the hum and swirl of bagpipes.

'Can you hear that?' Bunyan asked.

'Yeah,' said Williams.

'Do they pipe that music all over the whole country?'

'No,' said Williams, slowly. 'Someone nearby is playing bagpipes.'

They told the young PC on the desk that they were there to meet DI Hugh McAskill. He phoned upstairs. 'Be a minute,' he said.

'We heard bagpipes outside,' said Bunyan, leaning on the desk. 'Do they pipe that music all over the whole country, then?'

The PC smiled politely. 'No,' he said, his dry, brisk accent making Bunyan sound like a chirpy barrow-boy. 'The School of Piping is just down the road. They produce very good pipers.'

'I wouldn't know a good piper from a bad piper,' Bunyan told Williams.

'Yes, you would,' said the PC, tidying the posters on the noticeboard at the back. 'You'd know a bad piper if you heard one. DI McAskill,' he looked behind her, 'this is DI Williams and DC Bunyan from the Met.'

McAskill was tall and sad-faced. He reached out his hand. 'Hello,' he said, shaking theirs firmly. 'DI Hugh McAskill. I'm very sorry but we can't brief you just now. Bit of business. You've got the written brief?'

'Yeah, are we late?' asked Bunyan, shoving her hands into her pockets. 'That's a shame.'

Williams took charge. 'We'll come and see you in the morning,' he said. 'Will you be free then?'

'Aye.' McAskill looked solemn. 'Come in about eight.'

Williams nodded. 'Good luck with that then.'

'Aye,' said McAskill. 'We'll see ye in the morning.' And he turned and walked away through a set of double doors.

'We're all doomed,' trilled Bunyan, when they got to the car. 'What a misery that bloke was.'

'Don't be stupid,' said Williams, losing patience as he unlocked the car. 'Something's happened or they'd want to get it out of the way.'

He slid hip first into the still warm seat, and Bunyan climbed in next to him. 'How would you know?' she said, offended at being called stupid.

Williams reached around for his seat-belt and felt his tired back straining with the effort. 'The only reason a DI would be too busy for a briefing at seven at night and back in at eight in the morning is if something's happened. Otherwise he'd be at home watching *The Bill*, wouldn't he? That's why the bloke looked so grim, he was telling us that.'

'I see,' said Bunyan. 'Put Phil Collins back on.'

Chaos was king in James Harris's living room. He had four boys under ten all of whom were very excited about the arrival of the two visitors from London. The two older boys were jumping about on the only armchair in the room, taking turns to ride the high back like a horse. The two small boys, little more than babies, were sitting on the bare floor, playing with their plastic plates of spaghetti hoops, getting them all over their cotton trousers and in their hair. James Harris looked like a man about to crack.

'Will – ye – fuck – ing – chuck – it?' he screamed. The boys on the chair lowered their voices for a couple of minutes and then carried on.

'Mr Harris,' said Williams, noticing how soft his accent sounded by comparison, 'can't you get the boys to go upstairs? We need to ask you about your wife.'

Harris's response was bizarre. He opened his red eyes as wide as they would go and shook his head. 'No,' he murmured, but the boys on the chair had heard.

'Mum?' said the oldest one, clambering down from the chair and coming to stand by them in the doorway.

'Is Mammy coming home soon?' said his brother, coming over too.

The babies stopped throwing spaghetti at their faces and looked up. Williams couldn't believe it. The bastard hadn't told them. Bunyan opened her mouth to speak, but Williams stepped in front of her. 'All right now,' he said, speaking slowly and with great authority. 'I've heard that you two boys are very good at drawing.' He opened his notebook and ripped out two blank pages from the back. 'I have two sheets of paper. One for each of you.'

Williams held them above the boys' heads and they looked up at them. The longer the sheets of paper were out of their reach the more the boys were certain that drawing on these pieces of paper was the one thing they had been looking forward to for ages.

'What we need now,' he said, 'is for two very quiet, calm boys to tiptoe around the room and find one pen each.'

They scurried away.

'Tiptoe in a calm way,' ordered Williams loudly.

The babies were mesmerized. They didn't care about

their dinner any more, they wanted to do what the big boys were doing, they wanted to walk slowly around the room looking at the floor. The oldest boy ran back waving a biro—

'Got mine!' he screamed.

'Calmly,' emphasized Williams.

The younger boy came back clutching a purple felt tip with a broken nib. Williams gave them the paper, laying it on the floor in front of them. 'I want you both to draw a house and some children playing. Take your time. Start now.'

The boys sat on the floor, leaning over their bits of paper so enthusiastically it was as if they'd never had an organized task before. Williams turned back to Harris.

'How did ye do that?' said Harris, staring at the boys. 'I cannae control them at all.'

'Mr Harris,' said Williams, speaking with an adult voice, 'we need to speak to ye and it would be better if we were alone. Will the boys be at school tomorrow?'

'Aye.'

'Good, we'll come and talk to you then.'

They turned to leave but Harris put his hand across the door to stop them. 'What, um,' he licked his lips, 'what time will ye be coming?'

'About two? Does that suit you?'

'Aye, two's fine,' he lifted his arm away, 'I'll see ye then.'

Williams stepped on to the concrete veranda but Bunyan was holding back. 'Shouldn't we . . .?' She thumbed back into the room.

'What is it?' demanded Williams, losing patience.

'The boys are drawing for you,' said Bunyan.

The oldest boy stood up, holding his drawing in the air and shouted that he'd finished. He almost caused a fight by half stepping on to his brother's picture as he tried to get to the door and hand it to Bunyan. He had drawn a house with a roof and a boy standing in an upstairs window, waving out.

'That's great,' said Bunyan, in the indulgent, sing-song voice she spoke to her three-year-old daughter in. 'He's giving us a little wave, isn't he?'

'Aye.'

His little brother followed him and handed her a big purple square mess. 'I coloured mine in,' he said.

'This is lovely,' cooed Bunyan. 'Look at that beautiful house. I should like to live there.'

'We're off,' said Williams curtly.

Bunyan had no option but to follow him, waving back to the little boys standing on the windy veranda in their pyjamas. The smell of urine in the lift was disgusting.

'God,' said Bunyan, looking at the drawings. 'Those poor little bastards.'

'Why would the man not tell his children that their mother is dead?'

'Guilt,' said Bunyan and Williams agreed with her. 'Where did you learn to talk to children like that?'

'Used to be a teacher,' said Williams, 'before I got on to the fast track.'

Bunyan thought it made sense. Williams never listened to anyone and he was a bossy bastard as well.

25

Alan

The wind took on a shrill new vigour at the bus station, hurtling down the low streets, converging in the waiting area in front of the ticket building. The station was a solid concrete enclosure fenced in by a high brick wall. Until recently it had been a deserted corner of the town. The redevelopment had begun a few years before but already a big shopping centre, a multi-storey car-park, and a concert hall had been built. The bus station had been upgraded too. Glass walls had been erected at every bus stop around the square, designed to prevent pedestrians from wandering about in front of the double-deckers. The ticket centre had been redecorated and the renovations were reported to have cost a fortune but the bus station was still bleak. Most of the passengers were poor enough to be smokers and the new lobby was a smoke-free zone. Everyone likely to take the bus had to stand outside the brand-new structure, keeping it good for visiting dignitaries.

They waited for twenty minutes in the winding queue to buy the return ticket to London, leaving on the night bus at ten thirty. The return passage was open-ended. 'But you cannae just turn up, do ye understand?' The man behind the window spoke slowly, as if he was used to dealing with children. He had tapered hairs sticking straight out of his nose, as if an insect was about to step out of his nostril, heard a scary noise and froze.

'I understand that fully,' said Maureen, 'I need to book.'

'Ye need to book, that's right, ye need to book.' He took her cash and handed her the ticket, tugging it back a little when her hand was on it. 'There's the number,' he pointed to a phone number printed in red on the back, 'for when ye need to book.'

'I need to book,' nodded Maureen.

'Ye need to book,' grinned Leslie.

'That's right,' said the man. 'Ye need to book.'

As they left the bus station Leslie said she didn't like the idea of Maureen going away without being in touch. It was Thursday, the shops were open late, and she wanted her to buy a mobile phone, but Maureen said she'd rather eat her own still-beating heart. They compromised and Maureen agreed to buy a pager, promising to phone back any time Leslie sent her a message. She picked the most expensive one and said she'd take it but the salesman wouldn't stop his pitch.

'I'll take it.'

'It can be used in a variety of ways and comes with free batteries.'

'I'll take it.'

'It can also be put to a different setting so that you won't be interrupted during important business meetings.'

'I'll take it.'

'The one-year guarantee comes with a full parts and replacement clause and costs next to—'

Leslie leaned across the counter. 'Hoi, Mr Branson,' she said loudly, 'put it in a fucking poke and take her money.'

Within three minutes they were out of the shop and into the windy confusion in Sauchiehall Street. 'You're a cheeky cow, Leslie.'

'I know.'

Maureen stopped walking and looked at her. 'We're five

minutes away from the house and ye can't put it off any more.'

'I know.'

Jimmy opened the door wide at the fourth knock. His tired pallor was exacerbated by his wet eyes and slack despair. He stood, afraid to raise his head to look and see who they were, resigned to whatever was going to happen now.

'Jimmy,' said Maureen, dipping at the knees and bending down to make him look at her, 'it's me.'

He looked at Leslie. 'Jimmy, this is your cousin, Leslie. She's Isa's girl. They want to help you.'

'Isa? Isa?' Jimmy repeated the name, remembering a time long ago and unfamiliar kindness.

'Yeah,' said Leslie gingerly, 'Isa's my mum.'

Jimmy left the door open and wandered back into the living room. It was still early but the kids were already in bed; tiny clothes and shoes lay scattered on the bare floor. A bottle of MadMan, a cheap, sweet alcohol drink made to appeal to the under-twelves, sat on the floor by the chair. The bright bare bulb did Jimmy no favours. His skin was greying at the temples and jawline, as if he was dying from the outside in. He sat down in his only chair, lifting an old photograph of Ann off the arm, holding it carefully by the corner.

'I'm sorry, Jimmy,' said Maureen. 'Did ye tell the weans yet?'

Jimmy shook his head.

'Did the police tell ye what happened to her?'

'She's dead,' he breathed, as if that was the all and all of it.

Leslie settled against the far wall, staying near the door, and lit a fag.

'Did they tell ye she was killed?' asked Maureen, crouching down by the chair, afraid to speak loudly in case Jimmy shattered in front of her.

He nodded, bent over slowly and lifted the bottle to his mouth, sucking on it and swallowing hard. He was shaking: the tip of Ann's photo flickered like an insect wing. 'It's the only picture I've got.' He grinned at Maureen, displaying his vicious yellow teeth, and his eyes began to bleed tears. Jimmy covered his face with a taloned hand and sobbed silently, the sinews on his neck standing out like tent ropes, strings of saliva hinging his mouth open.

He stayed still for a long time and Maureen watched him, feeling she would hold him and pet him if she had been a better person and didn't find him so repulsive. She lit two cigarettes and slipped one between the fingers of Jimmy's hand on the arm of the chair. It was half ash before his neck went limp. He shuddered, taking his hand from his wet face, lifting the cigarette to his mouth. He took a long, deep draw. The ash spine dropped on to his lap and he brushed it slowly to the floor as he exhaled. 'The police were here,' said Jimmy. 'I don't know what to tell them.'

'Just tell them the truth,' said Maureen, thinking how it would sound to Leslie. She took the Polaroid out of her pocket and handed it to him. 'Do you know who this guy is?'

Jimmy wiped the tears from his face and looked at the well-fed, brutish man holding his son's hand. 'Nut. The wean told me. You asked about a picture.'

'I didn't want to ask you. I thought he might be Ann's boyfriend.'

'Aye,' said Jimmy, not giving a fuck about infidelity. He pointed at the man in the photo. 'He told the wean he needed a picture to send to his ma.' His chest trembled as he breathed in. He looked at the picture of his dead wife and his red eyes throbbed tears. He grinned, desolate again.

'Jimmy,' she said, pressing on, 'why would Ann want a photo of that particular boy? Was she especially fond of him?'

'Nut.'

He stood up slowly, holding his hand under his cigarette to catch the ash. He brought a cracked saucer in from the kitchen for them to use as an ashtray. Maureen took it from him and squashed her fag out, slipping Vik's lighter under the leg of his chair and out of sight. 'Did the boy tell ye when the picture was taken?' she said.

Jimmy sat back down. 'It was the day the Christmas holidays started. Look, ye can see his wee card that he made for me.' He pointed to the red fluffy card in the child's hand.

'Last day of school? What would that be, the twenty-first of December?'

'Aye.'

'Jimmy, will ye do me a favour? I want ye to ask at the post office tomorrow and find out if the child-benefit book was cashed today. Could ye do that?'

'Aye.'

'This is my pager number.' She copied it from the booklet on to the back of a bus ticket and gave it to him. 'Will ye phone and leave a message if they tell ye anything? A woman will ask ye what message ye want to leave and you tell her and it comes up as writing on this.' She showed him the pager and put the Polaroid back in her pocket.

Leslie stepped forward with a phone number written on the inside of a fag packet. 'That's my mum's number.' She handed it to him and Maureen noticed she didn't give him her own.

'Isa's wee girl, eh?' said Jimmy

'Aye.'

'You're her pride and joy. I like your mum. Isa. Nice person. Kind.'

Jimmy was speaking faster and higher, speeding towards another crying fit. A series of small thumps on the bare stairs drew their attention. Jimmy cleaned his face, scrubbing away the tears and smearing his thin hair back from his face. His oldest boy appeared at the living-room door, wearing a sweatshirt over his ragged pyjamas. Little grey school socks trailed from his feet. Leslie recoiled against the door-frame as if the sleepy boy had frightened her.

'Who is it, Da?' said the boy, not bothering to look at Leslie or Maureen, wanting his dad to tell him it would be all right.

Jimmy held his arms out. 'It's all right, son,' he said dutifully, and the boy ran over to him, climbing on to his knee, wrapping his arms around Jimmy's neck. The boy was nine. The last time Maureen had seen him he was acting like a hard man and he was too old to climb about on his daddy's knee. He was doing it for Maureen and Leslie, in case they had come to hurt Jimmy. Maureen imagined him sitting upstairs, listening to the knock on the door, trying to make out the conversation until the tension and worry reached a pitch and he had to come down and act like a child of half his age. She thought of her stepdad, George, at his cousin Betsy's wedding. George was appalled to find out that Maureen had never been danced. He took her on to the dance floor and let her stand on his feet while he waltzed her around the room. He made her feel like a tiny child, coddled and precious, but she wasn't, she was twelve, weighed about six stone and, in hindsight, it must have been murder on George's feet. She remembered him sweating and grunting as he lifted his feet for the next turn. He was making up for Michael, always making up for Michael. Jimmy Harris stubbed out his cigarette in the saucer, pulled the boy's legs round and sat him up in his lap. 'See this lady here?' He pointed to Leslie, hovering reluctantly at the door. 'This is your cousin, Leslie. Leslie, this is Alan.'

'Hello, Alan,' said Leslie, looking revolted.

'Hello,' said Alan, forgetting he was pretending to be sleepy and sitting up straight. 'You were here before,' he said to Maureen. He had Jimmy's teeth. 'Did ye find my mum?'

No-one knew what to say to him.

'Not yet, son.'

'Will ye?'

'Dunno, pal.'

Jimmy patted him on the back. 'Come on now, you should be in your bed. Ye can go up yourself.'

'I want you to put me to bed,' he said, clinging to Jimmy's arm.

'Now, Alan, I'm talking to people—'

'Jimmy,' said Maureen, 'we'll go.'

The boy smiled.

'Naw,' said Jimmy. 'He's old enough—'

'We'll go,' said Maureen. 'You take him up.' She stood up and Leslie lurched towards the door, desperate to get out. Maureen touched the boy's yellow hair. 'Cheerio, Alan, I'll see ye again.'

Alan wouldn't look at her. He was holding on to his dad, afraid to let go. He wouldn't even let Jimmy come to the door to see them off.

'See ye later, Jimmy,' said Maureen, looking back into the living room, but Jimmy had his hands full trying not to fall over his son.

She shut the door quietly and followed Leslie to the lifts. It was windy on the veranda and televisions blared behind the neighbouring doors. The smell of urine had faded in the lift, leaving behind it an acute bitter undertone. AMcC was still sucking cocks but had been joined in the endeavour by Rory T.

'God,' Leslie groaned, 'my mum'll be feeding them mince intravenously when she sees them. What was all that "Don't go down the mine today, Daddy" stuff?'

'There's money-lenders up threatening him every night, the wee boy's frightened for him,' said Maureen, trying to think of something positive to say, to stop Jimmy being Mr Pathetic Universe. 'They're a very close family.'

'They're a very frightened family,' corrected Leslie. 'That boy knows what's going to happen to his dad. He knows it better than his dad does.'

'Are ye going to take the pictures to the police?'

'I dunno,' said Leslie quietly, biting the inside of her bottom lip. She rubbed her eyes. 'But the first sign that he did it and I'll go to Peel Street myself and hand them over.'

Maureen grinned at her as the lift doors slid open into the empty foyer. Leslie stomped across to the door and Maureen followed her out into the dark and windy yard. She waited until Leslie had unchained the bike. 'Auch,' she said stagily, 'I've left my lighter up there. I'll just be a minute.'

She knocked very quietly so that the boy wouldn't hear her. Jimmy looked pleased when he saw her and even more pleased when he saw she was alone. 'What are ye back for?' he asked, opening the door wide.

Maureen looked up the stairs and saw Alan's ruffled hair above the solid banister on the landing. She called to him, 'It's just me again.'

Alan stood up and looked at her. His eyes were puffy and tired.

'Go back to bed, son,' she called softly. 'It's all right. I just forgot something.'

Jimmy looked up the stairs, apparently surprised that Alan was there. 'Away you to bed,' he said, raising his hand in a threat. 'Go.'

Alan got up and bolted back into his room, closing the door over-quietly, trying not to wake the other children. Jimmy led her into the living room, shutting the door to the hall so that Alan couldn't hear them. Maureen bent down and picked up Vik's lighter. 'Jimmy, why did ye fly to London last week?' Jimmy didn't answer. She pointed to the space by the wall where the bag had been. 'I saw your bag with the baggage sticker on it.'

Jimmy breathed in unsteadily. 'Do the police know?' he whispered.

'I don't know.'

Jimmy fell back into his seat, looking guilty and hunted. He smiled nervously up at her. 'Thought my luck had changed.'

'Why were ye there?'

'Someone put a ticket through the door,' he said. 'It was late at night. In an envelope. With a letter. It said I had to go to this lawyer's office in Brixton.'

'Why did ye go?'

He looked at her, not understanding. 'It was a lawyer's letter,' he said simply, as if it had the force of a papal edict.

'What was it about?'

'Some money.'

'What money?'

'From a will. Someb'dy'd died and left me money. If I didn't go I wouldn't get it.'

'Like in the movies?' asked Maureen sadly.

'Aye,' he nodded, 'like that.'

Maureen got her packet out and dished him a fag, lighting them with Vik's lighter. 'What happened when you went to the lawyer's office?' she asked.

Jimmy pulled the saucer out from behind his chair. He exhaled a thin stream of smoke and paused. 'I went to the address. It was a lawyer's office but it was a different office, different name. They used to be called that name a while ago but they changed it. They'd not written to me. There wasn't a will. It must have been a joke,' he smiled nervously, 'but I thought, Oh, well, at least I got to go on a plane, ye know?'

'Have ye still got the letter?'

'The one from the lawyer?'

'Aye.'

'I think so.' He rummaged through a pile of bills at the side of the chair. 'I've it here somewhere.'

He stood up, lifted the chair cushion and found an envelope with a printed address on it and no stamp. The letterhead read 'McCallum and Headie' and was printed in a typeface available on the most rudimentary word-processors. The text of the letter was in the same font as the heading and the paper was photocopy quality. They hadn't even spell-checked it: Jimmy was instructed to attend the office at 2 p.m. on the Thursday or he would lose his clam to the inheritance. He replaced the cushion and sat down on his chair.

'Jimmy,' Maureen was appalled by his naïveté, 'what possessed ye to go?'

'Thought my luck had changed.' He jerked his head at the letter. 'You'd've known, would ye?' He looked at her. She didn't want to say but Jimmy knew anyway.

'What day were you there?'

'A week ago today.'

'Last Thursday?'

'Aye. The polis said she'd been in the river for about a week. That means I was there when it happened, doesn't it?'

'When did ye get the ticket?'

'It came through the door the night before.'

Jimmy wasn't fly enough to dodge a glacier. The kids

might even be better off in care but Jimmy deserved one break in his entire fucking life. Just one break. She looked at the letter again. Liam had a lawyer. He used to lie about it if it came up in company, pretend he knew nothing about them if the firm was mentioned in the papers. He said you could tell the most intimate details of a person's life from the name of their lawyer, how much they earned, whether they were straight or bent, who they hung about with, what they were into. She jotted down the name and the address on the letter and put the bit of paper in her pocket. 'Did anyone see ye in London?' said Maureen. 'Would anyone remember you being there?'

'No, I was only there for the day. I couldn't have gone otherwise – the kids, ye know. I felt like a real jet-setter – flying down in the morning, coming back at night. The food was nice too. I saved my pudding for the wee ones.'

She thought about the mattress. 'Don't you know anyone in London, Jimmy?'

'No. I know Moe, but not well enough to go and see her. Should I just not tell the polis about it?'

'I don't know,' said Maureen. 'Don't volunteer the information, eh? Wait till they ask ye.'

'Okay,' said Jimmy, nodding wide-eyed, as if it was any kind of help at all.

Maureen suddenly, desperately, wanted a big drink of whisky. 'You know that Ann's sister lives in Streatham?'

Jimmy didn't understand the connection. 'I told you that,' he said.

'Streatham's right next to Brixton. Ann was seen in a pub down there.'

'Oh,' said Jimmy, 'I didn't know that. I knew it was London. That would be right because her man's a darkie.'

'Black people live all over London, Jimmy, not just in Brixton.'

Jimmy knew that she was correcting him and he knew he was in the wrong. His chin sank further into his chest. She felt like a sanctimonious prick.

'Moe's . . . a good-living woman,' he said.

'I'm sure she is. It's a coincidence, though, isn't it? The lawyer and Ann being in the same area? Was Ann close to her sister? Would she go and stay with her?'

'Oh, aye, they were close. Ye know how sisters are.'

Maureen didn't know how sisters were; she had two herself but she didn't know. She remembered that Leslie was waiting outside and did her coat up.

'I got money through the door the other night as well,' said Jimmy quickly, 'a lot of money. I don't know what to make of it.'

'How much money?'

'Two hundred and fifty pounds. What do ye suppose it means?'

'What did ye do with the money?'

'I hid it.'

She was embarrassed to admit to it. 'Jimmy, I gave ye the money. Ye can spend it however ye want. Just don't mention me to the police, okay?'

Jimmy frowned at his fag.

'Look,' she said, 'Isa and Leslie are going to look out for ye, they'll come around and get to know the boys in case, you know, ye have to go away. I'm going to London for a few days, see if I can find out what happened to her.'

Jimmy looked at her vacantly. 'Why are ye doing this for me?'

But she wasn't doing it for him.

'And you put that money through my door,' he said. 'Why?'

Maureen blushed. She was doing it because she pitied him, because he was the sorriest, saddest, most unsympathetic person she'd ever met, in or out of psychiatric hospital, because if life was any more cruel to Jimmy then Michael would live to a ripe old age surrounded by family and friends and she'd die soon. 'I've been stuck myself,' she said.

She drank her coffee in the living room and made up a small list of the things she'd need in London. Angus's letters were scattered all over the coffee table. She had been reading through them again, trying to work out the reasoning behind them, but she had sickened herself and now couldn't bring herself to touch them and put them away. She sat the cup on top of them and went into the hall cupboard to get her bag. It was a big rubberized cycle bag, black with a red stripe down the middle. She bought it for the little fish logo picked out in silver thread. The bag had a broad shoulder-strap that fitted across her chest. It was designed for a man, not a large-chested woman, and the strap sat across her breastbone, squeezing one tit up and the other down but it looked more casual than a rucksack and it could carry more. She pulled it out and crouched down, looking at the bloody stain on the floor, where the tender memory of Douglas and times behind her lingered. She stood up and looked through to the kitchen, out of the window, past the drizzling rain and the dark clouds to the grey shadow on Ruchill. She wasn't coming back to this, whatever happened. She wouldn't come back to a house where she was afraid to look out of the window.

She took the bag into the bedroom and began to pack. She was lying to herself, estimating a stay of three days to a week, packing pants and socks and spare jeans and a change of jumpers. In the bathroom she packed her toothbrush and Maxine's pricey cream and eye-makeup remover pads. She dropped the bag on to the tiled floor, sat down on the edge of the bath and cried. She felt the pull to London, the draw of the anonymous city without Ruchill and her family and the hospital and her history. She felt she'd never get back.

She ran a deep bath and undressed slowly, climbed into the scalding water and lit a cigarette, breathing in the moist nicotine. The damp atmosphere seeped into the paper and killed the light. She laid it on the side of the bath, looking down at her scorched red body and cried again, curling small with misery and grief, longing to be anyone but herself.

The phone rang out in the hall and Winnie spoke into the answerphone, sounding sober and sombre. 'Maureen,' she said, 'this is your mother.' Her voice had none of the melodrama Maureen was used to, none of the premature crescendos or the wavering high emotion. It was nine o'clock on a Wednesday night: she should be very drunk. 'I'm sorry for all the phoning before but I love you and want you to contact me. Please phone. Urgently.'

Maureen waited for a while, glad that something had happened and she had a task. She washed her face, scooping the vehement water on to her skin again and again until she was breathless. She wrapped the chain around her big toe and pulled the plug out, sat up and hauled herself out of the water.

She was sweating into the towel as Liam answered the phone.

'No, Mauri, she's fine.'

'I hardly knew her voice.'

Liam chuckled. 'She's sober, that's why.' Maureen could hear Lynn calling, 'Hiya, Mauri,' in the background. 'She's been sober for three days.'

'Three days? What about the nights?'

'I mean sober continuously for three days.'

'Fucking hell. How is she?'

'Well,' said Liam, 'she's just as mad as she was when she was drunk but she sleeps less and she's more articulate.'

Maureen was suddenly very glad that she had a good reason not to be in touch with Winnie. Winnie had tried abstinence several times before and they had been some of the family's saddest times. Maureen remembered playing cards with Winnie after school, keeping her busy until dinner-time, helping her shave another half-hour from the hellish day. Winnie trembled like a foal as the alcohol left her. Her eyes kept flicking to the clock and she cried as the stinging minutes scratched by, thinking perpetual discomfort was the alternative. She never lasted longer than a day because they had to leave her alone sometime.

'How's she managing to stay sober?'

'She's gone to AA.'

'With that bastard Benny?'

'No,' said Liam. 'Not with him. She said it's huge in Glasgow, she might never meet him.'

Benny had been at school with Maureen and Liam. He'd slept on her floor for three months when he was getting sober and he'd betrayed her so badly over Douglas that Liam broke his jaw. The last time either of them had seen him he was sitting in hospital with his arm in a stookie and a face like a waterlogged plum. Sober Winnie and the possible return of a traitorous childhood friend were two events too many. Maureen shut her eyes and made a conscious decision not to dwell or deal with either. Not for a while anyway. 'I bought a pager,' she said, pleased with herself for sounding light-hearted. 'Do you want the number?'

'Oh, yeah,' he said, and jotted it down. 'Are you off to London, then?'

'I'm going in an hour, on the night bus.'

'Fucking hell, I wouldn't get the fucking night bus for anyone,' said Liam, talking over the receiver and projecting his voice, talking for Lynn's benefit. 'Be careful down there. Don't mention Hutton to anyone.'

She was dressed and about to leave when her hand picked up the receiver again and dialled Vik's number. She got his answerphone. 'Pick up, Vik,' she said. 'Please pick up.'

She waited for a breath and he didn't so she told him she was getting the night bus down to London tonight and she'd phone later and she was sorry, again, really sorry. Please pick up? She had his lighter. Please? She felt ridiculous and dirty and ugly, as if everything Katia thought about her was true. As she hung up she saw a slit of blackness in the bedroom window. Michael was out there. He raised his razor finger, ready to make the first incision. Maureen caught her breath and waited until the horror subsided.

Jimmy was sitting in the chair, worrying about what to tell the police the next day and drinking the last of the MadMan when he heard the noise in the hall. 'Ya wee besom.' He stood up and stepped across to the door. Will ye get to your bed?'

Alan wasn't in the hall. Jimmy looked up the stairs. He wasn't on the stairs either. He looked up at the door to the boys' room and it was shut just as firmly as it had been when he'd let Maureen O'Donnell out. He looked down. A brown envelope was lying on the floor, dropped through the letter-box. Jimmy picked it up and ripped open the flap. He pulled the photographs out and looked at them. She had been badly beaten right enough but the injuries were healing. He could see that the bruises were yellow and green now, not black as they would have been. She was wearing a paper hat from a Christmas cracker, sitting at a table with a big dinner in front of her and four or five other women, smiling for the camera. She was sitting on a settee with a lassie with bad teeth and a flat nose. Ann was standing by a tree with a whole lot of other women and on the wall behind them hung a big sign showing where the fire exits were. It was Ann's last Christmas, Christmas Day in the shelter. Jimmy ran his finger over her dear face and wept, thanking Maureen O'Donnell once again for all her kindness.

26

Night Bus

Leslie slipped her arm through Maureen's and they made their way back to the bus station. It was cold and misty as they walked down the hill. Maureen's bag banged off her back as they hurried across the busy street.

The night-bus passengers were gathered together in the freezing concourse, smoking hard, trying to get enough nicotine into their systems to last the seven-hour journey. Apart from a couple of well-fed, healthy students, who were roughing it, most of the travellers were going to London to look for work, to fulfil errands or visit family who had moved away. The shoal of waiting passengers started at some invisible stimulus, grabbing their bags, shuffling quickly towards the glass wall, itching to get on. Maureen looked around but the bus doors weren't open and the lights weren't on. The crowd put their bags down again, lighting another last fag, bidding another last goodbye.

The night bus to London is a Glaswegian rite of passage. Most people try it once, attracted by the twenty-quid ticket, the comfortable seating and the promise of arriving in London as fresh as a daisy early in the morning. Only the poor or desperate do it twice. Maureen had done it many times. She always forgot how bad the journey was until she got to the station but her experience had given her a number of tips. The upstairs deck was the most comfortable because it was far from the smell of the chemical toilet and was usually warmer, which made it possible to sleep. It tended to attract the crazies but it filled up more slowly, making it easier to get and keep a double seat to herself. The double seat was the big prize: it meant she could stretch out and leave the bus without aching everywhere.

She took off her overcoat and put it into a poly-bag, pulled on a big jumper and took out a newspaper, a bottle of Coke and the bag of chocolate éclairs Leslie had brought for her. Leslie pulled the neck of Maureen's jumper straight and looked angry. 'Phone me. Take care when you're down there, okay?'

'I'll be fine, Leslie, don't fuss me.'

They stood close together, smoking and watching for signs of the driver. A gangly man wearing a blue nylon uniform sauntered casually down the side of the bus, keeping his head down, pretending not to notice the forty pairs of eyes behind the glass watching him like an aquarium of hungry piranhas. He leaned down to the side, unlocked the boot and the mob surged towards him, shoving and jostling to be first. He checked Maureen's ticket, took her bag and threw it into the hold.

'Right,' said Leslie. 'Take care.'

'I will.'

They hugged each other tight. Leslie backed away, stepping on to the shallow pavement in front of the glass wall as Maureen climbed on board. A different driver was waiting to double-check her ticket. He was short with a fags-and-sunbed-withered face, a jet black curly Afro perm and blindingly white false teeth. 'On ye go,' he said, in a strangled, nasal squeal.

She had to wait patiently in the queue, edging up the stairs one at a time. The top deck was full of people sorting themselves into the chairs. Maureen bagsied a double seat one down from the back row and sat by the aisle, putting her paper and sweets and Coke on the seat by the window.

She had learned that the best method for keeping a double seat was to look more obnoxious and unwelcoming than anyone else. She pretended to read her paper, sticking her elbows across the arm-rests, refusing to look at anyone coming up the stairs. The crowd outside the window diminished as the passengers filtered on to the bus, the aisle emptied and the passengers settled. Maureen was beginning to think she'd get the double seat to herself. Leslie stood on the pavement, watching her, looking very small and far away. She waved and Maureen waved back.

A mob of cheery drunk men appeared at the side of the bus, flinging their bags at the driver and piling in through the door. They climbed the stairs with difficulty, pulling at each other and laughing. The first man up the stairs spotted the empty back seat. 'Look, boys,' he shouted, 'the very dab.'

They fell up the aisle in a haze of stale smoke and beer, taking up the back row behind Maureen, tugging their jackets off and congratulating each other on their den. They were almost settled when a dishevelled wee man emerged from the stairwell. He was a good fifteen years older than the rest of them and wore thick specs and a dirty yellow anorak zipped up tight at the neck. He looked around, spotted his pals on the back seat and cursed. 'D'yees no' save a seat for me?'

Behind Maureen's head the men jeered at him, telling him to sit down.

'Cunts,' he said, spotting Maureen's precious extra seat. He stood next to her, waiting for her to move. Maureen sighed and stood up, moving over to the window, sitting the sweets and Coke on her lap. The man aimed his body and fell into the seat, landing heavily and clearing his throat. 'Right, hen?' he asked the head-rest in front of him. He turned and squared up to her, making a small, defensive mouth. The lenses on his glasses were so thick they distorted his eyes into tiny things, a blurry mess of blue and red and crumbs. 'Are ye no' fucking talking tae me? Too good fur me, is it?'

A bald man shoved his face between the head-rests behind her. 'Jokey,' he said, 'shut it.'

Jokey looked around the bus indignantly. He coughed and nonchalantly scratched his bollocks.

'Don't worry, hen,' the bald man said to Maureen, 'he'll be sleeping in a minute.'

Maureen was looking at a long night of Jokey snoring and dribbling, with nothing to comfort her but a bottle of Coke and a bag of chocolate toffees. Leslie waved from the pavement again and Maureen waved back at her. A speaker above the stairs crackled to life and the Afro'd driver spoke, sounding bored and telling them that they were in Glasgow but were going to London. He must have been doing the job for a long time because he had anticipated all their tricks. 'There will be no *smoking* on this journey,' he said. 'There will be no *drinking*.' The back-seat gang interrupted the announcement to cheer the mention of drink. 'There will be no *fighting*.' They cheered louder. 'Passengers are informed that they must keep their feet and bags out of the aisle *at all times*.' The men hoorayed and whistled. 'Anyone found to be breaking these rules,' continued the driver, 'will be put off the bus at the side of the motorway and left there.'

The men stopped cheering.

'We will be stopping at the Knutsford services at three thirty a.m. for refreshments. We will be leaving the Knutsford services at *three fifty* a.m. Any passengers not on board will be left behind. A member of the team will shortly be coming around to serve you tea, coffee and sandwiches. We hope you enjoy your journey with Caledonia Buses.'

The tannoy crackled to a stop and a frightened silence fell over the top deck.

'He's a bit fucking harsh, isn't he?' whispered the bald guy.

The engine spluttered to life, sending rolling bug-a-lug vibrations through the windows and seats. Leslie waved conscientiously from the pavement as the bus backed out of the loading bay and into the street.

Maureen was looking calmly out of the window, chewing the first chocolate toffee of the night, when she saw him. Vik was striding up the road to the bus station, his leather coat flapping open, checking his watch and walking fast. He had come to see her off. Maureen stood up, forgetting herself and dropping the bag of sweets to the floor. She banged her fists on the window and shouted, 'Oi,' but he didn't see her. She banged harder, turning, her eyes fixed on him as the bus sped away up Cathedral Street. He was a little liquorice strip on the pavement and the bus station receded to a strip of light below a black hanging sky. Vik had come to see her off. The bald man stuck his face through the head-rests again. 'I know,' he said, smiling kindly, 'I hate they Pakis too.'

'He's my boyfriend,' said Maureen.

Uncomfortable at his *faux pas*, the bald man sat back in his chair and puffed out his chest. 'Aye, very good anyway,' he told his sniggering pals, 'I was just trying to be nice.'

The road was clear. The bus rumbled through Blackhill, passing the chimneys of Barlinnie prison. They passed the fire-blackened flats of Easterhouse, boarded up with fibre-glass, and the driver dimmed the lights to let the passengers sleep. A hush fell over the cabin as the lights slipped past the window. They turned south at the Crosshill Junction, a knot of lanes and slip-roads in a bed of gentle hills. A spired church and cemetery sat on a summit, an angular protestation against the soft, snow-covered countryside. Vik had come to see her off.

As the bus warmed up Jokey began to give off a strange smell, like dirty hair and stale cheese mixed together. He was fighting sleep, nodding off and jerking awake again. After one particularly vigorous convulsion he turned around in the aisle and shouted, 'Cunts,' at the men in the back seat. The bald man reached his hand through the head-rests and patted Jokey's shoulder. 'Steady, Tiger,' he said, and Jokey surrendered to sleep, nuzzling his elbow into Maureen's soft side.

The driver who had packed her bag into the boot came up the shuddering stairs offering sandwiches and taking orders for cups of tea. Someone on the top deck started playing with a Game Boy, Maureen could hear the tingling, mindless tune. She realized suddenly that the music was coming from her pocket. She took out her pager, nervous that it might wake Jokey.

> Message is
> hope you are
> well lot*
> of love Leslie

She had been working her way through the sweets and reading the paper for an hour or so before the smell of Jokey became so distracting that she gave up. She looked out of the window at the dark countryside. They were crawling uphill, out of a deep glen. They were so high that Maureen lost perspective but then the wind shook the windows and scattered the mist below. An old drover's road appeared below them, paralleling the burn, a wavy pencil line through the foot of the hills. At the mouth of the glen stood an abandoned cottage, souvenir of a wild and lonely time. Vik had come to see her off but she was glad he had been too late. She wouldn't have known what to tell him. She was on the edge of her life, trapped on the spur by all the big questions.

She leaned her head on the vibrating window and thought of Ann standing in a cold office in her underwear, letting a stranger take pictures of her tired body, bruised and battered by the want of drink, as if her addiction was trying to scratch through her skin.

The announcement and the rush of cold air from the stairwell woke her up. The bus had stopped in a car-park. Hidden behind the rows of freight lorries were the bright lights of a service station. Jokey's pals woke him up and told him to come on. His smell had accumulated in his anorak while he slept and as he reached up for the back of the chair the stench escaped through the sealed neck in an ardent gust. Maureen waited until he was well down the stairs before getting up herself, stretching her stiff legs and running her tongue over her fur-coated teeth.

The cold was a shock after the nuzzled warmth on the top deck. She lit a fag in the windy car-park and followed the stream of passengers to the service station. The backseat men headed to the restaurant for hot food with Jokey at their heels. Maureen went to the newsagent's, looking for something to buy. The sandwiches cost a fiver and the crisps only came in ludicrously big bags but she was in a shop in the middle of the night and felt she had to buy something. She chose an *A–Z* of London and a spiralbound notepad to write things on. She went back to the bus, smoking another fag as she strolled across the windy car-park, looking out for the nice driver, the one who had packed her bag in the boot. She checked the cab but he wasn't there so she scouted around the bus and found him hiding in the dark shadows at the back, smoking. He nodded to her briefly, trying to shake her off.

'How are ye?' she asked, smiling.

'Aye,' he said, and went back to kicking the dirt.

'Can I show ye a photo of someone?'

The driver was intrigued. 'What for?'

'My pal went missing and I think she took this bus.'

'Ah, well now,' he looked wary, 'we get a lot of people on the buses, ye know.'

Maureen took out the photocopy of Ann's face, holding it up in front of the driver so that it caught the light from inside the bus cab. He looked at it for a moment. 'She had yellow hair and a red face,' said Maureen. 'Smelt of drink, a bit.'

He looked at the picture and was surprised that he remembered her. 'That's amazing,' he said. 'Up and down she was, just before Christmas.'

'Up and down?'

'I seen her a few times. I remember because she was up and down every few days and sometimes she'd keep her bag on her knee, a big bag.' He drew a one-foot square in front of him with his fag-free hand.

'When did ye last see her?'

'Months ago,' he said. 'Start of December. I remember because she was on the way up and got off the bus for the break and never got back on again.'

'She got left at this service station?'

'Aye, well, across the road.' He pointed to a covered walkway bridging the motorway.

'Was she just too late?'

'Don't know,' he said, wanting to be alone in the dark with his cigarette.

Aware that she was running short of time, Maureen

fumbled the Polaroid out of her pocket, 'Did ye ever see this guy with her?'

The driver shrugged, looking at the picture, getting impatient. 'I wouldn't know, hen.'

'Listen, thanks,' said Maureen. 'Thanks a lot.'

She backed off, leaving him to his break, and climbed the stairs into the cab feeling elated. Liam had been right. Ann was up and down and she might have been running for the loan sharks, she might have been running for Hutton. But if she was running for loan sharks she would only have carried the bag one way, not up and down again. She stretched out, enjoying the whole of her seat while she could, before Jokey came back.

The engine started softly, shaking her awake. She opened her eyes to see Jokey falling into his seat like a malodorous avalanche in an anorak. They were pulling out of the service station, leaving the big lorries and the bright lights and sliding along the slip-road on to the quiet carriageway.

It was five a.m. and the grey monochrome was broken only by the red tail-lights of overtaking cars. The land was very flat: they were in the middle of a plain so vast the edges were beyond the horizon. Farmhouses and tiny hamlets flashed by. They passed a small set of horse jumps in a paddock and then sudden banks of the motorway came up, enclosing the road. They passed a village, then through a town and into the country again. The towns began to blend together, meeting at their thinning outer edges, closer and closer until they were tumbling over one another, houses and houses and houses blanketing the shallow hills.

They left the motorway, following the broad road to the city, passing through Swiss Cottage. Houses gave way to small blocks of flats and the small blocks to bigger blocks to high-rises to massive glass and steel offices. The clumsy bus rattled through the dark city, stopping at lights and rumbling across roundabouts. They pulled slowly into King's Cross, stopping by the great blind arches of St Pancras. The Afro'd driver spoke over the Tannoy, telling them they were in London, so get off and thank you.

The bus emptied quickly. A crowd gathered by the boot while the other driver pulled out the bags and sat them on the pavement. Maureen lit a well-deserved cigarette, enjoying the feel of Vik's chrome lighter in the palm of her hand. She took off her jersey and rolled it up, pulling her overcoat out of the poly-bag, unravelling it and slipping it on. It didn't seem very cold, a little frosty, but not like winter at all. She spotted her cycle bag being thrown on to the pavement and stepped over a couple of suitcases to get to it. She waited until everyone else had claimed their baggage before she cornered the driver again. 'See about that girl . . .'

The driver looked up at her. His eyes were red-rimmed and he looked exhausted. 'Look,' he said, slamming the boot shut and locking it, 'I cannae mind the guy.'

'You look knackered,' she said, and offered him a fag. He took one and she lit it for him. 'No, I just wanted to ask about her bag. Did she always have it with her? Could she have just had it with her on the way down?'

The tired man exhaled. 'She put it in the boot sometimes.'

'Was it when she was going home or coming here?'

The driver took a draw and looked at the tip, frowning and trying to remember. 'Now ye say that, I think it was just the one way,' he looked up at her, 'but I cannae remember which.'

'Did ye have an unclaimed bag left in the boot in Glasgow,' prompted Maureen, 'the last time, the time she got left behind at the service station?'

The driver smiled at his fag and nodded. 'On the way up,' he said. 'She kept it on her lap on the way up.'

27

Indifference

It was half past seven in the morning and King's Cross was already gridlocked. Cars and buses on the Euston Road were jammed up close and exhaust fumes hovered over the stodgy traffic like smoke in a night-club. Across the road the Underground entrance hoovered streams of pedestrians off the pavement. Maureen realized that, for the first time in months, she was walking with her head up because the weather was so mild and Michael wasn't here and Vik had come to see her off.

She crossed at the lights heading for the tube. At the foot of the stairs stood a filthy old man with one agate eye. He smiled beatifically up at the ferocious river of bad-tempered people, enjoying the warm stream of heat from the vents, peeling an orange with one hand, his other arm cramped into his waist, his hand puckered and paralysed by a stroke. The torrent of commuters bustled past him, swinging to the far side of the tunnel to avoid even seeing him, rendering him invisible with their indifference.

It was oppressively warm downstairs. By the time Maureen arrived on the southbound platform the sweat was running down her back. After a gentle backdraft, a welcome cool breeze whispered from the tunnel. The crush of people shifted, looking to the left as a train clattered into the station. The passengers clotted around the opening doors, pushing from the back, shoving on to the train before the disembarking passengers could get off. The doors shut behind her, skimming Maureen's bag, and the train took off with a jolt.

Inside the carriage the commuters and tourists pressed tightly against each other, valiantly defending the fiction of unconnectedness. Those standing looked covetously at the seated. The seated looked relaxed and happy, reading books or staring contentedly into the crotch of the person standing in front of them. A Norwegian tourist shared an indignant observation with his companion, who agreed. Maureen wondered about Ann carrying up to Glasgow, wondering whether it meant anything. She couldn't think straight, her eyes burned hot and tired, and more than anything she wanted a wash and a sleep. Her coat was far too heavy, she was sweating into the gorgeous silky lining, straining a muscle on her side trying to reach the bar on the ceiling. The train stopped at a station and a fresh set of tired commuters, wearing their office best, clambered into the carriage.

The train was cooler than the Underground and brought her to Blackheath station. She followed the directions Sarah had given her, turning right out of the station, following the steep road up the hill and taking the left-hand fork. Blackheath was postcard pretty. The low shops had big bow windows with inappropriate red sale banners plastered across them. She walked on until she came to the corner of the heath. Restrained colonnades of high Georgian houses faced on to an extravaganza of empty land, which came to a little hill in the middle, like a pseudo-horizon, as if the grassy land was as infinite as the empire. Sarah Simmons lived in Grote's Place, one street back from the heath.

Maureen trotted up the stairs to number three but couldn't find a doorbell. She knocked with the heavy brass knob, heard the clip-clop of court shoes on stone, and the door opened. Sarah was dressed for work in a white blouse, navy blue skirt and matching tights and shoes. She looked Maureen over, took in her expensive overcoat, her cheap trainers and her heavy bag. 'Hello, hello, Maureen,' said Sarah, drawing it out as if she'd have nothing to say when the greeting was over. 'How are you?'

'Hi, Sarah, not bad,' said Maureen, smiling. 'How's yourself?' She noticed once again, as she had all the way through university, how rough her accent sounded.

Sarah stepped aside and invited her in. 'Come,' she smiled, 'come into the humble abode. Most welcome.'

Maureen walked into the hall and looked up. 'Oh, Sarah,' she said, before she could stop herself.

'Nothing much,' said Sarah, blushing with shame and pleasure. 'Granny's old house.'

The hall was fourteen foot high with black and white floor tiles, walls papered in textured *fleur-de-lis*, and hung with blue-black portraits of bearded men in naval uniforms. A high wooden staircase clung to the wall on the right with a black wood balustrade. The house was very still. Maureen pointed at the paintings. 'Who are these fantastic men?' she said.

'Relatives,' said Sarah. 'Deceased. Mostly from syphilis. Look, I have to leave for work in half an hour. I'd leave you here but I don't have a set of spare keys.' They looked at each other. Sarah smiled weakly and slid her gaze to the floor. 'I can give you a lift into town if you'd like?'

Maureen nodded. Sarah didn't trust her. All she knew was that she and Maureen had had little in common at university and Maureen had been mentally ill since then. 'That's fair enough,' she said, neglecting convention and responding to the subtext.

Sarah steered her to the back door, turned her round and lifted her coat by the shoulders, helped her out of it and hung it on a coat peg. 'Come,' she slipped her arm through

Maureen's, 'and have a little breakfast with me. Come and tell me everything that has happened to you. You must be famished. How's your hunky brother?'

The tentative pals walked into the Aga-warmed kitchen where Maureen sipped her tea and gave Sarah a disinfected summary of her last four years. Her time in hospital with mild depression, how Liam's business had done so well he could pay his way through uni, about her boyfriend, Douglas, who'd died of a heart-attack, and how her mother didn't keep terribly well at all. Sarah was sad for her, happy for her and sad again, as the story dictated. She put on her makeup at the table as Maureen finished spinning a tattered web of half-truths, then took her turn.

Sarah had been engaged to Hugo at the tail end of her university career but their relationship just hadn't worked out, they weren't as suited as they had imagined. Maureen had met Hugo briefly when he came up to attend the graduation ball. He was a thick-lipped, over-bred, rugby-shirted haw-haw. He didn't seem interested in Sarah, much less in love with her, and Maureen was glad she hadn't married him. Anyway, Sarah got her dream job at an auction house and was working hard and getting promotion and good work to do all the time, it was great and she had the house so money wasn't a worry. You see, she knew everyone here, in this area, so she had a ready-made circle of friends locally. And the local people were *so* friendly. They went out all the time. Sarah's lies were so bright and cheerful that Maureen felt sorry for her. She was a nice woman, and Maureen wished something nice had happened to her but the big house felt cold and Sarah seemed bereft and needy.

'Right,' said Sarah, taking a drink of tea and leaving most of the lipstick she had just applied on the rim of the cup, 'let's go. Where are you off to?'

Maureen said she was going to Brixton. Sarah frowned

at the mention of the area. She said she wasn't headed that way but Maureen could get a train straight there from the station at the bottom of the hill and insisted she'd drive Maureen and drop her. The station was a quarter of a mile away. Maureen wondered why she had agreed to her coming to stay at all. She could just have said no.

'Sarah,' lied Maureen, 'you're a pal.'

Joe McEwan sat back in his chair and lit his fifth smoke of the morning. He was thinking about her again. The harder he tried to avoid it the more she came to mind. His mother had died a month and a half ago and he knew he was coping badly, losing his temper, working too much, giving into the fags again. Whenever he relaxed or took his mind off his work for any length of time there was Patsy, waiting for him, her hand, her voice, her eyes. He had been sitting at home, alone and maudlin, sorting through her papers, the night before when the call had come through about Hutton. It was exactly what he needed: a big investigation with city-wide implications.

Hutton had been killed for dealing on his own. He was one of the new generation pushing their way up the ranks, one of the worst side effects of Operation No-go. The success of the operation was a mixed blessing. It pushed prices and profits up, turned already vicious men into animals and it meant more dead junkies in shopping-centre toilets. As new dealers sprang up to replace the old ones they sold virtually pure heroin to their first few clients so that word would get around that they did good deals. An OD brought the punters to the dealer's door like an advertising campaign. But the old powers were still battling for control, and the nature of Hutton's injuries was meant as a warning to other aspiring entrepreneurs.

McEwan knew Hutton. He had seen him in court several

years before when he had battered his neighbour. The Sheriff asked him why he was nicknamed 'Bananas' and Hutton's sodden junkie eyes darted around the room. 'I like bananas,' he said, and the public benches laughed. 'I could eat them all day.' He tried to bring his purported love of fruit into every answer thereafter, labouring the joke, playing up to the public, irritating the Sheriff and drawing the court's attention to his confused mental state. It was as if he thought the public benches were deciding his fate.

A sudden knock at the door heralded DI Inness's first visit of the day. Inness had been getting the brunt of McEwan's recent moods. He knew it was wrong, he knew he shouldn't allow himself the luxury, but he found Inness deeply annoying. And the more he bullied him, the more Inness sucked up to him.

'Sir,' he said, stepping into the office clutching a piece of paper. Inness always carried a bit of paper, as if his mum had given him permission to be in the police force. It was a standing joke at the station. When he was off duty and didn't have his bit of paper he always carried a plastic bag. 'The DI and the DC from the Met are downstairs. D'you still want me to handle it?'

'Yeah, I'll sit in. Take them to conference room two, please,' said McEwan, starting the day as he started every day, meaning not to pick on him.

Inness showed them in and DI Williams and DC Bunyan took their seats at the table without being invited. Williams was a pudgy man with a bald head and small gold glasses. Bunyan was a pretty little thing, petite and slim with short blonde hair and a modest trace of pale lipstick. They were dressed in smart dark suits, he in trousers, she in a skirt that just reached her knees, and McEwan didn't altogether approve. If they had been from any other region he wouldn't have bothered attending but they were the Met and he wanted them to know whose patch they were on.

'First of all, thank you for your co-operation, sir,' said Williams, and McEwan recognized the accent. 'It's been very helpful.'

'You from the south side?' asked McEwan.

'Aye,' said Williams, and he smiled. 'My da was a copper. Govan, 'sixty-two to 'seventy-nine.'

'Why are you in the Met?'

'Form of rebellion,' he said, and McEwan smiled at him. Regional forces resented the Met. They were considered arrogant and lax. Williams's dad would have hated it.

'Did you stay with your family last night?'

'No, they're all gone now. We stayed in a guest house in Battlefields.'

'That's a bit out of the way.'

''S familiar, though.'

'Yeah.' McEwan signalled to Inness to start the briefing.

Inness flipped through the notes in front of him 'There isn't much intelligence on the deceased,' he said, 'so I don't know how helpful we can be to you. The husband was interviewed when she was first reported missing and he claimed he hadn't seen her since November. Notes say he was a quiet man, very concerned for her safety. The area's not bad, poor but not bad.'

'Who's in the frame at the moment?' asked McEwan.

A little startled by the intrusion, Williams sat up. 'Well,' he said, 'the husband beat her up quite badly before, but we can't place him in London and we haven't had the chance to question him yet.'

'Didn't you go there last night?'

'Yeah,' interrupted Bunyan, 'but we couldn't question him because he hadn't told his kids yet.'

McEwan ignored the short-skirted woman and continued to look at Williams, answering him as if he was the one who had spoken. 'He hadn't told them she was missing?'

'He hadn't told them she was dead,' said Williams. He raised his eyebrows.

McEwan tipped his head to the side and sighed. 'How many kids?' he asked.

'Four,' said Williams.

McEwan shook his head at the notes. 'They've always got kids,' he said heavily. 'All these nightmare couples have got kids.'

'Yes, sir,' nodded Williams. 'Always got kids.'

Williams was quietly spoken, deferential but firm, and McEwan thought he might like him if they worked together.

Inness turned the page on his notebook and started reading again. 'They've got four kids, which you already know, and you know about the Place of Safety Shelter, obviously.'

'Yeah,' said Bunyan, sitting forward and leaning her hands on the desk. 'We're going there later.'

Hugh McAskill knocked on the half-open door and looked in. 'What is it?' said McEwan.

'They've got Hutton's girlfriend downstairs, sir.'

'Well,' said Williams, standing up, 'I can see you've got a lot on so we'll leave ye to it.'

'Right,' said McEwan. 'Well, let us know how you get on. If we can do anything, you know.'

McAskill stood at the door, holding it open for the visiting officers, and followed them out to show them downstairs. Inness lingered in the doorway.

'She's a bit of a hot-shot, isn't she?' said McEwan, assuaging his conscience by giving him credit.

'Yes, sir, she is.'

28

Coldharbour Lane

The passengers had thinned by the time the train reached Brixton. Maureen got off and climbed down the stairs, enjoying a bracing breath of cold air in the street. Everyone in Brixton was dressed for a mild spring and Maureen was ready for the height of a Siberian winter. The sweat from the Underground had dried out, leaving her feeling crusty and damp. She stopped by Woolworth's window and took out her *A–Z*. The lawyer's office was just beyond the high street and Moe Akitza's address was at the top of Brixton Hill, within easy walking distance. The pager in her bag began to sing and she felt for it, finding it at the bottom of her bag under a pair of pants. Jimmy said that the child-benefit book had been cashed yesterday.

She waited at the lights, crossed over to the Ritzy cinema and entered the mouth of Coldharbour Lane. The street ran around the back of Brixton high street, sloping away from it at a forty-five-degree angle. The start of the Lane was busy with bistros and wine bars, small restaurants and tasteful clothes shops. The brave push towards gentrification died suddenly at the intersection of Electric Avenue and the vegetable market. Coldharbour Lane crumbled into a ramshackle ghetto. A big police sign strapped to a lamp-post announced that someone had been shot and killed in the Lane at 2.09 a.m., three days ago, and appealed to the public for information. Next to a shop selling nothing but neon yellow chickens stood a subsiding Victorian inn with a sinking stone portico. It was the Coach and Horses, the pub Mark Doyle had seen Ann in before Christmas. It wasn't open yet but shadowy figures moved inside the small orange windows. It looked dirty and run-down and Maureen could easily see Ann drinking in there. Beyond the eroded brick railway bridge stood a row of pleasantly proportioned Victorian shops. On the corner, behind a bank of call-boxes, was a whitewashed pub called the Angel, and next to it a long office window was barred with vertical strip blinds. It was McCallum and Arrowsmith, Solicitors. Maureen opened the door, tripping a tinkling alarm bell as she walked in, and stood at the counter, trying to attract the attention of a secretary.

'Don't hold your breath.'

A tiny woman, in a fake-fur box jacket was sitting on one of the plastic chairs against the window. She had sun-brushed skin, thin brown hair and buggy, goitrous eyes. She was resting her head against the window, her eyes half shut. She looked like a tiny, very beautiful tropical frog. 'She'll take fucking ages,' she said, her accent a muted upper-class Glaswegian.

For all her worldliness, Maureen found the stranger a bit frightening. But she didn't look dangerous. Her hair was twisted into a loose roll at the back and her little slipper shoes looked expensive.

'Takes ages,' said the stranger.

'Aye, right enough,' said Maureen noncommittally.

Without sitting up the frog woman opened one blood-shot eye. 'Glasgow?'

Maureen nodded a little.

'Whereabouts?'

'Garnethill.'

The tiny woman shut her eye and smiled softly. 'Ah,

Garnethill,' she said. 'I was at the art school. Long time ago.'

Maureen wondered why she was in the lawyer's. She might be a criminal, or getting divorced. Divorce seemed more likely, somehow. She seemed fairly content. A phone rang out on the desk and was intercepted by an answerphone. Maureen remembered why she had come in and turned back to the counter. The office was shallow with two desks standing in front of a door leading to the lawyers' private offices. The young Asian secretary was alone, transcribing something from her headphones. Her hair was permed into tight spirals and hennaed burgundy. She was badly placed to see anyone at the counter but she was aware of Maureen and looked up at her a couple of times, nodding and lifting her hand briefly from the keyboard, letting her know she'd be with her in a minute. Maureen pulled a pen and the service-station notebook out of her bag, and stood at the counter, poised and ready to write, trying to look official.

'Wait till ye see her eyes,' whispered the fur-coated woman.

Maureen wasn't sure she was even talking to her. 'I'm sorry,' she said, 'are you waiting to be seen?'

'Just wait till ye see her eyes.'

Confused by the irrelevant mantra, Maureen smiled. Despite having her eyes shut the tiny woman smiled too and smacked her lips, nestling her head back against the window.

Six long, hot minutes later the secretary took off her headphones, picked up a clipboard and meandered over to the counter. She wore coloured contact lenses of such a pale blue that her pupils looked irradiated, as if the edges of them were melting into the whites around her eyes. Maureen almost let out a little gasp but caught herself. She looked at the frog woman. She still had her eyes shut but she sensed Maureen's intense discomfort and grinned to herself.

'Can I have your name,' asked the secretary, in a clipped lilt, 'the time of your appointment and the name of the person the appointment is with, please?' The dye, the perm and the contacts seemed designed to contradict her every feature, as if she didn't want to be her at all.

'I don't have an appointment,' said Maureen. 'I'd like to talk to you.'

The secretary looked up, startling Maureen again. 'I wanted to ask you a couple of questions,' said Maureen, trying to sound official. 'It'll only take about three minutes. Would that be okay with you?'

'You're not selling stationery, are you?'

'No.'

'Because I'm not authorized to buy anything.'

'No, no, I just want to ask you about something.'

'What is the nature of your inquiry?' she said.

'I wanted to ask you about a man called James Harris.' She let it hang for a minute. 'He came into this office a week ago yesterday. He was under the mistaken belief that this office was a different firm of solicitors.'

The secretary grinned. 'The little Scottish man who thought he was here for a will reading? Like in the films?'

'Exactly,' said Maureen. 'He spoke to you, did he?'

'Yes, he did. He showed me the letter and everyfink.' She smirked. "Course, it was made-up rubbish. We do criminal work and it wasn't even our name. We *used* to be McCallum and Headie but then, of course, Mr Headie left three months ago.'

'And Mr Arrowsmith came on board?'

'Yes.'

'Mr Headie left, did he?' Maureen looked up. The secretary looked uncomfortable but she wasn't giving anything away. 'Did he retire?'

The secretary didn't know what to say. 'Sort of.'

'Right,' said Maureen, jotting 'fuck' in her notebook. 'Did you get on with him?'

'He was a nice man to work for . . .'

'And where is he now?'

The secretary hesitated and glanced at the frog woman. 'He's in Wandsworth, I think,' she muttered.

'Could you give me the number of his new office?'

The secretary sniggered and held her clipboard up to cover her mouth. She tipped to the side to look behind Maureen and the frog woman giggled too. 'I haven't got the number of his office.'

'Well, thank you for your time,' said Maureen, closing her notebook. A shaft of sunlight hit her in the eye and she flinched. 'Thanks again.'

Out in the street the sun was warm and Maureen desperately wanted something sugary to wake her up. The door to the Angel pub was pinned wide to let in the morning air. She glanced inside to see if it was open. It was empty but someone was standing behind the bar, reading a paper and drinking out of a blue mug. 'You open?' she called.

'Naw, I'm waiting for a bus.'

The pub was tastefully furnished with dark wood cladding half-way up the walls and chalky white distemper over the ceiling. Plastic transfer etching on the windows softened the light. The person behind the bar was either a butch woman or a small man with nice skin. Little bumps under the T-shirt gave her away. She watched Maureen's feet as she walked up to the bar and waited for her to speak.

'Can I have a lemonade with ice, please?'

The woman slapped her paper on the bar. She sauntered over to Maureen and poured her drink from a big plastic

235

bottle with a 99p promise printed on the label. 'Quid,' she said, flapping her hand for the money.

'Where's the ice?'

'No ice.'

'You're charging me a quid for a glass when the bottle cost less than a quid?'

''S what it costs,' she said. 'Same price everywhere.'

Maureen gave her a coin. 'There ye are,' she said. 'Ye can restock your entire bar with that.'

The woman screwed the lid back on the bottle and sidled back to her paper. Maureen drank quietly, wondering about the conversation with the secretary and what could possibly be so funny about Mr Headie's new office.

'You in the Salvation Army, then?' The butch lady-man was calling over to her.

'Why?' said Maureen.

The lady-man nodded to her drink. 'Drinking lemonade in a pub.'

'I don't think the Sally Ann come into pubs, do they?'

'They do if they're looking for money.'

Maureen smiled at her glass and took another sip. 'It's nice in here.'

'Yeah,' the woman frowned, 'my friend just done it up. She's got good taste.'

'She has,' nodded Maureen. 'She really has.'

'Course, you can't choose your punters.'

'Rough crowd, is it?'

'Very rough. We were hoping for the lunch trade from the offices but they don't make it up here.'

'What's the Coach and Horses like?'

The woman waved her hand in front of her nose. 'Wild men. Scots and Irish mostly, and you know what they're like, duntcha?' The woman sidled back over to her. 'I know you Scots, tight as gnats' arses, the lot of ya.' She lifted the bottle of lemonade from below the bar and topped Maureen's glass up.

'What was that for?' asked Maureen.

'Don't want you starting fights and frightening away my other customers,' she said, suppressing a smile and shedding ten years.

The light in the doorway was dammed into shadow. It was the little frog woman from the solicitor's office. She walked over to the bar, took a seat five feet along from Maureen and ordered a mineral water. She paid for her drink and nodded to Maureen. 'Eyes, eh?' she said.

Warily, Maureen nodded back. 'Yeah, spooky.' She thumbed backwards to the office. 'Are you waiting for your boyfriend?'

The frog woman bit her tongue between her front teeth and laughed, dropping her chin to her chest. 'Yeah, kind of,' she said. 'Why are you asking about Mr Headie?'

Maureen turned to face her. 'I'm working for a lawyer's firm in Scotland,' she said, thinking fast. 'They asked me to find out about something down here.'

The woman stopped drinking and tipped her head back, looking down her nose at Maureen. 'That's crap,' she said. 'If you were working for a lawyer's firm they'd know about Mr Headie, they'd know where his new office is, they'd've read about it in Law Society newsletters.'

Maureen felt very tired and dirty. 'Mmm,' she said, and ran out of clever ideas. 'Do you know where his office is?'

The woman smiled wryly. 'You don't live here, do you?'

'No,' said Maureen, 'I'm just down this morning.'

'Yeah.' She drank again.

'You know this area well, then, do you?'

The woman smiled at her and leaned over, holding on to the bar. She held out her hand. 'Kilty Goldfarb,' she said.

Tickled, Maureen barked a laugh. 'Fuck off,' she said. 'That's not your name.'

Kilty laughed too, delighted at Maureen's reaction. 'It is,' she insisted. 'My family were Polish and my granny made up the name Kilty in honour of her new homeland.'

Maureen stopped laughing and mumbled an apology.

'You're well cheeky,' Kilty smiled. 'Who are you, anyway?'

'Maureen O'Donnell.'

'That's not exactly an exotic sobriquet, is it?'

'It is if you're from Swaziland,' said Maureen.

Kilty finished her drink. 'Hungry?'

'A wee bit.'

Kilty gestured down the road. 'I know an exotic wee place.'

The gang of skinny teenage boys in various states of customized brown uniforms were swinging their schoolbags around their heads, kicking at each other and laughing. Williams turned to stare them down and Bunyan cringed. 'Leave it,' she said, to the stippled lift doors.

'Leave what?' said Williams loudly.

'Leave it, don't say anything. Look, here's the lift.'

The metal doors slid open and they stepped in.

'I was just watching,' said Williams. He stood at the back of the lift and Bunyan pressed the button. 'You're not afraid of them, are you?'

'Having a fight with a gang of teenage Glaswegian boys isn't my idea of a light relief, sir.' She turned and looked at him. 'Are you sure he'll be in?'

'Yeah,' Williams said. 'He will be. He's not expecting us until two. He'll be in just now, though, getting the children off to school.'

They made their way along the windswept veranda and knocked heavily on James Harris's door. The oldest boy opened it. He was still wearing his pyjamas. He smiled up at Williams, a big happy smile, and said, 'Hiya,' through a rough morning throat. He coughed, clearing the phlegm away. The child sounded like a twenty-a-day smoker.

''Ello,' whispered Bunyan, in her silly childish voice. 'What are you doing still wearing 'jamas, then?'

The boy turned and ran into the living room calling for his da. James Harris had already been out. A shopping-bag sat against the wall by the kitchen and he still had his jacket on. He was sitting in his armchair, dressing the babies for a day out. The wee boys had matching hats and plastic capes on, thin as paper and dark green, not children's colours at all. Harris looked up and saw the police officers standing on the step. He rolled his eyes back and blinked slowly. Williams and Bunyan waited for him to speak. They waited a full minute.

'I thought you were coming at two,' he muttered, reaching out and pulling off the toddlers' hats.

'Why aren't the boys at school?' asked Bunyan.

'John's away already,' said Harris quietly, flattening the little woolly hats on his knee. 'Alan isn't well.'

'I've got a cough,' said Alan, staring adoringly up at Williams.

Williams ignored him. 'We need to talk to you alone, Mr Harris. Can you get the kids to play upstairs for a while?'

'They won't stay up there,' said Harris, staring at his feet.

Williams cleared his throat. 'Then we'll talk to you here, in front of the children. It's up to you.'

Harris looked defeated. 'Alan,' he said, 'take the weans up the stairs.'

'Auch, naw, I'll just stay here,' said Alan. He looked up at Bunyan. 'Ye can talk in front o' me,' he said eagerly, 'and the babies don't even understand words.'

Harris sighed and rubbed his eyes, dragging the thin skin back and forth. 'Take the weans up the stairs, son.'

Kilty Goldfarb took her burger out of the polystyrene box and pulled off the paper.

'Ah, McFood,' she said. 'Reminds me of bonny McScotland.'

Maureen sipped her Coke and nibbled at a cluster of salty chips. 'Have ye been away a long time?'

'Few years.' Kilty thought back. 'Five years? Just after I graduated. Came down to do a social-work course and stayed.' She took a bite out of her burger, stopped to scowl and felt in her mouth with her fingers. She pulled out a slice of green pickle, looked at it as if it was a hair and sat it on a napkin.

'Why did you study social work if you were at the art school?'

'Print-making just didn't seem as important as this. I was going to save the world.'

Maureen sat back. 'D'ye ever think about going home?'

Kilty sighed. 'All the time. It's hard to find a place for yourself down here, it's hard to meet people you have anything in common with. But everyone I knew's moved on, apart from my mum and dad. Don't really have friends up there any more.' She smiled. 'There's no patriot like an ex-patriate. What do you do, apart from the made-up job with the non-existent solicitors?'

'I just left my job, actually. I was working at the Place of Safety Shelters.'

'Right?' Kilty nodded, recognizing the name. 'Why did you leave?'

Maureen tried to think of a way to disguise it but gave up. 'I was shite at it and I was about to get rumbled.

Plus I hated it. Never seeming to get anywhere and the administrative grind, all that bollocks.'

'Not enough drama?'

Maureen nodded and sipped her Coke.

'Know what ye mean,' said Kilty. 'When I started I wanted to run into burning buildings and wrestle wild animals, not fill out forms to great effect. It's a bit of a disappointment, really.' She finished the last bite of her burger and brushed her hands clean. 'Do you have any cigarettes?'

Maureen got out her packet and put them on the table. Kilty took one, watching the tip as she held it in her mouth, and lit it with Vik's lighter, sucking the smoke into her mouth, exhaling it and immediately sucking again. Maureen watched her. 'You don't smoke much, do you?'

Kilty shook her tiny head. She stopped and looked at the cigarette. 'I so want to be a cynical smoker. I keep trying but I can't get the hang of it.'

Maureen reached out and took the cigarette off her. 'Give that to me before you hurt yourself. Who were you waiting for in the lawyer's?'

'Client,' said Kilty, sitting up straight and responsible. 'Young guy. Spot of bother.'

Maureen nodded. 'See, as a social worker, would you know a lot about the benefits system?'

Kilty looked at her, wary and guarded. 'Why?'

'What I'm actually doing here is,' said Maureen, wriggling forward in her seat, 'I'm looking for someone.'

Kilty's eyes urged her on.

'She came to us in Glasgow,' continued Maureen, 'came to the shelter in a terrible way, and then she disappeared but she was seen down here.'

'Are you trying to make sure she didn't go back to the man who beat her up?'

'Yeah,' said Maureen, relieved that her story was scanning out.

'Well,' said Kilty, 'what are you doing in the lawyer's office asking about changes in the partnership and Mr Headie, then?'

Maureen had forgotten all that. 'Oh, see, she got a letter from the firm on the wrong headed notepaper—'

Kilty interrupted. 'But if you're looking for her, who's the little Scottish man?'

Maureen couldn't think of another silly lie to cover up the other silly lies. 'I thought art-school people were meant to be thick,' she said.

Kilty raised each of her eyebrows alternately, wiggling them.

'I can't tell you all her business,' said Maureen, watching the eyebrows, hoping she'd do it again. 'I'm not in a position to do that.'

Kilty looked unreasonably annoyed. 'I'd better get back,' she said, standing up and gathering her fur and her handbag. 'What are you up to tomorrow?'

'Working,' said Kilty.

'On a Saturday?'

'I work Saturdays.'

'D'you want to meet for lunch?' Maureen was talking quickly and sounded desperate. 'I don't know this area at all and she disappeared somewhere around here.'

Kilty was standing over her, looking suspicious.

'I just thought you might know people,' said Maureen. 'Never mind.'

Kilty pulled her coat on and stepped out of the leg-trap table. She lifted her bag strap and swung it over her head. 'In here, tomorrow at twelve?'

'Yeah.' Maureen brightened. 'Twelve.'

'Sounds like you're sitting on a high-drama story.' Kilty

slipped past Maureen to the heavy glass door and used her weight to pull it open. 'I'll wheedle it out of you.' She stepped out into the street.

Maureen dug out Ann's sister's phone number and headed for a pay-phone. Pornographic photographs of vulnerable young women were papered over the inside of the box. The calling cards said the girls were schoolgirls, bad girls, dirty girls, barely legal, French and Swedish, call now.

'Hello, Mrs Akitza?'

'Yes?'

Maureen said that she had come to London on behalf of Jimmy Harris's family and she'd be looking around for the next few days, maybe a week. She wanted to come and see her in about ten minutes but she didn't know the area and she didn't know how to get to the house. The voice hesitated and gave her directions from the tube station. Ann's sister didn't seem very excited about seeing her. She hung up on Maureen without saying goodbye.

29
Gravel

James Harris had been staring at his feet for twenty minutes. A prominent purple vein throbbed under his eye. Bunyan and Williams stood near him, asking questions and waiting for answers that never came. The only times Harris seemed alive were the four times Alan had come back downstairs, banging loudly on the living-room door before opening it and coming in. The first couple of times he claimed he had forgotten something and went back upstairs slowly, carrying a broken toy or a pen. Then he started coming down to get things for the babies, a drink of juice and a bit of bread. Harris sat up when the boy came in, waking up, sitting tall and looking angrily at his eldest son for coming back to save him. At the last visit Alan started crying in the kitchen and wouldn't tell anybody why. He climbed on to his father's knee and refused to get down. Williams took Bunyan into the hall. 'Phone Carlisle on your mobile,' he muttered. 'Tell them we might need an interview room. And try and get hold of the emergency social work here, tell them about the kids.'

Bunyan looked back into the living room. 'Why won't he talk?'

'Jesus, I don't know, but he's obviously got something to say, hasn't he?' He stepped back into the room. 'Mr Harris, we're going to phone the social-work department so that someone can sit with the boys for a while, and we'd like to take you to Carlisle police station to conduct a formal interview.'

Harris stood up, letting Alan slide down his legs. 'No,' he said weakly. 'No. Don't. Please don't.'

'We need you to talk to us and we can't talk here with the boy coming in and out.'

'I'll talk,' breathed Harris. 'I'll talk. Isa'll sit with them. Try Isa.' He bent over and picked up the cushion on the chair. Underneath, in the hollow that springs should have filled, was a shallow pool of correspondence and bits of paper. Harris lifted some pages and found an unfolded fag packet with a number written in pencil. 'Here,' he said. 'She'll come.'

Bunyan slipped out into the hall and tried the number on her mobile but it rang out at the other end. She looked up. Williams and Harris were staring at her.

'Isn't there anyone else?' she said. 'A neighbour or someone?'

'Is she not in?'

'There's no answer.'

Alan stood on the chair and lifted up his arms. 'Mrs Lindsay's a neighbour,' he said simply. 'She's got babies anyway and I'll give her a hand. She likes my drawing as well.' He smiled up at Williams.

'Right,' said Williams hopefully. 'What number house does she live at?'

'Next door,' said Alan, trying to get between his father and the big policeman. 'I'll go an' chap her for ye.'

'Maybe your daddy should do that.'

They all looked at Harris. He walked over to the door with the energy and bounce of a sleepy octogenarian.

'I'll just come with you,' said Williams, trying to sound light-hearted so as not to frighten the boy, taking hold of Harris's arm as he came past.

Bunyan could hear them on the veranda, walking along to a door and knocking, waiting for the answer. In the street below someone was shouting as an engine revved furiously. The next door opened to a gruff female voice. Alan smiled up at Bunyan, a cluster of sharp teeth set in a little pink face. 'I'm not well.'

'You've got a cough,' said Bunyan.

'How can a lady be a debt man?'

'D'you think we're debt men?'

'Aye.' He was grinning, trying to appeal to her.

'Nooo,' she said, and felt her voice changing. 'We're not debt men, we're policemen.'

Alan's face fell and his eyes flickered to the front door. 'What do ye want him for?' he said quickly.

'Just a chat.'

The boy seemed panicked. His eyes darted around the room. If Alan was older Bunyan would have thought he was looking for a weapon.

'You're not gonnae ...' Alan caught his breath ' ... ye won't jail him, will ye?'

'We're just going to talk to him, here, in the house.'

The little boy frowned. 'What'll happen to the babies if ye jail him?' he said, but Bunyan knew what he was asking.

'You'll all be fine,' she said. 'We're just going to have a little chat, that's all. We won't be long.'

Williams and Harris came back through the door. Harris's eyes were redder than before: the purple pressure under his eyes was building. Alan ran forward and grabbed Harris around the thigh. 'I'll stay,' he said. 'I'll stay with yees.'

'You can't stay, darlin',' said Bunyan.

Alan smiled up at Williams, frightened and hopeful. 'Let me stay, I want to stay with yees, ye can talk to me, I'll tell ye things, I'll tell ye.' Harris tried to shake the boy off his

246

leg but Alan clung on. 'I'll stay, Mrs Lindsay only likes babies anyway. She doesn't want me.'

Harris put his hand on the boy's head and pushed him away. 'Get upstairs and dress,' he said.

Alan stepped back and looked at him, muttering a random string of dirty words under his breath. He turned and scampered up the stairs noisily on all fours.

'You should have told the children about their mother,' said Williams. 'This makes it very difficult for us.'

James Harris slumped against the wall, his mouth hanging open.

'Why didn't you?'

But Harris was staring at his feet. 'I just ... I couldn't,' he said.

They could hear the boy upstairs, singing loud mock opera in a kiddie baritone. A door slammed open, smashing off a wall and Alan clattered down the stairs carrying the smallest child, holding the little man under his arms, walking with his legs open so he didn't step on his feet and hurt him. He dropped the little boy on to his feet at the bottom of the stairs and the baby staggered into the living room, holding on to the wall.

'One more to go,' sang Alan, and ran back upstairs again.

Tearfully, Harris put the little hat on the boy and kissed his face as if he'd never see him again.

Bunyan took Williams aside, and pointed upstairs. 'That child is going mental,' she said sternly.

'He's just worried,' said Williams.

An upstairs door slammed open again and Alan shouted a strangled rendition of the climax to 'Ness'un Dorma'. He arrived at the top of the stairs with his laces undone, tugging a grey V-neck over his vest with one hand, holding the older baby's hand. He sang as the baby walked down the stairs one at a time, repeating his favourite bits when he got to the end. He was out of breath when he got to the hall and stood panting and looking at his dad. 'I'll stay,' he said.

'You can't stay,' said Harris, bending down and picking up the smallest baby. He took the other boy's hand. ''Mon,' he said, herding Alan with his knees, out of the door and into the neighbour's hallway.

Mrs Lindsay stood by the door, holding it open as she smoked a Super King fag. She was an eighteen-year-old with two small babies of her own and a voice like Orson Welles. 'When'll ye be back for them?' she gravelled.

They looked to Williams for an answer but he wasn't in the business of comforting anyone.

'Not too long,' said Bunyan.

''Cause I need tae go out later. I cannae watch them past five.'

'We should be finished by then,' said Bunyan.

'Thanks, hen,' muttered Harris, and the policemen took him next door.

30
Moe

Brixton Hill was a broad, fast road. Blocks of high flats lined it, set far enough back across grass or gravel to lend them the looming presence of ugly castles. Further up the hill the blocks were named after rough Scottish towns like Dumbarton, Renton and Steps. Dumbarton Court must have been the designer's dream when it was built. It was a stranded Deco cruise-liner with white balconies running the length of the block and metal railings accentuating the horizontal lines, rounded on the turn. Dead plants, bits of discarded furniture and strings of ragged washing shattered the straight lines of the verandas. Under attack from the sunshine and the exhaust fumes, the whitewash had turned a mottled grey and was peeling off in papery sheets.

Maureen took a turn at Dumbarton Road, as Mrs Akitza had instructed her, and walked round to the back of the block, looking for the entrance. In the back court a gang of teenagers shouted to each other, their squeals amplified in the concrete circle. The entrance to flats one to twenty-nine was a narrow stairwell with an open doorway in white-washed concrete and glass bricks.

It was the stairwell that gave it away. A soup spoon had been dropped when it was burning hot and was now stuck into the plastic flooring. Further up a splurge of vomit had dried on the lower wall. It was too cold to sit on the stairs, and the junkies had left their debris behind them.

She rang the bell, heard steps in the hall beyond the door

and felt herself being looked at through the spy-hole. The door opened and a skinny woman in her late forties looked out at her. Moe's short hair was thick and as yellow as Ann's but the livid pink of her skin had been mitigated by face powder. She was a handsome woman with large green eyes and eyebrows drawn on with brown pencil. She was dressed in a modest A-line brown skirt and biscuit-coloured silk blouse, tucked in at the waist to show off her slim figure.

'Hello, Mrs Akitza?'

'Hah, yes – Maureen?'

Moe shuffled backwards into her hall, swinging her legs as if her hip-bones were fused into her pelvis. She panted incessantly, turning shallow breaths into little 'halls', as if perpetually making tiny, amazing discoveries. 'Hah, thanks for phoning before you came up,' she said, her accent a fusion of open Glaswegian vowels and tiptoed English consonants. 'You gave me a chance, hah, to clean up a little bit. I have to ask you not to smoke, hah, I'm afraid.' She pointed to her chest. 'Bad heart.'

'No bother,' said Maureen, wondering if she could actually smell smoke or if she was remembering it. 'It's good of ye to see me.'

'Go into the front room,' said Moe, shivering at a pain in her arm, 'and sit down, hah. Would you like a cup of tea?'

'That would be lovely, thanks,' said Maureen, stepping into the bright mouth of the front room. She waited until Moe had hobbled into the kitchen before looking at the living room. It was a long, low rectangle with a horizontally barred window running the full length of the outside wall. A large green chenille three-piece suite filled the room. A vase of dead and moulting tulips sat on the windowsill, the black stamens spilt over the floor and sill like a cascade of spent matches. Sunlight shone into the room at an angle, lighting up the soupy dust swirling lazily in the atmosphere.

Evidence of Moe's disability sat around the room: a Zimmer frame stood in front of the sofa and a folded wheelchair leaned against the wall. Maureen went to sit down but found an Eazigrip stick standing upright in the chair. The claw looked sticky, as if someone had been picking up food with it. Maureen stepped away from the chair and saw a badly hidden ashtray tucked under the fringe of the chair. It had a dead cigarette in it. She bent down, holding her hand over the stub. It was still warm. She stood up and smiled.

A concealed panel in the wall shot up and the top of Moe's head appeared in the hatch. She shoved a tea tray on to the shelf. 'I'll, hah, give ye this through if ye don't mind ...'

Maureen took the tray, but couldn't find anywhere to set it down. She had to wait for Moe to hurple into the living room and, bending over with considerable effort, pull over a leather-embossed pouffe. Maureen sat the tray on it, listening to Moe panting hard. 'D'ye not keep well, Moe?' she asked.

Moe patted a hand to her chest. 'Hah, angina,' she said. 'Terrible, hah, affliction.'

'It is,' said Maureen.

'Hah. You said you know Jimmy Harris's family?'

'Aye. I know his cousin and his auntie.'

Quite suddenly, Moe grabbed the back of the armchair and clutched her left shoulder, struggling for breath. Maureen watched her impassively. Moe thought she was from the social. If she was prepared to put on a disability display for a total stranger she must be screwing the brew for a bundle. Angina was worth eighty or ninety quid a week. Plus mobility if she claimed she couldn't walk, hence the fused hips. Moe's attack passed and she looked at Maureen for sympathy, patting her chest. Maureen wanted to slap her leg and challenge her to a hula-hoop competition. 'You sit down, let me get the tea,' she said.

Moe dropped into the armchair, landing on top of the sticky Eazigrip.

'Milk and sugar?' asked Maureen.

'Uh-huh.' Moe watched the tea, looking worried.

Maureen guessed at two sugars, stirred and held the cup and saucer out for her. Moe grabbed hold of the chair arms and pulled herself forward to take the cup. Behind her the sticky Eazigrip toppled against the arm-rest, its tacky claw touching the arm. Moe took the cup and sat back again, pressing the dirt into the chair.

'I'm awful sorry about your sister, Mrs Akitza.'

Moe nodded sombrely. 'Yes, hah, call me Moe,' she said. 'Does Jimmy know you're here?'

'Oh, aye. I wanted to ask ye about Ann.'

'Yes,' Moe sniffed with a dry nose and looked at her lap. 'They took me down to Horseferry Road to identify her.'

'That must have been terrible,' said Maureen, thinking of Douglas.

Moe leaned forward, reaching for a Garibaldi biscuit. Her outstretched fingers missed the plate by three feet. Maureen watched her for a moment, wondering about her, before reaching forward and holding up the plate of biscuits. Moe took one and thanked her, smiling reproachfully, resentful of the pause.

'Did Ann come and see ye when she came to London?'

Moe nodded. 'Yes,' she said, taking a bite. 'Always.'

'Did she come this last time?'

'Came to borrow money. I haven't any money. I can't work because of my condition.'

'When did Ann come?'

'New Year's Eve, hah, the Friday.'

'And that was all she said, could she have money?'

'Yes, she was very scared, hah,' Moe said solemnly, talking slowly. 'Someone was after her. She was running for her life.'

Maureen nodded back.

'Well, she's dead now,' said Moe, and frowned as if her sister had missed a bus. She sipped her tea.

'Jimmy said she was in some state,' said Maureen.

Moe shivered. 'Oh, aye, terrible, hah.'

'He said she was shot.'

'No.' Moe sounded certain and pointed to the back of her head. 'Fractured skull. Hah, her feet was all burned, her hands too.'

Maureen watched her, remembering the morning when she had found Douglas dead in her living room. It had been six months but Maureen still shuddered at the image. Moe had seen her sister less than a week ago. She was trying quite hard but she didn't seem very upset.

'Oh, he told me she was shot in the head.'

'Hah, no. The river made a mess of her face but she wasn't shot. I've never seen anything like it, hah. They'd cut her legs.' She drew little lines around the back of her knees. 'Still had her bracelet on. Our mother gave that to her, as an heirloom. Ann was named for her, you see. Been through all that and, hah, still had it on ... She was never without it. Wore it everywhere.'

She gestured around her wrist, running her fingers slowly over the flat bone. Maureen nodded again, but she had a pretty firm grasp of the whole bracelet concept already. 'Is this the gold one?'

'Hah.'

Outside the dirty window an ambulance me-mawed down the hill. Moe sipped her tea, looking at Maureen. She didn't speak.

'Ye know Ann was in a shelter for battered women before she disappeared?'

'Hah.'

'The police are going to think Jimmy had something to do with her murder—'

'Nice, hah, man, Jimmy,' she interrupted.

'Aye,' said Maureen. 'He is a nice man. Do ye think he hit Ann?'

Moe looked at her Garibaldi and shrugged. 'Hah, I don't know. Ann could be difficult, hah?'

'Because she drank.'

Moe swallowed hard and looked into the shadows. 'It was the drink that killed Ann, really, hah?'

Maureen nodded.

'The company, hah, she kept.' Moe looked sad. 'She was a good girl. She wouldn't have been in that company otherwise.'

'The police phoned Glasgow to tell the home for battered women that Ann was dead and they asked for someone very specifically. Would you know how they got that name?'

'Leslie Findlay at the Place of Safety Shelters. Ann told me when she came here and I told them.'

'Why did she tell ye that name, do ye think?'

'Hah, in case anything happened, I suppose.'

'It was lucky that you remembered her name so well,' said Maureen carefully, 'because otherwise the police might never have known Ann had been in a shelter.'

'Yes, it was. Lucky.'

Maureen pulled the Polaroid out of her pocket and handed it to Moe. 'Do you recognize this man?'

Moe looked at the picture closely. 'No.'

Maureen reached over to take the picture back but Moe was reluctant to give it to her. 'Can I keep it?' she said.

'Why would you want to keep it if you don't know the man?'

'It's got my nephew in it. I might never *see* Ann's children again. I can't hardly go out of the house. I don't keep well.'

'I'm afraid I'll need to keep it.' Maureen had to tug the picture to get it back off her. 'I'll get Jimmy to send you a set of school pictures. Have you got her child-benefit book, Moe?'

Moe was so startled she nearly kicked the tray over. 'No, I haven't, hah, hah, hah,' she panted, her eyes darting around the floor.

Maureen leaned forward and patted her arm. 'Hey, calm down, I'm sorry, I'm just asking.'

'But why are ye asking? I wouldn't do that, it's against the law.' The sunlight spilled over the edge of the windowsill and caught Moe's forehead. Specks of sweat were soaking up the pink face powder.

'I'm upsetting you,' said Maureen. 'I'm sorry. I can see you don't keep well. I hope you've good friends and neighbours down here.'

Moe pursed her lips in disgust. 'They're animals here,' she said. 'Bloody animals. Nothing's safe. A woman was mugged at lunchtime the other day. Broad daylight. They're animals.'

'Oh dear. Well, you've got your man.' Maureen looked around the room. There were no signs of a man at all, no odd shoes left lying around, no jackets, no special armchair positioned in front of the television with the remote balanced on the arm.

'Hah,' said Moe smugly. 'Hah, we've got each other.'

Maureen didn't think she could listen to another incompetent lie without calling her on it. She gave Moe a copy of her pager number and stood up to leave.

'It's nice tae hear your accent,' said Moe, burring on

the Rs with wide-open vowels, showing herself. 'You're Glaswegian.'

Maureen smiled. 'Aye.'

'I married a Londoner. He can't live in Scotland – we couldn't even go home to visit for a long time. He's black, ye see.'

'Aye,' said Maureen, thinking of the bald man on the bus and feeling the shame of her people. 'I'm sorry about that. Have ye been married long?'

'Fourteen years. They're terrible racists, the Scots.'

'Well,' said Maureen, 'I'm sure you're right.'

Moe hoisted herself out of the armchair and led her through the hall to the front door.

'Hah. Ann led a terrible life,' she said heavily.

Maureen patted her arm and thanked her for her time. She walked down the first flight of stairs, hearing the regular pant, pant of Moe behind her. Moe had been married to the same man for fourteen years and rarely left the house, but she still took good care of her appearance. It was as likely as peace in Africa.

She would have sold her soul for a lie-down. She walked back down the hill, down the high street and up the stairs to the overhead train station. When the Dartford express arrived she found a seat near the doors. She sat on the warm train, wishing to fuck she could smoke, her ankles burning from the hot radiator under her seat, the chilly breeze from the open window making her eyes water. She closed her burning eyes for a moment. It was lovely to be here, lost in Ann, away from Michael and Ruchill, where Winnie couldn't find her and Vik couldn't demand an answer.

She tried phoning Leslie's house from Blackheath station but couldn't get an answer. Without making a conscious choice she pressed follow-on call and dialled Vik's house.

'Hello?' said Vik.

'Hello, how are ye?' said Maureen, her heart thundering in her throat, distorting her voice to a quiver. 'I thought I'd give ye a ring and see how ye are.'

'I'm fine.'

'I've, um, got your lighter.' She was trying to sound breathy and casual but it wasn't working. She sounded as if she was about to cry.

'Oh,' said Vik stiffly, 'I left it.'

'Yes. It was under the settee.' She nodded into the phone and they waited, each for the other to say something and make it all right between them.

'Did ye think about what I said?' he said.

'I did, Vik, I did.' She blanked out again, cringing into the receiver and wishing she hadn't phoned.

'Why did you phone me?'

Her heartbeat was so loud she could hardly hear him. 'I thought about what you said, Vik, I want that too. I don't know if I'm capable. I miss you here.'

'Are you in London?'

'Yeah, I'm here, yeah.' She shouldn't have phoned. She took a deep breath and shut her eyes. 'Vik, I want to be happy and content but I'm not. I don't know what to do about it.'

'I'm not asking you to get happy for me, Maureen, I just don't want to get all the shit for you not being happy.'

'How's your tummy?'

''S okay.'

They listened to each other breathing for a while.

'My money's running out,' she said, as the urgent beeps began.

'Gonnae phone me again?'

'Tomorrow?'

And the phone cut out.

31

From C to T with N and U

Black rainclouds were gathering outside the window and the air temperature in the damp flat had dropped dramatically. Bunyan and Williams both had their coats done up and they were cold. Bunyan wondered how the family managed to live in these temperatures. Williams was losing patience with Harris and had changed tack from curious stranger to bullying shit. Dakar was right, he was very good. Kindly interest hadn't worked on Harris, they both wanted to get home for the weekend and Jimmy Harris was not a difficult man to be unpleasant to; in fact, he was a hard man to like.

'Jimmy,' said Williams, 'what we need to know now is what happened to Ann between her leaving you and arriving at the shelter.'

'I never hit her,' said Harris.

Williams sighed. He had been standing for over an hour and his feet were throbbing.

'Jimmy,' he said softly, 'we can't keep just going over the same bits. Can we leave aside whether or not you hit her for a minute – just a minute? We'll come back to that—'

Harris interrupted him. 'But I never.'

'That is as may be,' said Williams, 'but what we are concerned about just now is finding out what happened to Ann when she left you. It seems that she was up and down on the bus to London. Now, her sister saw her each time but she wasn't staying with her. Can you think of anyone

258

else she knew down there?' Harris looked blank. 'Any friends or workmates? Relatives maybe?'

'She owed a lot of money,' said Harris.

'So you've said.'

'I never hit her.'

Williams sighed again. 'So you've said.' He tapped Bunyan on the arm and motioned for her to give Harris a fag.

She opened the packet and leaned across, flicking open the packet. 'Want one, Jimmy?' she said.

Jimmy Harris's eager eyes caressed the packet of Silk Cut. His tongue slid past the sharp teeth and licked at the corner of his thin lips. 'Yes, please,' he said, without having the wit to reach out and take one.

Williams didn't like him at all. There was something sly about him, something small and base. Williams liked to place interviewees in the classroom, imagine where they would come in the natural order of things, how they would relate to others and react to authority. Harris was one of nature's victims. The other children would take the piss, hit him, kick him, and he'd get up smiling and try to play with them.

'Well, take one, then,' said Williams softly.

Harris reached out slowly, watching Williams and Bunyan, as if he expected them to slap his hand away. He fumbled a cigarette out of the packet and retracted his hand quickly. Williams didn't smoke himself but it was an interesting feature of the interview, the sudden, misplaced sense of community that came in a fag break.

Bunyan leaned across to give him a light and something on the floor caught her eye. 'Sorry,' said Bunyan, leaning down by the side of the chair. 'May I?'

Harris nodded his consent and Bunyan picked up a bundle of photos from the floor.

'Jimmy,' said Williams, 'what can you tell me about Ann?'

Harris shrugged and inhaled. 'She drank. A lot.'

'She was badly beaten, very badly beaten. She told everyone that you did it.'

'I never. I'd never ever hit her.'

'Do you think it's wrong to hit a wife?'

Harris nodded, shaking his head up and down. His thinning hair fell over his ear and he brushed it back.

'But sometimes,' Williams was talking softly, siding with him before the pounce, 'a wife might do something unforgivable, like hurt the kids or go off with someone else.'

Harris was shaking his head again. He was disagreeing before he'd even heard what Williams was going to say.

'Would it be wrong,' said Williams, 'to hit a wife who spent the food money on drink, for example?'

Harris looked up and realized that they were staring at him, expecting him to speak. 'Shouldn't hit people,' he said.

'You should never hit people?' said Williams indignantly. 'You mean if someone was hurting your kids you'd just let them?'

Jimmy Harris stared at the floor. He was there, someone was hurting his kids, the bruises around his eyes darkened, the tremble in his hand magnified. 'God, no,' he said.

'You'd let people hurt your children and stand by and do nothing?'

'No. No.'

'What would you do then?'

Harris opened his mouth to speak and realized the trap. He kept his pointed little teeth together to stop himself from speaking and dropped his eyes to his lap.

'It's not always wrong to hit someone, is it?' said Williams

Harris looked at the floor and took a drag on his fag. His eyes began to fill up. He was going to cry, it was good, it was good, he was going to cry and a crying man has no defences. Wet guilty tears gathered in his piggy eyes. He was playing with his fag, tapping it frantically into the saucer, he was about to break.

'Where did you get these?' said Bunyan. Williams stared at her. Harris was about to break and she was changing the fucking subject. Bunyan handed the photos to Williams and he looked at them. They were pictures of the dead woman.

'They're Christmas pictures, aren't they?' Bunyan asked Harris. 'It's Christmas at the Place of Safety Shelter.'

'Aye,' said Harris.

She looked at him curiously. 'But, Jimmy, you said you hadn't seen her since November.'

Harris looked confused. 'It's just pictures.'

Williams smiled. 'Jimmy,' he said, continuing to smile with his mouth long after his eyes had stopped, 'you said Ann hadn't come back to the house after she went into the shelter?'

'That's right,' Harris nodded emphatically, 'she didn't.'

'So, you haven't seen her since before Christmas, have you?'

'Not since November.'

'No.'

'No contact at all?'

'No.'

'Now, listen carefully,' said Williams, speaking slowly, 'if a person left point A with item X ...' He held the photos over to his right, looking up to see Harris's face. He was watching the photos. ' ... and the person goes to B ...' He moved his hand and the photos to the left and Harris's eyes followed them carefully. ' ... how could item X ...' Williams threw the photos into Harris's lap. ' ... be found in C?'

Harris was staring at the photos, puzzled by the sum.

'The photos,' Williams spoke as if he was sharing a

confidence, as if he was on Harris's side, 'how could they be in your house if Ann hadn't been back?'

Harris looked up. 'But they came through the door,' he whispered. 'I thought – a girl I know – she put them through the door.'

Williams shook his head. Harris's eyes glazed over and he looked up. The game was up. He was going to confess.

'They were put through my door,' he whispered. 'I never seen her.'

'You never saw her,' said Williams, correcting his grammar without meaning to. 'Like you never hit her?'

'I wouldn't hit her,' said Harris, squirming on his chair, panicking, losing what little composure he had. 'I wouldn't ever, never hit her. I wouldn't.'

'Wouldn't you hit her if she was hurting the kids?'

But Harris was crying, staring at the ashtray, baring his yellow teeth and sobbing. The kids were the problem. He'd confess if he thought the kids were safe. He wanted to confess or he wouldn't have kept the photos.

Williams gave her the nod and Bunyan slipped out to the hall and phoned ahead. The receptionist at Carlisle police station told her to come any time this afternoon. He said there was no need for them to book an interview room, they were usually quiet on Friday evenings. Getting through to the social worker was much harder. Bunyan got through to an answerphone message, which gave her the number of another answerphone, which gave her the number of a mobile that rang out for thirty-odd rings. She slipped back into the room and muttered to Williams that she couldn't get through.

'Jimmy,' said Williams, 'we're going to take you to Carlisle police station for a formal interview now. Before we phone the emergency social-work department and get them to send someone over, is there no-one who could sit with the kids?'

'Auntie Isa?'

'She's still not in, Jimmy. Your kids'll be fine with the social worker.'

'I'm worried about them.'

'Why are you so worried?'

Bunyan shifted against the wall. Williams didn't have kids. If he had kids he wouldn't have asked that question. Williams seemed to think there was something sinister about Harris's fear of the social work but Bunyan understood. She provided a clean house for her family, cupboards full of food, central heating on all the time, judging by the bills, and she still wouldn't want her parenting assessed by a government official.

'Don't phone,' said Harris, crying and trying to talk through his gaping mouth. 'Please ... for fucksake.'

Williams stepped forward. 'Who don't you want us to phone, Jimmy?'

Harris was sobbing now and they were ashamed for him. He could hardly catch his breath to speak. 'Please don't.'

'Who, Jimmy? Who don't you want us to phone?'

'Social work,' he said. 'Don't phone the social work.'

Williams glanced at Bunyan and crouched by the chair. 'Why don't you want us to phone them, Jimmy? Do they know you? Have they been here before?'

'Jimmy,' interrupted Bunyan, 'is there someone else we could phone? Someone else who could sit with the boys and set your mind at rest?'

Harris sat up. 'Leslie,' he said, 'Isa's daughter, but I don't know her address. She'll live in the Drum.'

Bunyan nodded encouragingly. 'Is Leslie married?'

Harris looked even more bewildered.

'Has she married and changed her name?' asked Bunyan.

'Oh, no. I don't think so.'

'So, her surname's Findlay too?'

Jimmy Harris nodded eagerly. 'She'll live in Drumchapel. All the Findlays live there.'

Bunyan slipped out into the hall again. She was trying directory inquiries when it occurred to her that the name was familiar. She'd heard it recently, in connection with the dead woman's sister in Streatham, but she couldn't recall the context. The operator gave her the number and as she called the house she repeated the name over and over to herself. 'Hello, Leslie Findlay?'

'No,' said Cammy, 'Leslie isn't in just now.'

'My name is DC Bunyan from the Metropolitan Police. I'm trying to contact Ms Findlay in relation to her cousin James Harris. Could you tell me how I could get hold of her?'

'Ye could phone her work.'

'Where is that?'

'Place of Safety Shelters. If ye can't get her they'll take a message.'

Sarah was very tired. Her crisp blouse was flaccid, her hair looked dull and she had changed her shoes into a pair of badly burst men's leather slippers. She couldn't even get excited by the fresh Chelsea buns Maureen had bought in the village and they used to be her favourite. She showed Maureen upstairs to her bedroom. 'This should do you,' she said.

The cornicing on the ceiling was a continuous run of delicate leaves and grapes. The bed was large and soft. At the foot of it, balanced on a stool, stood a white plastic television with a rotation knob. A little door at the side of the room led up a step into a black marble *en suite* bathroom with blistered mirrors on the wall and verdigris stain dribbling from the taps. 'Perhaps you'd like a wash before dinner?'

'I don't think I can stay awake for dinner,' said Maureen, and Sarah looked relieved.

'Well, feel free to go straight to bed,' she said. 'Make yourself at home. There's hot water and plenty of towels.'

'If I ever go into labour in anyone's house, I want it to be yours.'

Sarah didn't understand the joke but she saw Maureen smiling and mirrored her. She must have had a rotten day.

'Thanks for letting me stay,' said Maureen.

'You are most welcome,' said Sarah.

Maureen took a bath but the water was so hard she could barely muster a head of foam from the soap and an oily husk formed on the surface of the water. She dried herself with a towel and her skin felt scaly, squeaking like a glass fresh from a dishwasher.

When she came out of the bathroom she found a silver galley tray on the little table by the bed. Sarah had brought her a big mug of tea and a lukewarm plate of strong kedgeree. As Maureen ate, her eye fell on the bedside table and a crumbling black leather Bible held together with elastic bands, set at an angle, pointing at her bed. Sarah must have a hundred family Bibles. Maureen climbed across the bed, turning on the black and white telly before lifting the cold linen sheets and sliding in. She fell asleep listening to a television consumer programme warning her to be very, very careful which dealer she bought her Land Rover from.

Leslie knocked at the door softly and stepped back. The sharp wind whirled down the veranda, gathering the litter and dust into rustling bundles in the far corner. If it wasn't to save Isa she wouldn't have promised to come over after work. She knocked again and the door was opened by a small blonde in a severe suit.

'Hello, Leslie?'

'Yeah, are you Bunyan?'

'Come in.' She opened the door wide and Leslie saw Jimmy sitting in his armchair, looking knackered and terrified. He raised his hand in a limp greeting and she nodded back. His eyes were very red. The babies were sitting on the floor in front of him, and Alan, the boy she had met the night before, was standing behind him holding on to the top of Jimmy's arm as if he was huckling him. A fat bald guy with gold specs stood in the middle of the living room, holding a bunch of photographs and watching her. The wee boy from the Polaroid looked around the door at her. 'Hiya,' he said, and looked at her crash helmet. 'Are you a polis?'

'No.' Leslie stepped into the hall. It was freezing in the flat and she wished to fuck she'd brought a jumper. She looked at the woman. 'Why do ye have to go all the way to Carlisle?'

'Oh,' the woman rolled her eyes, 'we want to tape the interview and because we're an English force it has to be in England.'

'That's a bit mad, isn't it?'

'Yeah.'

'Leslie,' said Jimmy, 'thanks for coming over.'

'No bother, Jimmy,' said Leslie. 'Are ye just off then?'

The woman in the suit looked at the fat guy and he looked at Leslie. 'Actually, Ms Findlay, we wanted to talk to you as well.' His accent was tempered Glaswegian and he breathed in as he spoke, swallowing his words.

'Tae me?' said Leslie, sensing that something was amiss. 'What about?'

'I understand you work at the Place of Safety Shelters?'

Leslie frowned.

'Could I ask you to step outside with me for a minute?'

Leslie looked at Jimmy's blank face. The fat guy led her back through the hall and on to the windy balcony, pulling the door shut behind him. 'I'm very sorry,' he said, and smiled, 'I didn't introduce myself. I'm DI Williams, Arthur Williams, from the Met.' He leaned on the balcony ridge and looked out over the traffic, at the big orange buses stopping to pick up passengers and the cars trapped behind them. 'Do you know anything about the circumstances under which Mrs Harris left the shelter?'

'Yeah, I do, I told you guys about it on the phone. She got a letter or something and disappeared a couple of hours later.'

The fat guy clicked his fingers and pointed at her as if he had just remembered. 'That's right, it came in the post and you couldn't understand how anyone would know the address.'

Leslie took out her fags and cupped her hand around the lighter as she lit up. 'I think I know what she got in the letter as well.'

'What?'

'A photograph. A Polaroid that was left among her things. It's a picture of her kid,' she thumbed back to the house, 'the second one. He was with a pretty heavy guy.'

'Do you still have the Polaroid?'

Leslie took a draw and exhaled into the wind. 'Ah, no, I don't, my friend's got it.'

'Can you get it for me?'

'Well, I can't contact her just now.'

The fat guy nodded over the street. 'I see, I see.' He reached into his pocket. 'I've got one of you, actually.' He pulled out a handful of photos and looked through them, his face lighting up when he found what he was looking for and he handed it to her. 'See?'

Leslie looked at the picture. It was Christmas Day at the shelter. Ann and Senga and the other residents were standing stiffly in front of the plastic tree. Leslie was behind them, growling at the camera, her pupils fiery red. The timer had run out but the camera had failed. She was cursing and just about to come round and see what had gone wrong when it finally went off. 'That's right,' she smiled, 'that's me. Where did you get these?'

'Where do you think I got them?'

'From the office?'

'Nope.'

He was smiling quite benignly, seemed quite personable, and Leslie didn't feel a threat. She handed the picture back to him. 'Well, you must have got it from the office. We only had eight copies done, one for the office and one for each resident.'

'Are you sure?'

'Yeah, I'm sure. I had the copies made. I know there were eight copies.'

The fat man stood up straight and licked the back of his teeth. 'These,' he said, pointedly, 'are Ann's.'

She snorted a laugh. 'Nah,' she said. 'Ann left hers at the shelter. I've got Ann's copies.'

'We found these in Mr Harris's house.'

She was suddenly aware that it was no accident. The fat guy had placed himself between herself and the stairs.

'If I was working on the assumption that Mr Harris killed his wife,' he said, his quiet voice barely audible above the traffic, 'I'd have to explain how he found her again after she went into hiding, wouldn't I?'

Leslie leaned heavily on the balcony and took a long, deep draw on her fag. 'Look, I've been working there for four years, paid and unpaid. D'ye think I'd jeopardize all that to tell him she was there? I just met this joker for the first time last night.'

Fat bloke was very surprised. 'Last night?'

'Yeah,' said Leslie aggressively. 'Last night.'

'But he's your cousin.'

'*We lost touch.*'

'So, an attractive young woman like you would drop everything on a Friday night and come over and babysit for him? Offer to stay the night if necessary? He must have made quite an impression.'

She shook her head adamantly. 'Listen, I'm not doing it for him. If I don't babysit my mum'll do it and she's got a heart condition.'

But he wasn't listening, he was looking at the bundle of photographs in his hand. 'You had the copies made, did ye?'

32
Smoky Lemon

Maureen woke up at six o'clock and found the television still on at her feet. She hadn't dreamed of anything but still couldn't get back to sleep. She knew Sarah would be uncomfortable if she wandered around the house on her own so she stayed in her room and had another bath. After watching half an hour of Stock Exchange news on breakfast TV her sense of probity gave way to her desire for a coffee and a fag. She put the dirty dishes from last night's dinner on the tray and crept quietly downstairs to the kitchen.

The Aga had cooled during the night but still gave off a little warmth and Maureen pulled a chair over to it, sitting with her hip against it, hanging over the griddle with her cup of coffee. Sarah had left a bundle of Jesus pamphlets on the table. Each had a catchy title on the cover and mesmerizingly bad drawings of Aryan Jesus telling some black people what to do, Jesus having a laugh with some sheep, baby Jesus chortling in a manger. Sarah had never been into religion, as far as Maureen knew. She vaguely remembered her referring to her family as high Church of England, implying that in some way this was Catholicism by another name.

The windows at the back of the kitchen looked out on to a long, immaculate lawn with deep borders, cloaked in freezing fog. Sarah's life must be an aesthetic delight; she must cast her eye over lovely things every day. Maureen had been so busy keeping her head above water that she had forgotten the significance of having beautiful things around her, things she wanted to touch and look at. She thought of Jimmy and the paucity of charm in his life, the incessant nag of need and want. The child-benefit book had been cashed and she felt sure that Moe, the Giro Magnet, would know something about it. Maureen was still sure Jimmy hadn't done it. He said he'd only been in London for a day and the mattress still bothered her.

She searched all the cupboards and set the table for a formal breakfast. She warmed the tea-pot and put out thick-cut marmalade and cereal bowls. She brought two small camellia blossoms in from the garden and put them in a glass of water, sitting them on the table as a centrepiece. The red flowers clashed with the blue striped Cornishware, making the table look Christmassy and cheerful.

Carrying her fags and Vik's lighter, she pulled open the back door and stepped out into the restful garden, lit a fag and looked around her. In the very far distance she could hear the distant rumble of the city. The milky fog was lifting from the ground, floating above the grass, rising up to meet the morning. Maureen inhaled and felt the nicotine trickle into her system, tickling her fingers, opening her hair follicles, placating the angry rims of her eyes, kicking her into the day. She looked back into the kitchen and saw a three-foot-high pile of old newspapers tucked away into the recess by the back door, awaiting recycling. She finished her fag quickly, rubbing it out on the stone step and binned the ragged filter.

She lifted out all the *Evening Standards* for the previous week, Monday to Monday, and took them over to the clear end of the large table. She skimmed through, looking for some mention of the murder. It would have taken the police a few days to identify Ann and trace her back to the shelter. They had phoned the office looking for Leslie on Tuesday so Maureen checked last Thursday's edition but found nothing. She went back and checked the Friday edition again and found nothing. She checked Monday, poring over the smallest story, trying to get a lead. She was reading a tiny story about an art fair when she looked up to rub her eyes and spotted it: 'Bike Crash Leads to Gruesome Find'. A guy on his way to work had been involved in a motorbike accident and landed on a mattress on the riverbank with a body inside it. The man had no comment but a member of the Thames division said that the body matched the description of a missing woman. The police were treating the woman's death as suspicious. The next day's edition named her as Ann Harris, a woman reported missing by her sister only days before. Maureen tidied away the papers and went back out to the garden for another smoke.

She found it bizarre that Moe had reported Ann missing. Ann didn't live with her, she had been missing before, and Maureen knew a bit about the reality of living with a drinker. If Ann was away on a binge, and the police found her and brought her back, she'd be looking for money and bringing trouble. Mood swings and grandiloquent claims went with the territory in alcoholic families and Ann saying she was running for her life was probably a monthly occurrence. If Moe was screwing the brew she definitely wouldn't want to draw official attention to herself. It didn't make sense for Moe to report her missing.

Sarah appeared at the kitchen door in a man's old tartan dressing-gown and the exploding leather slippers. 'Good morning, good morning,' she said. 'Oh, you've set the table?'

'Sarah, you've been so sweet to me.' Maureen stood up. 'I'm making you breakfast this morning.'

Sarah all but clapped her hands with glee. 'Oh, how lovely,' she said, and sat down at her place while Maureen made the toast. They were half-way through breakfast when

Sarah put her fingertips on the bundle of Jesus pamphlets and pushed them across the table to Maureen. 'Why not have a read while you're eating?' she said.

Maureen smiled. 'You're fucking joking, aren't you?' she said, and the atmosphere deteriorated from there.

Maureen was on the wrong train. She got off at London Bridge and began the long walk to Brixton. It was only nine o'clock and she didn't have much to do before she met Kilty Goldfarb again. As she walked she looked up at the office blocks, a thousand windows with forty, fifty workers behind each of them every day of the week, each one trying to believe that they were the central character in the big movie, heads down, pretending that no-one else existed, as if the knowledge of their number was too much to bear. And it was. Maureen was utterly convinced of her own insignificance.

She walked through the underpass at the Elephant and Castle, enjoying the sense that nothing really mattered, not the truth about the past, nor whether they believed her, not Winnie's drinking or Vik's ultimatum. It was the perfect place to escape from a painful past. She could waste years at home trying to make sense of a random series of events. There was no meaning, no lessons to be learned, no moral, none of it meant anything. She could spend her entire life trying to weave meaning into it, like compulsive gamblers and their secret schema. Nothing mattered, really, because an anonymous city is the moral equivalent of a darkened room. She understood why Ann had come here and stayed here and died here. It wouldn't be hard. All she had to do was let go of home. She would phone Leslie and Liam sometimes, say she was fine, fine, let the calls get further apart, make up a life for herself and they'd finally forget.

She heard the noise and continued walking, expecting it

to pass her, but it remained constant and she realized that it was the pager. Liam wanted her to phone him at home. Her pulse quickened at his name, as if she had been lost and reclaimed immediately.

'Come home right now.'

'What?'

'Maureen, Neil Hutton's been found dead. He was assassinated.'

Maureen frowned. 'Like what? By a sniper?'

'He was shot up the arse. I think even Mossad would have trouble making that shot.'

'But I've just this minute got here.'

'Look, the way they killed him is a warning about something, and until we know what it's a warning about, you have to come home.'

'Keep your knickers on, Liam. I'm asking her older sister about her debts and stuff like that, I'm not getting into a drugs war.'

Liam sighed and she could feel him thinking hard. 'Please, Mauri,' he said quietly, 'please come home.'

'What is it really? Is it something to do with Michael?'

'No,' he shouted. 'It's about Hutton!'

'Don't you shout at me.'

'You wanker!' shouted Liam. 'They shot him up the fucking arse, Maureen.'

'God, keep the head, I'm not doing anything dangerous down here.'

'Maureen, if she was muling for him and you're asking about her they'll kill ye!' Liam sounded almost hysterical. 'They shot him up the arse, Mauri. Think what they'd do to you.' It took four pounds in small change for Maureen to convince Liam not to panic, that Sarah's house was safe and she would be home really soon, next couple of days tops. He made her promise that if she got a scare of any kind she would phone him, he'd book a flight on his credit card and she could be home within three hours.

'I've got loads of money,' she said. 'I can book it myself.'

'And listen,' he said, 'don't mention my name to anyone. Don't even tell anyone your name.'

'Why?'

'They might connect us with each other.'

'Right,' she smiled, ''cause we're the only two O'Donnells in Britain.'

Liam paused so long that she thought they had been cut off. 'Hello, Liam? Liam, are ye still there?'

'You have no idea,' he was muttering, almost to himself, 'no fucking idea what goes on.'

Maureen passed the door, trying to look inside and antici-pate the clientele, but the small windows had been back-coated with orange reflective plastic and any apparent move-ment inside was actually a reflection of the street. She opened the door and walked in, standing tall, trying to make an impression. The pub split into two rooms just inside the door with a continuous bar running through both. To the left was a room for the serious drinkers, with tables and ashtrays and little else. The room on the right had pictures on the wall and a dartboard, closed over like a travelling altarpiece. The pub smelt strongly of stale cig-arette smoke tainted by an industrial lemon scent. Maureen remembered the smell from her time working in the Apollo box office. It was industrial spray sold in gallon containers, guaranteed to cover any smell. The cleaners at the Apollo used it when members of the public messed themselves or spilled milk on the soft furnishings.

Maureen went into the social room and sat down at the bar, shaking off her overcoat, waiting for the barman to get round to her. Sunshine spilled on to the tiled floor, forming little yellow puddles and showing up the filthy grouting. The wooden bar was badly scarred with fag burns and water marks. She could see through the arch into the serious-drinking room. A lone man sat crouched over his beer, asleep, his dirty brown anorak pulled over to one side by the weight of loose change in his pocket. She couldn't see his face. The less serious room was empty. It was eleven thirty on a Saturday morning and the drinking day had yet to begin.

She lit a cigarette as the barman came round the corner and asked him for a lemonade and a whisky in separate glasses. He was middle-aged, black, dressed in jeans and a blue silk shirt open at the neck, displaying little hairy Afro bobbles on his chest like a dot-to-dot puzzle. He poured the lemonade from the gun, drew a tiny measure of whisky from the optic and put the two glasses on the bar. Maureen lifted the lemonade and sipped. The oily mixer syrup swirled in the water, catching the light. He was watching her, wanting to talk, busying himself with the hopeless task of cleaning the bar-top. Finally, he nodded at the untouched whisky and asked her if she was waiting for someone.

'No,' said Maureen, between gulps of flat lemonade, 'I just came in because I'm thirsty.'

It was pretty unlikely. The Coach and Horses was a different world, not a small deviation from the street. He wiped the taps near to her, rubbing them with a ripped beer towel, and caught her eye three or four times.

'You worked here a long time?' asked Maureen, trying to sound casual.

He said he'd been there two or three years, then went back to cleaning the bar and glancing at her. She picked up her whisky. There was hardly anything in the glass, just enough to discolour the bowl. She felt sure she was being ripped off. Maybe that's why he was watching her. 'It seems a shame to mess a glass with a measure that small,' she said.

'You just come from Glasgow?' the barman asked.

Maureen nodded.

'Yeah,' he said. 'A lot of the pubs up there sell whisky in quarter-gill measures. In here we sell them in an eighth.'

'Is that legal?'

'Oh, yeah,' he grinned at her, 'we charge the same as well.'

'Bet you don't get many Scots in here.'

'Actually, we do, 'cause we do the Tennent's.' He illustrated his point by gesturing to a pair of lager taps.

'Ah,' said Maureen, smiling and pretending she gave a shit.

They had nothing else to say. Although keen to chat, the barman seemed incapable of saying anything that didn't bring the conversation to a grinding halt. Maureen looked around the room.

'You're just off the train, aren't you?' he said.

'Aye.' She tried smiling at him again. 'Why? Because I didn't know the whisky measure?'

'No,' he said, indicating her overcoat. 'They always dress too warm, just off the train.'

Maureen held out her hand. 'Maureen O'Donnell,' she said.

He shook her hand with a limp squeeze. 'Hello,' he said, neglecting to give his name.

She suspected that he did know better. She let go of his hand and picked up her drink again. 'Lot of Scots come in here, do they?' she said.

'Yeah, they do.'

'Bet I'd know half of them, as well. Does Neil Hutton ever come in here?'

The barman sneered as if she had told him a dirty joke. 'No.'

'What about Frank Toner?'

'Who?'

'Frank Toner – big guy, wears glasses?' She pulled out the Polaroid and showed it to him. 'See that guy?' she said. 'Does he come in here?'

'Why?'

She tucked away the photo in her pocket. 'I was told to meet him,' she said.

The barman twisted his mouth to the side enigmatically as he pushed the dirty flannel over the bar. Maureen watched him for a minute. She didn't like him at all. She flattened her cigarette in the ashtray and slid off the stool, picking up her coat.

'He drinks in here,' said the barman quietly.

'Most nights?'

'Some nights.'

Maureen held up the photocopy of Ann's face. 'Is that his girlfriend?'

The barman flinched from the picture. 'No,' he said, watching the bar as he cleaned it.

'How can you be so sure?'

He thought about it. 'Maybe,' he puzzled over it, 'maybe she was his girlfriend. I don't keep track.'

'Was?'

'Eh?'

'Well,' said Maureen, 'I said "she is" and you said "was".'

He looked her in the eye. 'I 'aven't seen her for a while.'

'Oh,' said Maureen. He knew Ann was dead and he wasn't planning to tell Maureen. 'But you saw them together?'

He shrugged and smiled to himself. 'Long time ago,

before Christmas. Maybe she was his girlfriend ...' he glanced up at her ' ... maybe.'

'Did she come in here?'

'She used to come in a lot. Came in with him. Then she came in on her own just after Christmas. She was wasted.' He shrugged again.

Maureen waited for a moment but it was obvious that he didn't know anything else. She wrote her pager number on a sheet from her notebook, put it on the bar and covered it with a fiver. 'Wet the tip of your tongue with that,' she said, trying to sound pleasant but coming over as fly. 'I'll see ye again.' Then she walked out of the pub into the shaming sunshine, leaving the smoky lemon behind her.

33

Mr Headie's Holiday

Kilty Goldfarb was sitting by the window, sipping a milk-shake, wearing her fur coat and a ski hat, looking worried and jumpy. She watched Maureen cross the road and come in through the doors. She looked at the table and gathered a thin smile before looking back up.

'I'm sorry if I'm a bit late,' said Maureen, sitting across from her. 'I nipped over there to the Coach and Horses to check it out. D'ye know it?'

Kilty looked faintly disgusted. 'Jesus Christ, I wouldn't go in there. It's full of heavies from home.'

'Oh?' Maureen arranged her coat on the seat and put her packet of cigarettes on the table. 'It was quiet when I went in.'

Their lunch appointment suddenly felt like a bad date. Maureen pointed at the milkshake in front of Kilty. 'Can I get you something to go with that?'

'No, I'm short of time,' said Kilty, firmly, putting a Woolworths polythene bag on the table, signalling her readiness to leave. 'Why don't you just sit down and ask me the questions you want to ask and I'll be on my way?'

Maureen looked at her. 'I am sitting down,' she said.

'Oh,' said Kilty, 'good. I've got to get back to work, I'm running late as it is. Ask me the questions and I'll go.'

'Look,' said Maureen, 'ye didn't need to turn up if you were that reluctant to talk to me.'

'It's just I don't really know why I'm here,' Kilty said

stiffly. 'You know, in London no-one asks to meet a stranger without a reason.'

'I've got a reason,' said Maureen. 'I want to know whereabouts in Wandsworth Mr Headie's new office is.'

'Why?'

'I want to see him, I want to know what sort of cases he deals with and who his clients are.'

'And what would knowing Headie's clientele tell you?'

'I want to know what sort of people were familiar with that firm's old name. The headed letter was hand-delivered in Glasgow and the person who sent it might be an old client.'

'And what do I get in return?' asked Kilty.

It was a peculiar question. Maureen had the feeling that she was being asked for money but she didn't want to pay her. There would be any number of people who knew about Mr Headie and the benefits system.

'I can teach you how to smoke,' said Maureen.

Kilty smiled at the window.

'Look,' said Maureen, 'forget it, it doesn't really matter, I can look him up in the phone book or ask someone else.'

Kilty picked at the handle of her poly-bag, pulling the two layers of plastic apart. ''Kay,' she said sombrely. 'But I don't want to get into anything here. I don't want to be your new best friend or anything.'

It was ludicrous: Maureen was going home in a couple of days, she was certain that she'd never see the little frog woman again anyway, and she still felt rejected. 'Okay. Okay. We'll never see each other again after this.'

'And you have to tell me the story about the woman,' said Kilty. 'The woman who's disappeared.'

Maureen held up her hands. 'I don't know what to tell you. I'm down here because I don't know what's happened to her. She's got two kids, a husband who works in a shipyard as a welder and she likes to play the piano.' Kilty watched her, wanting more. 'The last time anyone saw her she was in the Coach and Horses.'

Kilty sat with her hands below the table and stared at Maureen's waist.

'That's all I know,' said Maureen.

Kilty nodded to her waist and Maureen saw that she was staring at the packet of cigarettes. She had been teasing when she said she'd teach Kilty how to smoke but Kilty was serious. Maureen gave her a fag and a light. Kilty sucked in the smoke, puffing like an over-wound automaton, watching the tip of her fag and going very slightly cross-eyed. Maureen was going to tell her to inhale just a little at first, not draw her cheeks in so much and keep her eye off the tip but she still felt slighted at the suggestion that she was going to trap Kilty into a lifelong friendship. 'That's fine, actually,' she said, 'you're doing that fine.'

'Really?'

'Aye.'

'It doesn't feel the same as what everyone else does.'

'Maybe you're just thinking about it too much.'

Kilty looked bewildered. 'Hm, maybe. You won't find Mr Headie in the phone book. He doesn't have a new office. He's in Wandsworth prison.'

'What?'

'Yeah, few months ago the whole of Coldharbour Lane was an open drugs market. But now look.' She pointed across the street at a tall grey pole with a high steel box aimed down the Lane. 'They had a big clean-up and put CCTV all up and down it.'

'So now the nervous junkies have to go up dark alleys with their tenners and twenties?'

'Yeah,' said Kilty. 'Mr Headie was one of the first casualties in a big clean-up operation. He was arrested with half a kilo of uncut cocaine in his briefcase.'

'Mr Headie was into that, was he?'

'He was skimming money, yeah, legally and illegally. He represented everyone and gave some of them special services. Anyway, he got done.' She looked at her watch and seemed concerned. 'Is that all?' she said quickly.

'Do you know anything about a trade in benefit books?'

Kilty waved her fag about, getting the feel of it. 'I know there is one. They pay a small portion of the value to the person up front. They buy them from alkies and junkies. It's about as low a scam as you can get.'

'The woman's child-benefit book is missing. Could anyone cash the book?'

'Not unless she'd signed the back,' said Kilty. 'When they buy the book they get the person to sign the agent clause on each cheque. If she'd signed and dated them all in advance they could cash them.'

'How much would it be for four kids per week?'

Kitty thought about it. 'About fifty-odd quid. I thought you said she had two kids?'

Maureen looked at Kilty and Kilty stared back.

'I didn't say it was her book. Did I?' The question wasn't rhetorical.

'No,' smiled Kilty, 'you haven't said that yet. But I think you're about to.'

Maureen avoided insulting her with the obvious. 'If the book was made out to a Glasgow address, could she cash it down here?' she asked.

'She'd have to give notice that she was moving,' said Kilty. 'She'd have to let the post office know in advance where she was moving to and when the first cheque would be cashed. Like I said, if someone else is cashing the thing they'd need her consent.'

If Ann had sold it in London she must have known in advance she was going to run here.

Outside the window the street was busy and shoppers spilled into the road from the market.

'Well, Kilty, that's really all I wanted to know,' said Maureen, standing up. 'Thanks very much for coming to meet me, despite your misgivings. You've been really helpful.' She slid two cigarettes across the table to her. 'Keep them to play with.'

Kilty reached out and took them. 'You really haven't kept your side of the bargain,' she said. 'You haven't told me anything that wasn't a total lie—' But her reproach was interrupted by the tune from Maureen's pager.

> ... About ...
> ... Ann. I Am
> ... 2/1 631 Argyle
> Street. Brixton
> Hill come now.

Maureen sat down again and stared at the message, reading it through and through, trying to understand how anyone could have heard about her within one day of her arrival and how they could have got her pager number. The only people who had it were Jimmy, Leslie, Liam and Moe. And the barman from the Coach and Horses. It was the lying barman.

'You haven't told me about the woman.' Kilty saw her looking puzzled. 'Don't you understand the message?'

'Yeah,' said Maureen. 'I just don't know how they got my number.'

Kilty twisted around and read the address over her shoulder. 'Jesus,' she said. 'You're not going up there on your own, are ye?'

'Why?'

'I wouldn't go up there,' said Kilty. 'Don't go.'

Maureen tutted. 'Look, I was up at Dumbarton Court the other day. There's a gang of teenagers hanging around but it's not that bad.'

'Dumbarton Court's fine. The Argyle, that's a different country. When they broke up Coldharbour the trade moved up the road. Don't go up there.'

It sounded like an order but Maureen couldn't imagine why Kilty thought she'd do what she said. ''S no big deal, I know the guy who sent the message.'

'D'you know him well?'

Maureen wanted so much to be right that she almost lied. 'No,' she said, 'I don't know him at all but I'm going anyway. You can come with me if you're that worried.'

Kilty put her Woolies bag on the floor and took out the cigarettes, sitting them on the table. 'Give me the address,' she said. 'I'll wait here for you and if you're not back in an hour I'll call the police.'

Maureen showed it to her. Kilty shut her eyes and said it over and over to herself.

'I thought you had to get back to your work?' said Maureen.

Kilty lifted one of the cigarettes, sitting it between her fingers. 'I don't work Saturdays.' She looked at her prop cigarette and smiled up at Maureen.

'So, all that clock watching,' said Maureen. 'You've just lied to me continuously?'

'You tell me the truth and I'll tell you the truth.' Kilty spread her hand over her tiny grinning face, pretending to puff on her unlit fag like a movie star. 'See ye in an hour,' she said, exhaling imaginary smoke through her teeth.

34
Scarface

Williams had gone off for a piss and left the tape-recorder running. They were in a small interview room. The pale grey walls were tinged with yellow smoke. The smell of a hundred frightened punters clung to the wall and Bunyan felt that she could smell their sweat, the desperate lies and nervous resignations. Jimmy Harris was smoking and looking at his hands. He had sat silently all the way to Carlisle and had gone meekly into the holding cell. When they went to get him in the morning all he asked about were his kids. Harris wasn't working to a game plan, that much was clear already. He was making it up as he went along, stumbling over his story, backing up when he got caught out and telling them the truth when the tears came. The lies weren't meant to get him off, he didn't give a shit what happened to him, but he cared about his kids.

He looked up at her now and crumbled his chin into a polite semblance of a smile.

'You all right?' asked Bunyan, able to be kind without contradicting Williams now that they were alone.

Harris sniffed and nodded.

'The kids'll be all right, you know.'

Harris nodded again, nervously, and took another draw.

'You're lucky with your family,' she said. 'I don't know if I could find a family member ready to sit with my kid over a Friday night.'

Harris exhaled. 'You got kids?'

'Yeah. Little girl. She's three. Called Angie.'

Harris softened. 'Nice name. My wife,' he gestured to the past and took another drag, 'she wanted a wee girl. Kept trying because she wanted a girl.'

'I'd like a boy now.'

'Boys are hard work. They're not obedient like girls.'

Bunyan laughed softly and sat back. 'You really haven't got a girl, have you? They're terrible. Whatever you tell them they do the opposite. Just like when they grow up.'

Harris smiled and showed his horrible little teeth but Bunyan didn't notice. She was looking at his eyes. Alone with four kids and no money. Jesus. Harris's face fell suddenly sombre and he glanced at the tape. 'Will ye promise to keep the social work away from my boys?'

'I can't promise that, Mr Harris, but I'll try.'

Harris drew a deep, trembling breath, and propped his elbows on the table, resting his forehead in his hands. 'I was in London,' he muttered to the table-top. 'Someone put a ticket through my door and I went down on a plane for the day.'

Startled by the vital piece of information, Bunyan forgot how she sounded. 'Who would do that?' she breathed.

'I don't know. But I think I better tell ye because if I don't they will.'

Kilty was right about the Argyle. It was a short, narrow road but the yellow-brick block of flats was dirty and less cared-for than Dumbarton Court. Maureen looked through the small glass panel on the door to block six and knew she didn't want to go up there. The stairwell was littered with burnt juice cans, fag butts and empty crisp packets. At the very foot of the flight sat what she hoped was a dog turd. She could hear someone walking slowly down the stairs, their footfalls uncertain and irregular. She backed away from the door and walked across the road, standing at the bus stop, watching. The door opened and a skinny woman emerged, walking uncertainly, her eyes glazed and troubled. She wore a sweatshirt with 'Viva Las Vegas' written on it in a rubberized transfer, the kind that peels off in a hot wash. She made her way out to the hill, steadying herself against the bus-stop wall. She didn't look any more able to handle herself than Maureen. Tentatively, Maureen approached the entrance and walked up to the second floor, reminding herself that it was just the boring barman and she had nothing to fear but long pauses.

There was no welcome mat in front of flat 2/1. The door was coated in sheets of bolted metal, and a protective outer door, constructed from seventies hacienda-style wrought-iron, stood half a foot out from the wall. A big three-dimensional spy-hole, like a marble, stuck out from the door in a way that would allow the viewer to see downstairs and into every dark shadow on the landing. The doorbell at the side was drilled into the wall. She pressed and stepped back, waiting for the answer.

'Who're ye?' It was a man's voice, a Scottish man, and he sounded nervous.

Maureen had been expecting the barman.

'I got a message to come here.'

'Who from?'

'On my pager.'

Four or five metal locks of different types snapped, crunched and slid back. The door opened with the chain on. A man's eye looked out at her, checking her out, looking behind her. The door shut, the chain came off and he opened it, swinging the bars out, beckoning her indoors while he kept his eye on the stairs. He was white and in his forties, with a twisted stab scar on his left cheek. The contused skin had contracted as it healed, dragging the cheek down and in. An older, cleaner slash line ran from the soft skin on the outside of his left eye, across his cheek, ending in an artful twist on the tip of his nose. Face-slashing is a Scottish gang custom, used to teach lessons and mark opponents. No wonder he was nervous. No wonder he'd left Glasgow. 'Come,' he whispered, flapping his hand urgently, calling her in.

Maureen didn't want to go in. She didn't like the bars on the door or the dirty stairs or the locks. 'Who are you?' she said, crossing her arms and shifting her weight on to one foot, letting him know she wasn't moving.

'Tam Parlain,' he said, and pointed at her. 'You're from Glasgow, eh?'

'Yeah.'

'You'll have heard of my family.'

'No,' said Maureen. 'I'm sorry, I haven't.'

Tam Parlain was still watching the stairs. 'Ah, come on,' he said, 'you've heard of the Parlains. From Paisley.'

'No, I haven't, I'm sorry. Why would I have?'

He looked at her and seemed disappointed. 'Well,' he said, acting modest, 'we're in the news a lot.' He smiled and the stab scar on his cheek puckered, dragging the skin into a pointed nipple. He remembered what he looked like and let his face fall. Maureen guessed that the Parlains didn't grow prize marrows.

'Come in,' he said. 'I can't keep the door open.'

'Why?'

'There's guys after me.'

'D'you know anything about Ann?'

'Ann? The poor girl who was found? Aye, come in.'

She was wary and unsure, but Maureen thought of Kilty and squeezed the stabbing comb in her pocket. She sidled past him, turning through the half-foot he left for her. Parlain shut the door and Maureen watched as he did up the locks again. She tried to remember the order and method of each but by the time she had walked through the hall to the living room she'd forgotten the second and third locks.

The living room was a long rectangle with a fitted kitchen at the back and a breakfast bar marking out the territories. The flat-pack kitchen cupboards had been badly put together and several of the doors were missing. The cupboards were empty. A fussy dark green leather sofa with loose cushion attachments sat against the wall and next to it a coffee table, recently washed and still wet. The room was ridiculously clean. The walls had been painted with glaring white emulsion. There was no carpet on the floor, just big squares of immaculate bare hardboard, painted black. The picture window was barred from the inside. 'Sit down.' He motioned to the tattered leather sofa.

Maureen took a seat, resting her hands beside her on the leather sofa and looked up at him. Tam Parlain twitched like a heavy smoker and his eyes were hollow and insincere.

'Tam,' said Maureen, 'did you page me?'

'Yeah.'

He sat down next to her on the settee, turning to face her, his arm outstretched behind her, like a gauche teenager angling for a snog. He half smiled and pointed at her. 'Sorry,' he said. 'What's your name again?'

She didn't want the creepy fuck to know her name. The barman had probably told him already. 'Marian,' she said. If they cross-checked the name each would think the other had misheard.

'Marian.' He took time to think about it and she knew the barman had told him it was Maureen.

'Whereabouts in Glasgow are ye from, Marian?' he said, trying to place her in the city and work out whether she was connected.

'Just Glasgow,' she said, sitting forward, taking her fags

out of her pocket. She didn't want to offer them in case Parlain touched her. 'The barman at the Coach and Horses gave you my pager number, didn't he?'

'Oh, aye.'

'Do you know something about Ann?'

'Aye, Ann. Poor Ann.' He hung his head. 'That was terrible.'

Maureen lifted the fag to her mouth, and as she lit it she noticed that her hands were damp and giving off an odd smell, like a detergent. They felt gritty. He had been washing his leather sofa with watery detergent. He had washed the floor too and the coffee table, and the kitchen cupboards were empty. He had washed every surface in the house. He was exactly the sort of paranoid lulu Liam would have turned into if he hadn't stopped dealing. She turned back to him, pitying him his life, nodding along with him. 'Yes,' she said, 'it was terrible. And how did you know Ann?'

'We drank in the same pubs around here.' He let the conversation falter.

'Do you know her sister?' asked Maureen.

Parlain shook his head and again they found themselves staring blankly at one another.

'She lives a few streets up,' she said.

'Naw, I don't know her.' He stared at Maureen as if he was waiting for her to do something.

'What is it you want to tell me, Tam?'

'Oh.' His eyes slid to the floor and he looked very serious. 'You were asking about a guy. Thought I might know him.'

'Do you know him?'

'Is there a photie . . . ?'

He waited, leaning into her expectantly. The most paranoid man in Brixton had called a stranger to his fortress flat to see if he could be of any assistance. Maxine had warned her about this: she had told them to get rid of the picture.

'I'm afraid I've lost it,' she said innocently, 'but how about if I describe him to you?'

Parlain didn't like it.

'Would you be able to identify him then?' she asked.

Parlain didn't like it at all.

'He's quite distinctive,' she said.

'How did ye lose it?' he snapped.

'How did I lose what?'

'The photo.' He was nearly shouting at her.

'I was in a bar today and I showed it to someone and they asked to keep it.'

'In the Coach?' His face was turning red and he was on his feet, pacing up to the barred window with his hands behind his back.

'No.' She tried to think of another pub. 'It was the one down by the . . .' She pointed and frowned as if she couldn't quite remember. 'By the . . . Opposite the railway station, across the road.'

He was next to her, leaning over her and frowning. 'The Swan?'

'Could be, I don't know this area well.'

She really wanted to get out. She felt sorry for Parlain but she didn't know what this level of paranoia would make him capable of.

He leaned in closer and she could feel his breath on her forehead. 'Big bar, long bar, bald guy serving? Talks like a poof?'

'I think so,' she said, because she wanted out. 'That's right, there.'

'What was the guy like?'

'Which guy?'

'The guy who took the picture?'

'Wee, English accent, wore a dark coat—'

'Fat?'

'Yeah, he was quite fat.'

'Right,' he said, his arms hanging by his side, his fingers wriggling like a bushel of worms. He walked back to the window and looked out. 'And he was there when ye left?'

'Yeah, this was like fifteen minutes ago. Ye paged me when I was with him.' Parlain was going to leave the house and go to the Swan. He was going to leave her in here. 'I'll take ye to him. He was a nice guy, I'm sure he'll give me the photo if I ask him.'

He looked at her. 'Aye.' His neck twitched nod after nod. 'You come with me.' He stormed into another room and came back with a battered leather jacket.

Maureen wondered if he had taken the precaution of washing it with soapy water too. She stood up, smiling stupidly. 'Let's go then,' she said happily. 'I'll buy ye a pint if ye like.'

But Parlain was beyond being touched by courtesy. He ignored her offer, unlocked the door and they stepped out in to the stairwell. Maureen felt the updraft of warm air and knew she was lucky to have got out of there. Parlain peered down the stairs as he locked up carefully. He led the way, turning back occasionally to make sure she was still with him. He led her down the stairs and out of the door to Argyle Street.

'I'm not sure it's called the Swan,' said Maureen, thinking on her feet. 'It's past the Underground and over the road a bit.'

Parlain stopped. 'That's not the Swan.'

She pulled him by the elbow, trying to give the impression that she was keen to stay with him. 'Come on anyway, and I'll show you. Down here.'

They took the road straight down to the high street. Parlain's paranoia was not confined to the house, he kept his head down, looking straight forward, anxious not to be seen.

'Straight down and across the road,' she said.

She walked alongside him all the way down the hill, wittering shit about home and how cold it was and she liked it here and the people were really friendly. Parlain stopped responding after the first two hundred yards and Maureen gradually let her chatter peter out. When they got beyond the long social-security building she began to drop back, walking in the edge of Parlain's line of vision for a little while, slipping back when they got to the mouth of a small lane. She let him get a couple of feet ahead of her and then she bolted, walking as fast as she could at first and then running, skipping around the corner, running and running to get the fuck away from him. She ran down Brighton Terrace and cut down a series of small streets before heading back to the high street and scurrying into McDonald's. She sat at the far table with her back to the window. Kilty Goldfarb watched her come in. She looked around, giggled and stood up, tiptoeing over to the table like a panto villain. 'Hiya,' she said. 'Are you avoiding me?'

'Kilty,' said Maureen, sweating and staring at the table, 'do you like to drink?'

'Yeah.'

'Will you go out to the road and hail a cab to take us into town?'

'You look terrified.'

'I am terrified,' whispered Maureen.

Kilty stood up and disappeared. Two minutes later she tapped Maureen on the shoulder. 'Come,' she said, watching the distance like a bodyguard. Maureen stood up and hurried outside to the waiting taxi. 'Where are we going?' asked Kilty, shutting the cab door and sitting down next to her.

'Busy place with pubs,' said Maureen.

'Covent Garden,' called Kilty to the driver.

The taxi sighed as the handbrake came off and they drove away along the high street.

35
Drunk

Leslie had sleft all night in the armchair. She was desperate to get out of the cold house for an hour or so but she couldn't handle the kids at all. They were hungry and there wasn't any food in the house, apart from white bread. She had decided to dress them and take them to a café but Alan had hidden their clothes so that no-one could take them anywhere.

Six-year-old John was playing nicely with the babies, talking to them and trying to make them wear Leslie's crash helmet, but it was big and black and it scared them. He pulled it on himself to show them it wasn't scary and sat in front of them, stroking their little legs. Alan was still in his pyjamas, sitting in his daddy's chair, his little hands spread over the sticky arm-rests, looking up at her like an evil child genius.

'Tell me where the clothes are, Alan,' said Leslie, for the fourth time in fifteen minutes.

Alan smirked at her.

'Where are the fucking clothes?' shouted Leslie, pressing her face into his.

'Hey, they're weans, ye can't talk to them like that,' said Cammy, pulling her back by the arm. 'They've had a bad fright.'

Leslie glared at him. 'Don't you raise your hand to me.'

'I'm not raising my hand to ye, Leslie. I'm just saying ye'll upset them if ye shout like that.'

As if on cue Alan started to cry. 'I want my daddy,' he said. 'Where's my daddy?'

John whimpered under the helmet. The babies picked up the panicked theme and began to howl.

'See?' said Cammy. 'You've upset them.'

Leslie poked him hard in the chest. 'No, Cameron, you've upset them.'

Just then the front door opened and Jimmy came in, flanked by the two police officers. In silence the children ran, staggered and crawled over to their dad, clinging on to his legs and hands, holding on to each other when they ran out of limbs. John was the last to get there. Blinded by the oversized helmet, he banged into the door-frame and bounced back, staying on his feet. He grabbed his daddy's jumper, pulling it down at the side, baring Jimmy's skinny yellow shoulder. Jimmy calmed them all down with a pet and a hush each, but the children hung on tightly, tethering him like a rogue Zeppelin.

'Where's the ticket, Jimmy?' The fat guy looked very tired now. His hand was tucked under Jimmy's armpit and he looked as if he'd like to smash him off a wall. 'Is it under the chair?'

'Aye.' Jimmy looked exhausted.

The blonde woman lifted the cushion and began to rummage through the papers.

'Jimmy,' said Leslie, 'why are ye back here? Are they letting ye go?'

'We're just here to pick up some evidence,' said Williams. 'Mr Harris flew to London the week his wife was killed.'

'Aw, get real,' said Leslie. 'Where would he get the money to fly to London?'

Williams raised an eyebrow and looked at Leslie's leather trousers. 'There's always someone to lend a hand, isn't there?' His phone rang out the theme tune from *The*

Simpsons in his pocket. He took it out with his free hand. 'Hello?' he said formally and paused to listen. 'Speaking,' he said and nodded intently at the floor as the caller spoke. 'Thanks. We know about that now. Yes. Heathrow.' He glanced up at Jimmy and nodded at the floor again. He looked up at Leslie, caught his guard and motioned to Bunyan to get hold of Jimmy's arm. She did as she was told and Williams opened the front door, stepped out onto the balcony and pulled the door shut behind himself.

Bunyan looked at Leslie. 'How did you manage with the boys last night? All right?'

Out on the balcony Williams leaned into the receiver. 'Listen,' he said to DI Inness, 'can you check and see if you have any intelligence on a Leslie Findlay? She lives in Drumchapel—'

Inness sounded excited. 'Has she got a motorbike?'

'Yeah.'

'Why are you asking about her?'

'She seems to have been involved in this case. Do you know her?'

'We all know her. She came up in an investigation a while ago. An assault case. Her and another woman. She works at the women's shelters, doesn't she?'

'Yeah.' Williams glanced at the door. 'You said it was an assault? Is she violent?'

'Could be,' said Inness. 'They messed someone up really badly.'

'Was she prosecuted?'

'Can't get any evidence on them, but I'll tell you what, if she's done it again you'll've made my DCI's day.'

The bar was quiet. The few big town shoppers frittered the afternoon away, missing their connecting train, not quite making it home. Two men at a table laughed unhappily and sipped at brown drinks. Maureen thought about Parlain asking for the Polaroid. Frank Toner was something to him. Toner might have crossed him. Parlain might be looking for a photo to identify him, to show to people and ask about him. None of the scenarios she came up with sounded right: Parlain was paranoid, he was hardly going to carry out a revenge attack and who ever heard of gangsters showing each other photos? They all knew each other.

'There you are,' said Kilty, putting the glass down in front of her. 'Whisky and lime. Now, relax.'

'I just got a bit freaked, that's all.' Maureen drank deep.

'It was mad of you to go up there,' said Kilty. 'You don't know the area at all.'

'Do you live there?'

'Yeah, well, in Clapham. I rent a room in a Victorian terrace near the common. High ceiling, gorgeous open fire from the fifties, it's lovely.'

'Can't you afford a house on a social worker's salary?'

'I'm not that settled.'

'Why don't you come home?'

'Why don't you stop barking questions at me?'

'I'm sorry,' said Maureen. 'I'm rattled, that's all.'

'He gave you a fright, did he?'

'God, yeah, I don't even know why. He was just a paranoid wanker. He wanted a photo I've got and I could have given it to him but I didn't.'

'Why didn't you?'

'I dunno.'

'Let's have a cigarette,' said Kilty, taking her second fag out and sitting it on the table.

'Fuck.' Maureen breathed out heavily and rolled her head around her neck, trying to relax a little. 'That was scary.'

Kilty used Vik's lighter and began producing banks of smoke from her fag. Maureen watched her and was thinking that it would be criminal to correct her when it suddenly occurred to her that she hadn't cried once in four whole days. She had been shit scared this afternoon but she hadn't felt weepy or out of control. It had been months since she got through a day without her eyes transgressing. Maybe it wasn't infinite. She sat up, feeling odd and hopeful, and lit a cigarette. Kilty smiled at her. 'Right, you,' she said. 'It's payback time. Tell me the story.'

So Maureen told her about Ann in the mattress and about Jimmy and the kids, about Moe's unlikely missing-persons report, about the child-benefit book and about Hutton being shot up the arse. She went on as the drink warmed her and told her about the thin babies and Alan on the stairs and about the wee boys in their Mutant Ninja Turtle pyjamas. When she looked up Kilty was staring into her drink and looking distraught. 'Jesus Christ,' she said, 'the Turtles were ten years ago.'

And they drank on. Kilty hated her job too. She'd been inspired by what Maureen said and had been toying with chucking it all last night. 'I'm not going to try and save the world any more. From here on in,' Kilty stabbed the table with her finger for emphasis, 'I'm tending my garden. And you tend yours.'

'I think saving the world's easier in my case.'

'Why?'

'My garden's full of drunk buffalo.'

Kilty tipped her head and smiled wryly at the phrase. 'Oh, right?' she said, as if she'd understood. 'Well, what do you want, then?'

'I want beautiful things around me,' said Maureen, 'and I want a nice man to have a laugh with. And I want to feel content.'

'And you think seeking justice on this earthly plain will do that for you?'

'Everyone wants things to come right in the end, don't they? It's a fundamental human desire.' Maureen thought of Sarah rattling around her big house with the ghosts of naval syphilitics. 'That's what attracts wronged people to religion and politics, isn't it?'

Kilty grinned. 'I thought they just liked getting on and off minibuses.'

'No, but, you know, the true religious are never happy campers, are they? I bet your social-work department is full of people with sorry histories.'

'You're probably right,' said Kilty, stubbing out her half-smoked fag. 'They'd hardly tell me. I'm the luckiest girl in the world. My mother's a delight and my father's utterly charming. The only reason I'm in London is to dodge a good marriage to a big fat advocate.'

'Really?'

'Christ, yeah. They're desperate for me to consolidate their social standing. It's a *nouveau riche* immigrant thing.'

'But you don't want that?'

'Fuck off,' she sneered. 'I've got better things to do with my life than choosing chintzy curtains at Jenner's.'

Kilty sipped her drink and Maureen realized where she was from. She could hear the traces of the private school in her accent. She was attracted to her calm acceptance of the world around her, as if no-one had ever been a real threat to her and everyone was of interest. She'd like that for herself. Everyone she knew was chippy. Kilty sat forward. 'You see, down here coming from a posh background is considered a good thing.'

'But back home?'

'Nice people won't talk to you. They think, quite rightly, that you've had a bigger slice of the pie.'

'And social work is your penance for that?'

'Catholicism hangs over you like a shroud, Maureen O'Donnell.'

They got round after round in, drinking slowly and enjoying the company, watching television sometimes, sitting quietly with each other. They moved on to another bar when some ridiculously young men tried to chat them up, packing Kitty's bag of shopping into Maureen's cycle bag. By the time they hit bar three Kilty was taking a lemonade every second round so that she didn't pass out and was slurring heavily. They made crazy, drunken plans together. Kilty would come home and live at Maureen's for a while. She couldn't go home to her folks – they'd want her to spend all day horse-riding and attending ghastly parties. She'd come home and try being an artist, and she said Maureen should let the buffalo out of the garden. She sang 'Don't Fence Me In' in a precariously high octave all the way to Brixton. The taxi-driver was glad to see the back of them. He was dropping them outside the Coach and Horses before they had fully considered the other options.

'It'll be fine,' said Maureen, taking half an hour to find the right change in her hand and pay the taxi. 'Come on.'

'It will be many things,' slurred Kilty sombrely, 'but it won't be fine.'

The Coach and Horses was eerily quiet. There was no pretence at socializing, no crowds of chatting acquaintances, little effort made to disguise the business of drinking. The barman who had dubbed her up to Parlain wasn't working. Maureen was feeling slightly sick. She took a deep breath and led Kilty into the serious-drinking room on the left. They stepped up to the bar and Maureen ordered a triple whisky with lime and ice.

'I'll try that as well,' said Kilty.

The barman poured the drinks without asking if they were sure they wanted triples and Maureen knew that she was drinking in a pub that suited her. The customers were nearly all men and, strangely for the area, predominantly white. They heard accents from home, east and west coast, some broad, some mild. The few women had a sad, junkie look about them, wearing clothes they had happened upon, standing vacantly, glancing round as if they were waiting for someone to come and get them. Ann belonged here among these lost people.

'Jesus,' muttered Kilty, 'it's a fucking hole.'

Maureen saw a man and a woman sitting at a table across the room. She recognized them and the man was watching her. He was nursing a pint. The table kept disappearing behind a smog of drinkers and appearing again. She was trying to remember where she knew them from when the door to the ladies' toilet opened. A woman paused there, swaying gently and wiping her hands on her stone-washed jeans. It was the woman who had come out of Tam Parlain's close; she still had her Vegas sweatshirt on. Moving slowly, she made her way across the floor towards Maureen and Kitty and sat on a stool, concentrating hard on the tricky business of sagging over the bar, her head hanging limp on her skinny neck. Keeping her eyes shut, she lifted her leg to her hand and roughly tugged the leg of her jeans up over one calf, scratching at a spot behind her knee, running her broken fingernails over a deep open sore. It was a baby ulcer, a septic track mark.

'Fuck me,' muttered Kilty into Maureen's hair. 'I'm sorry. I can't stand it here. Come on.'

'No,' said Maureen, 'I wanna see some'dy.'

'Just come. Crash at mine.'

'No.'

Kilty ceremonially handed over the packet of fags she had bought for herself. 'Give that back to me tomorrow.' She patted Maureen on the tit by accident and swerved her

303

little froggy body away from the bar and out of the door. Two minutes later she came back with her phone number written on a bit of paper and put it in Maureen's coat pocket. 'Tomorrow,' she said, and left again.

It was later and busier and warmer. Maureen rolled limy whisky around her mouth. She felt superior to the other people in the bar and wondered how they could stand it. She was from a shitty background, she'd had a crap life, but standing here in the Coach and Horses she felt like Lisa Marie Fucking Presley. She went to the loo and found the source of the sharp lemon smell. A broken mirror was bolted to the stained wall, its shattered guts missing. She left the first cubicle because menstrual blood had been smeared on the wall spelling out a 'T'. The seat was broken in the second loo and there was no paper.

She was very drunk now, leaning on the bar, reckless of her good coat on the sticky surface. A tinny tune began behind her and played and played until it played itself out. She saw the man and woman sitting at the far table again and was trying to concentrate hard enough to work it out when she turned and saw Frank Toner coming in from the street. The crowd parted for him. He was shorter and stockier than he had seemed in the Polaroid and moved like a retired boxer. Behind him was the staggering Vegas woman who had been leaning over the bar earlier. Maureen hadn't seen her leave. She seemed much brighter now, happier and lighter, ready to laugh and give and receive. The couple came to the bar and Maureen moved nearer, nodding to the woman. The woman recognized Maureen from somewhere and nodded back.

'How are you now?' said Maureen. 'Feeling a bit better?'

'Oh, yeah,' she said, pretending she remembered. 'Much better now. Nice now.'

She was well-spoken. She might have been a beauty once.

Her face was as slender as a Modigliani; her thick brown hair had a natural sheen of auburn through it. She moved with grace, stepping from one foot to the other, letting her hips lead the sway. She might have been young, the deep wrinkles in her forehead and under her eyes looked premature; the rest of her skin was soft and fresh. Frank Toner looked at Maureen and Maureen nodded at him. 'Good,' she smiled, 'let me get you both a drink.'

'What would I want to take a fucking drink off you for?' he said, speaking with a harsh south London accent.

It suddenly occurred to Maureen that she was far too drunk to deal with this. She backed off. 'Forget it,' she turned to the bar, 'doesn't matter,' as if ending the conversation was her choice.

Toner announced to the gathered crowd that the day he took a drink from a bit of Scottish cunt was the day he'd fucking retire. He ordered his round and told the barman to give Maureen one as well, adding a wee joke, that he didn't mean fuck her. He guffawed like a bitter child and the moat of sycophants around him laughed too.

'Don't want your drink,' said Maureen quietly, feeling like a defiant cowpoke. Everyone ignored her. The barman put the drink down by her hand. 'I don't want it,' she said.

He gave her a manic look and pushed the glass towards her. 'Just fuckin' take it,' he said. 'Save us all the trouble.'

Maureen wasn't going to drink it but in the end she did because it was there and she couldn't get served quickly enough. She was playing with Vik's lighter and wanted to turn suddenly and set fire to the back of Toner's coat.

The skinny woman sidled up to her. 'Are you all right?' she said, smiling, mellow now, like a different woman again. Maureen had been insulted, and she was trying to mend the damage with the tenderness of a woman who had known

305

humiliation herself and wanted to soften the pain for other people.

'I'm Maureen.'

'I'm Elizabeth.'

A rattle of laughter emanated from a table in the corner. Maureen nodded to Frank. "'S that your boyfriend?'

Elizabeth glanced round to see who Maureen was looking at. 'Oh ... no ... I haven't seen you in here before.'

'I'm looking for my pal. Did you know Ann who used to drink in here?'

Elizabeth smiled hard at her. 'Ann. She didn't really drink in here.'

'No?'

'No.' Elizabeth stood casually on one leg, looking at her puffy hands. The thick skin was hopelessly scarred, red and shiny on the knuckles, on the joints, around the slippery forked vein on the back of her hand. 'Ann drank in different places, mostly.'

'Do you drink in here all the time?'

'Yeah.' Elizabeth relaxed a little, now that they were off the subject of Ann. 'Yeah, it's nice in here.'

'Is it?' asked Maureen, testing to see if she had a sense of humour.

Elizabeth smiled, getting the joke. 'It looks really grotty,' she said, 'but they're a good crowd in here.' She nodded around the room at the drunks and the bums. 'These are good people. We all look after each other, you know?'

Elizabeth wasn't lying. She honestly believed that staggering about in the Coach and Horses was a lifestyle choice.

'How do you look after each other?' asked Maureen, curious about the way her justifications operated and wanting her to elaborate.

'Oh,' said Elizabeth, getting stuck, 'lots of things ...' She couldn't think of any. 'Lots of little things.'

Maureen guessed that Elizabeth probably did lots of little things and got fuck-all back.

'Yeah,' said Elizabeth vaguely, losing her way a little. 'You're Scottish.' She smiled suddenly. 'I like Scotland.'

'Oh?' said Maureen. 'Have you been there?'

'Yeah, I go sometimes,' said Elizabeth, remembering neither sad nor happy times. 'Not now, but I used to.'

'On the train?'

'Sometimes.' She was getting vaguer, zoning out.

'Ann was killed,' said Maureen.

'I know.' She came to. 'I know.'

'Did you know her well?'

'Not well.' Elizabeth smiled nervously. 'I don't know anything about that ...'

She backed off into the crowd. Maureen had lost her fags. She looked up again and saw the man and the woman at the table. Maureen looked at him. He was a big man, beefy next to the scrawny drinkers. She felt angry with him but she couldn't remember why. She couldn't place either of them but the woman was especially familiar. She thought about it. She definitely knew them from somewhere and then it hit her: the woman was Tonsa.

Tonsa was an elegant middle-aged woman with blonde-streaked hair. She always dressed beautifully in suburban designer clothes. Liam knew her because she was a professional mule, carrying backwards and forwards to Glasgow once a month. He'd introduced her to Maureen once in Glasgow. Tonsa's eyes were the only real giveaway: they were blank. Liam said you could run at her with a spear in each hand and she wouldn't blink, which was why she was so good at her job. Tonsa had almost managed to get Liam arrested a few months before: for no reason at all she'd told the police he'd beaten her up, retracting her statement at the last minute. Maureen fell across the floor towards them. 'Hiya,' she said, sitting clumsily at the table. 'D'ye 'member me?' She slapped Tonsa on the arm. 'Tonsa, Tonsa, d'ye not remember me? My brother, Liam? He introduced me to ye.'

Tonsa ignored Maureen and pulled at the cuff of her Burberry overcoat absentmindedly.

Maureen looked at the man He sat back. 'What you doing here?' he said. He was Scottish and she knew she knew him from home.

'Just, ye know, kicking about.' She wanted to hit him and she couldn't remember why. Frank Toner was still holding court at the bar. 'See that baldy guy?'

He stared at her. 'What about him?'

She shook her head, thinking maybe she had known once but had forgotten. 'What is it with that guy?'

'Never you mind about him.'

Without acknowledging Maureen, Tonsa stood up and left the table. Maureen looked at the man and remembered why she hated him so much, why she was so angry with him, why he was Michael. It was Mark Doyle.

'You,' she said loudly, slumping over the table. 'Who killed Pauline?'

Mark Doyle leaned in, his blistered red face suddenly vivid and alive. 'You're gonnae get yourself a sore face. Get the fuck out of here.'

Maureen was too drunk. She blinked at him. Mark Doyle jutted out his jaw, looking as if he could take a punch and not flinch.

'I'm not looking for trouble,' she said, with a dawning consternation at her own drunkenness, 'I'm just drinking.'

'You here 'cause I telt ye Ann was in?'

'No,' she said. 'I'm here to see her sister and have a drink.'

Doyle looked around the bar, sniffing the air. 'Does her sister drink in here too?'

'No.' Maureen reached into her pocket and pulled out the Polaroid, cupping it in her hand to hide it. 'I'm here because of this.'

Doyle was on his feet, wrapping his fingers around Maureen's elbow, digging in deep to the soft skin between the bones, making her feel faint and breathless. He stood her up. 'Get the fuck out of here,' he growled, lifting her from the seat and directing her towards the door. '*Get the fuck out of here.*'

They were all watching him lift her with an apparently gentle touch to her elbow, seeing her almost crying with the pain. Mark Doyle opened the pub door and threw her out into the street. Maureen didn't fall over, she staggered forward, scratching her knuckles on the pavement, bumping into a black couple who were walking past, nearly pushing them into the busy road. 'Aye,' said Doyle, 'an' fucking stay out.'

Sarah was not pleased to see her. She was dressed for bed and told Maureen over and over that it was half one and she had to get up in the morning. Maureen sat on the bed while Sarah shouted at her that she couldn't stay any more, no more, not any more. She lay down on the bed fully dressed, promising herself never to drink like that again, never again. She held her bloodied hand to her chest, and Sarah's voice receded into the background as the Grecian leaves spun a dance above her and Michael hovered in the black bathroom.

36

Rumbled

The cold in the hall enveloped her and the syphilitic sailors glared down from on high. Sarah was yanking Maureen into her overcoat. She had come into the room while Maureen slept and packed up all her stuff into her cycle bag. She woke Maureen up and poked and prodded her downstairs. Added to the discomfort of a terrible hangover, the knuckles on Maureen's hand were badly scratched and her elbow throbbed when she tried to straighten it. Sarah threw the bag on to the floor by the door. 'I just can't have it, Maureen, I'm sorry. This is my home.'

'Christ, Sarah—'

'Don't you say that.'

'I'm sorry. I'm sorry for coming home in a state, I got a bit drunk—'

'A bit drunk?' screeched Sarah, and her voice felt like a needle in Maureen's eye. 'You're an alcoholic!'

Maureen cupped her sore hand. 'Fucking calm down,' she said. 'God, I've got a hangover, have ye no pity?'

'I have pity, I have plenty of pity for people who don't bring misfortune on themselves—'

'You're just pissed off because I wouldn't read your Jesus pamphlets.'

'*Get out of my house.*'

The bright sun attacked her and her eyes were bursting. She felt ashamed as she sloped through the quiet village to the station. She'd been completely pissed and she'd said the only curse word that was guaranteed to upset Sarah. She got herself to a newsagent's in Blackheath village and bought a packet of fags. The guy behind the counter was tilling them up when she saw a rack of cheap sunglasses. She impulse-bought the cheapest-looking pair. They were reclaimed stock from the 1970s, with brown lenses and a soft, orange plastic frame. The man charged her a tenner for them, correctly guessing that she was too hung over to argue. She got outside and slid them on, lit a cigarette and silently thanked humanity for the miracle of tobacco.

She was groaning at the bumpy train when she checked her pager and found an old message sent the night before from Leslie: Jimmy had been arrested and she must come home immediately. Maureen tried to phone her from a call-box in London Bridge but couldn't get an answer at home. She looked away down the road. Cars and lorries passed in front of her, whipping the air into wind. She wanted to be cold again and to see familiar buildings, to have her home to go to, her bed to hide in, fresh clothes to wear, to see some noble fucking hills instead of this endless flatness. But she couldn't go home; she couldn't go back to Ruchill.

They were having a break. Leslie smoked yet another ciga-rette and looked around the grim room, at the yellowed walls and the rubber flooring. She had been smoking for hours without anything to wet it. A giant ulcer throbbed on the end of her tongue and she couldn't stop biting it. Isa was looking after the kids and Jimmy was downstairs in a holding cell.

Leslie had knocked back the offer of a lawyer initially, thinking it would make her look suspicious, but she was beginning to wonder about the wisdom of that. She didn't think she had anything to hide: all she had done was omit to tell Ann that she knew Jimmy, but she had done it because she knew whose side she was on. She knew how it would look if the police spoke to the committee members and heard that Leslie had requested Ann as a resident. She should have declared an interest when Ann was first mentioned. If the committee even suspected that she had told Jimmy that Ann was in the shelter she'd get the sack, at best they'd move her to the big smelly office. She'd be sitting across from that twat Jan, feeling as miserable as Maureen. She should have told the committee she was Jimmy's cousin. She should have told them.

The police didn't believe in the Polaroid and she couldn't tell them where it was. She couldn't mention Maureen or they'd want to know why she had taken it and why she was in London. When she told them it was of a guy called Frank Toner the fat guy laughed and the woman smiled up at her. 'What has he got to do with this?'

'I think he was her boyfriend,' Leslie'd said.

The policeman had sniggered. 'Well, I know what Frank Toner's girlfriends look like and Ann just wasn't his type.'

Leslie bit the tip of her ulcer again and blanched at the convulsive needle pains in the root of her tongue. If she could just speak to Maureen and find out what was happening she might be able to lie convincingly. The English woman came back in and sat down across from her. 'Would you like something to eat?' she said.

'No,' said Leslie. 'Listen, I didn't know Ann was Jimmy's wife until after she left.'

'I see. When did you realize?'

'After she left.'

'When after she left?'

But Leslie wasn't used to lying and she didn't have any of the basic equipment. She couldn't visualize herself or build on existing facts to make a lie sustainable. She sat back, drawing the last of her cigarette and stubbing it out in the pie-tin ashtray. 'What's going to happen to me?' she asked.

'What do you mean?'

'Are you going to charge me?'

'We're not sure yet.'

'If you do, what will you charge me with?'

'Depends.'

'On what?'

'If we can prove you could foresee he was going to hurt her and you aided that in some way. Then ... well, then it's murder.'

Leslie still wasn't home. Maureen nearly phoned Vik again but lost her bottle half-way through the area code. Outside the glass of the telephone box the car exhaust was forming a gritty haze above Brixton Hill, the fumes and the dirt suspended in the sunlight like salt in solution. It was early afternoon and the day was turning out to be another warm one. She put on her sunglasses and stepped out of the box, heading up the hill to Moe's. Her bag was heavy and pressed on her shoulder, making her feel worse. She stopped and rested the bag on a low wall, ripped the Velcroed flap open and looked inside. She still had Kilty's shopping. She picked out the heavy stuff and left two cans of beans and a tin of corned beef on a wall. She kept the things that couldn't be replaced from a corner shop; two giant bars of Milka chocolate, a packet of rice cakes and a box of firelighters. She'd explain to her later. She cringed as she remembered the night before. The Las Vegas woman, Elizabeth, had said she didn't know anything about *that*. She wouldn't have said that unless there was something to know.

Someone had tipped a wheelie-bin over around the back of Dumbarton Court, disseminating the putrid smell of week-old ready meals and shitty nappies. Maureen took the stairs slowly, stopping to catch her breath on each of the landings. By the time she got to the door she was half hoping Moe wouldn't be in, but she was.

'What do you want?' asked Moe, adding a 'hah' as an afterthought.

'I'm not from the brew,' said Maureen, softly, more concerned with nursing her hangover than setting a kindly tone. 'Ye can stop all that puffing and panting.'

'Hah, I don't know what you mean, hah.'

'Where's Ann's child-benefit book, Moe?'

Moe stood up straight, glared at her, opened the door and pulled Maureen in by the lapels. Her angina had cleared up a treat. She slammed the front door shut and turned to face her. 'Who the fuck are you?'

The darkness was a comfort to Maureen and she rubbed her itchy eyes. 'Have you got the child-benefit book, Moe?' whispered Maureen.

'Are you from the police?'

'No,' said Maureen. 'I'm just a friend of Jimmy's family. Look, Ann died a week and half ago and her book's still being cashed. Have you got it?'

'If you're just a friend of Jimmy's I don't have to answer any questions, do I?'

'No, Moe, you don't, but I know about the book and I know about her trips to Glasgow with the big bag and I know why you want the Polaroid. What should I do with that information?'

Moe's chin crumpled and she began to cry, tugging at her wedding ring. Her face turned pink, like Ann's. Maureen was glad of the dark hall and the cool walls but her knees were feeling shaky. 'Come on, sit down,' she said, and led the crying woman to the living room.

Moe cried for a long time, hiding her face in her hands

and each time the crying subsided the sight of Maureen made her sob afresh.

'Moe,' said Maureen quietly, 'you've got an alcoholic sister who doesn't live here. She comes to visit ye, goes away and two days later you report her missing. She could have gone home and not phoned, she could be lying drunk somewhere in the middle of a binge. It's ridiculous for you to report her missing.' Moe was looking at the carpet, dabbing her wet eyes. Maureen sighed. 'Do you mind very much if I smoke?'

Moe shook her head. Maureen took out her fags and lit one, leaning over and feeling under the chair for the ashtray. She found it and pulled it out, sat it on the arm of the chair. Moe watched her, sniffing quietly. 'Would you like a cigarette?' asked Maureen gently.

Moe shook her head again and gestured to her heart, sobbing and turning away. Too hung over to fight with a woman about her heart condition, Maureen waited patiently until Moe had cried herself out. She gave her a hankie.

'Thank you,' said Moe, in a little-girl voice, glancing up at her. 'Can I make a phone call?'

'No. I want you to sit and talk to me for five minutes and then you can make a phone call.'

Moe dabbed at her nose. 'But I want to phone my husband.'

'After.'

Moe looked up to see if she meant it and saw Maureen's red eyes and scratched knuckles. "Kay.' She shrugged. 'What do you want?'

'Tell me about the book.'

Moe picked at the chenille on the arm of her chair. 'I've got it,' she said. 'I didn't think it would matter, now she's dead.'

'It does matter. It means that the children are going without. Burn it.'

''Kay.' Moe sniffed. 'I'm sorry, I just didn't think it mattered.'

Maureen drew on her cigarette and looked at her. 'Have you ever heard of a guy called Tam Parlain?'

'Of course I have. Everyone knows about him. It's men like him that make this estate hell to live on. They buy drugs from him and they come round here to use them.'

Maureen took a drag. 'I know Ann was a courier,' she said softly. 'What's the story, Moe? Why did she really tell you about Leslie Findlay?'

Moe began to cry again, covering her face and panting, making a passable impression of herself earlier. 'No, come on, stop,' said Maureen lethargically. 'I know it's not real this time, stop it.'

Rumbled as rumbled could be, Moe sat up straight, sniffing and blushing and watching Maureen's cigarette. 'Can I have one?' she said.

'Course ye can.' Maureen gave her one and lit it for her, moving the ashtray to the other arm of the chair to save Moe reaching over. 'Now tell me. Who was Ann carrying for?'

'I don't know,' said Moe. 'Someone bought her debt and they made her do it. She knew she was in danger, she told me about the photo and gave me the address of the shelter so that I'd be able to tell the police if anything happened. She was very concerned about the kids . . .' she broke off for a genuine sob '. . . she was worried about them, worried anything would happen to them.'

'Didn't she know the police would think Jimmy beat her?'

'No,' said Moe. 'She thought the truth would come out.'

'She should have told the shelter people the truth.'

'But if she'd told them the truth they wouldn't have let

316

her stay, would they? They'd have sent her to the police and she couldn't go to them.'

Moe was right, Ann couldn't have told them that. They'd have turned her away immediately.

'Why did they beat her up at all?' asked Maureen.

'She lost a whole bag of their drugs.'

'She *lost* them?'

'She was mugged.'

'What's the story with the Polaroid?'

'He was her boyfriend,' said Moe. 'He was going to protect her. She said I should contact him if anything went wrong.'

'What's his name?'

'I don't know. She said she'd left a photo and I'd be able to find him through that.'

'And that's why you wanted to keep it?'

'I just want to know what she was doing,' said Moe desperately, 'why she was working for drugs . . . people. Our family have never been involved in anything like that. We're from a decent family. Can I have the picture?'

'No,' said Maureen. 'I haven't got it any more but the guy's name is Frank Toner and he drinks around here.'

'In Streatham?'

'No, in Brixton. Coach and Horses.'

'I thought he lived in Scotland. What happened to the picture?'

'I gave it to a guy I met in a pub.'

Moe was very offended. 'Why did you give it to him when I asked for it?'

'I had the feeling you were lying to me, Moe, and I didn't want to give it to you.'

Maureen stubbed her cigarette out in the ashtray and as she did Moe lurched across in the chair and grabbed her hand, squeezing too hard, crushing the scratched fingers together. 'I'm sorry I lied,' she said, pointedly making eye-contact. 'I just don't know who to trust. Thank you for being kind to me, I'll never forget it.'

Maureen disentangled her hand and stood up. 'Look, take care of yourself. And burn that book.'

'I will,' sighed Moe unsteadily. 'I will.'

'You can make your phone call now.'

Moe shut the door behind her and double-locked it from the inside.

The sunlight and the mild weather heightened the smell from the bins and Maureen held her breath as she hurried out of the enclosed courtyard. Another message was coming through on her pager. She dug it out and found that Leslie had left a mobile number and asked her to phone urgently. She took a side-street to the station and soon found herself in a pretty road of low, terraced houses with climbing plants around the doors and shallow gardens. She lit a cigarette and walked slowly. A car crawled past her, lilting over the speed bumps, speeding up in the pauses. If Moe had the book then Ann must have signed all the cheques for her in advance. She must have known, thought Maureen suddenly. She must have known she was going to die.

The receiver in the phone-box in the high street had been smashed and she had no choice but to move nearer to the tube station. The Hebrew Israelites were shouting through a megaphone at a small crowd of bewildered listeners standing five feet away. They had constructed a small platform for themselves and were dressed in what appeared to be old costumes from an amateur play about Hannibal, studded belts and trousers tucked into knee-length leather boots. Two stood on either side of the speaker, their arms crossed, looking over the heads of an imaginary vast crowd. The speaker had been shouting about the evils of homosexuality and handed the megaphone to his pal. 'And they shall be put to death!' he shouted. 'And they shall be put to death!'

She tried the mobile number recorded on her pager but found it engaged.

'Liam?'

'Mauri?' he shouted. 'When are ye coming home?'

'I'm a bit rough, Liam. Don't shout again, okay?'

A bus passed the phone-box, sending a gust of air under the door.

'Are ye hung over again?' he said, sounding a bit worried.

'No, I've got flu or something.' She felt like Winnie, telling a hopeless lie to cover up her drinking. 'I think I got it from someone on the bus,' she said, digging herself in deeper and deeper, wondering why the fuck she was lying.

'Hutton was trying to move out on his own,' said Liam. 'That's why he was hit.'

It took her a couple of minutes to remember why she cared about any of it. 'Oh. That's good, isn't it?' she said. 'Means Ann had nothing to do with it.'

'Probably. No-one knows where he got his stash from. She might have been carrying up to him.'

Maureen tried to think of something intelligent to say but blanked. 'My head's bursting,' she said.

Liam paused. 'Why are you outside, then?'

'Sarah chucked me out for getting drunk and bad-mouthing Jesus.'

'So, you got drunk while you had the flu or you've got a flu with exactly the same symptoms as a hangover.'

She laughed softly, trying not to shake her head or breathe out too much. 'Oh, God,' she whispered, 'I feel so bad. I've hurt my hand.'

'Well, you shouldn't drink so much,' said Liam. 'I heard they arrested that Jimmy guy.'

'Yeah. Look, Liam, your druggie pals down here, are they nice people?'

'Yeah, they're nice enough.'

'Can I go and see them? I want to ask them about something.'

'I can't give you their address, Mauri. It's a confidential relationship, you know.'

'Come on, Liam, you're not a priest.'

'They won't be chuffed if I send you there. They're a bit, you know, careful.'

'Can't you phone them first and ask?'

'They might not be in.'

'Well, ye can tell me whether they're in when I phone back in a minute, can't ye?'

'They won't like it.'

'I'll phone ye back in twenty minutes, Liam.'

Liam tutted and muttered 'fucksake' before hanging up. Maureen looked around at the soft porn in the phone-box, wondering what the children who came in here thought of it. A lorry passed by outside and the cards on the cheaper paper fluttered, whipping up like curling fingers. The Hebrew Israelites were chanting threats through a megaphone. She would have given anything to be at home, before Mark Doyle had grabbed her elbow, before Sarah had called her an alkie.

37
Martha

Martha's voice was a drawling syrupy balm and her soft eyes were a solace. She wore a colourful wrap-around skirt, a short red T-shirt and big trainers. 'Alex is away for a couple of days,' she said, blinking slowly, as if she'd just had a smoke or was about to have a smoke. 'Anyway, babe, Liam said you had a really bad hangover and I had to look after you.'

Maureen lay back on the settee and looked at the ceiling. Martha lived just across the road from the Oval underground station. It was a poky flat, gracelessly shaved from a more illustrious whole. The odd-shaped rooms were too high, the cornicing stopped abruptly at walls like a discontinued stanza and the galley kitchen was shaped like a streamlined map of Italy, splaying out at the end to avoid cutting the big window in half.

Martha and Alex had not spent a lot of money on decoration but their entire flat seemed specifically designed to appease a hangover. The front room was dark and the heavy curtains were drawn, even though it was four in the afternoon. Damp patches on the ceiling were covered with Paisley shawls and a dim deflected light shone out from underneath a floating umbrella in a high corner. A collection of 3D postcards of dogs wearing hats was displayed on the fireplace. Compared to Sarah's house it was the most cosy, welcoming place she had ever been, and Maureen never wanted to move from here. Martha sat down next to her on the sagging sofa.

'Do you own this flat?' asked Maureen.

'No,' said Martha, in her breathy English accent. 'We rent it from a bloke who lives in Ireland. He owns the building. He's cool when it comes to rent and dates and stuff.'

'It's nice. Very calming.'

'Would you like something to eat? What about a cup of tea and a chocolate mini roll?' said Martha, well versed in the chemistry of comfort.

'Oh, that would be perfect.'

'I've got some Valium too, babe,' said Martha, heaving herself up. 'You could have one or two.'

Maureen declined. She desperately wanted to stay on the sofa but she thought it might be rude to sit while her host attended to her so she wrenched herself out of her seat and put her shades on again as she followed Martha into the bright kitchen. She wanted to use the phone but thought it might be cheeky to call a mobile in Scotland. The kitchen was homely and comfortable: the cupboards had been painted pink and yellow with matt emulsion, and the fridge had a big picture of Lionel Ritchie, *sans* beard, varnished on to the door, looking as if his mouth and jaw had been manipulated in a special computer program. It hadn't. Martha filled the kettle from the tap.

'It's very kind of you to look after me like this,' said Maureen, suddenly aware of the sorry spectacle she must present.

'No trouble.' Martha turned off the tap and plugged the kettle in. 'How's Liam?'

'He's fine,' said Maureen.

'Yeah, is he still with Maggie?'

'No, they split up at New Year.'

Martha stopped still and blinked at the worktop. 'When?' she said, the breathy freshness gone from her voice.

Liam had a knack of inspiring obsessive interest in certain types of crazy women. Maureen put it down to his constant low-level aggression. 'Not long ago.'

'Yeah?' Martha tried to smile. 'Well, he told me on the phone that they were still together.'

Liam, it seemed, did not reciprocate the interest. 'Oh,' muttered Maureen, 'maybe they got back together, then.'

Martha turned back to the kettle. 'Yeah,' she repeated. 'Back together.'

'He doesn't tell me everything,' said Maureen, afraid that Martha would turn against both O'Donnells and refuse to let her back on to the settee. 'I wouldn't know if they were.'

'If they were what?' challenged Martha. 'If they were together? Or if they were apart?'

'Well, if they'd got back together, I wouldn't know. He wouldn't tell me. I don't get on with Maggie all that well. I don't see them together much.'

Martha lifted two clean mugs from the busy draining-board. 'Don't you like her?' she asked, in a snide undertone.

Maureen could understand Martha not liking Maggie. Maggie's father was an actuary and the family lived on the south side of Glasgow in a big new house with a garden. She probably wouldn't sit down in Martha's house. Plus Martha wanted to fuck her boyfriend.

'I do like her,' lied Maureen. 'I just don't have a lot in common with her. Does Liam come here a lot?'

'Not any more. Not since he retired.'

Maureen thanked fuck that the conversation was over. Martha pulled a packet of chocolate mini rolls out of the cupboard and peeled back the crunchy Cellophane, exposing the row of soft cakes. 'Have a couple, there, babe,' she said. 'Worst thing you can do for a hangover is starve it. Your body needs sugar.'

Maureen unwrapped the foil and sank her teeth into the spongy roll. It melted in her mouth, she hardly had to chew.

'Liam said a friend of yours is missing, is that right?'

'Yeah, I wanted to ask, do you know most of the dealers in Brixton?'

'Some,' shrugged Martha.

'Tam Parlain?' asked Maureen. 'Argyle Street?'

'Yeah, he's not a very nice man. How did you hear about him?'

'Well, I was asking about a solicitor called Headie and his name came up.'

Martha smiled. 'Coldharbour Lane?'

'Yeah.'

'Poor old thing.' Martha frowned and petted her lip with mock concern. 'Mr Headie drank,' she said, as if that explained everything. It probably did.

Maureen took the photocopy of Ann out of her pocket. 'Have you ever seen this woman?'

Martha unfolded the photocopy and looked at it closely. 'No,' she said. 'Was she a user?'

'Don't think so.'

Martha looked closer. She was the only person so far who'd looked at the picture of Ann without flinching. She held the photocopy at arm's length. 'Yuch,' she said disdainfully. 'What a mess to get yourself into.' She smiled as she handed it back to Maureen.

'I don't think she did it to herself,' said Maureen quietly, taking the Polaroid out of her pocket. 'What about this guy?'

The kettle had begun to boil and Martha turned it off before taking the picture from Maureen. She looked at it and her face fell. 'Where the fuck did you get this?'

'It was among the woman's belongings after she disappeared.'

Martha threw the picture on the work-top. She didn't even want to hold it. She held up her hands, wiggling her fingers in panic. 'Have you showed this to people?'

'One or two,' said Maureen.

Martha forgot about the lovely tea she had promised Maureen, forgot that Maureen had just had a chocolate sponge on an empty, rebellious stomach. 'Get rid of it,' said Martha, poking it away with her finger like a dead rat. 'Fucking bin it, get rid of it. Do you have any idea what this picture is?'

'No.'

'It's a threat. Whose kid is it?'

'The woman who disappeared.'

Martha looked at the picture again. 'In a playground, that is un-fucking-human.'

Maureen didn't know what unhuman was but she had an inkling 'Why is it a threat?'

Martha leaned forward and pointed at the Polaroid. 'He knows where the kid is. He's been near the kid once and he can get to him again. He's going to hurt her kid.'

They settled back in the living room on the seductively sagging sofa and Maureen sipped the tea and ate more chocolate mini rolls. Martha said that the Polaroid was a way of flushing Ann out and making her come to him. She wasn't surprised when Maureen told her that Parlain was after it. Parlain worked for Toner and anyone who dealt with Toner would want it: returning the Polaroid to him would be a way to curry favour, keeping it back would give them leverage. She said that if Toner knew Maureen was holding the Polaroid he'd have marked her already. Maureen looked at the picture, at Toner's spiteful smile and the strain in the boy's forearm as he tried to pull away. Ann must have been terrified.

'What had she done to deserve that?' asked Martha.

'I'm not certain. I think she was carrying for him and she lost the lot or sold it and then he beat her up and she got away. If she was carrying for him, who'd she be carrying to?'

Martha shifted uncomfortably in her chair and sipped her tea.

'You know, don't you?' said Maureen.

'It's not a big secret or anything.'

'What isn't?'

'Toner's got a relationship with some people in Paisley.'

'Parlains,' said Maureen.

Martha smiled faintly into her cup. 'Liam would be so worried if I told him about this.'

'Oh, God, Martha, please don't tell him. He'll be worried sick.'

Martha shrugged.

'No, please, don't, Martha. I'm going home in the morning anyway.'

38

Anagram

Michael had slipped through the window as a smoky vapour and was hanging in the air near her bed, close enough to touch her if he wanted to. Someone was tapping her feet and calling her name. She opened her aching eyes and slowly made out the figure of Martha across the room. She was sitting in the big wicker armchair and had put on a lot of makeup. She smiled sexily at Maureen. 'Hello, sleepy,' Martha drawled, lifting a big spliff to her smudged red mouth. 'Daddy's here.'

Maureen scrambled to her feet, staggering on her wobbly legs, trying to scratch the sleep out of her eyes and make out the figure standing stiffly at the end of the sofa.

'Fucking hell,' said Liam

'Liam?'

'Are you okay?'

'How the fuck did you get here?'

'I flew.' He looked very concerned. 'Are you okay?'

'I got a fright.' She pointed at Martha.

'But she's all right now, aren't you, babe? She was so ill earlier,' said Martha, keen to give Liam the impression that she and Maureen had bonded.

'Look, Mauri, there's a flight back tonight,' said Liam, 'and I've booked two seats.'

'I'm not going back,' said Maureen. 'I'm not finished.'

'Maureen,' he glanced sidelong at Martha, 'I've come all the way down here to get ye out of trouble.'

'I'm not coming home yet.'

Liam sat down on the settee, sinking to within three inches of the floor, and looked up at her. 'Come here, come and sit down,' he said, patting the seat next to him.

'I don't want to sit down.' She sounded like a sullen teenager.

Martha stood up, acting embarrassed, as if she was so fey she'd never seen siblings squabble. 'I'll go and put the kettle on,' she said, and went into the kitchen with an affected, wiggling walk. Maureen waited until she was out of the room before going back to the settee and falling into it. Liam offered her a fag but she refused it.

'The game's a bogie, Mauri,' said Liam. 'The police found stuff in Harris's house, his wife had been back—'

'What stuff?' interrupted Maureen.

'A set of photos belonging to the woman. In Leslie's shelter place at Christmas.'

'But Leslie's got them! She wouldn't have two sets.'

'Hey,' shouted Liam indignantly, 'don't fucking shout at me, I didn't put them there—'

'I didn't shout!' she shouted.

'Mauri, listen. Harris had been in London as well. They've got evidence that he was here when she died. Isn't that proof enough?'

'I'm not going home yet,' she said simply.

'Look, Mauri,' he said softly, 'there's no point sulking about this. Take it from me, Frank Toner is a very scary man. If you've been showing that picture around you need to come home. Did ye show the picture to anybody?'

She shrugged.

'Did ye show it to anyone who could trace ye to home?'

She vaguely remembered showing it to Mark Doyle, or Tonsa, she couldn't remember.

'Tonsa?' she said. 'I think I showed it to Tonsa.'

Liam was horrified. 'Tonsa?' he said, slapping her leg and leaning over her. 'Maureen, they'll think you're working for me.'

'But you're retired.'

'No-one retires, you silly cow. If Tonsa realizes who you are and tells Toner, I'm fucked. God,' he sat back and looked at her, 'wee hen, you've got to come home before ye do some real damage.'

Vaguely, vaguely in a distant place within her shrivelled brain, she remembered telling Tonsa she was Liam's sister. She'd said his name to Tonsa, of all fucking people. She looked up at the umbrella floating on the ceiling. He had told her not to mention him. He had specifically told her.

Liam nudged her gently. 'Let's go home.'

'I need one more day to make it right,' she said, panicking. 'I need to see her sister again. She's a wee old lady, she doesn't keep well. One more day? Can't we stay tonight and leave tomorrow?'

Liam looked hurt. 'Promise me that's all you're going to do.'

'I promise.'

Martha was leaning on the door-frame, her forearms wrapped around her waist in a way she imagined was slimming. She smiled at Liam. 'Looks like you're staying,' she said, and laughed gaily.

'We're not staying here,' said Liam bluntly. 'There isn't any room.'

'Alex is away for a couple of days,' said Martha casually. 'There's loads of room. Maureen's comfortable on the sofa, aren't you?'

'Yeah,' said Maureen. 'It's just one night.'

Reluctantly, Liam went out to the hall and phoned the airline, changing the flights for the next evening. Maureen and Martha sat together on the settee, listening and relaxing when they heard him confirm his details. Martha smiled. 'It's comfortable, isn't it?'

'What?'

'The sofa. Nice and comfortable.'

Confused, Maureen smiled back at her as Liam came back in. 'Tomorrow night,' he said. 'But we can't change them again, right?'

Maureen nodded. 'I'd better go back to Sarah's,' she said, staring meaningfully at Liam, 'and let her know I'll be staying here.'

'Good. Come on, then,' said Liam, deliberately not inviting Martha.

Maureen said she wanted to see Kilty to give her back what was left of her shopping. In fact, she had been so drunk the night before that she wasn't sure how they had left things. A twitching pang of hangover insecurity nagged at her and she wanted to see her to make sure it was all right. The young landlord let them into the narrow hallway and said that Kilty was upstairs, last door, knock loud.

'She knows we're coming,' said Maureen.

'You'll still have to knock loud.'

The door to Kilty's room trembled with the reverberating theme tune from the *Money Programme*, and beyond the wall of noise a trilling little soprano voice sang along badly, following the notes a step late and pausing for breath mid-bar. Maureen banged on the door as hard as she could but felt the sound being swallowed beyond the door. She banged again and the singing stopped. Moments later the theme tune flickered to a dead stop. 'Did someone knock?' asked Kilty politely.

'It's me.'

The door opened on a grinning Kilty. Her room was large, with a big oriole window at the far end and wooden shutters like the ones in Liam's house. She had very little furniture: a single bed, a leather armchair and an ottoman. On the far wall a semicircular fireplace built of orange tiles looked like a decorator's take on a sunset. It was stacked with smoke-free fuel, little burning black boiled sweets. A gold mesh fireguard stood in front of it.

'This is my brother, Liam.'

Kilty smiled and held out her hand. 'Kilty Goldfarb,' she said, shaking Liam's hand.

Liam looked bewildered. 'What is that?' he said. 'An anagram?'

Kilty wiggled her eyebrows alternately at Maureen, and Liam watched them, hoping she'd do it again. Kilty turned off the television and made sure the fireguard was as close to the fire as possible before slipping on her fur coat and turning off the light. She said that the best place for a quiet chat was the Alhambra restaurant and the coffee was beautiful. On the way round the corner Maureen chatted anxiously and managed to glean that Kilty had had a good night the evening before and Maureen had neither said nor done anything spectacular in her company, apart from convincing her to have a drink in the Coach and Horses.

The Alhambra was a North African restaurant decorated with a desert-theme mural. It looked as if the artist could only draw people from a side-on view but they had exploited their limitations to the full; men carried heavy bags and led camels backwards and forwards across the wall while the women stared straight at them or watched their backs. Kilty took a table near the window and began talking to Liam, asking him about himself. They knew the same crowd of people from the Glasgow Tech disco and worked out that they had probably been at several of the same parties when they were in their late teens but had somehow managed never to meet each other. At Kilty's insistence they ordered three coffees. Maureen sipped hers. It was delicious, the bitterness of the coffee tempered by the subtle perfume of cardamom seeds and other hints and flavours too complex for a heavy smoker's palate. Maureen asked Kilty to smoke a cigarette. Liam and Maureen sat and watched her puff-puffing over her coffee, giggling and nudging each other. Maureen didn't expect Kilty to enjoy the negative attention quite as much as she did, but Kilty didn't mind people laughing at her because Kilty thought she was great. And so she was. Kilty stubbed out her fag, finished her coffee and pulled on her jacket, saying she'd better go home and get ready for work tomorrow. She invited them both out for dinner the following evening.

'We're going home tomorrow,' said Liam.

'Oh,' Kilty looked crestfallen, 'what a shame. You will come back, though, won't you?'

'I'll definitely come back and see ye,' said Maureen. 'I promise.'

Kilty leaned across the table, grabbed Maureen by the ears and pressed a smacking kiss into her cheek. She stood up. 'I had a fucking top time last night.' She pulled her ski hat down over her eyebrows like a cloche. 'It was lovely to meet you. Both.'

'She's a turn and a half,' said Liam, when she had gone.

'She certainly is,' grinned Maureen.

Liam had ordered two plates of lamb couscous. Maureen didn't want to eat but the cardamom coffee had given her an appetite. When the food arrived the smell from the meat was rich and heady and the couscous was as light as air. Tentative, she tried eating a little couscous on its own, then with a spoonful of gravy over it and finally got stuck in. Liam ate his dinner and kept an avaricious eye on hers, discouraging her where he could, telling her that dinner was the worst meal to eat with a hangover and lamb could prolong the pain for up to a week.

'How's Winnie?' said Maureen. 'Still sober?'

'Sober as a very jumpy judge. She won't have Michael in the house any more either and her and George have remade their bed together.'

'That's great.' Maureen smiled. 'Una'll be pleased anyway. She won't keep having to fend a drunk granny off the wean.'

Liam looked suddenly at the table. 'Yeah,' he said. 'That's right, yeah.'

'What?' said Maureen, knowing the look of old. 'Una's not seeing Winnie or what? Has Alistair finally put his foot down or something?'

'Alistair's, well, Alistair's gone.'

'Gone?'

'He's left.'

'What do you mean he's left?'

'Una's chucked him out. They're getting divorced. He'd been having an affair with the upstairs neighbour.'

Maureen sat back and looked at him. '*Alistair?*'

'Yeah, Mr Steady Eddie Alistair.'

'But he was the only nice one out of all of us.'

'I know,' said Liam. 'Changes things, doesn't it, if Una's bringing up the child alone?'

'Is Michael still hanging about at Una's?'

'Like a persistent bad smell. She's the only one who's kept faith with him. I think that's why Winnie got sober. I think she's worried about the wean.'

'Jittery Winnie's going to protect the wean?' said Maureen, her voice cracking mid-sentence.

Behind the counter two men shouted over each other angrily until one of them slammed a frying-pan down on the work-top. An intense quiet fell over the café. It wasn't born yet, Maureen told herself, not yet. She didn't want to care about that, she didn't have room to care about that. She wanted to nuzzle her face into the abstract problem of Jimmy and Ann and never think about Michael again.

'See if someone's carrying drugs up to Glasgow? Do the people buying them pay before they arrive or do they pay on delivery?'

Liam giggled at her. 'On delivery.'

Maureen frowned. 'Why are you laughing at me?'

'You're very naïve, Mauri. The trip's the dangerous bit. We'd all be broke if we paid before.'

Maureen clicked her tongue at him. He was very patronizing sometimes. 'This woman,' she said, 'was killed in a really bizarre way.'

'How?'

She watched Liam shoving couscous into his mouth. 'D'ye really want to hear about it when you're eating?'

'Doesn't bother me,' he said.

'Well,' she said, 'her feet and hands were burned, her legs and arms were cut and her skull was fractured. Does that sound like a gangster killing to you?'

Liam wiped his plate clean with a chunk of lamb.

'Not really,' he said. 'Not unless they were torturing her for information.' He looked at her meat dish. 'They'd probably be disguising her identity.'

'That's the one thing they weren't doing. They left her identity bracelet on.'

'They must have been torturing her, then. Where did they cut her on her legs?'

'The backs of her knees.'

Liam sat up and looked at her curiously. 'Really?'

'Yeah.'

He gazed into the mid-distance and mapped the injuries on his body, moving his lips and gesturing to his legs, his feet and finally his hands, like a tiny genuflection. 'Those are all places you inject yourself,' he said.

'Eh?'

'The veins junkies inject in, arms, hands, feet and behind the knees, that's a bit later.'

'Maybe she became a user?'

'Maybe.' Liam lit a cigarette and sat back, rubbing his swollen belly. 'That was fucking lovely.'

'You know who I feel really sorry for?' said Maureen. 'Hutton's girlfriend. She's pregnant.'

Liam huffed at his plate. 'I wouldn't waste my energy feeling sorry for Maxine Parlain.'

Maureen dropped her fork to the table. 'She's a Parlain? From Paisley?' Liam nodded. Maureen sat forward, shaking her finger in his face. 'Her brother's down here, Tam Parlain paged me to go and see him.'

'Ye didn't go, did ye?'

'I didn't know it was him till I got there. He's a dealer—'

'Keep your fucking voice down,' muttered Liam.

'Sorry, sorry,' she affected a whisper, 'but he's down here and he's involved in this somehow. Martha says he works for Toner.'

'Well,' said Liam sceptically, 'he won't work for him but he'll distribute for him.'

'Why won't he work for him?'

'Well, he's a Parlain and they're a team so Tam is always going to be one of them. Toner might get him to work for him but he knows his loyalty will be with the family. He'd only have taken him on to build contacts with them. It's like the idiot son who used to get taken on by another firm as a goodwill gesture.'

'So Toner'll have a lot of contacts at home?'

'Yeah.'

'She must have been muling for Toner, not Hutton at all.'

'Well, there you are, she'd be carrying up to the Parlains, then. That Tam's got slash scars all over his face.'

'I know,' said Maureen. 'Is he quite heavy?'

'Naw, everyone says he's a prick. He kept getting slashed for annoying people. He's probably down here out the way of harm.'

Maureen gave Liam the rest of her dinner as a reward and sat back watching him eat. The Parlains could have put the ticket through Jimmy's door. Senga could have given Maxine the photos and Toner would have an army of lackeys in Glasgow happy to fake letters for him. She wondered about Las Vegas Elizabeth. She'd been to Scotland on the train, she might have been a courier too. Liam finished the meat and sat back, picking at his teeth with a complimentary toothpick. Maureen went to the back of the restaurant to use the pay-phone. The mobile was answered before it rang out. 'Hello,' called Maureen, sounding jolly.

'Maureen, for fucksake come home,' said Leslie.

'What?'

Leslie dropped the phone to her shoulder but Maureen could still hear her asking permission to take it outside. She heard the shriek of a chair being pushed back and Leslie muttered, 'Hang on, don't hang up,' before walking somewhere and shutting a door.

'Are you all right?'

'No. The police are going to arrest me. They don't believe me about the Polaroid.' She was whispering quickly and sounded terrified. 'They think I told Jimmy where she was, and gave him the money to fly to London. They found the shelter Christmas pictures in Jimmy's and they think she was back there.'

'But you've got Ann's set.'

'I've told them that, they don't believe me. Even if I don't get charged I'll lose my job if the committee hears about it, fuck.' Her voice was rising to a tearful pitch. Leslie dropped the phone to her shoulder to gather herself together and the receiver crackled in Maureen's ear as she rubbed it against her jacket. Leslie cleared her throat and came back on. 'He was in London, Mauri, he was in London when she was murdered.'

'Ye haven't given them the CCB photos, have ye?'

'Are ye fucking joking? They're gonnae charge me and I'm going to do that?'

'Look,' said Maureen, 'tell them Maxine Parlain's brother lives down here and knew Ann.'

'What's that to do with anything?'

'Just tell them. I'm coming home tomorrow.'

'Don't lose that fucking Polaroid.'

'I won't, I promise I won't. Sit tight, it'll be okay, I promise.'

'Even if they don't sack me they'll never trust me again. I'll end up working in that fucking office with you.'

Maureen coughed and hesitated. 'I'm not going back there, Leslie. I'm going to do something else.'

'Aye,' said Leslie, looking around. 'Well, ye might have to save me a seat.'

'Listen,' said Maureen, feeling relieved, 'what's Jimmy's story about the Christmas photos?'

'He's saying they came through his door, like the ticket. He thought you'd put them through.'

'Senga fucking Brolly.'

'That's what I thought,' agreed Leslie.

They dragged themselves back to Martha's expressionist house and spent a horrible evening flicking through the television channels looking for something watchable and listening to Martha carp on about how great she was and how everyone mistook her for a model. They watched a nasty, gossipy programme about JFK and Martha talked over the most salacious bits. Alex was away for a couple of days – in fact, Martha and Alex weren't getting on at all well and Martha wondered if they'd break up. Maureen smoked until her tongue went numb. She wanted to leave and go to Brixton and lose herself in Ann again. Martha had been with Alex for over six years, that was a long time, wasn't it? Una and Alistair splitting up must have been worse for Liam than it was for Maureen; Una would talk to Liam, rely on him and make him spend time in the house with Michael. Martha wished she had hair like Maureen and Liam's, lovely curly hair. She stood up and walked over to Liam to touch it and comment on the texture. She'd love hair like that. The prospect of a new baby in the family had never seemed real to Maureen, even though Una had been trying for years. The enormity of it began to sink in. Una was having a baby without the good sense and protective presence of Alistair. In all the years they'd been trying for a baby none of them had imagined that Martha was going to get her hair cut, really short—

'Martha!' snapped Maureen. She was up for a fight but Liam glared at her.

'What?' said Martha, smiling for Liam.

'Don't cut it!' exclaimed Maureen, maintaining a furious face for the sake of continuity. 'Keep it long!'

'Really?' Martha was very pleased. She didn't notice Liam turning away from her and grinning into the ashtray. 'Yes! It's nice!'

Liam sniggered out a trail of smoke and started coughing.

It was twelve o'clock and the mediocre programming took a downturn. Martha insisted that Maureen sleep on the sofa, because she liked it so much, didn't she? She brought out a sleeping-bag and a pillow and gave Maureen a T-shirt and pyjama trousers to wear. She demanded that Liam sleep on the floor in her bedroom. He tried to resist but Martha persisted shamelessly. 'Are you frightened of me?' she said, smiling at Maureen for support.

'No, Martha, I'm not frightened of you but I'd rather sleep in here.'

Martha laughed. 'But there's more room in there. Don't be silly, I'll set up the camp bed for you,' she said, and skipped lightly out of the room.

Liam sighed and lifted his jacket from the floor. 'I'll see ye in the morning, Mauri.'

Maureen settled on to the sofa, fully dressed, feeling disgusted at Martha and her tawdry flat with its regressive hippie shit décor. She knew she had to make a choice. She could abandon Una's baby to its fate, stay away from them all and live her own life with her eyes half closed among decent people like Vik. Or she could stand up and face it. She wanted Vik and nights out at the pictures and seaside days and the odd bottle of wine. She wanted normal, decent company. She wanted Vik.

She had been thinking about Michael and Una's baby for over an hour when she heard creaking from the next room and Liam groaning loudly. She banged on the floor to remind them that she was there but it didn't make any difference. She tried closing the door to the front room but the sloping floorboards and subsiding frame held it open.

She sat up by the window, as far away from the open door as she could get, watching the lorries and the black cabs stopping at the lights outside while Liam shagged Martha to get her off his back.

She woke up in the sagging armchair, convinced that she was home and Una was breathing baby blood through the window. She'd dropped her fag and it had burned a long chewy black stripe in the rug. She couldn't face Martha or Liam – she didn't think she could hide her disgust. She gathered her bag and left a note for Liam, saying she'd meet him at the airport. She tiptoed out of the flat, down the stairs and into the breezy street. She wanted to find Elizabeth.

Following the route in the *A–Z*, she made her way from Martha's house to Brixton. The clouds were sparse and ribbons of sunshine filled the street. It was warm. Lynn would be at home in Glasgow, waiting for her Liam to come home. She thought of Liam and tried to remember what she had said to Tonsa. She needed a good sleep. She stopped for more fags and a half-pint carton of milk, drinking it as she walked from the Oval to Brixton. She was struck by a sudden image of Michael holding Una's baby, cutting its little legs with his razor fingers.

She was standing at the edge of the pavement on the high street, waiting to cross over, when she looked up and saw Frank Toner swaggering along the pavement with a woman on his arm. The woman was tall but frighteningly young, like an elongated child with big breasts. Toner grabbed her around the waist and pulled her to him, buckling her ankle as he nuzzled his face into her rich hair. The girl feigned a big smile, opening her mouth and showing all her teeth, but her young eyes were frightened. As Toner lifted his face from her hair he turned and looked straight at Maureen. He stopped and Maureen caught her breath.

He was coming chin first across the road, pulling the girl off the pavement, dragging her by the hand. The cars slowed and the child ran after him on tiptoe, precarious in her stilettos. Toner speeded up, swinging his free hand as ballast. The child was slowing him down so he dropped her hand, abandoning her in the middle of the road; she staggered to a stop, her thick hair falling over her eyes as a

Volvo screeched to a halt in front of her. Frank Toner was coming.

Maureen stood quite still on the pavement, watching him. She should have run but she was sweating and exhausted and knew she couldn't run any further. If she died now she would never go home, never see Ruchill or have to save Una's child, Liam would be safe and Vik would always be a possibility. She held her breath and he reached out for her, tucking a rigid hand under her armpit, lifting her off her feet and scuffing her toes, pulling her along through the crowded pavement. Behind them the lost girl teetered on her heels and cried, 'Frank, Frank!' The air smelt like water, like the breeze back at the window in Garnethill, and Maureen resigned herself.

Toner was dragging her towards the mouth of Coldharbour Lane. He was hurting her, pressing the tendons tight together, pinching the bones apart, holding tighter than he need have. Pedestrians watched them pass, Toner striding up the road with his jaw foremost and a small, ragged woman in his grip. She didn't seem alarmed, didn't seem bothered, just hanging at the side of him like a little doll with a mop of curly hair.

They turned the corner and up Coldharbour, past the nice boutiques and businessmen's bars, towards the Coach and Horses. But Leslie needed the Polaroid. Leslie needed it. Maureen began to struggle, scratching at his hand and drawing his attention as they passed the mouth of Electric Avenue. A shadow moved closer and Toner toppled over on the pavement, dropping Maureen and landing on his face. An arm wrapped tight around Maureen's waist, lifting her off her feet, turning her sideways and running down the lane, carrying her into the market, blending into the stalls.

Mark Doyle put her down on her feet and grabbed her forearm, scratching her skin with his callused hands. He dragged her into a shallow doorway, through a narrow close open to the sky, through another door and up a set of worn wooden stairs. He pushed her in front of him and she ran as fast as she could, suddenly awake and afraid, suddenly caring. They ran up four flights of stairs until they came to a door. Doyle unlocked three heavy bolts and opened it, shoving her in. It was a tall, shallow room, completely bare, flooded with startling sunlight from a high arched window at the narrow end.

Maureen approached the window carefully, standing on tiptoe to peer out, afraid that Toner would be standing outside. They were three storeys above the shops in the high street. She turned and looked around her. At the other end of the narrow room a red sleeping-bag lay crumpled on a dirty mattress, an ashtray spilling on to the floor next to it. They were panting with excitement, their faces varnished with sweat and apprehension. She was about to ask him why he had saved her when she turned and saw him rubbing his hands together. 'You're heavier than ye look,' he said.

She was alone with Mark Doyle in a room no-one knew about, with one exit and three locks.

'Much heavier.' He smiled and walked towards Maureen, panting alone by the window.

39
Death

Doyle sat four feet away from her on the bare concrete floor, smoking a cigarette. 'Why didn't ye struggle?'

Maureen reached into her pocket with a trembling hand and took out her cigarettes. She put one in her mouth, and the sight of Vik's lighter made her want to throw up. 'I didn't know it was you,' she whispered eventually.

He looked at her curiously. 'I meant with Toner. Why didn't you struggle when he grabbed you? I saw ye standing on the road, watching him come across. I thought you were going to pull a gun or something, the way you were looking at him.'

She didn't answer. She had been prepared to die at Toner's hands but not this, not Mark Doyle. She didn't want to be dead Pauline under a tree, she didn't want to die with spunk on her back. It was bright in the room and his skin was worse than she had realized. Open yellow sores pitted his face, punctuated with patches of red flaking skin. They were sitting on the cold floor under the window with their backs against the dead radiator. Doyle had his feet flat, his elbows resting on his knees, his big red hands hanging limp. Smoke from his cigarette snaked through the shadow, blossoming into lively white clouds in the brilliant sunshine.

'You hurt me the other night,' she said quietly. 'My elbow was aching all day.'

He nodded hard, sinking his chin into his chest, but he didn't apologize. 'The photo,' he said. 'It would've taken two minutes for Toner to find out you had it. You need rid of it.'

She pulled her coat tight around her. 'Is that what he was after?'

'Probably,' said Doyle. 'He must have thought you were a real hard nut, showing it around the pub then standing on the pavement waiting for him.' And he tittered, laughing like a nervous girl.

Liam had a ticket home for her and she'd never get there. She was waiting for Doyle to sidle closer to her, wriggle along the floor and make the first burning touch. He sat up and looked out of the window behind him. 'How well did you know Pauline?' he said.

Maureen held Vik's lighter in her hand and thought of Hutton torching his rival's house to obliterate him. She could set fire to him, just lean across and hold Vik's lighter to his jacket. She looked at his sleeve. It was wool. At best it would leave a bad smell. She started crying, holding her forehead with one hand, scratching her scalp hard. 'We were in hospital together,' she said, holding her breath to stop herself sobbing, making her blood pressure rise. Doyle didn't bother to try to comfort her. He looked away and drew on his fag. If she had to die she wanted it to be quick, not a long slow rape and battery with Doyle coming and going out of the room, leaving her there to visit when he wanted. Of all fucking ends, not this. If she had to die like Pauline she wanted it to be quick. Hot blood rose in her chest. 'Pauline told me everything,' she blurted. 'About her dad and her brother. At the funeral—'

Doyle was mesmerized, watching her, his jaw hanging open, his eyes half closed.

'We all knew what ye'd done to her. I put acid in your dad's pint to fuck him up.'

He raised his eyebrows in surprise and tittered again,

edgy this time, turning back to his fag. Maureen felt herself getting righteous and hot, angry at everyone who had shut up and made it all right for Doyle to be alive and Pauline to be dead. She threw her fag into the corner. 'She was lovely.' Her bubbling voice reverberated around the tall room. 'She was kind and sweet and thoughtful, and she never fucking told because she wanted to protect your mum, did you know that? Did ye know that's why she never said? That's how much she thought of her. She'd rather go back to that, rather go home and die, than hurt her mum.'

Doyle's mouth turned down in a disgusted frown and he touched his heart with the tip of his thumb. 'And me,' he said. 'She was protecting me.' He gawked morosely at the floor.

'No, she fucking wasn't.' Maureen stood up and bent over him, shouting into him, her fists clenched at her side, her voice wet and hysterical. 'She wasn't fucking protecting you. She fucking hated ye. If she hadn't been so sick and feeble she'd've gone to the police and reported ye, ye sick fuck. Then you'd be fucking in prison and kept away from other Paulines, like ye should be.'

Doyle wasn't reacting: he was sitting calmly, watching her shout at him, watching the tears, letting her taunt him.

'You ruined her life,' she said. 'She told me once that she left a trail of filth behind her. Can you begin to imagine how that feels? You took her life and made it squalid. Every fucking thing she did felt dirty to her because of what you did.'

Doyle was watching her rant with detached disinterest, blinking heavily, not getting annoyed like he should. He shut his eyes, squeezing the rims together. Maureen's anger dissipated suddenly and she found herself back in the soundproof room with the most frightening man she'd ever met. She breathed in unsteadily, her bottom lip flapping against her teeth. Doyle wasn't righteous or indignant the way he should have been.

He dropped his cigarette on to the floor and stubbed out the burning head with his callused fingertip. 'She never telt yees,' he whispered, watching as he scattered red flecks on the concrete floor. His head lolled forward and when he looked back up he wasn't looking at her. 'I can't believe her. She never telt.'

'What?'

He shook his head slowly. 'Wasn't me,' he said eventually.

'What do ye mean?'

'Wasn't me,' he said.

She stepped back and looked at him. Doyle wasn't a social animal; he wouldn't lie for approval. The sunlight illuminated flakes of scalp impaled on his hair. If Mark didn't hurt Pauline then the other brother did. Maureen stood in the shaft of hot sunshine, looking into the shadows, trying to make out his face. 'Mark,' she said quietly, 'what exactly happened to your brother?'

'Brother's dead,' he said glibly, picking at a scab on his neck as he stared at the floor.

'How did he die?'

Doyle looked straight at her as he picked at his jugular. The tips of his fingers were tanned a deep, polluted yellow.

'When did that happen?' she asked.

"Bout a month after Pauline,' he said quietly.

'What happened to your dad?'

'Came out of hospital, after what ye did.' He pointed to her, his dry finger catching the light. 'Then ... he died too.' He looked at his hand, frowning, grey and pained.

'Mark?' she said. She bent down to make him look at her but he couldn't. 'Mark, I think that's brilliant,' she said softly.

But Doyle shook his head. 'It was a mistake.'

'But you did it for Pauline.'

'I did it for myself,' he said loudly, as if they'd had this conversation before. 'I was angry. If I'd had Pauline in mind I'd've paid more heed to her when she was alive. I felt no different about Pauline before nor after. Made no difference to her. I did it for myself.'

'But, Mark, ye did something.'

'Stop saying my name.'

'I'm just saying, most people don't do anything.'

'Most people are right,' he said quietly, touching a scab on his face. 'All I've done is waste myself. Is that why you're looking for the people who killed that Ann? You going to do something?'

She shrugged. 'The husband's been arrested,' she said.

'Why d'you care? Is he your man?'

'No.'

'Well, why d'you care?'

'He deserves a break.'

Doyle looked up at her. 'No-one deserves anything,' he said.

'But your father and your brother, didn't they deserve what happened to them?'

'And they thought Pauline deserved what they did to her. I spend time with men. I hear them. Know what they say about women like Pauline? She deserved it, asking for it, must've done something.'

The direct sunlight was making her hot and her fags were lying on the floor but she couldn't bring herself to sit down in the comforting shadows with Doyle. 'This guy,' she said, 'his kids'll go into care if I don't turn up anything. I think Frank Toner killed her.'

Doyle tittered again and she watched him. He held his mouth tight, keeping the lips tightly under control, but his brown eyes curled into perfectly geometric half-moons, lined by dark lashes. Tittering wasn't a creepy habit – Doyle couldn't laugh out loud: if he stretched his face he might split the dry skin on his cheeks. He took out his battered packet of cigarettes and lit up. 'Frank Toner never killed her,' he said, pocketing the packet without offering them. 'He wouldn't waste himself on that. And he wouldn't be so careless after, either.'

'But he was going to kill me just there.'

'No, he wasn't. He might have hurt ye a bit to scare ye but what he wants is the photograph.'

'But if he hurt me and let me go, I could give evidence against him.'

Doyle looked sceptically at her feet. 'He'd deal with ye if ye did.'

Maureen ducked into the shadow and whipped out her packet of cigarettes. She looked at him as she lit up, feeling angry with him again, wanting to hurt him. 'You don't care who killed Ann, do ye?'

'Naw.'

'Why not?'

Doyle shrugged carelessly. 'I told her to be careful. If ye run with dogs, ye hear about a lot of things.'

'Why do ye run with dogs?'

'I'm not fit for anything else.'

'Since when?'

Doyle blinked a couple of times and took a deep breath. Maureen calculated that it was as close as she would ever come to seeing him cry.

'Since Pauline,' he said, quietly.

He was like her. He was sad and soiled by what he had seen, a melancholy ruin like Douglas.

'Give Toner the photograph. Ye'd be safe enough,' said Doyle. 'Leave it in the pub or with someone. Ye could leave it with me.' He narrowed his eyes.

'I haven't got it on me,' she lied, still unsure of him. 'But I will. Mark, if you're only fit to run with dogs, why did ye grab me there, from Toner?'

Mark Doyle blushed under his blistered skin. 'Seen ye, in the main street.' He rolled the tip of his cigarette on the floor, watching it carefully, wanting to talk about something else. 'Ye dying tae know what happened to Ann?'

'Aye. I'm going to see Elizabeth.'

He looked up at her, surprised and approving. 'Good, aye. If ye want the edge, tell her about the guy's weans.'

'Where will I find her?'

'Coach? Don't go in without the photo. Frank'll kick your head in. He'll get in trouble if he doesn't get it back.'

'From the police?'

Mark's eyes smiled wearily. 'The police are nothing to him. He'll be in trouble from his boss. Frank is muscle, that's all he is. Rubbish like us never see the real bosses.'

Maureen looked at him sitting in the shadow. She wanted to tell him that she wasn't rubbish, she wasn't like him, that she didn't belong here in Brixton with the Elizabeths and the Toners and the young girls with long hair and stiletto clamps on their feet. She wasn't ruined, she wasn't spending the rest of her life running with dogs, she was visiting, just visiting, and Vik was still a possibility. Doyle's mournful hopelessness was making her feel ill. She wanted to get away from him. She was edging towards the door and Doyle was pretending not to notice. 'How did ye find this place?' she said.

'Guy I know loans it to me when I'm down here.'

'How did he get it?'

Doyle looked at the floor. 'Won it.'

40

Toilet

The instruction booklet wasn't helping at all and Maureen was having to guess at how the camera worked. She was in the damp toilet in Brixton tube station, sitting in a locked cubicle, trying to fit the film while she balanced the instructions on her knee. She'd had the brilliant idea of making a Polaroid of the Polaroid and giving Toner the new one so she could give the old one to the police to prove Leslie hadn't been lying. She fitted the box of film into the gaping mouth of the camera and shut the little door. The insides flipped over and the camera jerked noisily as it spewed out a plain sheet of black plastic.

She pocketed the instructions and stood up, propping the photo of Toner and the boy on the cistern. Standing close and looking through the view-finder, she tried to frame the picture. The flash flooded the cubicle with white light, the camera whirred and clunk-clicked noisily, oozing the picture out of its mouth.

The first picture was useless: the detailing on the cistern was remarkable but Toner's face came out as a blur and the boy's arm and face were hidden behind a bald white rectangle of reflected flash. She tried again, using the close-up button this time. Flash and whir and clunk-click and the camera spewed out another smeared grey photograph. Eight photographs later Maureen realized it was impossible, the details weren't coming out at all. She'd wasted a tenner on film and forty quid on a cumbersome camera. Gathering the blurry pictures together, she tucked them into her bag next to Kilty's forgotten shopping and tried to come up with another plan as she unlocked the door.

A black woman in a white coat was standing in the doorway of a small office, looking horrified. She jumped when Maureen came out of the cubicle with the camera in her hand. 'Can't do that in here,' said the woman disdainfully, shrinking from the camera.

'What?'

'You can't do that in there,' repeated the woman, staring at the camera. She backed off into her cupboard office, slamming the door. Her shadow appeared behind the strips of reflective mirror on the window, watching.

Puzzled, Maureen washed her hands and face. She was drying them on paper towels when she realized that the woman thought she had been taking pornographic photos of herself. She ran away up the stairs to find an office supply shop, her face still damp.

It was busy in the market. She left the bustle of Electric Avenue and turned down the lane towards the Coach and Horses. She could see the front door, the small orange windows and the shimmy of the light reflected from the street. She stopped in a doorway, taking deep breaths, feeling in her bag for her stabbing comb, hoping Doyle hadn't lied and that Toner really only wanted the photo. She stood the comb up in her pocket with the teeth foremost and practised drawing it. The weight of her bag was restricting her elbow so she lifted the strap over her head, hanging the bag diagonally to the left instead, patted her pocket and headed for the pub, telling herself to stay calm. She hurried on, strengthened by the presence of the comb and the promise of Elizabeth.

Across the road a drunk man stepped out of the pub and

held on to the portico column before attempting a turn into the road. Maureen knew she could be seen from inside. She hoped Toner would be in there, that she wouldn't have to sit about, waiting for the barman to go and phone him, waiting and getting nervous and trying not to drink. She stood up tall and walked quickly across the road, pushed the door open and walked in. Toner was in the left-hand room, standing at the bar, the central event in a crowd of flies. The snide black barman was smiling behind him, his hand behind his head, smiling and scratching the nape of his neck. Elizabeth wasn't in the bar but Maureen couldn't leave now. Sweat trickled down the valley in her back. She walked straight over to Toner and stopped ten foot short. Toner looked up and saw her. 'I've got something that belongs to you,' she muttered.

He stepped towards her, raising his hand above his head and brought it down hard on her face. Maureen's teeth sliced into her cheek, her left eye flashed blankets of white light and her mouth was suddenly filled with salty blood. A heavy hush descended in the pub as each man computed the difficult equation of why a small woman with blood dripping from her chin was nothing whatever to do with him. Toner slid his fat hand under Maureen's arm as he had before and lifted her, carrying her to the door of the ladies' toilet. The chat started again, a little higher, a little nervous, as Toner kicked open the door and threw Maureen face down into the piercing smell of piss-filled lemons. The strap snapped and her bag skidded across the floor, spinning as slowly and as gracefully as a curling-stone, stopping an inch short of the far wall. Maureen lay rigid, blood falling out of her mouth on to the floor. Doyle had lied. She wasn't safe. She reached back in her mind, trying to remember why she had thought it would be safe to come here as Toner kicked open first one cubicle door and then the next.

Elizabeth was sitting on the toilet in the second cubicle, her trousers gathered around her knees. She jumped to her feet when the door crashed open, startled awake and trembling.

'Get!' barked Toner.

Her jeans slid to the floor, baring her bony legs and her wet and tattered fanny.

'Get!'

Automatically, Elizabeth bent down to pull up her trousers, banging her head hard off the cubicle wall. She pulled her trousers up over her bare bum and ran to get out, banging into walls and the door in her hurry to get away, running into the pub with her fly undone and her pubes on display. Maureen watched Elizabeth leave and groaned into the stinking floor.

He wrapped his fat hands around Maureen's throat and pulled her on to her feet, choking the breath from her. She remembered. She reached for the comb in her mind but her hand was frozen. She was so afraid she couldn't move. She couldn't move. He pushed her over the sinks, pressing the back of her head into the wall and squeezed her throat hard, baring his teeth as if he was going to bite her face. She couldn't move. The pressure was building in her eyes and her tongue began to swell.

'Give it me!' he roared, flecking spit.

Maureen reached into her coat pocket, sliding her hand past the stabbing comb, and handed him the Polaroid. He looked at it, smiling as if remembering a happy holiday, and hid it in his coat. Maureen's hand returned to her pocket, settling on the comb, her fingertips running across the ferocious teeth. If she stabbed him she'd have to kill him. One more squeeze of her neck and he'd kill her.

'You should have given it to me in the first fucking place,' he banged the back of her head off the wall, 'shouldn't you?'

'I meant—'

'Shut it!'

Toner retracted his fingers and the pressure from his palm relented, leaving Maureen to find her footing, scrabbling on the slippery tiles. He seemed very pleased.

'Cross me again and you'll fucking know about it,' he said, smiling to himself. He straightened his coat and flattened his hair, checked in the shattered mirror to make sure he looked flash before he walked out of the ladies' toilet.

Maureen threw up. Blood and milk splattered her coat skirt. She hung over the lumpy pink puddle, breathing heavily, trying to negotiate the sharp hot pain in her throat and eyes and the throb at the back of her head.

She turned on the tap to wash out her mouth and looked at herself in a broken shard of mirror on the wall. Her chin was smeared with burgundy blood, her pale blue eyes were pink and cracked. A livid red bruise around her throat tapered away to fingermarks at the side. Blood was soaking into the shoulder of her coat. She'd crapped it. She had a fucking weapon in her pocket and she'd crapped it.

She wanted to stay in the toilet, wanted to wait until Toner had left, but she knew that might be never and the longer she stayed in there the more frightened she'd be. She washed out her mouth, poking at the cut in her cheek with her tongue. The long, deep gash was bleeding heavily. She wiped the vomit from her coat and pulled up her collar to cover the marks on her neck, picked up her bag and slowly tied a knot in the strap. She spat out a last mouthful of blood into the basin and kept her head high as she walked out into the pub.

Toner was back at the bar. He looked up at her as she came out, leering as if she'd sucked him off. He said something to the flies and they looked over at her and laughed. She walked unsteadily across the room, every eye watching her.

She walked through the little doorway and into the empty leisure drinking room and stopped at the bar, telling herself that she would have a whisky, just to show him she wasn't scared. But it was a Winnie lie. She needed a whisky to get straight again and she couldn't hold out until she got somewhere else. She stuck her tongue into the cut, feeling along the edges of the rip, trying to guess how long it was. The barman came around to her. 'What can I get you?' He smirked nervously.

'Large whisky,' she said, keeping her eyes down, scratching the gash in her cheek against her razor teeth as she spoke. The barman leaned over and emptied the optic twice, dropping the glass in front of her. Maureen only had a twenty and some change. She picked out the right money with tremorous fingers, certain he wouldn't come back with the change if she gave him the big note, knowing she couldn't come round the bar looking for him.

'You're not staying here,' he muttered, as she counted it out into his hand, 'because I don't want trouble in here.'

She lifted her glass, swallowing a big mouthful of bloody whisky, and felt the spiky liquid sate the wound, as gentle and comforting as a kick in the tits. She dropped her empty glass.

'You're a cunt,' she said, her voice strangled and rough.

The barman lifted the glass and wiped the bar under it. 'Get out,' he said, and watched her until she did.

She wanted to forget Ann, she wanted to go and get Liam and leave here. A sharp breeze swirled along the pavement, carrying dust and city filth, making it difficult to see. She couldn't face the busy high street with people looking at her, smelling the vomit from her coat, seeing her broken neck. He had hit her in front of all of them, fifteen men in a room, and not one of them had flinched. They thought she deserved it. She wondered if Toner had killed Ann in front of them, if the audience of mute men had seen that too and done nothing. As much as she wanted to go home she knew she couldn't just let him get away with it. She needed to find Elizabeth. She stopped and looked up and down the lane, trying to imagine where a woman would run to with her madge hanging out. Elizabeth had had a fright, a big fright, and she was jumpy anyway. She'd be looking for comfort and calm. Maureen looked up Brixton Hill. Elizabeth'd be in Argyle Street; she'd be at Parlain's house.

Maureen walked up the hill, staying on the opposite side of the broad road, urging herself on. Parlain had no reason to come after her now: she'd given the Polaroid to Toner and there was nothing he could do about it, but she was scared anyway. She thought she'd stay scared for a long time.

She didn't want to go up the stairs or even wait outside. Her throat was aching and she sat on the low wall behind the Perspex bus stop, watching across the road, lighting a cigarette and swallowing blood, watching the street for signs of Elizabeth. The moment she had frozen in the toilets she knew she couldn't handle herself. Like Leslie, she couldn't fight everyone, and knowing that had made her deeply afraid. She remembered the sensation of her hand slipping past the comb to the photograph, the cold metal on her palm, and being too afraid to lift it and use it. She saw a shadow coming out of Tam Parlain's block.

Elizabeth fell out of the door and sloped across the muddy grass to the road, her knees weak, her jumper pulled to the side, looking as if she'd been attacked. Maureen stood up and Elizabeth saw her. She darted across the road without checking the traffic and ran up to Maureen. 'Will you help me?' Elizabeth looked desperate, she glanced back at the door. 'My friend won't help me, will you help me?'

'What happened?' said Maureen.

'He pushed me out, my friend, he pushed me. Will you help me?'

'What's wrong?' But Maureen knew what was wrong. It was obvious from Elizabeth's quivering panic and her damp skin.

'Lend me some money?' said Elizabeth.

Maureen shook her head. Elizabeth pointed down the hill. 'Buy me a drink?'

'Okay.' Maureen's voice came out as a rasp. 'Talk to me?' Elizabeth was looking at Maureen's neck. She nodded. Maureen wanted to get the fuck away from here to somewhere relatively safe. She spotted a black cab coming over the hill and asked the driver to drop them at the Angel. She saw the driver watching them in the mirror, worried, knowing something was very wrong.

They pushed open the door and found the butch lady-man behind the bar, sipping from her blue mug, reading a newspaper. Elizabeth sloped off to a table as far from the bar as she could get but the barwoman recognized her. She looked from Elizabeth to Maureen and seemed disappointed. 'What happened to your neck?' she said, putting her mug down.

Maureen blushed and lowered her head to hide her shame. 'I got in a fight,' she said.

The landlady came over to her, keeping her eyes on Elizabeth cowering in the far corner. 'One drink,' she said. 'I'll give you one drink and then you have to go.' Maureen turned to Elizabeth. 'Vodka,' said Elizabeth. She didn't specify how much or what she wanted in it, she just said vodka, spoken with an open ending, making it sound as if it could go on for ever.

'Large,' said Maureen. 'And a large whisky.'

The woman gave them the drinks reluctantly. A trembling junkie and a battered Scot wouldn't exactly draw in the business lunch trade. As she walked across the empty room and sat the glasses of succour on the table, Maureen saw the lady-man watching her and she knew what she was thinking, that Maureen and Elizabeth were the same. And maybe she was right.

They huddled over the table, two frightened women hiding from the men, wasting the day getting out of it.

41

Little Pats

Maureen's throat hurt when she spoke and she couldn't swallow properly. She was having to sip her whisky, let it slide down her throat and numb her cheek. She wanted to gulp it down and lose herself in it. She had stood limp and let him slap and throttle her. She was frightened and she hated everyone. She wanted to go home.

'Where are you from, Elizabeth?' rasped Maureen.

'London,' said Elizabeth, looking at her drink

'Where are your family?'

Elizabeth smiled churlishly. 'Where I left them, I suppose.'

'Have you got brothers? Sisters?'

She sat up a little. 'A sister. She's a designer. Furniture. She makes it all herself. In a workshop. In Chelsea.'

'She must be doing well to afford a workshop in Chelsea.'

'No, we had trust funds ...' She tried to smile again. 'All gone now.' She frowned at her glass, the light shining in through the softening etched windows.

Maureen couldn't tell how old she was. Her long hair and hopeful smile fitted a different life, a crazy deb living life her own way, with real people, making all the wrong choices. Elizabeth didn't want to talk. Whatever she was feeding into the back of her knee wasn't working for her today. She was trembling inside her dirty Vegas sweatshirt and her hairline was damp. Maureen looked at her and thought of kind Liam sitting at Martha's, waiting to whisk

359

her home to safety. She'd never made the connection between Liam and these people, never acknowledged a causal connection between his big beautiful house and bony bodies like Elizabeth's.

'Remember Ann who died?' whispered Maureen.

Elizabeth tore herself away from the mess in her head and looked up. 'Yeah.'

'She had kids. Her husband's looking after all four of them but he's been arrested for murdering her. They'll go into care.'

Elizabeth nodded slowly, taking it in. 'I had a kid.' She sat up, remembered, then her back bent and she slumped. 'Nice kid.'

'Boy or girl?'

'Boy. Joshua. He never cried. He was a good boy.'

'When was that?'

Elizabeth brushed her hand into the past but her mind went with it and she stared vacantly at the table.

'Is he in care?' asked Maureen.

Elizabeth shook her head. 'Died. House fire.' She took a deep, deep drink of liquid eraser.

'Sorry,' croaked Maureen, and Elizabeth shrugged, as if she'd heard the word a thousand times and was sick of hearing it. She took another drink.

'If I knew what happened to Ann,' said Maureen, 'he might not go to prison. The kids could have a normal life.'

Elizabeth drank again, looking at her glass.

Doyle had misjudged her: mentioning the children had had no impact; all that mattered to Elizabeth was what she could get and where she could get it.

'I've got five hundred quid. If you tell me what happened, I'll give it to you.'

Elizabeth sat up.

'Five hundred.' Maureen sipped her whisky and Elizabeth stared at her.

'What for?'

'Ann. Tell me what happened.'

Elizabeth tried to find the catch. 'How do I know you've got five hundred quid?' she said.

'In the bank,' said Maureen.

Elizabeth hesitated so Maureen reached into her pocket and found an old cash-line receipt. The account balance at the bottom was faint but Maureen showed it to her and Elizabeth smiled and relaxed when she saw the figures. She gave it back to Maureen and looked at the floor, thinking.

'Can we get it now?'

'No. Once you've told me.'

'But we might miss the bank.'

'Tell me quickly, then.'

'You're not the police, are you?'

'D'ye think I'd have this mess on my neck if I was the police?'

Elizabeth hesitated, staring at her drink, then looked up suddenly. 'It was an accident,' she said. 'She fell over.'

Maureen snorted, and regretted it immediately. 'She fell into the river?' she said, holding her throat and trying to swallow.

'No. She fell over and banged her head. We were trying to look after her.'

'Where did she fall?'

'Dunno. Do you know Tam Parlain?'

'I do, yeah.'

'Tam said she fell and banged her head. She was on the couch when I got there. She was in a mess, her face was all bloody. No-one wanted to look at her.'

'Who was there?'

'Ann, Tam, Heidi and Susan. Heidi came up with

me – she used to be on the methadone programme with me up at Herne Hill. It was closing time.' She took a sip of vodka. 'Tam came and told us we had to go to his house. She was on the sofa. And then she died.'

'Why did he want you all up there?'

'For Toner. He was teaching us all a lesson for Toner.' Elizabeth sipped again.

'What was the lesson?'

'He was teaching us not to steal. She'd stolen from Toner and Tam was doing him a favour.'

'What did she steal?'

'She stole a lot. A whole shipment. She went missing after that but Toner found her. Tam was teaching us not to steal.'

'Do you carry for him?'

'Not now.'

'What about the mattress and the river?'

'Well, we got a fright so Tam got some of his friends to come and put her in a mattress and put her in the river.' Her skin was so white and damp it was beginning to turn silver. 'Is that it? Can we go to the bank now?'

'No. Why burn her feet? Who cut her legs?'

Elizabeth sat up straight, as uncomfortable as if Maureen had accused her of farting at dinner. 'Oh,' she said, 'that was the others. Tam made them do it, to teach them. I had to go out and see the doctor.'

'In the middle of the night?'

'No,' said Elizabeth, trying to put the times together. 'That was later, the next day, or the day after, I think.' Elizabeth didn't think she was lying: she was so divorced from reality she genuinely believed that mutilating and killing a drinking partner constituted a bit of an accident.

'They did it when you went to the doctor's?'

'Yeah,' she said. 'See, she was on the sofa and Tam got

362

really fed up with her being there and he got Heidi, I think it was Heidi, to burn her feet to wake her up, but she didn't wake up.'

'What about her legs?'

'Oh, Tam told them to cut them, I don't know why. I was out.'

'She was wearing a gold bracelet. Why didn't you take it off her?'

Elizabeth looked guilty. 'Tam said leave it.'

Maureen leaned in to her, dropping her aching voice. 'Elizabeth,' she said, 'did Toner ask Tam to get her?'

'No,' she moaned, cringing and afraid. 'That's why it was such a big deal. Tam did it to teach us a lesson. He thought Frank would be pleased but he wasn't. It wasn't what Frank wanted. And now Tam's crossed him but we were there.' Elizabeth glanced out of the door. She lifted her glass to sip but was trembling so much she had to put it down again. 'And Tam might say we were there. Tam comes from a big family, he's got people behind him. Frank won't hurt him but he'll hurt us.'

'The little fish?'

'Yes,' nodded Elizabeth, dipping her chin down and looking up at her, making herself the victim. 'The little fish.'

'Toner didn't mean to kill her?'

'No, no, he wanted to ask her about the bag and there's a photo of him and it's missing now. It's very bad for Frank.'

Maureen looked at her glass, at the thousands of tiny scratches on the surface. 'Why would he want to ask about the bag? She said it had been stolen but he didn't believe her, did he?'

'Not at first, no, but then he put out the word that he wanted to talk to her about it.' She tried to smile. 'Frank doesn't talk to people about things like that, not usually.'

'What made him want to talk to her?'

Elizabeth took a deep, impatient breath. 'I don't know, it turned up in the wrong hands and I guess he thought it had been stolen after all.'

'But she died before he got the chance?'

'Yes,' said Elizabeth, shaking her legs under the table like a small girl desperate for the toilet. '*Please can we go?*'

'We'll go when I've finished or we won't go at all. Who stabbed her in the legs?'

'Tam told them to do it,' she said.

'But, Elizabeth, why did the women do what Tam asked them?'

'It was her or us.'

But Maureen knew there had to be more to it. 'Did he feed you while you were there?'

Elizabeth reached out a bruised hand and held Maureen's wrist, looking at her watch. She gestured towards the door. 'We should go.'

'It was a vicious thing to do, Elizabeth. She had four kids.'

'Well, I was out. At the doctor's.' Even Elizabeth was having trouble believing in a doctor's appointment that lasted several hours. She blinked, looked at the floor, blinked again and looked back.

'Ye can't have been out for all of it,' said Maureen. 'It must have gone on for hours.'

Elizabeth gave it some thought but the terrible cold was driving through her muscles like frozen needles, cracking her bones. 'There was a queue,' she said feebly.

'There was a queue?' repeated Maureen, her high voice pushing the battered rings of cartilage against the bruised muscles, sending a searing pain through her neck.

Elizabeth knew how stupid it sounded but she wasn't used to being talked to, or listened to, or taking responsibility. She played with her glass, running her finger down the side and around the rim. She lifted it and drank deep into it, looking for blindness and peace. Maureen knew that if she tried to make Elizabeth admit her part she'd never find out what had happened. She tried again.

'So, when you came back from the doctor's, did ye see what happened to Ann at the end?'

'Oh, I was in then.' She sat forward. 'That was Tam. Tam did that at the end. He kicked her.'

'Where did he kick her?'

She pointed to her face. 'In the chin. She was lying on the floor and he kicked her. She held his leg, held on while he kicked her with his other foot.' She looked away wistfully. 'She was hitting his leg, little pats, you know, like, slapping him, over and over, while he kicked her. I thought that was brave of her, hitting back. Can we go now?'

Maureen thought back to the missing flooring and shuddered when she remembered the grainy texture of the damp leather settee. 'Who did he get to put Ann in the mattress?'

'A fat bloke and a bloke called Andy.'

Maureen drained her drink. 'Let's go to the bank.'

The butch barmaid watched them leave, sadder than she had been before, certain she'd be watching the cheeky Scottish girl die inch by inch over the coming months and years.

Elizabeth was shaking so intensely that she had to sit on a chair at the side while Maureen went to the counter. The queue was long, busy with shop managers depositing end-of-day bags of small change and office workers paying their bills. Maureen looked over at her. The white lights in the bank glinted off her sweaty face. Elizabeth gathered her hair with her shaking hands, twisted it into a rope at the front and threw it over her shoulder, keeping her eyes down like Maureen did when she was dying, concentrating on breathing in and breathing out. Maureen looked away and followed the rest of the line, shuffling forward. She needed to get to the airport, she needed some cash herself for a cab.

She thought of Ann with her split lip and her battered fanny, coming to London to give herself up gladly for her kids. But Ann fought back at the last, refusing to go gently, a dying woman with burnt feet and cuts on her legs and a fractured skull, hitting back as she was kicked in the face. Maureen wanted to fight back before it was too late, before her head was broken. She thought about Winnie playing cards, crying because she was sober, of Elizabeth running into the pub with her straggly fanny on display, hedonistic casualties.

The clerk made no secret of his scepticism. He didn't think a bedraggled woman like Maureen could take out six hundred quid. He read carefully as Maureen's account details came up on screen and watched as Maureen typed in the pin number. He asked her how she wanted it.

'Any way.'

Elizabeth was excited and on her feet. She watched the wad of notes with cloudy, absent eyes and Maureen recognized the tranquillizing calm of anticipation. Elizabeth took the money, shoving it deep into her pocket, plugging the hole in her soul with the readies, and her panic evaporated. She stood up tall and straight, flinching slightly at muscle pains, flicking her hair back over her shoulders again. She knew she'd done a bad thing. 'You won't tell anyone, will you?' she said, quite casual.

But Maureen couldn't lie to her. 'Don't kill yourself with that money.'

'Please don't tell,' she whispered close. 'Frank doesn't know I was there. He'll be really angry. I'm only a little fish.' She dipped her chin down again and looked up. At best she had stood by while the rest, as vicious as frightened children, had ripped and burned Ann to death.

'Don't worry,' said Maureen. 'I won't tell Frank.'

When they got outside Elizabeth said goodbye and walked quickly away, melting into the crowd. Maureen watched her skinny shoulders swaying, her hair roped and tucked into her sweatshirt, and she felt exhausted. It was so pedestrian. She didn't have the sense of having met with something evil. It was so normal, so within the scope of what she knew. She couldn't set herself apart from Elizabeth or from the crowd of greedy users, helping themselves as a mother of four bled to death on the settee.

Maureen lit a fag, inhaling with her tongue flicking over the cut in her cheek. She wanted to tell someone who couldn't have done this, seen this, heard this without feeling different and separate. The police. She wanted to tell the police.

'Excuse me.' She stopped a man and could see him taking in the bruises on her neck and the smell of whisky on her breath. 'Could you tell me if there's a police station around here?'

'Yes, dear,' he said, 'down there, under the bridge, third on your right. Canterbury Crescent.' His accent was African and his yellow and brown eyes were sad and sorry for her. Maureen looked down the street towards the bridge. 'You want me to take you there?' he asked.

'No,' said Maureen, laughing as if it was nothing, as if she'd lost her poodle. 'I'm – I can find it okay.'

She was beyond the bridge when her mind settled. She couldn't walk into a police station and give her name. If she went in and said she'd found a gang of murderers they wouldn't let her go home with Liam, they'd keep her there for hours. If she didn't leave London now she would never get home, and Douglas's money wouldn't last for ever. She knew her place here, next to Elizabeth and the men on the pavement, afraid like them, floating for years, another fun-seeker picking at scabs on the back of her knee. She turned up Electric Avenue, following the railway arches back to Coldharbour Lane and the phone-boxes outside the Angel. She went into a newsagent's for a ten-quid phone card.

'Maureen,' Martha whined reproachfully, 'he was so worried about you. He's gone to the airport. He didn't have your pager number with him and he was counting on you being there.'

'What time's the plane?'

'It's at seven thirty. You'd better set off now if you're going to get there on time.'

'Cheers, Martha,' said Maureen; because she couldn't bring herself to thank her properly, and hung up.

Hugh McAskill wasn't at his desk. The man who answered the phone wandered away to look for him. Maureen listened down the line to some men laughing and people walking past, watching as two and a half quid ticked away on the crystal display. The man came back over to Hugh's desk; she could hear him sniffing and chatting to someone near the phone. It took him twenty pence to pick up the receiver again. 'Sorry about the delay,' he said. 'He's left the office for the day. Can I help?'

'Well,' said Maureen, speaking fast, 'someone I was drinking with has just confessed to witnessing a crime and I don't know what to do about it.'

'Whereabouts are ye?'

'In London.'

'Did the crime happen in London?'

'Yeah.'

'Well,' the man sounded completely uninterested, 'you're through to the wrong division anyway. Have ye tried the

Crimestoppers hotline? Or the City Police? Or what about the Metropolitan Police?'

'Okay,' she said, surprised by his cavalier lack of concern. 'Well, thanks anyway.'

'Yeah, 'bye,' he said and hung up.

She phoned directory inquiries for the number and called New Scotland Yard. She told the switchboard operator that she had information relating to the murder of Ann Harris and they put her through to a phone queue. A screechy voice from the East Midlands told her that she was being held in a queue and her call would be answered as soon as a communicator became available. The phone rang out blindly at the other end. The voice came back on several times, one and a half quid's worth of times, and each time returned her to the ringing phone. Maureen was running out of money. When the phone was finally answered a pleasant man asked her for her name and address. Maureen didn't want to get involved, she just wanted to pass on the information and go and find Liam. 'Marian Thatcher,' she said. 'I live in Argyle Street off Brixton Hill.'

'What number?'

'Six three one,' she said, feeling clever.

'Well, Marian, why don't you come in and tell us what happened?'

'Look, I've got kids, I can't come in. Can't I just tell ye and ye can come and interview me later?'

The policeman paused. 'Um, okay, let's do that first. What happened?'

'I'm running out of money here. Will you phone me back?'

'Can't you come—'

The phone clicked and she was listening to the dialling tone. Maureen checked her watch. It was going on twenty to six and her throat was killing her. It shouldn't be this fucking hard to dub someone up. She dialled 999.

'Fire, police or ambulance?'

'Police,' she said, trying to make her strangled voice sound urgent.

The operator told the police that Maureen was in a call-box and told them what the number was. 'Hello, caller, what is the nature of the emergency?'

'There's a woman called Ann Harris, she's being held in flat six three two in Argyle Street in Brixton Hill. I think they're going to kill her.'

'Who is going to kill her?'

'Tam Parlain, Elizabeth, Heidi and Susan. She's on the settee, they're going to throw her in the river.'

'What's your name, caller?'

'Please help her.'

'Caller, I need your name.'

'Marian Thatcher.'

'And your address?'

'Six three one Argyle Street off Brixton Hill. Tam Parlain's going to get two of his pals, a fat guy and a guy called Andy, to come up and put her in the mattress and throw her in the river.'

'Caller, your name isn't coming up at the address you've given me.'

Maureen hung up and backed out of the phone-box. Liam would be frantic. She stepped into the street and hailed a black cab. She had forgotten that the close-circuit camera was hovering high above the road, watching the street, keeping it clean.

42

Knutsford

Maureen watched the slow traffic snake ahead of them on the motorway and saw the fare clocking up on the meter. The taxi driver's eyes flickered towards her in his rear-view. He had tried speaking to her, managed to get as far as she was going to Glasgow because she lived there when Maureen's throat began to hurt so much that the conversation ran out.

'It's bad traffic,' he shouted, over the noise of his engine, his eyes smiling. 'Getting worse all the time in London.'

'Will ye get me there for seven thirty?'

'I don't know, darlin'. I'll try. This time of day you can't tell, being honest wiv ya.'

She was going home and she was going to fight back before the last gasp. She patted her bag sitting next to her on the seat. She knew what she was going to do. She wasn't afraid of Ruchill any more.

The taxi drew into Terminal One at twenty past seven. Maureen gave the cabby sixty quid and bolted up the escalators, pushing past bewildered gangs of tourists standing with their luggage, her throat aching with every heavy step. She couldn't see a sign but stumbled through an archway and found herself facing the BA check-in desk. A long, tired queue snaked around an elaborate maze of Tensabarriers. She skipped along it, glancing down the aisles, looking for Liam. He wasn't there. She found the gate and had to queue to speak to the woman on the desk. 'Listen,' she said, rasping for breath, 'my brother's got my ticket for Glasgow and I think he's in there. Can I go and see him?'

But the immaculately made-up woman couldn't let her through without a ticket. 'Sorry,' she smiled. 'For security reasons.'

'Can't you put a call out for him?'

'Which plane was he on?'

'The seven thirty.'

'Well,' she said, smiling slowly, 'the seven thirty has just left. It's taking off now, so I'm afraid you've missed him.'

'Put out a call,' said Maureen, close to tears. 'Call him. He won't have gone without me.'

'I'm afraid you'll have to go to the information desk to put a call out,' she said, and pointed to a separate desk with its own queue.

Maureen waited. A man in an expensive suit bought a ticket to Edinburgh using a credit card with a disputed limit He gave the dolly-bird behind the desk another card and she tried that one, swiping it with long pink fingernails. 'Yes,' she said, stretching her Peach Party lips across her peroxide teeth. 'This one's fine, sir.'

They paused to smile at each other. Maureen lit a cigarette. 'Excuse me,' said the woman, standing up and reaching for her arm. 'I'm very sorry but you can't smoke here.'

'Why?'

'Because it's a no-smoking area. There are designated smoking areas.' She pointed to the signs hanging from the ceiling.

Maureen dropped her fag and stood on it, wishing she could fill her lungs just once more. The businessman was staring at her. 'You going to leave that there, then, are you?'

'Leave what?'

'That cigarette end. Are you proposing to leave it on the floor?'

'Aye,' said Maureen, sounding as hard as she could, 'I am.'

The businessman looked at the woman behind the desk and rolled his eyes. 'Smokers,' he said, and she stared at his credit card.

Her hand hovered over the printer for a month as his ticket emerged. 'There you are, sir,' she smiled, 'thank you very much.'

'No,' the man addressed her tits, 'thank *you* very much.'

He picked up his briefcase and gave Maureen a dirty look before walking away.

'Can I help you?' said the woman, smiling hard at Maureen, employing the best of her training.

'I want to buy a ticket for the next flight to Glasgow.'

'I'm afraid that flight is boarding now.'

'Well, the next one, then.'

'That's the last flight to Glasgow tonight, I'm afraid.' She smiled, and Maureen knew she was enjoying it.

'What about Edinburgh?'

'No. I've just sold the last ticket on the last flight.'

A hot impotent tantrum shot up Maureen's neck and she leaned her dirty face across the desk. 'Fuck you,' she said, chalking up another triumph for Glaswegian diplomacy.

She walked downstairs, quivering with the craving for nicotine. She took the wrong lift and found herself at the Paddington Express station. She bought a ticket anyway, afraid that if she went back upstairs she'd get lost in the airport. The ticket cost a tenner. She was the only poor person on the platform. The tunnel was encased in sleek aluminium sheeting and the chairs were stark moulded pine. She tried to affect the look of an eccentric millionairess and cupped her hand over her throbbing red throat. An immaculate high-speed train pulled into the station and Maureen climbed on, sitting down just inside the door. As the train slipped from the station all of the passengers within a ten-foot radius were staring at her. It was only when they arrived in Paddington and she stood up to get off that she saw the flickering television above her head. She ran across the concourse, following the signs for the cab rank. She opened the door and threw in her bag. 'Victoria coach station,' she said.

Despite having left it to a couple of hours before the bus left Maureen managed to queue in the smelly ticket office and book her return for that night. The bus station was far poorer than Glasgow's. Desperate travellers from all over the country gathered in it with their poor luggage, waiting for the buses to take them away. Glass walls had been erected all over the coach station as well, part of either a fast-spreading fad in bus-station design or a nationwide push to lower the number of passenger-on-concourse deaths.

Maureen used the phones to call Vik. She could hardly hear his answer-machine message because a very fat man sitting near the kiosk was listening to music on headphones and warbling along to Mariah Carey at the top of his voice. She shouted over the racket that she'd be in touch. She was coming home. She'd phone him when things were more settled. Definitely phone him. She'd keep his lighter for him and give it back when things were settled. She whispered that she was thinking about him, that she was going to make things right, but the background noise was so high she doubted he'd hear it.

It was ten minutes before the bus left and she finally managed to get Liam at home. 'Mauri, I wasted over two hundred quid on that fucking ticket.'

'I'll pay it back, Liam, I'm sorry.'

'I'm not made of money, ye know.'

'I know, Liam, I'll pay ye back.'

374

'I'm a poor student.'

She could tell that Liam had been rehearsing the fight all the way home. 'I'll give it straight back to ye tomorrow,' she said. 'I'm really sorry.'

Liam hesitated for a moment. 'What time ye getting in?' he asked.

'I don't know,' said Maureen, looking around the coach station. 'About six thirty in the morning.'

'Well, I was going to come and meet ye but ye can fuck off,' he said, as if she'd timed the bus deliberately. 'Listen, I'm sorry about Martha. I heard ye banging on the floor.'

'Yeah, and I heard you banging on the bed.'

'Sorry,' he said quickly.

'It's not me ye need to be sorry to,' said Maureen.

The moment she sat down on the itchy seat she knew that she was going to be okay. The coach was less than half full and Maureen managed to get half of the back seat to herself. An elderly woman took the other side, squashing herself up against the window, arranging her refreshments in a tidy spread on the seat next to her.

The bus rumbled out of central London, up through the deep valley of Swiss Cottage and out on to the vast M1. Maureen settled back, resting her head on the shuddering window, watching the individual people in their individual cars pass the window, the individual houses with individual strips of gardens, poisoned by collective exhaust fumes. She watched the dirty grey city slip into the past, saw the low houses on the shallow hills leave the frame of the window, and she suddenly knew how close she had come to dying. She changed her mind and fought back at the last minute, like poor Ann. Poor Ann, lying on the settee with her fat lip and ugly children.

Maureen was close to crying but the bruised rings of

cartilage in her throat resisted. She was going home to face them all, knowing that her brittle courage had shattered. She was going home to Glasgow and for the first time remembered that she had a life beyond her present troubles. She loved the colours of the city, she had a place and history there, she understood the obscure kindness of the people and the rationale behind the brutal weather. She'd missed the cleanness of the air, the archaic turns of phrase and the rasping guttural speech. She could have a bath in her own bathroom soon, without the intrusion of Ruchill, and sleep soundly in her own bed. Leslie would be safe and Liam had been saved. She didn't care about Ann any more, didn't care that Moe didn't make any sense.

The motorway left the city behind it and entered a dull, flat landscape stretching beyond the horizon punctuated by grey villages and shadowy gymkhana runs. Maureen pulled her legs up and wrapped herself up tight in her dirty coat, no longer too good for the bus or for her, and watched middle England's bland suburban plain coast past the window.

Joe McEwan had been at work for eleven hours and he wasn't feeling well. He was drinking a lot of coffee and smoking twenty-five a day, or so his doctor thought. The office was almost empty; only the obsessive and divorcees were still in. The Hutton investigation was dragging to an unsatisfying conclusion. The evidence they'd amassed didn't pan out. Terrified witnesses changed their statements from stupid lie to stupid lie and the case had swallowed up their overtime budget for the next three weeks. Rumour and retracted witness statements had given them the pick-up place, the pub where he'd been killed, the name of the driver and, by implication, the boss who'd ordered it. They even had the name of the guy who stole the taxi. What they didn't have was a shred of usable evidence, not a single witness. Inness kicked open the door and stormed into the room. He was grinning, his stubby teeth half hidden under his moustache, his excitement clashing with everyone else's worn apathy. He spotted McEwan and almost ran across the room. 'Look at the e-mail noticeboard,' he said, beckoning him over to a desk and calling up the system and the page. 'Look at this.'

It was a message from the Met in London. The text explained that they were trying to trace a Scottish woman called Marian Thatcher. She had dialled 999 and had given important inside information about the Ann Harris murder. A call had been made from the same phone-box to Stewart Street directly before the 999 call but it might have been unrelated. The taxi had been traced and the woman tried and failed to get on the last plane to Glasgow. Inness clicked on an attached file and a colour picture slowly unravelling in strips from the top. Three strips down McEwan was grinning. It was a scratchy colour shot of Maureen O'Donnell coming out of a phone-box and hailing a taxi. 'Eh?' smiled Inness. 'Told you.'

'Fucking lovely,' smiled McEwan, and lit himself a congratulatory fag.

It was much later and Maureen woke with a start at the pains in her neck. She looked around her and saw the grey road and the red tail-lights and the old woman sitting upright on the other end of the back seat, looking out of the window. It was three o'clock and they would be stopping soon. She could have a cigarette. She looked out of the window at the chill night and spared a thought for everyone who went to London and never came back. For the poor men and women looking for work and brighter futures and for the maddies like herself, who went to fix the world and got lost. She felt a nudge to her elbow and found the woman on the far back seat handing her a plastic flask cup of orange juice. She thanked her, but the woman had shuffled over to the other side of the bus already, glaring resolutely out of the window. Maureen drank and the acid juice washed away the flavour of stale cigarettes and blood and sour milk.

The bus hurried up a slip-road without losing velocity and hit the car-park at fifty. The frightened passengers sat up straight, looking out of the window, holding on to the seat in front of them. The bus slowed and eased to a stop. Maureen stood up and scrambled for the door. As her feet hit the concrete she had a fag in her mouth and was lighting it. She filled her empty lungs.

It was cold and windy in the car-park, properly cold and windy, making her nose run and her skin tingle. She walked slowly to the service station, straggling behind the other passengers, taking time to enjoy the weather, smoking and letting the wind peel the ash from the tip. The automatic doors slid back and Maureen found herself facing a sign welcoming her to Knutsford service station. The name reminded her of Ann, but she couldn't remember why.

She went to the loo and washed her face and hands, thinking her way through Moe and Tam and Elizabeth. Moe still bothered her. She looked at her throat in the mirror. The red marks were turning dark blue. Frank Toner's thumb had impressed a perfect imprint on the right-hand side of her small neck. She remembered. This was where Ann got off the bus and never got back on again. She had probably met someone and got a lift, but if she was ferrying drugs up to Glasgow she wouldn't be that careless. Just out of interest Maureen fished around in her pocket, found the battered and cracked photocopy of Ann and went into the shop. There were two members of staff on but neither of them had been working here before Christmas. They were both new starts. Thinking how reckless it was of the management to leave two new starts running a shop together, Maureen made her way to the restaurant. She stopped and realized that there were CCTV cameras everywhere. The new starts could have been safely left in charge of the Brazilian national debt. Out in the foyer she saw a sign for a pizza bar. She turned the corner and found a café area with red plastic chairs and tables cordoned off from the stairs. A waitress in her fifties was cleaning the chipped plastic with more care than it deserved.

'Excuse me,' said Maureen, finding her voice more rough than before. 'Have you been working here long?'

'Yes, love, I've been here for five months.'

'I'm trying to find out what happened to a friend of mine who was on the night bus to Glasgow. She got off for the break and never got on again about a month ago.'

'Oh, yes,' said the woman, folding her cloth to a flat surface. 'I know.'

Maureen got out the picture and showed it to her.

'I know,' nodded the woman. 'Wasn't it awful? We were all shocked, actually.'

Maureen was surprised that news of Ann's death had reached Knutsford. 'How did you hear about it?'

'I saw her, dear, I saw her coming out of the toilet and going into the ambulance. It was very sad. We were very shocked.'

'Into an ambulance?'

'Yes, she was mugged, dear, in the ladies'. Beaten very badly. Had her bag stolen.'

'Her bag?'

'Yes, her handbag. She wasn't found for half an hour. The men that did it were probably long gone by then.'

Ann's bag. She'd taken the bag everywhere with her, afraid of it being stolen, drawing attention to herself everywhere she went. If Tam Parlain told Maxine when it was coming in, Hutton could have been waiting for her at the service station, watching for her, waiting to do what he did best, annihilate the weak. They must have known she was going to get off and come in with a handbag worth tens of thousands. Parlain and Maxine were going out on their own, siding with Hutton against their own family and Toner. Toner would know Maxine lived with Hutton and he must have realized what they'd done before Hutton was killed over a mystery stash. Elizabeth said Toner had wanted to talk to Ann, and Senga had told Leslie that Ann had recognized Hutton's picture in the paper. Parlain had killed Ann to stop her talking. Poor witless Ann. Toner could afford her no protection here – in Glasgow and London maybe, but not in this wilderness. The CCTV evidence might have been kept, and even if it hadn't, the ambulance would have a record of it.

She went back to the bus early, standing outside on the grass verge, smoking a final fag, wondering about Ann. How desperate would a woman have to be? How much money would she need to owe to take a chance like that? But that's what Frank Toner had been counting on, someone desperate enough to take those chances.

Williams was out of bed and pulling on his trousers before Hellian had finished the sentence. '. . . under the sofa which give a superficial match to blood and hair samples from the deceased. Obviously we won't know for certain until the lab have a look at it.'

Williams balanced the receiver on his shoulder and knelt down, feeling under the bed for his shoes. The guesthouse carpet was a hideous hangover from the seventies: it flowed and spiralled like a melted box of crayons and smelt of dog. 'Parlain ye said?'

'Yes, Tam, t.a.m., Parlain, p.a.r.l.a.i.n. Works for the Adams family.'

'Those bastards again. Who's Parlain under, did Intelligence tell ye?'

'One Frank Toner, f.r.a.n—'

'And she bought a ticket up on the overnight bus?'

'Yes, but we can't confirm whether she's on it. DCI Joe McEwan knows her and has volunteered one of his officers to give a visual.'

'She'd better be on it. You realize that if this gets out before we interview her she's dead?'

'Won't get out this side, sir.'

Maureen couldn't sleep. The cigarettes and the story about Ann had woken her up and she was desperate to get home, home to the cold and the red and yellow tenements, the big sky and the rude children. She knew who she was in Glasgow and she was going to fight back before the last and make it safe. It was half four when they reached the wild hills. Steep slopes of mud and jagged rock were capped by creeping snowbanks and the bus felt suddenly colder. She looked at the bare hills and saw the families driven from their homes to make way for sheep, a thousand Coach and Horses all over the world, serving succour to souls who couldn't go home, who didn't even know where home was. Maureen leaned her head on the window and cried for the beautiful land, sobbing and covering her face with her hands, trying not to sniff. The woman on the back seat was at her elbow. 'Why are you crying?' she asked.

Maureen sniffed. 'Scotland,' she pointed out of the window. 'It's so beautiful. I haven't been home for so long.'

'That's well seen,' said the woman quietly. 'This is the Lake District.'

*

The bus hurtled into the reluctant dawn, through lowlands and into the flat Clyde valley. A cloudless electric blue sky was marred in the distance by a patty of thick black cloud and in its dark grey shadow sat Glasgow, her Glasgow, and she began to cry again.

43
Ruchill

The air was very still in the bus station. Maureen's breath hovered in front of her, swirling as she pushed past the other passengers, picked her bag from the growing pile and walked out of the automatic doors. The pavement shimmered and the buildings strained against the cold. A white mist filled the tall street and Maureen cut a swath through it, leaving black footprints in the frost. A black cab glided past her, turning for the city centre and the stations. She lit a cigarette. Her raw throat throbbed and she looked like shit but she was home. A sudden flurry of snow bleached the colours out of the city as she passed the foot of Garnethill and walked north. She was tempted to go home first, to dump her heavy bag, but she was sure she'd never come out again. Maureen pulled her scarf around her head and walked on.

Williams parked across the street from the station.

'Here, just here,' said Inness. 'That'll be fine.'

'Are you sure?' asked Williams, cranking up the handbrake and making Bunyan sigh. 'We're on a yellow.'

'Yeah.'

They walked across the road and took the grey concrete stairs down to the bus station. It was almost empty. Local double-deckers were parked in tidy lines along the centre of the concourse. A single bus, stopped in front of the ticket building, showed signs of life. A driver in a blue nylon uniform walked around the bonnet and disappeared behind it. Williams bristled. 'It's already in,' he said, and jogged over to it, his suit jacket flapping open. He stopped a withered wee guy with an Afro hairdo. 'Is this the London bus?'

'Aye.'

'Look, I'm a police officer.' He pulled the grainy printout photograph of Maureen O'Donnell out of his pocket. 'Was this woman on the bus?'

The wee guy looked at it and asked his pal to come and see as well. 'Think so,' said his pal.

'Aye,' squawked the first driver nasally. 'I recognize the hair. She was on the bus, right enough.'

'Where is she now?'

'How should I know?'

'Did you see anyone come and pick her up?'

The ugly man shrugged. 'I don't watch them all leaving, we've to get the luggage out.'

'Did ye see anyone grabbing her?'

The men stood apathetically and Inness pulled Williams by the arm. 'She might just have gone home.'

'Do you know where it is?'

'Yeah, it's up the road, two minutes up the road. Top of that hill there.'

It was a long walk. The snow thickened as the sun came up, enveloping the city in a heavy grey light. It lay on her sleeves and shoulders, catching on her scarf and eyebrows, deadening the noise of the cars and traffic as she made her way up the Maryhill Road. She got angrier as she walked, working up a sweat as she approached the turn-off to Ruchill. The lazy blizzard stopped suddenly under the disused railway bridge. Maureen walked on, stepping out of the envelope of calm into the white sheet and up the steep hill.

Ruchill was a dead area. A single row of buildings stood against the steep road. Behind it, ten acres of wasteland were criss-crossed by overgrown roads. Street after street of damp and rotten tenements had been demolished. On the other side of the street a high fence barred entry to the park, a tall grassy hill pitted with skeletal trees and the looming hospital tower. Maureen ignored it, willing herself not to look as she passed the black machine-gun nest pub, and walked on. The first of the hospital outbuildings appeared on the shoulder of the road, a modest red bungalow with an outsized Dutch gable façade.

Maureen paused at the foot of the steep driveway, hot and trembling. She shifted the scarf on her head to get some of the snow off and looked up. The drive curved sharply and disappeared behind a high bank of bushes. Shards of broken glass scratched the Tarmac beneath her feet and she walked on, past the bushes, and followed the road to the tower. The vandals had been there night after night. Single-storey buildings were dotted around the campus; their wooden onion domes lay on the ground, burnt and smashed. Crazed Venetian blinds hung forlornly in broken windows and net curtains flapped lazily at the muffled wind. She walked on to the top of the hill and looked out over the city dawn. She could see her house.

Maureen narrowed her eyes, blinking and catching snow-flakes in her lashes as she looked up at the jagged tower. silhouetted against a crumbling white sky. She crouched, picked up a stone, ran towards the building as she aimed, and threw it, her feet skidding on the slushy snow. The heavy grey stone hurled through the air, spinning and scattering the snowflakes falling gently in its path. She gasped as she saw where it was headed. The high window shattered and fell like a curtain. She picked up another stone from the overgrown grass verge, ran again and chucked it as hard as she could. Her scarf fell off her head, trailing down her back, baring her head to the weather. The stone shattered another window. Maureen smiled. She dropped her bag on to the wet ground and felt inside for Kilty's shopping. Her cold, stiff fingers relaxed when they found the rough cardboard of the box of firelighters.

The heat left her as soon as she reached the bottom of the stairs. She was smiling and happy, chewing squares of Milka chocolate and feeling safe and home. She must never, ever tell anyone what she had done. She let the tension leave her. All she had to do now was phone Leslie and wait for the police to come to see her. Then she was looking forward to a wash and a sleep and a day in her pyjamas, sitting on the settee in front of the television, sipping tea. Grinning and excited, she skipped up the stairs, taking them two at a time, until she got two steps away from her front door and stopped.

The front door was hanging on the hinges, two inches ajar. The lights were on in the hall. Noiselessly, she slid her bag to the floor and reached into her pocket for the stabbing comb. She pushed the door open with the tips of her fingers. She couldn't see into the living room but she could hear. Someone was in there, she could hear a voice muttering something, a short question, followed by a curt answer. Footsteps came towards her along the wooden floorboards, pausing in the living room. They stepped towards her, pressing on the back of the door to shut it. Maureen kicked the door with the flat of her foot, banging it against the wall and found herself staring at a startled, sleepy Inness. She dropped her bag. 'What the fuck are you doing in my house?'

Inness was standing in her hallway, grinning out at her with the blue morning behind him. 'Mrs Thatcher, I presume? I've got some pals here who are dying to meet you.'

A man and a woman in smart dark suits were standing in her living room. Angus's letters were scattered over the table. Every one of them had been pulled from their envelopes and read. 'You bastards.' She lurched into the hall, reaching for the letters but Inness grabbed her by the arm and pulled her roughly round to face him He screamed at her, 'Calm down!'

Over his shoulder, out of the kitchen window and beyond on the north horizon, the Ruchill fever hospital tower was burning like a Roman candle, the turret windows belching black sparking clouds of dead men's ashes. Below, in the quiet city, siren screams rushed to a fire too well set to be sated. A door opened in the close and Jim Maliano appeared in her doorway pulling his purple dressing-gown shut. 'What is going on in here?' he demanded, his bouffant trembling with fury.

Inness held on to Maureen and put his other hand on Maliano's shoulder, pushing him out of the door. 'We are police officers,' he said, 'and we are here to speak to Miss O'Donnell. Go back inside, please, sir.'

'You can't go through my stuff,' said Maureen stiffly. 'Those are my letters.'

'Well,' shouted Jim, 'if you are police officers you should know better than to come into a domestic close at this time of the morning, making that sort of noise.'

Inness pushed him with the flat of his hand. 'Back inside, please, sir,' he said, pushing too hard and making Maliano stumble over the step.

Maliano slapped his hand away and turned to Maureen. 'Maureen, are you all right?'

Maureen didn't like Jim Maliano and he had made it abundantly clear that he didn't like her or her lifestyle, but whenever there was trouble Jim came running across the close and looked out for her.

'I'm fine, Jim, I'm really fine. You go back to bed and I promise we'll keep it down.'

Maliano glared at Inness insolently. 'Call me if you have any trouble?'

'I will, Jim, thanks.'

He turned and looked at her. 'Ruchill's on fire,' he said, somewhat gleefully, as if he were having an everyday chat with his neighbour.

Maureen and Inness looked down the hall to the kitchen window and the column of fire on the horizon, and Inness muttered an awed curse.

'Neds,' said Maliano, and looked accusingly at Inness. 'Ye should be out stopping that sort of behaviour instead of harassing her. I keep a diary of all your comings and goings up here,' he gestured to his spy-hole, 'so,' he said, pointing at him, 'just you watch it.' Jim's bottle snapped and he blushed and scuttled back across the close to his own door, giving Inness a last warning look before he shut the door. Maureen knew he would be standing, watching. She shut her front door and darted into the living room, gathered up all of Angus's letters and held them to her chest. 'These're mine,' she said.

'We asked you about them,' said Inness sternly, 'and we're seizing them, so you can put them down. They're not even yours any more.'

'What gives you the right to break into my house?'

The fat guy in the dark suit stepped over to her. 'Miss O'Donnell,' he said, 'where have you been since you got off the bus? We thought you were dead behind the door in here.'

'I don't have to fucking tell you anything,' she said.

'What happened to your neck?' asked the little blonde woman, staring at it.

Inness stepped closer and Maureen could tell from the flush around his eyes that he was furious with her. 'Those letters'll be going to the fiscal.' He was trying to threaten her but in the last few days she'd been trapped in Parlain's, she'd been strangled by Toner and she'd made her home safe from the evil eye and had chosen her path. Inness couldn't frighten her with a moustache and a stare.

'Get out,' she said, trying to shout but sounding strained and weak.

The fat guy was staring at the bruise around her throat. 'What happened to your neck?' he asked.

'Get out,' said Maureen.

He touched her arm gently. 'Miss O'Donnell? I'm Arthur Williams from the Met.' His face was kind and nervous. 'I understand that you have information about Ann Harris's murder.'

Maureen was folding the letters, shoving them back into their envelopes, dizzy with the desire to be alone and home and safe. She ripped an envelope trying to shove a letter into it and that was enough. 'Fuck it,' she shouted, her throat throbbed and stabbed with the effort. She dropped all the letters and kicked them out of the way. 'Fuck it.'

Inness was staring at her. 'What happened to your neck?' he said.

The plump man stepped forward. 'We really need to talk to you, Miss O'Donnell.'

44

Rosenhan

Williams insisted that Maureen have some tea to warm her up, and Bunyan made her a mug and brought it through from the kitchen. She hadn't put any cold water in it and Maureen managed to scorch her tongue, but the heat soothed her throat a little so she persevered and sipped at it anyway.

Bunyan lit a cigarette and shoved the packet across the coffee table. Maureen couldn't resist her hollow camaraderie. She lifted the packet and took one. She could have cried for ever now she was home. Arthur Williams sat calmly, smiling dutifully whenever she looked at him.

'Have you charged Leslie and Jimmy?'

'Not yet,' said Williams softly. 'We might still, we'll have to see how this pans out.'

'Did you go to Tam Parlain's house?' asked Maureen.

'Yeah,' he said. 'We're questioning Parlain and Elizabeth Woolly.'

'You found Elizabeth?'

'She was at his house when we got there. They've both been arrested on another charge, so we've got all the time in the world.'

'What other charge?'

'Possession.'

Williams watched Maureen looking downcast at the table, drawing on her fag. Her throat was a red and black mess; he wouldn't be surprised if she had broken something.

She looked skinny and bedraggled, and judging from the letters in her house, life wasn't too sweet at all. He leaned over the table and tapped his fingers softly on the table in her line of vision. 'Why don't you just tell us what happened?'

So Maureen sat and smoked Bunyan's fags and told them the story about Ann's big bag, the debts to the loan sharks and the attack at Knutsford, about the letter from the non-existent law firm and Tam Parlain's damp settee. She left out the troubling inconsistency of Moe and the benefit book, left out Mark Doyle because she still didn't know what to make of him. She was getting to the end, to Maxine and Hutton and the service station. She had just phoned Hugh and New Scotland Yard and 999 when Williams interrupted. 'What was the story about the Polaroid?'

'It was a picture of Toner and her son. He sent it to her to flush her out of the shelter.'

'But you don't have it?'

Maureen shook her head and reached into her pocket. 'I've got something, though.' She pulled out the photocopy she had made of the Polaroid in the copy-shop in Brixton high street. Bunyan leaned in as Williams unfolded it and they looked down at Toner holding the small boy's hand.

'Nice bloke, isn't he?' said Bunyan, lowering her voice. 'Did you get a fright?'

Maureen hung her head and drew on her fag.

'These people,' said Bunyan, nodding gently, 'are very frightening.'

Maureen noticed that she was talking to her as if she were a child, as if she could make it better with a glass of orange and a chocolate biscuit, but Maureen needed that certainty now and she responded to it. She nodded back. 'I got a fright,' she said.

'I'm not surprised,' said Bunyan, leaning towards her. 'I get a fright when I talk to these people.'

Maureen looked at her. 'Did you come all the way up to see me?' Her voice was high and nervous.

'Yeah.'

'How did you know I'd be here?'

'Didn't know.'

'How could you possibly know it was me that phoned?'

Bunyan tapped her nose playfully. 'Copper's instincts,' she said, and smiled a consolation.

Maureen smiled back. 'Thank you,' she said:

Williams sat back. 'It's still possible that Jimmy Harris did it, you know.'

'I know.'

'He was in London.'

'I know,' she looked at Bunyan, 'but you've spoken to Jimmy, you know how passive he is. I'm sure Tam did it. Why else would he wash a leather settee?'

Williams nodded at the floor. 'But that's not evidence. We can't get a conviction on the basis that he mistreated his leather sofa, can we?' Williams smiled sadly again, and Maureen realized that nice, plump, unthreatening male was his catch, they must send him in to question all the mental birds.

'We'll have to take you to Carlisle to interview you formally,' he said.

'Why Carlisle?'

Williams sighed and looked very tired. 'It's a long story,' he said.

A soft knock on the door heralded the creeping return of Inness. Hugh McAskill was behind him, his gold and silver hair splitting the grey morning as he looked into the living room and caught Maureen's eye. For the briefest moment he looked very sad then dropped his eyes to the floor. He looked up again with a blank expression.

'Is this the officer you were trying to phone?' asked Williams.

'Aye,' said Maureen.

Hugh stood in the living-room doorway and nodded solemnly at his feet. Williams and Bunyan took the hint, stood up and went into the kitchen with Inness to wait. Hugh watched them leave and turned to her, his china blue eyes suddenly lively. 'You all right?'

'I'm fine,' said Maureen, feeling like a hard case. 'It's nice to be home.'

'They taped the phone-call from London,' said Hugh. 'They went around to Tam Parlain's house and found bits of blood and hair under his settee. There's a superficial match with the hair from the body.'

'Will they let Jimmy go?'

'He's out already,' said Hugh. 'They hadn't charged him yet.'

'Right? What about Leslie?'

'She's out too. That Elizabeth woman's in a bit of a state. She's telling them everything on the promise of a methadone course.'

'Yeah,' said Maureen. 'She told me everything for five hundred quid.'

'Desperate.' Hugh nodded at his feet and looked at her. 'Farrell's been writing to you all this time?'

'Yeah.'

He sighed. 'Maureen,' he said, 'I can't believe you didn't tell me.'

'It's your job, Hugh, you'd've been honour-bound to tell Joe.' They looked at each other and Hugh nodded quietly. 'He's only pretending to be mental,' said Maureen. 'He's having ye on. I didn't understand why he was writing at first but then I realized. It was too easy for you to trace the letters here. He's drip-feeding Joe information about his mental state. He knows that the harder Joe has to work to get it, the more likely he is to believe it.'

'I don't know . . .'

'What will ye do with the letters?'

'We'll have to give them to the fiscal now. We don't have any option – they're material evidence as to his state of mind.'

'He'll get out, Hugh,' she said. 'He's a fucking psychologist, he knows exactly how to act to get off.'

'I know. It's a tricky one.' He turned to look at her neck. 'Let me see you.' She stretched her chin up as high as she could. 'You should get an X-ray,' said Hugh. 'I'll take ye up to the Albert if you want.'

'Naw,' she said, 'I'll go after. Would you like a cup of tea?'

Hugh blinked slowly and smiled. 'I would love a cup of tea.'

He followed her into the cramped kitchen. Bunyan was sitting down at the table and Williams was standing in the corner, smiling as Inness mumbled a story to him. They stopped talking as the door opened, stiffening when they saw it was Maureen.

'Hello, again,' said Williams pleasantly.

'Excuse me,' said Maureen, 'I was just going to make a cup of tea.'

Williams shifted on his feet and glanced sideways at Inness. 'I understand,' he said, 'that you were in a psychiatric hospital for a while.' He looked at her innocently but the question was never innocent.

'So what?'

Williams shrugged. 'It's just, you know, interesting.'

Maureen lit another cigarette and her heart heaved at another lungful of harm. Hugh was here and she didn't need the fellowship of this pushy man any more. 'No,' she said, flicking the kettle on, 'you're wrong. It wasn't interesting.'

'While you were in there—'

'I'm not answering questions about myself. I'm answering questions about Ann Harris and London, not about myself.'

Williams pointed at Inness. 'My colleague here tells me that your brother was a drug-dealer. Did he have any connection with Frank Toner?'

'No. None.'

'It's interesting, though, isn't it? That Tam Parlain is found with a houseful of drugs and your brother used to be a dealer? Is that why you went to London?'

If she hadn't been to Ruchill she would have thought it was strange herself. She would have wondered but she was sure of everything now. The kettle reached a pitch, spluttering before switching itself off.

'This is a magnificent view,' sighed Bunyan. The men looked at her. She was sitting down, her hand resting on the table, a vertical cigarette burning between her fingers. She was smiling softly to herself and looking out over the rugged north side of the city and the flaming fever tower. 'Magnificent,' she breathed.

'We'll be keeping the letters,' said Inness, stepping forward, reasserting his authority.

Maureen turned to him. 'Look,' she said, 'see those letters? He wanted me to give them to you. He wants you to think he's mental so he'll get a short sentence in a low-security facility.'

'Really?' Inness glanced a snide, silent aside at Williams. 'You're a doctor now, are ye?'

She fucking hated him. 'Have ye ever heard of the 1971 Rosenhan study?' She waited, making him say it.

'No,' he said finally.

'These people went to mental hospitals and said they'd been hearing voices. They behaved normally apart from the retrospective claims. They were lying, there was nothing wrong with them.'

'Why did they do it then?'

'For the study,' said Maureen, with forced patience. 'They were all diagnosed as schizophrenic and everything they did after that was put down to their illness; taking notes for the study, watching people, asking about their case. Some of them were kept in for days, some for weeks. The only people who knew there was nothing wrong with them were the other patients. Now, I am a certified mental case.' She looked at Williams. He was biting his lip and listening. 'And there is fuck all wrong with Angus Farrell.'

Williams raised his eyebrows and smiled at Inness. 'Smart lady,' he said.

Inness didn't smile back.

They were leaving. Inness was making a great play of being grateful for her help but he didn't like her and she didn't like him, and it was getting harder for both of them to hide it.

'Goodbye,' said Inness. 'I'm sure we'll be seeing each other very soon.' He gave her a disgusted look and turned down the stairs, walking away before he said something he regretted, leaving Maureen and Williams alone.

Williams looked faintly amused. 'You're not exactly in his good books, are you?'

'Personality clash,' she said.

'You're in my good books,' he said. 'You're not planning on leaving town again, are you?'

'No,' she smiled, 'not for a long time.'

'We'll be back tomorrow to take you to Carlisle. About twelve, okay?'

'Yeah.'

'Get it X-rayed,' said Williams, backing off and pointing at his neck. 'Little bones in there.'

'Yeah,' she touched her throat softly, 'it'll be all right.'

'Okay,' said Hugh. His breath smelt of bitter tea. 'I'll be seeing ye.'

'Take care, Hugh,' she said, trying to look up at him without bending her neck.

'Get an X-ray.'

'I will, Hugh, I will.'

She watched them pile down the stairs. The little blonde English woman trailed behind the men, looking up at her as they disappeared below the landing. She smiled and lifted her hand, slapping the fingers against the palm, as if she was waving to a child.

Maureen used the mobile number.

'Oh, Mauri, fucking hell, fucking hell, I've never been more scared in my life.' Leslie paused and Maureen could hear a little 'phut' as she took a draw of her fag.

'They've let you go?'

'They've let me go and I'm home and so's Jimmy, thank fuck. They told my work. I'm getting sacked but I don't care. I just fucking don't care.' Cammy called impatiently in the background for Leslie to come here and harhalfingfom. Leslie sighed into the receiver and turned to speak to him. 'I'm on the fucking phone, Cameron. Can it, will ye?'

'Well,' said Maureen, 'they've found blood and hair in someone's house so I think they'll be dropping the charges.'

'They'd never have made a case. It was ridiculous in the first fucking place,' said Leslie, and realized how she sounded. 'Surrounded by Injuns I was, but wasnae feart, oh, no. Let's set up a business together now we're both free agents.'

Maureen giggled, glad to have Leslie back on form.

'A business? Doing what?'

'Roaming vigilantes,' said Leslie. 'I'll be your driver.'

'That's crazy. I've never even been to Rome.'

'Maureen,' said Leslie seriously, 'punning causes cancer.'

45
Equal

The Equal café was serving lunches. Hungry office workers and students from the art school were cramped together at the black and gold fleck Formica tables, eating their rolls and sipping tea from smoked-glass mugs. Maureen and Liam managed to find a small empty table near the back. It was under a sloping ceiling of cheap pine, which hung so low that Maureen's seat was really only suitable for a midget with a hump. Previous patrons of the café had carved their names into the sloping soft wood. The middle-aged waitress who approached them had a very prominent limp, which worsened dramatically when an order was sent back or anyone asked for anything tricky. She seemed to have developed some sort of fungal complaint on one of her feet as well, because she was wearing what appeared to be a slipper with the toe cut out.

'Hello,' nodded Liam.

'Whatd'yeswant?'

'Two all-day breakfasts,' he said. 'I'll have tea with mine. Mauri?'

Maureen was tired and wanted coffee but didn't trust it to be anything but reused grounds. 'Tea as well.'

The waitress shuffled off to the adjacent table to take a lone businessman's order.

'Sorry about the Martha thing,' said Liam, casually watching the waitress and nodding, as if his apology brought the whole episode to a satisfactory conclusion.

Maureen sat back indignantly, banged the Toner bruise on the back of her head off the ceiling and sat forward again. 'Liam, what are you going to do about Lynn?'

'She doesn't need to know,' he said briskly. 'What happened to you in London?'

'Look, ye can't harass her into going back out with ye and then do things like that. You can't treat her like that. Lynn's too good for you, she always has been.'

Liam turned to face her, exasperated. 'What exactly do you expect me to do?' he said, unreasonably annoyed for a transgressor.

'Um, well,' she said sarcastically, 'start with not fucking other women?'

'Look, if it wasn't for you I wouldn't have done it. I only came down to London to get ye. It was you who wanted to stay the night there.'

The businessman shifted in his seat, pretending not to listen but savouring every word.

'Hey,' she said, 'ye can't blame that on me, it was you who got your fucking tager out.'

'Fuck off, Maureen.'

The businessman looked up and smiled sweetly at the far wall.

'That is so unreasonable,' Maureen said. 'Anyway, I've been fighting people all week, I'm not going to say any more about this. But it wasn't my fault.'

'Let's say no more about it,' said Liam, adding quickly, 'But it wasn't my fault either. What happened to your neck?'

The waitress shuffled over to them, carrying two mugs and two oval plates. She dropped the cups on to the table and slid a plate in front of each of them, walking away before the runny egg yolks had stopped quivering. The bacon, eggs, sausage and black pudding were cooked to perfection. Fried potato scones, swollen and glistening with hot oil, sat on either end of the ovals like inverted commas. Liam bagsied the tea. For some reason Maureen had been given a cup of hot orange squash but she was pleased with it.

'Tell me about your neck,' said Liam, eating a slice of Lorne sausage dripping with yolk.

'London was heavy, you know?' She nodded. 'Really heavy. There's some bad people in the world.'

'I know, wee hen.'

Maureen remembered Elizabeth. 'And some sad people too,' she said.

'Yeah,' said Liam. 'God, I'd rather deal with the evil ones any day, they just try and fuck ye. The sad ones make ye feel miserable and then they try to fuck ye. Did ye find out who killed her?'

'Tam Parlain. She was robbed of a big bag of drugs she was carrying for Toner. Tam told Maxine she was muling and she must have told Hutton. I think he ran down there and robbed her. He kicked the shit out of her.'

'Yeah,' said Liam. 'He would do. He was a right sicko.'

'Anyway,' said Maureen, a little annoyed at being interrupted, 'Toner was putting two and two together and put out the word that he wanted to talk to Ann, and Tam killed her to stop him finding out.'

'Are you sure?'

'Yeah, in front of a whole lot of people.' She squashed crumbly black pudding on to a portion of square sausage and covered it with runny yolk.

Liam was looking at her and trying not to smile. 'He killed her in front of people?' he asked.

'Yeah. He made them all help him.'

'So,' he smirked, 'Tam Parlain killed a woman in front of loads of people because – what? He wanted to cover up another misdemeanour?'

Maureen stopped eating and looked at her plate.

'Well,' said Liam sceptically, 'maybe it's random enough to be true.'

'They were all junkies,' said Maureen, irritated by his supercilious tone. 'I never really knew what that world was like before. How could you, Liam, knowing what it's like?'

Liam paused and stared at her, instinctively angry and defensive. He used to look like that all the time. 'Dunno,' he said, clenching his jaw. 'It's not like that for most users. Lots of people use socially. Ye start off doing a favour for a friend, and then favours for several friends and then it's for friends of friends. Before ye know where ye are, you've become this big demon and the police are strip-searching ye and you're to blame for everyone who misuses or ODs. You don't hold wine merchants responsible for Winnie's drinking, do ye?'

He sat up and looked at her. Liam had never done anything but right by her and Maureen had no right to cast up his past to him. 'I'm sorry,' she said, 'I was annoyed. I'm very tired.'

But Liam continued. 'I like not living like that,' he said. 'I like putting my rubbish out the front like everyone else and not being worried when the door goes. I was good at it, they were choosing to use it, and if they hadn't bought it off me it would have been from someone else. But I've got a house out of it and I'm at university and I can fly to London at a minute's notice looking for you so I can't lie and say I'm sorry. I did a bad thing and I'm not sorry.'

The businessman called the waitress over and asked where his hot orange was. Maureen cupped her hands around the drink, afraid they'd take it away. 'I shouldn't have asked about that,' she whispered. 'It's in the past and I shouldn't have.'

The waitress insisted that she'd already brought the hot

orange and accused the businessman of losing it. He said how could he possibly lose a drink when he'd been sitting at the same wee table since he came in? The waitress tutted, muttered a bowdlerized curse and hobbled away.

'Know what you were saying about alcoholism being genetic?' whispered Liam, leaning over the table. Maureen nodded. He pointed at her hot orange. 'There's a gene for criminal behaviour as well.'

Maureen laughed at him, choked immediately and used the last of her hot drink to soothe her throat. She hid the cup behind a stand-up plastic menu.

'D'you know what I find amazing?' said Liam, dipping into his yolk with a slice of scone.

'What do you find amazing?' said Maureen.

'The fact,' he pointed his fork at her, 'that you know two people who've been murdered in the last six months.'

'Mad, isn't it?' she said.

'I mean, that is unbelievable,' said Liam. 'In fact it's more than unbelievable. It's statistically implausible.'

Maureen looked at him, remembering Elizabeth saying Toner wanted to speak to Ann, the cuts behind Ann's knees, and Moe, who remembered Leslie's name and work address perfectly and reported her drunk sister missing after a day. 'Bitch,' she said.

'Who?'

'The fucking lying bitch.'

Liam looked over his shoulder. 'Who are ye talking about?'

'Finish, finish,' she said suddenly, poking at his plate.

'Why?' he said, pulling it away from her.

'You're driving me to the airport.'

46

Fucked Both Ways

The plane lifted off the Tarmac, pressing Maureen back in her seat. An excited small boy in front lost control and undid his belt, standing up on the seat and giving out a high happy squeal. His nervous mother grabbed his leg and sat him down, nodding apologetically to the stewardess who was staggering towards them down the aisle, ready to quell the boy's air joy.

Within minutes they were blinking at the sunshine and looking down at a molten white landscape. The flight took an hour and ten minutes but felt much shorter. The cabin crew came down the aisle dishing out drinks and pretzels, followed it with a small meaningless meal and chased that with tea or coffee. By the time the passengers had stopped fretting that their neighbour was getting something they weren't, the plane had already begun its descent. They made a quick, bumpy landing and pulled to a stop. The passengers stood up, cluttering the aisles and standing with aching knees pressed into the seat in front, waiting to get out and get away. It was raining gently outside the window.

It occurred to Maureen as she stepped on to the industrial carpet at Heathrow that the information lady might be there, somewhere, waiting to tell her to fuck off herself. She kept her head down and walked quickly to the express shuttle. The spacy silver platform was quieter this time and the train was waiting. She climbed on and sat down, closing her eyes to relieve the stinging. She saw the Ruchill fever hospital tower belching sparks over Inness's shoulder and smiled all the way to London, feeling like Kilty in the lawyer's office.

The train pulled into Paddington and the sounds and smells of the city brought her back round. As she made her way to the tube station she was struck by the creepy conviction that the city had tricked her into coming back and she wasn't getting away this time. But she hadn't been tricked. She knew she was right. She was certain of it.

She took a taxi from Victoria. She shouldn't be seen in Brixton, not now, and the ride gave her the chance to decide what she was going to say. She pulled her hair back and pinned it down so that she wouldn't be as easy to recognize.

Dumbarton Court echoed to the sounds of children playing before their tea. A crowd of teenagers stood around at the entrance gate, kicking the ground and posing for each other. A couple of boys played football against a wall. Maureen walked straight past them and took the stairs for Moe's flat, running up them two at a time, her tired heart pounding when she got to the door. She waited until she had caught her breath and knocked lightly, trying to sound like a casual caller. She turned away, looking down the stairs so that Moe would only see the back of her head through the spy-hole. The door creaked open just a little and Moe called out to her, 'Hello?'

Maureen swung round and jammed her foot in the small space. 'Let me in, Moe, I have to speak to you. Toner knows.'

She could see in Moe's eyes that she wanted to slam the door shut, ram it against Maureen's foot until the pain got too much to bear, but worry wouldn't let her. 'What are you talking about?' said Moe.

'She's in danger.'

Moe looked out on to the landing. She let Maureen in, shut the door and looked out through the spy-hole again, checking that Maureen had been alone. She turned and pursed her lips, planting her hands on her hips. 'What's going on? I thought you were on Jimmy's side?'

'You fucking lying cow,' she said. 'He was going to prison for the rest of his fucking life and the kids were going into care. Don't you give a shit about that?'

Moe's eyes were damp and glassy.

'Don't give us the tears again. Ye had a choice!' Maureen was shouting, as loud as her broken voice would go, and she saw Moe's eyes flicker to the ceiling. Some kindly neighbour upstairs might hear and come to help poor Mrs Akitza. 'You had a fucking choice,' she repeated, more quietly.

Moe stepped back and looked Maureen over. 'What the fuck has it got to do with you?' she said.

'Where is she?'

Moe folded her arms. 'I don't know what you're talking about.'

'West Country?'

Moe flinched.

'For fucksake,' said Maureen, 'it's the most obvious place for her to go – away from London and Glasgow – there's a big trade down there. The West Country's crawling.'

'Where else is there?'

'Somewhere else, anywhere else.'

It was dark in the hall, light from the living-room window hardly making a dent in the gloom.

'They'll kill the children if you tell,' said Moe, eyeing Maureen up, weighing her in.

'Whose idea was it?'

Moe shuffled her foot, watching it as she pointed to the centre of a big swirl in the carpet. She was thinking her way through it, seeing what she would give away if she told.

Maureen looked at her, poking her tongue into her cheek, feeling the ragged lines of the cut. 'It was yours, wasn't it?' she said. 'And Tam agreed to go along with it. Did you pay him or are you fucking him?'

Moe looked coy. 'I'm a married woman,' she said.

'You're married to the invisible man,' said Maureen. 'Mr Akitza's long gone, isn't he?'

Moe shifted uncomfortably.

'You gave my pager number to Tam, didn't ye? And ye told him I had the Polaroid. Was he going to kill me too?'

'She's my wee sister,' she muttered. 'I couldn't turn her away. She's my sister.'

'Who was she?'

'The girl that died?'

'Yeah. The junkie.'

Moe shrugged. 'Someone.'

'And ye cut her legs and burnt her hands and feet to hide the marks because everyone knew Ann was a drinker.'

'Not me,' said Moe, shaking her head indignantly. 'I never touched her.'

'Who cut her face up before the others got there?'

'Not me,' said Moe.

'Nothing's you, is it, Moe? She was someone's daughter, for fucksake. She must have been a mother too or they'd have known it wasn't Ann when they did the post-mortem.'

Moe hissed at her and stepped across the hall to the living room. She had been sitting in the dark. The blue dusk hovered in the long window and a fag was burning in the ashtray. Moe bent down and picked it up, taking a draw.

'They were gonnae kill the children,' said Moe, blinking in the gloom. 'They'd have killed them one by one. What else could we do?'

'What about the woman who died? D'ye even know her name?'

'What else could we do?'

'That was some poor soul you killed. You're fucking animals.'

'She was killing herself, anyway.'

'You're animals. Did ye even stop and think what it would do to Ann's children? They think their mum's dead. They think she was killed and thrown in the river. They've been told their dad could have done it and they'll always wonder, that'll always be at the back of their minds. Did neither of ye stop to think about that?'

Moe bit her lip. 'What else could we do?' she whispered.

Maureen didn't know. She didn't know what they could do. 'You lied to me,' said Maureen. 'You lied to me twice.'

Suddenly infuriated, Moe turned and slapped Maureen's arm. 'And who the fuck do you think you are?' she spluttered. 'An interested party? My sister was going to get killed, they were going to kill her fucking kids and how dare I lie to you? You fucking silly twat.'

Maureen leaned back against the wall to get away from her. Moe was trembling as she took another draw. 'What'll happen now?' she asked.

'Jimmy'll probably go free,' said Maureen. 'You know they've charged Tam and other people. They might mention your Ann, he might tell.'

'Tam won't tell. Frank Toner'd kill him if he knew,' she said, and added, 'I'm glad Jimmy's going to be okay.'

'Fuck off, you don't care about him,' said Maureen spitefully.

'Listen you to me.' Moe narrowed her eyes. 'I like Jimmy. I like him more than I like my sister. Before their wedding I took him aside and said to him, "Jimmy," I said, "she's a drinker. You watch yourself." I did. That's how much I think of him. I warned him about her.'

'Well, that must have kicked the nuptials off on a happy

note. Did Ann know Leslie Findlay was Jimmy's cousin?'

'No, she didn't,' Moe said. 'She'd have left her out of it, if she'd known. All she wanted Findlay to do was tell the police she'd been there, he'd hit her and give them the compensation pictures. She said she was a right feminist. She'd make sure they chased him . . .'

They stood in the dark living room, unable to resolve anything.

'But she didn't because he was her cousin,' nodded Maureen. 'The woman you killed—'

'Not me,' insisted Moe. 'Not me.'

'She was someone's family too.'

'Yeah,' nodded Moe defiantly, 'but not mine.'

Maureen shoved her hands in her pocket. Moe didn't know. She didn't know what he'd done to her. 'You think Tam killed that girl for you, don't you? To protect your sister.'

Moe folded her arms, looking at the floor.

'Moe,' said Maureen quietly, 'did ye know that the guy who battered the shit out of Ann and took her bag was called Neil Hutton?'

Moe looked nervous. She knew something was coming but she couldn't work out what it was. 'No,' she said finally, shifting on her feet. 'I didn't know that.'

'Hutton was shot up the arse for dealing on his own, did ye know that?'

Moe frowned hard. 'No,' she said more quietly, 'I didn't know that either.'

'Tam didn't tell ye that?'

Moe looked frightened.

'Well,' said Maureen, moving out to the hall and over to the front door, 'that was very remiss of Tam because he knew about it. He should have told ye, really, shouldn't he?'

Moe followed her out into the hall, confused and wanting to know more.

'How d'ye think Hutton knew Ann would be in Knutsford that night? Will I tell ye? Hutton's bidie-in was a sour-faced cow called Maxine Parlain.'

The expression on Moe's face didn't change but, rather, slid a fraction to the side, making her look old and vulnerable.

'Maxine's Tam's wee sister,' Maureen paused. 'What d'ye think Toner would have made of that? If he'd managed to speak to Ann he'd have found out, wouldn't he? She could've described Hutton to him. She knew what he looked like and Toner would've worked it out. He'd know Tam had told Hutton where Ann would be on the bus. He'd know Tam had planned it all.'

Moe had a shocked red flush around her eyes and Maureen imagined she saw blood on her lips. 'If Ann ever comes near Jimmy or those kids, I'll kill her myself. You tell her that. And for fucksake tell her to stop cashing the fucking child-benefit book.' Maureen unclipped the Yale and swung open the door. 'Fucked ye both ways, didn't he, hen?'

Maureen headed further up Brixton Hill. She turned, walking backwards and looking down to the lights of the high street. It was dark and the orange street-lights throbbed awake. She was leaving, she was going home, and the ugly streets and vile buildings and the men in pubs and the hungry beggars couldn't keep her here. She hailed a cab. 'Heathrow,' she said. 'Can ye get me there for seven o'clock?'

'I can get you there for half six.'

47
Jimmy, Jimmy

She didn't know. She'd been thinking about it for days. She thought she'd already decided back at the house. She was going to tell Jimmy that Ann was alive because it wasn't right for her to know and not tell him. But now, in the stippled, pissy lift, she'd changed her mind again. She remembered what Angus had said about the blood and how that one scrap of information had haunted her for months. Jimmy and the kids were just reaching some sort of equilibrium. If she told him, Jimmy might go looking for her, and Ann could end up on a murder charge with the rest of them. But at least the kids would have a mum, and a mum in jail is still a mum. She didn't know.

Alan opened the door to her, but he wasn't playing the helpless child any more. He held the door tight to his face and looked out at her. 'Whit d'ye want?' he said, eventually.

She wanted to say something unpleasant to him, pull him up about his manners or something, but she couldn't find it in her heart.

'Why have ye got that on your neck?' he said, staring at her neck brace.

'I fell. Is your father in?' she said.

'Aye.' He didn't budge.

'Alan, son, there's nothing clever about being ignorant. Go and get your da.'

Alan's eyes slid to the side, listening to the living room,

and he pressed the door tighter against his face. 'Da's busy,' he said quietly.

'Hey,' Jimmy was shouting at him from the living room, 'is that someone at the door?'

Alan sighed and looked at Maureen's feet for a huffy moment before opening the door and slipping back into the house. Maureen heard him whisper something as the door fell open.

Jimmy was sitting in the big chair, changing the babies into their pyjamas. 'Oh,' he smiled, 'it's you. Hello.'

'Hello, you, yourself,' she said, and they grinned at each other as if it was Christmas and Santa was real.

He dropped the sweatshirts and climbed over the little people standing around his chair, coming towards her with a big smile. As he got closer she saw his uncertainty. He didn't know whether to hug her or kiss her or what. He squeezed her shoulders, stood on tiptoe to reach across the plastic frame of the brace and planted a chaste little peck on her cheek. She stepped into the hall and the first thing that struck her was the damp warmth. 'God,' she said, taking her hat off, 'it's warm in here.'

Jimmy pointed to a Calor-gas fire standing in the middle of the room. It was on full and the babies were watching the little orange blanket of flames, mesmerized as if by television. 'Eh?' said Jimmy, smiling.

'Oh, yeah,' she said. 'Where did you get that?'

Jimmy nodded out to the hall. 'Eh, out of the door money,' he said, a little embarrassed.

'Ye charging to get in here now?' she said, watching Alan standing in the kitchen doorway eating a margarine sandwich. She nodded to him. 'All right, wee man?'

Alan looked irritated. He stormed past her out to the hall and up the stairs, leaving Jimmy shaking his head in exasperation. 'That wee cunt,' he muttered. He looked at her. I've telt him and telt him, we owe everything to you and Isa and wee Leslie, and he still won't mind his manners.'

'But ye don't owe us, Jimmy, ye don't. You're the one that does the hard work.'

Without seeming to have moved, the babies had some-how got closer to the fire. It was obvious that they had been told not to go near it; they were watching Jimmy's legs out of the corner of their little eyes, their backs stiff with naughty apprehension. Maureen pointed to them and Jimmy swung round. 'Get away,' he said, slow and threatening, raising his hand over his head.

The babies scuttled backwards, grinning and keeping their eyes on the gorgeous flames as they held on to the armchair. Maureen told Jimmy to finish dressing them, and would he mind if she went up to see Alan? Jimmy cringed. 'It's no' very tidy.'

She climbed the narrow staircase to the cold landing. The bathroom door was lying open. The noise of an anxiously dripping tap and the sickly-sweet smell of mildew filled the air. The bedroom door had a Radio One sticker on it and a slit of light below. She knocked. Alan shouted that she couldn't come in but she opened the door and called into the crack that she'd travelled all the way up the stairs to see his room. He didn't answer her. The smell of baby pee and mildew mingled in the doorway. She opened the door a little more and looked in. Two sets of unmade bunk beds on either side of the room left a narrow three-foot strip of floor between them. The aisle was full of little shoes and clothes, broken second-hand toys and the tails of rough blankets. Alan sat cross-legged on the far lower bunk, watching the door like an angry convict. She should have decided before she came. 'Are ye all right, son?'

'Don't you "son" me,' he said, furious but keeping his

voice down so that Jimmy wouldn't hear him. 'I'm not your son. My mum's dead.'

She looked bored. 'Doesn't mean that, anyway,' she said, staying in the doorway and checking out the comics on his bed. 'It's just a thing ye say. What do your pals call ye?'

'Mental Harris,' he said, his eyes flashing in the shadow. He was lying. Maureen had known kids like him at school. They probably called him Smelly.

'Well,' she said, 'I'll call ye . . . Alan.'

He almost smiled at that.

'D'ye like comics?' she asked.

He touched them with his fingertips and said aye, he did, and she stood there for a bit. She wanted to say that she'd been a sad and angry wee girl and she knew how he felt but she didn't know how. Even when Michael was hitting Winnie they'd always known that she could handle herself and provide for them. 'Ye know, Isa and Leslie don't mean ye any harm.'

'I don't want anything from them,' he hissed.

She looked around the room. 'Where's John?'

'He's at Granny Isa's,' he said quietly.

John was sweet and handsome and loving, he was the nice one, the wee boy they'd want to care for. John wouldn't understand until he grew up, he wouldn't know what had happened, but Alan knew. Angry, ignorant Alan knew. She nodded at him 'You could come to mine one day,' she said, trying to sound casual. 'I've got cakes and we could watch the telly and have tea and then I'll bring ye back.'

He slapped his hand flat on the open comic in front of him, ripping the page, crumpling it in his fist. He threw it on the floor. 'Don't play with girls.'

He turned to the wall, digging his finger into a crumbling hole in the plaster. It was quite a big hole, it looked as if he'd been worrying it for a while.

'I've got a big brother,' said Maureen. 'He could come as well.'

Alan stuck his finger into the wall, twisting on the bed to get the better look at it, turning his back on her. She waited. He dug deep, twisting his elbow wide to get a good hold, grunting. He was so unsympathetic she could have cried for him, for all the crews at school that would reject him, for all the exams he'd fail, for all the lassies that wouldn't go with him, for Billy Harris chasing the girls from the dancing and Monica Beatty's eye.

'Does your brother work?' asked Alan.

'He's at university,' she said. 'He makes movies.'

Alan stopped digging and swung around on the bed. 'Does he make cartoons?' he said quickly, breathless at the possibility.

'No,' she said, wishing he did. 'Just films.'

Alan looked disappointed and turned back to the wall. He dug and grunted again. 'When?'

It was the smallest question she'd ever heard. 'Tomorrow?' she said.

''Kay.'

She shut the door behind her and took the stairs slowly, wondering how much more damage it would do to Alan if he found out Ann was alive. But Ann might come back in a few years' time, just reappear one day, and a dead mother's return would fuck anyone up.

Back downstairs Isa was everywhere. There was a light in the kitchen, the sink was empty and sparkling and a giant box of tea-bags was sitting on the clean work-top. Even the strips of off-cut carpet had been rearranged into a block formation representing a rug, and the hardboard floor had been scrubbed clean, right up to the corners.

Jimmy had finished dressing the babies in matching sets of cheap but new pyjamas. He was holding their dummies above their heads, hypnotizing them into standing still while he ambushed them with a wet flannel and wiped their faces. Maureen stood in the doorway and lit a cigarette as Jimmy picked up a baby in each arm and brushed past her. 'Can I have one of them when I come back?' he said, gesturing to her fag.

'Aye.'

Jimmy took a deep breath and climbed the stairs. Alan would probably come back down as soon as the babies went to bed, and Maureen wouldn't get a chance to speak to Jimmy alone tonight. She could put it off, it didn't have to be tonight. Could be any night. She had wanted to talk to Leslie about it before she decided, but Leslie was still captive in Cammyland and she was such a loudmouth sometimes that telling her would be as good as making the decision.

'Give us one, then.'

Jimmy was behind her, rubbing his hands and staring at her cigarette. She handed him the packet. 'That was quick,' she said.

He nodded, walked over to the chair and lifted the cushion, took out a box of matches and lit up. He turned off the fire and Maureen looked out into the hall. 'Isn't Alan coming down?'

'Naw, he likes to sit with them till they fall asleep.' He blew out a stream of smoke, holding his head back, standing tall. 'A smoke's just what ye need sometimes, isn't it?'

'Aye.' She looked at her cigarette, as if it knew what the fuck to do.

Jimmy sat down in his chair. 'What ye did for me and the weans,' he said, smoking and squinting at her, 'I'll never be able to thank ye for it. Ye were brave to go down there.'

'That's not brave, Jim. Bringing up four weans on benefit, that's brave.'

Jimmy looked into the dying fire. He took a draw and sucked it down, deep to the pit of his stomach. 'I lied to ye,' he said, whispering so the children wouldn't hear him, 'I do miss her.' He took a deep draw. 'I even miss her being sick and being missing. I miss her being in trouble and blaming me and hitting the weans and bringing parties back to the house and passing blood. I miss her. I miss her all the time.'

'She's not dead, Jimmy.'

He shook his head at the floor and Maureen wondered if he'd heard her.

'I miss her,' he said.

'Jimmy,' said Maureen, 'it wasn't Ann. She's not dead.'

Jimmy shuddered and closed his careworn eyes tight. 'I miss everything about her,' he whispered.

48

White Martyr

Siobhain's face was twenty-foot high and she stared angrily down at them. She was standing too close to the camera, her face spilling over the edges of the frame. 'I am Siobhain McCloud, of the clan McCloud.' A self-conscious snigger rippled through the audience as the more insecure let their neighbours know they'd got the reference.

Siobhain stepped away from the camera. She was standing in her beige living room and all around her on the floor, on the big telly, on the sofa, on the windowsill were her cutout pictures. There were pictures of babies in baths and dogs and food and models and readers' pictures and home baking and top tips and holiday resorts. She told the audience that she had kept the pictures that pleased her and liked to collect them in books. She held open her album and Liam's lighting brought the image to life. It was a picture of a horse-drawn wedding carriage with a grotesquely unattractive couple in full wedding regalia. The camera zoomed in on it. 'This,' said Siobhain, 'is Sandra and John from Newcastle on their happy day,' she turned the page, 'and here is my favourite picture of a crab.'

Her delivery was strange and stilted, she was talking too loud and sounded simple. She showed the audience a picture of a plate of fish and explained about her people. They were Highland travellers. She described how they would dredge the rivers in the summer months, wading and looking through boxes, past the choppy surface to the still waters below, finding pearls and selling them in the cities. The camera turned to the painting above the fire and she told the story of her young brother, Murdo, and how he drowned in a shallow burn in the autumn and grief made her mother leave the land. She turned to a picture of an Italian holiday resort and pointed to the flag fluttering above a castellated battlement, explaining that according to the old church there were three types of martyrdom. Red was death, green was leading the life of a hermit in the woods and white martyrdom was exile, leaving the land and your people for the preservation of the faith. Her accent sounded thick and she didn't look pretty at all. Her face was fat and her chin dissolved into her chest, leaving her with a small Hitchcockian chin. 'I look very fat in this,' she whispered indignantly to Maureen.

The other shorts had received a quiet ripple of applause but when the lights went up on Liam's film everyone applauded, some politely, some sincerely. A couple of attention-seekers at the back cheered and whooped. The audience stood up and began to file out. Maureen tried to look around for Lynn but her neck brace was restricting.

'I looked very fat,' said Siobhain, staring at the darkened screen.

'What did ye think?' Maureen asked Leslie.

'Went on a bit, didn't it?' said Cammy, as if he wasn't sitting in an art-house cinema wearing a Celtic Puffa jacket.

'Jesus Christ,' said Kilty Goldfarb, shaking her half-eaten Cornetto at him in exasperation. 'It was nine fucking minutes long. What are you? Brain-damaged?'

'Still,' said Cammy, uncomfortably, 'I thought it did . . .' He looked away around the cinema, knowing he'd got it wrong.

'It went down well with the audience, anyway,' said Leslie, covering for him.

Liam had been right about the three-month honeymoon. Maureen saw Leslie looking annoyed when Cammy said stupid things. She seemed to have changed her mind about having kids as well but she hadn't told Maureen why. Liam came in from the back, fighting his way through the flow of the crowd and stood next to Maureen, flushed and proud. 'What d'ye think?'

'Brilliant,' said Leslie.

'Fucking super,' said Kilty.

'I looked fat,' said Siobhain, annoyed, as if Liam had tricked her and used a special lens.

'I thought it went on a bit,' said Cammy, assertive now that a man was there.

Liam blanked him. 'I think it went quite well,' he said, looking around. 'Lynn was working late but she should have been here by now.'

Leslie took Maureen's elbow and said that Cammy had his car and they were going to drop Siobhain and stop off at Jimmy's to bring Isa home, did she fancy coming and seeing the boys?

'Can't,' said Maureen. 'I've promised to meet someone.'

Cammy could hardly contain his delight. 'Brilliant, okay.' He grinned. 'See ye later, then.'

Leslie and her entourage were swept away in the flow. Several members of the audience recognized Siobhain and stared at her as she made her way out, thinking her a very clever actress. Kilty watched them leave. 'You were right about him, Mauri,' she said. 'That guy's a prize arse.'

Maureen sighed with dismay. 'What makes her stay with him?'

Liam shrugged. 'Her family go for idiot men, though, don't they?'

Maureen nodded. 'Aye, right enough.'

'And here,' he said, 'is someone else who goes for idiot men.'

Lynn had watched the film from the back and was shuffling sideways along a row to get to them. Maureen felt implicated in Liam's betrayal of her. She hadn't felt the same about Lynn since Martha. She was letting her down by not telling but she couldn't, it wasn't her business. She'd tried to trip Liam up by saying that Martha might be HIV positive, but he said he'd been careful. Lynn climbed over the last seat and called to Liam. 'Your film made Siobhain look like a prick.'

'No, it didn't,' he said.

'Actually,' said Kilty, 'she looked like a bit of a nutter.'

'It's the best film you've made so far,' said Maureen.

'D'ye think so?' he said.

'I do. Have ye got your key, Kilty?'

'Yeah,' said Kilty. 'Aren't ye coming for a drink with us?'

'Can't,' said Maureen, 'I'm meeting someone.'

As Vik parked his car he thought of Maureen up on her hill, sitting in her cosy little house with the heating up and the big curls in her hair dancing as she laughed at something on telly. He walked up Sauchiehall Street, digging his hands deep into his jacket, lowering his head to keep his neck warm. The pubs were busy for a Monday. The *Issue* sellers and the beggars were working the cinema queues and the drinkers filtered up and down the street, finding a bar for the night. An excited crowd of women in sweat-shop nylon outfits gathered at Porter's door for the karaoke and the students were hanging about outside the Baird Hall.

Mark Doyle was waiting in the Equal Café. He had kept his donkey jacket on, a big dirty man sitting alone at a small table by the window, smoking. He nodded when she came in. 'Right?'

'Were you early?' she said.

'Bit, aye.'

'D'ye want something to eat?'

He shrugged. He didn't look comfortable. Maureen didn't know if he'd ever been in a café. 'What is there?' he said, behaving like a nervous spy.

'Cottage pie?' He shook his head. 'Fry-up?'

He shook his head again. 'Bad stomach.'

'Soup?'

'What kind?'

'Minestrone.'

'Aye. I like that. I'll have that.'

The waitress was busy at another table. Maureen looked at Doyle. He wasn't an easy man to make light conversation with so she didn't try. 'Do you think Pauline would be pleased that we know each other now?'

He touched the broken skin on his face. 'Think she would,' he said. 'But, then, she never mentioned you tae me. For all I know she mibi couldn't stand the sight of ye.'

He raised an eyebrow and Maureen smiled at his joke. The sullen waitress limped over to the table and Maureen ordered them a bowl of soup each and some bread.

Vik turned to cross the road and looked into the Equal Café. Maureen O'Donnell was sitting in the bright white light behind the window, wearing a skin-coloured neck brace, looking relaxed and happy. Across the table from her was a tall, dark-haired man with broad shoulders. He wasn't her brother: he didn't look anything like her. Vik walked on and crossed further down the road. When he got to the Variety he ordered a pint and found that he was trembling with disappointment. She would have to pass the doors on

422

her way home to Garnethill She'd know he was in there. He was always there on Mondays. He and Shan were always there.

'Elizabeth,' said Doyle. 'She's dead.'

'What happened?'

'Out on bail. Went for a hit. OD'd.' He told the story as if he was passing on a social arrangement.

'God,' said Maureen, 'that's awful.'

'No, it's not,' said Doyle.

The waitress brought over two plates of soup garnished with greasy croutons and a plate of spongy white sliced.

'What did ye want to see me for?' asked Doyle, resting his big hands on the table, leaving the cutlery undisturbed.

Maureen stopped with her spoon an inch from her mouth. She put it down in the bowl. 'My father is back in Glasgow.'

Doyle nodded as if he already knew that.

'He's a bad father,' she said. 'He's like your father.'

He caught her eye. 'Don't,' he said.

'But—'

'Ye can't go back, after. Ye think they're in your head before, but when ye cross that line, then they've really got ye. You're no better than them.'

But she hadn't been weakened by Millport, she'd felt better afterwards, stronger, more powerful. If she could keep her nerve this time and not freeze like she had with Toner, she could do it.

'Whatever he did to me,' she said, 'is in the past.'

Doyle nodded. 'It's over,' he said.

'That part's over.'

They looked at each other. Doyle lifted his spoon and sipped his soup.

'What's this part?' he said.

'My sister's expecting. I want to know what to do.'

'Warn her.'

'I have warned her. She doesn't believe me.'

Doyle shook his head, looking at the table. 'Don't do it, hen.'

'What else can I do?'

'Run away. Leave. It's not your business.'

'I can't leave.'

'Ye can't stop it.'

'But I can stop it. You know that. We both know that. I can stop it.'

Doyle shook his head again. 'You'll ruin yourself.' He wrapped his big hand around the handle of the spoon and flexed it anxiously, splitting the skin at the joints into red slits on the papery skin. He began to eat his soup. Disappointed, Maureen watched him. She'd wanted him to say yes, make suggestions, or even offer to help her. 'Nothing's ever over, is it?' she said.

'Nut,' said Doyle, and crushed a crouton between his teeth.

Vik waited all night. He sat on a bar stool, watching the door for four hours, pretending to chat to Shan about Gram Parsons and Motherwell's line-up. Every time the doors opened he felt sick and nervous. He waited and waited until the bar staff were shouting time, but Maureen never came.

THE END